"Be careful, milady, that you do not confuse lust with love. Both are dangerous to the inexperienced."

Catherine drew in a shaky breath. "As I have little experience with either emotion, I shall have to trust in you to guide me."

Alex looked stunned. Then he gave a soft, amazed laugh. "Is that not too like trusting the wolf in the sheep pen, milady?"

"Perhaps. But 'tis all I can do. . . ."

As her words trailed into a whisper, he shook his head. "You have undone me, my lady. I am confounded."

"Are you?" She dragged a fingertip across the smooth expanse of his lower lip. "Yet you look like a man very certain, and very much in control."

In a swift motion, he bent to cover her lips with his in a searing kiss that stole her breath and left her clinging to him weakly. It consumed her. . . .

In memory of Dolly Kinnison Gibson, who lent a fourteen-year-old girl the courage to spread her wings.

THE SCOTSMAN

PROLOGUE

Scottish Borderlands
October, 1313

A cold, fierce wind as foul as a demon's breath sucked the clouds from the western sky and spat gray sheets of rain toward the distant bristled spires of Kielder Forest across the border. Alexander Fraser reined in his lathered mount atop a rocky summit where the wind was the fiercest, and watched in angry disbelief as the riders vanished over the crest of a bare knoll. Sassenach, though they were too far away for him to see the pennant that identified them. They would be well across the border into England before he could reach them. Curse them. He was too late . . . too late.

A crackling boom split the heavens, drowning out the relentless drum of futility resounding in his ears, and Alex looked up into the blackness overhead. Thunder rumbled in the skies, an ominous pounding like the English hooves on Scottish soil. Rain fell harder. Rivulets streamed over his face, plastering his long black hair to his head like a monk's cap, clumping his eyelashes together and blurring his vision as he stared at the distant border. He huffed a long breath that formed frost clouds in front of his face, but the demon wind whipped them away.

He curbed both his restive mount and the temptation to follow the enemy across that invisible line between Scotland and England. It had been overlong that he had bided his time as Robert Bruce bade him do, and now he was weary of engaging the English only in swift skirmishes or lightning raids that availed them heavy tributes from the villagers but not their freedom. Would a decisive battle ever come? Too many Scots lay among English dead strewn about the summit in boneless sprawls, waning steam slowly rising from their lifeless forms. He nudged his horse forward to survey the dead with dread anticipation, but did not see his own men among the fallen. Nor did he see Adam de Brus, dead or alive. Bitterness rose. Curse Robert Bruce's cousin for confronting the English with too few men at his side. Aye, even after Alex had warned him. Now Scots lay dead on their own turf, testament to foolish de Brus pride and hot temper.

A savage flick of rain-thick wind curled the edge of his plaid and knifed through the jagged rips in his sherte. Alex barely felt it. The stench of death was too strong, defying even the wind, seeping into him with powerful premonition. It was all much too familiar, the moans of the dying, the peculiar sickly sweet smell that pervaded even his dreams—had he ever had a day without it? It did not seem so now. All he could remember was struggle and battle and the screams of those hurled into eternity in the blink of an eye and the flash of a sword—Alex drew in a deep breath to clear his head and sweep away the images that haunted him.

The metallic clink of harness was muffled by the relentless keening of the wind as Robbie MacLeod rode up beside him. Robbie's horse snorted, crimson nostrils flared and blowing frost clouds like dragon-smoke.

"It was the Earl of Warfield. He has Adam de Brus."

Robbie's rough announcement only confirmed what Alex already suspected, and he nodded tersely.

"Aye, curse him. Doubtless, 'tis vengeance for the Bruce's raids over the Solway two years ago, his burning of Haltwhistle and most of Tynedale. Bruce will not be pleased to hear the English have yet another of his kin captive."

"Alex—they have Jamie as well."

A splinter of shock pierced Alex, sharp and suffocating in its intensity as the Gaelic words were whipped away by a gust of wind. "I left Jamie behind at Castle Rock."

"He did not stay behind." Robbie jerked his head to indicate a bloody form being wrapped in a wool plaid and borne to a litter. "One of de Brus's men just said that your brother joined them late last eve, and was taken captive with de Brus."

Alex did not move, for it would betray the tension that rendered him almost immobile. "Christ above! I gave Jamie strict orders to stay where I left him."

"Och, you know Jamie's a braw lad with not a dram of caution in him." Robbie spat onto chewed turf that was rife with battle litter. Rain molded his thin sherte to his body and dragged his woolen plaid down with its weight. His light hair was dark from it, and water streamed over features as sharp as an ax blade as he regarded Alex with glum resignation. "He was angry because you said he was too young to fight the English. Now he has fought his first battle."

"So it seems." Alex drew in a breath saturated with the smell of fresh blood, wet earth, and grim despair. "By God, I will have his hide for this!"

"Aye," Robbie said soberly, "but Warfield will have his head."

Alex sucked in another sharp breath. "Yea, 'tis true. This feckless decision will cost Jamie his life."

"Alex, you cannot mean we will do nothing about it." Robbie's tone was angry, amazed. "The bloody Sassenach have your brother . . . do we not go after him? Christ above, Alex, you know what will happen once Warfield gets Jamie to England."

Numbly, Alex swung his gray gaze to Robbie. A light of desperation glinted in Robbie's eyes and made his decision more difficult, yet no less resolute. "Yea, I know well what is like to happen. I am not willing to let Jamie die, but I am not willing to defy the Bruce. He bade me stay my hand and arms for the moment, and until I confer with him, I must abide by my oath."

Robbie groaned. "May God help Jamie then. Warfield is a ruthless man, and boon companion of King Edward. Though Longshanks's spawn may not be the hard king his father was, he is still as dangerous as a snapping cur."

"I will negotiate with Warfield—"

"The bloody earl holds the English king's ear, and will not listen to you," Robbie growled.

"But he does want money." Alex regarded him grimly. "My coffers are near empty, but I am worth more as hostage than Jamie."

Flames of real fear leaped high in Robbie's dark eyes, and his ruddy complexion turned scarlet as he searched Alex's face for a long moment. "Do you think Warfield will pass up the chance to slay you both? He will not. We have ravaged his lands and exacted too many tributes from him not to know he will seek vengeance where he can. Nor will Bruce want to risk your certain death."

"I have fought fifteen years for Scotland's freedom and have supported Robert Bruce well." Alex's jaw went taut, and he shoved roughly at the wet loop of dark hair the wind dangled in front of his eyes. "The Bruce holds English prisoners for ransom. If he is loath to risk me, surely among that lot there are some important to Warfield." He drew in a deep breath. "Or to the English king."

"More important than holding Bruce's cousin?" Robbie shook his head dolefully. " 'Tis doubtful, Alex."

"You have met Warfield. What think you of him?"

Robbie spat on the ground again, and his lips curled. "He is a powerful lord, to be certain, but not a man I would trust with the life of my kin. He backs King Edward, just as he backed his father, and 'tis said he would deliver his own mother to the king if 'twas asked of him."

Alex was quiet. The wind howled around his head and his horse pranced restively beneath him. At last he said, "Think you that if negotiation fails, you could remember the lay of Warfield keep, Robbie?"

A grin split Robbie's craggy face. "Aye, 'tis more what I wanted to hear from you, by God! I have been to the earl's keep, and can recall well the lay of it. We should call up our men and ride hotfoot to England now—"

"Nay, first I will counsel with the Bruce."

Wrenching his mount around, Alex spurred the lathered animal down the steep, rock-studded hill. A forked lightning tongue speared the darkening sky, briefly bringing noonday brightness to the rocky summit. The air shimmered with the pungent scent of wet turf and blood. Behind him, he heard Robbie following at a reckless pace.

Despite his words, Alex had more doubts than he would allow Robbie to see. Would Bruce allow him to negotiate for Jamie's release? Of late, the Scottish king had avoided direct battle with the English, preferring to raid towns and lay waste to the English countryside, exacting heavy tributes for his protection. Those who did not resist were spared, but those who turned to fight met swift ends. Noble English hostages were a valuable commodity, ransomed for hefty sums.

But if Warfield demanded ransom instead of an exchange of hostages, Scottish coffers could not bear the fine. The coin paid by the northern counties of England to purchase truce was spent too swiftly in the provisioning of an army.

With a sick heart, Alex feared Robert Bruce's reply. Jamie's future seemed grimly short.

PART ONE

CHAPTER
⚬ ONE ⚬

England, 1818

*T*hick woods crowded the lonely road as the royal carriage and its phalanx of armed outriders pounded on through the black autumn night.

Inside the coach, seated across from her lady-in-waiting, the raven-haired Princess Sophia of Kavros stared out the window at the dark tangle of gnarled tree trunks and scraggly branches whizzing by. The tiny candle sconces inside the carriage cast her reflection on the window glass—a face of exotic beauty, with an expression of brooding intensity, lost in her thoughts.

Not much longer now.

In another few hours, they would reach the castle for tonight's secret meeting with the British diplomats.

The rhythmic jouncing of the coach set the beat as Sophia continued mentally rehearsing the impassioned speech she meant to give the Foreign Office lords.

On this, the very eve of her destiny, they could no longer deny her, for at the stroke of midnight, she would turn twenty-one, attaining her legal majority; then they could not brush her off anymore with their excuses and protestations that she was too young to rule.

The time had come for the British government to keep

its promise and restore Sophia to her family's throne. Her people would have it no other way, and God knew, they had suffered enough.

Restlessly, she glanced at her attendant. "What is the hour, Alexa?"

The striking blonde jumped when Sophia addressed her.

Of course, they both were nervous about this night, so long in the planning.

There was so much at stake.

Alexa checked her locket-watch. "A quarter past nine, Your Highness. Ten whole minutes since the last time you asked," she added, with a taut smile.

Sophia knitted her eyebrows and flicked an impatient scowl toward the carriage window, but took no offense at her companion's irreverent tone. Alexa had been with her too long to stand on ceremony; her ancestors had been courtiers to the royal family for generations, and had even followed them into exile here in England when the kingdom had fallen to Napoleon. Alexa had been assigned as Sophia's lady-in-waiting when both girls were barely fifteen.

Besides, Alexa always made cheeky jokes when she was on edge.

"Must you look so glum?" her friend attempted again with an air of vague distress, though striving for levity. Not every girl gets a crown and scepter for her birthday, you know."

"We're not there *yet*," Sophia answered matter-of-factly.

When one had survived as many shocking twists of fate as she had in her brief years, one learned to take nothing for granted.

The cooperation of the English, for example.

She did not think at this point that they would refuse her outright, now that conditions on Kavros had deterio-

1

Lady Catherine Worth braced herself against the wind. Her fingers curled into the rough stone of the high curtain wall that encircled Warfield keep as she gazed over crenellated parapets into the distance. A heavy mist dampened the air and curled her unruly mane of coppery hair around her face in dark-fire ringlets that tickled her cheek. An impatient flick of one hand brushed them aside; violet-blue eyes narrowed against the moisture that obscured her vision.

"Where *are* they?" The wind whipped her fretful words away on wet currents. Clouds stacked in a towering black and gray mass raced by overhead. The keening sob of the wind grew louder; it sounded to her like the mournful despair of lost souls. The maudlin thought sent a shiver down her spine. Catherine tugged the fur-lined edges of her cloak more closely about her. Aye, 'twas true she was far too fanciful, as her mother oft lamented. And just as often, her father cursed her for it.

The earl made it abundantly clear that he had no patience for the whims of a female, even his wife. And

especially his daughter. Her lips tightened. Robert
Worth, Earl of Warfield, was not an affectionate man.
Nor was he a man who considered it important for a
female to know more than how to sew altar cloths or
brew medicinal herbs. Nay, 'twas not for her father's return she had come to the turrets to watch this dreary day,
but for her brother.

A faint smile replaced the grim slash of her mouth.
Nicholas was far too frequently all that stood between
her and their father's wrath, for she was not at all the
dutiful daughter the earl demanded. Her mother had
once complained that she had inherited far too much of
her father's obstinance, but it was not said in front of
him. The countess would not dare imply criticism of him
so openly. Only Nicholas dared that.

Restless, but preferring the worsening weather to the
mundane chatter of the women beside the fire, Catherine knotted her small hands into fists beneath the warm
fur lining of her cloak as she strained to see through the
gray gloom stretching beyond Warfield. Hills rolled down
from the knoll upon which Warfield Castle squatted like
a great hulking beast keeping watch. Which it was. The
earl was known to many as the Border Lion, for he kept a
close eye on the marauding bands of rebellious Scots that
frequently crossed the border between England and
Scotland. That boundary lay only a few miles from Warfield.

A small frown knit her brow as Catherine studied the
lip of horizon beyond the spiky tree spires of Kielder
Forest. Warfield was so detached from the rest of the
world it seemed, her life here an anonymous blur of days
sliding one into the other. Yet she knew something more
existed beyond these walls, heard whispered tales of
strife and bloodshed, of the Earl of Warfield's fierce reputation . . . of brutal Scots raids on surrounding villages

the earl would not protect. Was it true he did not defend his own people, or only idle malice? No one would tell her. They kept her as sheltered as a child.

Not even Nicholas would tell her more than vague tales of border raids by the Scots, though at times she saw thick plumes of smoke in the distance and knew another village had been destroyed. Even Lanercost Priory had been sacked by the ruthless Scots, and 'twas said that the savage rebels had made the nuns dance naked. But it was futile to ask questions, for she would be sharply rebuked for it. 'Twas as if they all feared her delicate female constitution would warp and fray from the horror of truth, or perhaps even—

"Milady?"

Catherine half turned, and saw her handmaiden peering out from the arched shelter of the tower doorway. How vexing! Had Bess been sent to fetch her? As if she were naught but a small girl? Poor Bess shivered, blinking away the wind and rain, and looked so miserable that Catherine's irritation eased. She lifted her voice so she could be heard over the keening wind, speaking in the maid's familiar vernacular, a blending of Welsh and English.

"If thou hast come to fetch me inside, Bess, I am not ready. I watch for my brother. Perhaps 'tis the day they return."

"Mayhaps not . . . milady, thy lady mother sent me to fetch thee inside before thee catch thy death from the raw wind. Wilst thou not accompany me?"

"Nay, Bess, I will not. Tell my mother thou could not find me." Catherine glanced again across the parapet toward the distant murky line of sky and land, seamed together by gray mist and rain. It beckoned her, elusive and vague, a mere promise of freedom. "Yea," she muttered crossly, "I much prefer solitude to the constant harping prattle of my mother and those other tiresome ladies."

The squelching sound of wet shoes in rain puddles marked Bess's progress as she inched her way to the parapet wall, carefully keeping her distance from the wide ledge. Her dark eyes were wide with anxiety. " 'Tis dangerous to stand here so close to the brink in such a wind, milady! What if the Tylwyth Teg should snatch thee away? I beg of thee, come with me. . . ."

" 'Tis safe enough, for your Welsh spirits do not come here. Tell me, Bess—" Catherine turned suddenly, her abrupt movement startling a squeak of alarm from the maid. "Is it true what some say?"

Bess was shivering, her thin wool dress clinging damply to her spare frame. "S-say, milady? Of what?"

"About my father—that the Earl of Warfield is ruthless with his enemies. That he is greatly feared by even his own villeins . . . yea, it must be for thou art shaking like the last autumn leaf in the wind and looking as pale as a boiled owl. Never mind. I know 'tis forbidden to discuss such matters with me. Go inside, silly goose. I shall be down presently, and 'twill satisfy my mother if I feign deep repentance."

"Truly, milady, I d-dare not go back without thee. Lady Warfield will be most distressed."

"Pah! She cares about naught but her lace tatting or tapestries. She will not miss me. I daresay she will not notice my absence until my father's return, and then only when he takes notice." Catherine drew in a ragged breath. She had not meant to sound so bitter, and saw from Bess's earnest face that it had not gone unnoticed. She managed a bright smile. "Ah, Bess, thou shalt suffer no ill. I shall come in soon. I just thought that perhaps today they wouldst return. It has been a fortnight, when

Nicholas said they wouldst be gone only two days. I worry, 'tis all."

"Lord Devlin is very important to thee, is he not, milady? More important even than thy betrothed?"

Catherine stiffened. "I do not know Ronald of Bothwick, nor do I care to wed him. 'Tis my father's choice, not mine. I think I wouldst rather retire to a nunnery than wed a stranger. There, at least, I could be at peace, and none wouldst think it improper if I chose to read or write, or study philosophy—"

She halted, and drew in a deep breath. It would never do to have *that* repeated about the keep! If the earl were to hear of it, he would no doubt have her wed to Ronald within a sennight.

Dredging up her most aristocratic tone, she said, "Inform my lady mother that I will join her anon, Bess, then thou dost hurry to the kitchens and tell Cook that I will need a cup of hot spiced wine to chase away my chill."

"Aye, milady. At once, milady."

Bess bobbed a curtsy, half lifting her drenched skirts in one hand as she turned away, obviously delighted at the thought of going to the warm cavern of the kitchen. It was one of the girl's favorite spots, and Catherine knew she would linger there as long as possible. *Neatly done,* she congratulated herself with a faint smile as Bess disappeared amid the turret shadows, leaving Catherine in peace.

Another gust of wind snapped the hem of her cloak, a loud popping sound like the crack of a whip. The heavy wool and fur slipped from one shoulder, and she had to grab for it swiftly before the capricious wind sent it sailing over the edge of the parapet into the turbid waters of the moat below.

Rain began to fall harder, pelting her upturned face

with stinging droplets. Tiny cold rivers streamed over her brow onto her cheeks, chilling her. Wet lashes closed over her eyes, blotting out the gray sky and bare tree limbs. There had to be another future for her. She did not want to wed a man she did not know just to align two powerful houses, and could not bear the thought of spending the rest of her life as her mother spent her days, quaking at an unkind word from her husband, always so anxious to please, so afraid of his displeasure—

Drawing in a deep, shaky breath, Catherine opened her eyes again and stared across the rolling land stretching away from the keep. Thunder? No, the escalating sound of hooves against solid turf, a low, steady pounding that could be heard above the sobbing moan of the wind. She blinked away rain, and in a moment could make out the shadowy forms of mounted troops approaching along the muddy track that snaked over the hills and through the towering trees. The line of horsemen briefly disappeared from view into a shallow ravine that harbored a winding stream, then appeared again, much closer now. Warfield's banner flew before them, a red lion against a white field, and to her relief, she saw Nicholas, his uncovered head dark and glistening with rain beneath the unfurled standard of the earl.

Relief flared, dispelling her gloom and anxiety. Even at such a distance, she knew her brother. His cocky demeanor set him apart from the other muddy riders, a laughing rogue who had his way with far too many village maidens, charming them into haystacks and corn cribs or wherever he fancied. Nicholas—older by six years—her brother, her confidant, her only refuge, and now he was back at last.

Turning, Catherine flew across the slippery gray stones of the battlement and ducked into the musty shadows inside the turret. Blinking at the abrupt absence of proper light, she made her way down steep, winding stairs only dimly lit by sputtering torches stuck into iron holders on the newel walls. The smell of burning pitch was acrid in the close air. Darkness yawned beyond the hazy, wavering pools of light as she descended the narrow steps into the great hall, then hurried through the vestibule and out a heavy door onto the open staircase guarded from the bailey by a massive stone forework. Smoke stung her eyes, and the ordure in the moat seemed heavier than usual. No one tried to stop her as she scurried across the bailey toward the gatehouse.

Was she too late? No, there was the groaning rattle of the portcullis being lifted, the shriek of the winch chains and the inner drawbridge being lowered to admit the earl and his sons, home from Scotland.

Heart pounding, delight drowning her turmoil, Catherine dodged a woodsman with a heavy load of faggots atop his bent back, and reached the gatehouse just as the first riders thundered over the wooden bridge. Nicholas saw her, as she'd known he would. It was a ritual. She always waited for him here, anticipating his return as she had done since she was small, and he watched for her. Now he bent slightly from his huge, snorting destrier to scoop her up beside him, ignoring their father's disgruntled oath.

"It is raining, kitten, do you not know that?" Nicholas teased, laughing as he pulled her against his side.

Catherine held tightly to him, her fingers sliding over the rough metal links of his mail to grip the thick wool surcoat. He smelled of rain and mud, and other vague odors that she preferred to ignore. She leaned slightly away, her voice accusing to hide the choking relief that he had safely returned. "You are near a fortnight longer than you said you would be, you know."

"Aye, so we are." His arm tightened around her. "But

the rebels were more troublesome than usual. Thick as fleas on a camp cur, and near as vicious."

Catherine's hand closed on a handful of wool and wet hair, and she pressed her mouth against her brother's ear. "I must talk to you. Will you meet me later?"

"Yea, kitten, so I will." His voice was gruff and low, his squeeze quick before he reined in his great destrier and lowered her to the muddy ground by the forework. With a wink, he bade her go inside to ascertain their evening meal was hot. "I will eat no cold meat tonight, by God!"

Catherine made a face at him, keeping a wary eye on the agitated warhorse as it pranced in a tight, nervous circle. Those lethal hooves could bash a skull in quickly if one got too close. She backed away, skirts lifted in her hands to clear the muck of the bailey, and swept a brief glance toward her father. The earl ignored her. His attention was trained elsewhere, and she caught a glimpse of scarlet and blue against the anonymous drab of mud and mist.

Pausing, Catherine peered through the tangle of horses and men toward the flash of color. An angry curse rose into the air, followed by the unmistakable sound of a blow. At once, horses neighed and reared, and men began to shout. In the confusion, no one noticed as Catherine crept closer, her curiosity stronger than even dread of her father.

She was startled to see that one man was the source of all the chaos, and he was shackled with heavy chains about his wrists and ankles, standing in the midst of the heaving mass of shouting men with his garments awry. Oddly, he did not look at all afraid, but rather contemptuous of those around him. His hair was dark with mud and rain, but she could see that it was a lighter color, almost as pale and coppery as her own. He was forced to his knees, and she saw then that he was shackled to another prisoner, who was being dragged down into the muck beside him.

With a shock, Catherine realized the second captive was young, even younger than herself, and cuffed as brutally as the older man. Both were hauled roughly to their feet again. The boy glanced up, and she saw the youthful features twisted with ancient hatred. A thin trail of blood trickled down from his brow to his chin as he turned to regard the earl with contempt.

"Murderin' Sassenach swine—"

One of the guards struck him, a backhanded blow of his mailed fist that caught the boy across the face and sent him staggering to one knee. More blows followed, raining down on both prisoners, and Catherine gasped with horror. Or perhaps she cried out, for her father turned toward her with his brows lowered over his colorless eyes in a scowl. His voice was low and tight:

"Go inside, Catherine."

"But what have they done? If they are prisoners, should they not be treated more kindly?" The words were out before she knew it, and she realized at once that she had done the prisoners no favor by questioning her father in front of his men. It was all she could do not to turn and flee when she saw fires of rage leap in her father's eyes. White lines bracketed his mouth with tension.

"This is none of your affair, daughter. Get inside with the other women, and do not dare speak of matters that do not concern a maiden."

Rebellion flared in her, and might have spewed unwisely forth had Nicholas not intervened, leaning from his great mount to say in a soft voice, "They are my captives and I will see to them, kitten. Do not tweak our father's nose for what you cannot change."

"Very well, but only because you ask it of me." With a

fleeting glance at her father, she turned angrily on her heel and ascended the stairs of the forework.

Lady Warfield met her just inside the entrance to the great hall, and a glance at her expression made Catherine sigh inwardly. Were there never any secrets at Warfield?

Exasperation edged Lady Warfield's cool rebuke: "Must you behave like the lowest scullery maid, Catherine? Look at you. Garbed in a filthy gown, hair uncovered, flying loose and as wet as cat's fur—hardly the conduct of a lady."

Catherine held her tongue and stared down at her ruined slippers. Sodden velvet toes peeped from beneath the frayed and muddy hem of her gown. The contrast between her appearance and her mother's could not be more vivid—Lady Warfield was elegant in the gilt barbette atop her head and thinly woven gold threads of the crispinette that held her hair, down to her small embroidered slippers encrusted with pearls and gilt. Her mother's grandeur made her achingly aware of her own disheveled state. She focused on her feet while Lady Warfield delivered a scathing lecture, allowing the French language preferred by her parents to drift over her head until one particular remark captured her attention.

Catherine's head snapped up with consternation as the countess finished, ". . . and hardly suitable should your betrothed witness your unbefitting demeanor. God grant, he is not yet arrived, but with the date so soon now—"

"Soon? What date do you mean, my lady?"

Lady Warfield's elegant features remained stern and unlined. "It is unseemly to be so rude, Catherine. Must you interrupt me?"

"I crave your pardon, madam, but I do not know what you mean by the date being so soon."

"No doubt. Nevertheless, you will go immediately to your chamber and allow Bess to ready appropriate garments for the morrow. Wear the blue velvet gown, as we expect important guests. You are required to behave with decorum and not as if you are no more than a rebellious serf. I am certain that you understand me."

"Of course, madam, but I—"

"Your father will wish to see you in the solar right after Prime is rung in the morning. I insist that you heed the customs you have been taught, and act accordingly."

Catherine stared after her mother as the countess turned to move away in a familiar, silent glide, as if her feet did not touch the floor. No one would listen to her. She was trapped, and her freedom was slipping further and further away.

2

Lord Warfield did nothing to lessen her apprehension the next morning when Catherine stood silently awaiting his attention in the solar. Her father pored over a parchment, goose quill in one hand and a pot of ink at the ready. The family seal and a carved box of sand waited at his elbow; when the document he studied had been signed, it would be sanded and sealed. After what seemed an eternity, the earl looked up at his daughter.

"Bothwick's envoy arrives today to sign the nuptial agreement. You will make ready to move to Bothwick keep, and your wedding will take place on Saint John's Eve."

Catherine blanched. "But I do not wish to marry!"

"Do not be foolish, Catherine. You are female, and this is your purpose in life. Indeed, 'tis long past the time for it. What else is there for you to do."

He made it sound like a statement instead of a question but she answered: "I could live on the estate my grandmother left to me. As it borders the Solway Firth, I—"

"What crackbrained notions do you entertain in that head of yours, girl?" His brows lowered, and despite his angry tone, a glimmer of amusement lit his eyes. "Do you intend to fish for your supper? Land is not free. It costs coin to hold property."

Her chin came up. "I am not so foolish as to think I could live off fish, sir. But I could live off fishermen. Off merchant ships. There is a busy harbor in the village that belongs to the land, and I am well aware that tariffs must be paid by those ships that wish to dock there."

The earl's eyes narrowed slightly. "This is not a matter for female discussion. You are near past marriageable age—a veritable spinster. When the Earl of Moray defected to the Scots, it destroyed the nuptial negotiations we had long held with him, and made you more of a liability than an asset. It has taken time and delicate negotiations, but I have at last arranged an excellent match for you that will cement relationships with Bothwick as well as the king. They are distantly related, and that is a vital connection."

"It is said that you already have the king's ear. Why is Bothwick so important that you would sell your only daughter to him?"

Lord Warfield's palm crashed down on the table with a thundering crack that made the ink pot quiver. "Enough! You are rebellious and insolent. You will wed Bothwick's son, and there is no more to be said about the matter."

"I do not wish to wed anyone, and especially not a man I do not know." Dangerously close to tears, Catherine drew in a deep breath. "You care more about position and profit than you do about my desires, and I protest."

"It is not your place to protest, but to do as you are told. Where is your mother?"

Rising from his chair behind the long table, the earl

strode across the solar to the door and flung it open to bellow for his wife. Then he turned to Catherine. "You will go to your chamber and ready yourself. Bothwick's envoy is due to arrive shortly."

With her head held high and chin resolutely firm, Catherine strode silently past her father and out the door. But instead of going to the winding stairwell that led up to her chamber, she went to the doors that led to the bailey. Her mother was not yet in sight and luck was with her. No one spoke to her or otherwise delayed her as she descended the steep stairs of the forework, nor even commented as she crossed the wide, open area of the bailey to the postern door.

It creaked on oiled hinges as she slipped through it with a reassuring smile for the dubious guard. They knew her well, for she had oft used this door as a child. What must they think now? She was far too old to be going on such a lark, as if escaping her nurses as she had done so many times, usually in the company of her brothers when they were being tolerant of her presence. But that was a long time ago now, and one by one her brothers had departed Warfield to be trained in other keeps. As heir, Nicholas frequently returned from one of his other holdings to tender his knight's service to the earl, who was, of course, his overlord. He was her only ally, yet even Nicholas saw nothing wrong with an advantageous marriage.

Catherine sighed and turned her face upward as she circled the keep and crossed the outer bridge that stretched over the moat. Sunlight danced over the meadow that dipped down and away from the keep. After the chill rain of the previous day, the unexpected warmth was enticing. A rare autumn day, indeed. Golden light shimmered, beckoning her to return to the places where she had played as a child. So long ago, or was it only a few years? But the blithe innocence of those days was gone forever.

Slipping a little on the still-damp grass, Catherine glanced behind her when she reached the meadow's edge. Warfield's turrets spiked into the sky, white banners snapping in the wind. From the bottom of the steep slope, the castle looked forbidding and impregnable, a reminder of how insulated she was from the world. Sorrow and fear for the future dogged her, and her steps grew slower as she neared a copse of hawthorn hedges bordering a swift-running brook that flowed into the Lyne River. These hedges were familiar, though much taller than she remembered.

She parted the branches cautiously so as not to prick her skin on the sharp thorns, and slipped through the hedge to walk along the bank. It was pleasant to recall the times she had come here, sailing crude boats of wood-chip down the cascading stream, or in summer, wading into the middle to wet her bare feet in the cooling waters.

Those had been carefree days, filled with idle dreams of the future—was her own special place still there, in the midst of the brook? It was distinctive, a large flat rock with springy moss to cushion it, a small island in the center of rushing water that had lured her as a child. Nicholas had always teased her, but nothing daunted her when she was upon her rock. It was her citadel, her refuge from the world, a place where she was solitary queen.

As she wandered idly, the day grew warmer. It was a mild October day festooned with brilliant-hued leaves that lent splashes of color to the air. Birds chattered briskly in the trees and hedgerows, busily searching for food. It soothed her to be free, even for this brief time, and she relished the too few moments while she could. Soon, she must return to Warfield, to the knowledge that she was to wed a man she did not know. Perhaps her mother was right when she scolded her for heeding the forbidden tales of romantic love—Lady Warfield had once remarked they were all foolish dreams with not a shred of truth to them. And 'twas also true that many of the tales ended with the lovers dying instead of being reunited . . . was she yearning for what would never be?

Sighing, Catherine paused to pluck a violet from its nest of heart-shaped leaves. The delicate color was faded now, but would be bright against the winter snows that would soon blanket the land. She twirled the tiny blossom between her fingers and let her mind drift as she walked.

A bird cried out overhead, a strident cry that alerted a flock of nesting rooks, and she glanced up with a start as the sky was immediately dark with feathered flight. She waited, suddenly tense with apprehension at what may have frightened them, but when several moments passed without incident she relaxed again. Rooks were notoriously skittish, oft fleeing at the slightest noise, she told herself.

As the black-hued birds began to return to the hedges crying their dissonant annoyance, she resumed a meandering path along the bank. When she spotted a large flat rock in the center of the foaming water, she paused. Green moss was draped in an inviting pillow atop the gray stone. Her emerald island in the midst of the rushing currents.

Smiling as she yielded to temptation, Catherine bent to remove her shoes and stockings before wading out to the center of the stream. She gasped a little at the icy chill of the water rushing around her bare legs. It thoroughly wet the hem of her blue velvet gown even though she held her skirts nearly to her waist. The currents were much deeper than she recalled, and faster. When she reached the rock, she climbed up a bit clumsily, feeling a little foolish but delighted at revisiting her childhood. It seemed so short a while before, when in truth it had been ten years since she had been allowed to romp freely with her brothers.

Her velvet skirts were heavy with water now, and she wrung them out as best she could, then smoothed the folds around her to dry in the soft air. After a furtive glance around assured her that she was quite, quite alone, she tugged her skirts up to her knees to let the sunlight dry bare legs and blue velvet. It took only a moment to undo the pearl-encrusted crispinette that encased the heavy weight of her hair, freeing it to drape over her shoulders. Then she leaned back on her palms and reveled in the rare moment.

For several minutes, she sat quietly while the water tumbled melodically around her and sunlight dappled the trees and rocks. She tilted her head back to gaze up at the blue sky visible beyond shifting patches of autumnal leaf, blinking against the brightness. The rhythmic wash of water and warmth of the sun lulled her into a dreamy haze of gentler memories—the innocence of childhood. It was restoring to the soul. Her eyelids closed slowly as she let her mind drift into pleasant oblivion broken only by the sweet murmur of birds.

So pleasant, with the splashing water sending small sprays of mist up and over her bare toes and legs. If only she could stay forever, and never return to Warfield keep. Bess had often whispered to her of the fairies that were said to haunt the meadows and dance in flower rings, of how they were known to capture humans foolish enough to seek them out. Those people were never seen again, stolen by the magical little creatures and spirited away to live forever in enchanted lands. Perhaps if she wished hard enough, she could vanish as well. . . .

She smiled wryly at the fanciful direction her thoughts had taken. Foolish, of course, to even dream of such things. As her father had so bluntly reminded her, she was merely a pawn and must do what she was born to do. That thought summoned a shudder, and she resolutely pushed it to the back of her mind and stretched out more fully upon the rock, lifting her arms over her head so that water spray wet her fingers.

Gazing upward, she listened to the water racing over the rocks, much louder now that she was lying down. She lay quietly in a pleasant reverie of suspended time and thought until interrupted by a loud splash and cold droplets spattering her face. Blinking them away, she sat up with a jerk, suddenly aware of how distant she was from the keep, and how alone.

Heart pounding, she half turned toward the noise. When she saw its source, the breath caught in her throat and her muscles constricted, freezing her in blank terror.

A tall, dark man strode toward her through the water, the wet red plaid that swathed his frame identifying him as one of those murderous Scots her brother referred to as savage devils. For what seemed an eternity she sat immobile and watched him approach. When he was a scant yard from her, a scream welled up from deep inside her, gathering strength as it erupted from her throat with visceral force.

The man halted, and his dark brows winged upward. He put out a hand as if expecting her to take it. "Quiet, lass. Come easily and you will not be hurt."

The English words sounded strange, spoken in a thick burr that was nearly incomprehensible through the thudding of her heartbeat, but she perceived the danger of her situation clearly enough. Before the echoes of her scream faded, movement returned to her frozen limbs in a rush and she floundered from the rock and into the water. The current grabbed at her and she stumbled against it, choking as cold water filled her mouth and nose. Panicked, she fought to her feet and toward the opposite shore, water blurring her vision and the sound of pursuit growing closer.

When broad hands descended upon her shoulders, she twisted free, but the soggy velvet gown gave way at the seams as he grabbed for her. She fell forward into the brook and went under before somehow managing to claw her way up, gasping for breath. It was no use. The Scot was upon her again, hauling her from the water and into his grasp. He held her tightly, his hands hot against her chilled flesh.

"Did I not tell you not to run, lass? I should have, I see . . . ah, be still now before you drown us both. Ah, Christ—will you be still!"

"Re . . . lease me . . . at once!" Her stuttered words were less than effective, and the big Scot just grinned down at her with infuriating mockery.

"Nay, I think not."

She struggled, pushing against him and twisting like a slippery eel in his grasp, sputtering angry demands to be freed. One of her flailing hands caught him against the jaw, and with a muttered oath, he swung her into his arms and suspended her over the water. Catherine pushed desperately against him, then grew still as she became aware of the hand cupping her buttocks beneath her skirt. Startled at the feel of his rough palm on her bare skin, her gaze riveted on his face.

A subtle difference altered his features as his mocking grin faded into a tense set of his mouth. The amused light in his eyes darkened. His eyes were gray, she thought distractedly, as gray as summer storm clouds, and fringed with a thick brush of black lashes. How odd, that the devil should have such beguiling eyes. . . .

The muscles in his arms tightened, bringing her up hard against his broad chest, and his voice was rough. "Well now, lass, taking you might be more pleasant than I thought 'twould be."

3

Alex held her close against his chest, fully aware of the thudding beat of her heart, and even more aware of the satiny feel of her soft curves in his hands. She gazed up at him with the stricken expression of a startled doe, eyes wide and filled with fear and shock, and her trembling lips parted. Sweet Jesus, he had not expected such a beauty when they had first spied her upon the rock.

But it seemed to be a day for surprises, most of them nasty. Though Bruce had given permission for him to barter for Jamie's release, he had no hostages left to offer, or coin to spare. So Alex had crossed the border with a small band of men, hoping fate would be kind. A single glance at Warfield's well-fortified keep was enough to convince any sane man that siege would be long and unfeasible. Assault would be futile.

And then fortune had smiled upon them, for when they paused to water the horses and plot their strategy, this angelic creature was there, perched like a water sprite in the midst of the stream. It was Robbie who recognized her, having seen her a few years before in the company of her father, the earl. Her appearance was providential. Now he had the key to his brother's release in his arms.

She blinked at him, and he felt her muscles tighten as the moment of immobilized shock vanished. He barely had time to tighten his grip before she began to thrash about and he almost lost his hold on her. He heard Robbie hoot with laughter from the muddy banks of the swift-running burn.

"Och, lad, you have mistaken a hawk for a dove, it seems!"

A little grimly, Alex recognized the truth to the taunt. The maid was no docile dove in his embrace. She alternated between aristocratic English and French, railing at him to put her down before she boxed his ears for him.

Alex slogged through the currents toward the bank without loosening his hold on her, swearing when she almost twisted free. "Curse you, I have no intention of putting you down. Be still and you will not be hurt."

"Release me, you black-hearted knave!"

One of her flailing arms swung around and her palm slammed against the side of his head, delivering a ringing blow that caught him off-guard. His ear exploded with pain, and at that moment he stepped into a hole and bent to one knee in the water. Boisterous laughter erupted from the banks, and he did not need to look to know that Robbie and the rest of his men were enjoying this far too much for the comfort of his dignity.

Angry now, Alex ignored the temptation to duck the squirming girl beneath the cold water until she could not struggle. Instead, he lurched upright and dumped his captive on her feet in the stream, then grabbed her arms by the wrists before she could swing at him again. He held tight to her as the rushing water billowed beneath her skirts to puff them to the surface.

Undaunted, she glared up at him with eyes the vibrant color of violets. Through her winded panting, she got out, "My family will hardly view this in a kind light, sir. Are you so foolish as to risk your life for a moment's pleasure?"

Grudging amusement tempered his fury, and Alex grinned. "What a vain lass you are. Do you think me so taken with your bonny face that I need to steal you away? If 'twas only a few moments of pleasure that I wanted from you, I could drag you under yon hedge. And as far as your family is concerned, I pray most heartily that your father views this in the worst light possible—'tis what I depend upon."

A flicker of uncertainty crossed her face, but her chin rose in a defiant gesture somewhat diminished by the slight chattering of her teeth. "Then you are indeed a f-fool, sir. My father will rend you limb from limb—if I do not d-do so before him. If you dare to lay a hand upon me, you will draw back a stump instead of that hairy p-paw you now use."

More guffaws from the banks, and from one corner of his eye, Alex could see Robbie bent double with laughter. Devil take her . . . she was making a fool of him in front of his men, yet he was at a loss as to what to do. He was not in the habit of mistreating females, but neither was he accustomed to being abused by them. Alex stared down into her upturned face, at the dark violet eyes, elegant line of nose, and lips parted over chattering teeth, then let his gaze drift lower. The drenched gown was ripped at the shoulder seam, baring creamy flesh, but that was not what drew his attention. Wet material clung snugly to the rounded curve of her breasts, revealing the small hard pucker of her nipples beneath the velvet. He looked back up at her face, and saw her eyes widen with sudden awareness of her appearance.

"You would not d-dare touch me!"

"Would I not?" His smile felt tight. "Do not tempt me, lass."

"Tempt a Scots savage? I would sooner die!"

His smile vanished, and a surge of anger shook him at her stinging contempt. Did she think herself so above him that his mere touch would soil her? Curse her. Curse her. . . .

A small gasp escaped her and she took an involuntary step back, but she was too late. Alex bent his arms to bring her up hard against him, catching her wrists in one hand. With his free hand, he spread his fingers in her damp wealth of hair and held her head still as he kissed her full on the mouth. Her breath was warm against the cold clatter of her teeth, and for an instant he allowed himself the luxury of nothing more than appreciation for her soft femininity. It was arousing, and her struggles were even more stimulating as she writhed against him. The water-saturated wool of his plaid was bunched between his thighs in a wad, rubbing against his bare skin with her every movement. He deepened the kiss, ignoring her resistance and the loud hoots of his men on the bank, ignoring all but her surprisingly sweet mouth and the arousing contrast of cold water against his heated body.

When at last her resistance faded and she grew limp in his embrace, Alex tightened his fingers in the silky spill of copper hair and gently tugged her head back to break the kiss. She stared up at him with sun-dazzled eyes, silence replacing her rebellion. 'Twas the same with all women—once they learned who was master, they became amazingly docile. He smiled slightly at her capitulation, and freed her arms.

Still holding his gaze, her eyes narrowed slightly as she

rubbed at her wrists. Her lips were moist and parted, and a deep flush stained her cheeks. Alex allowed himself a moment of self-satisfaction. Aye, she was thoroughly chastened, and should be no more trouble to him now that he had proven his mastery—

"Whoreson!" The brutal word exploded with savage intensity from the lovely mouth he had just kissed, no less shocking than the lightning-swift blow that followed.

Alex escaped the full force of her hand by a mere hair as he jerked back, but her long nails caught his cheek, raking furrows in his flesh. He felt the blood well even as he retaliated by snatching her to him with a rough force that knocked the breath from her lungs in a loud rush of air. Cursing harshly, he gave her a brief hard shake that tumbled the hair into her eyes and should have rattled her to the very marrow of her bones.

Then he slung her over one shoulder and snarled a warning: "I will not tolerate another blow from you without giving back in kind, so you had best think on't most carefully if you intend to try it again."

Shrieking at him as she dangled over his shoulder, she beat on his back with her fists, pounding blows that did no damage save to vent her fury as he slogged toward the muddy banks. Not even another snarled warning dissuaded her from her course, though he doubted she could hear him through her own piercing shrieks of fury.

When he reached the bank, Alex dumped her roughly to the ground where she sprawled in a tangle of wet red hair, blue velvet, and hissing curses. Breathing hard, he looked up at his men. Robbie did not meet his eyes but his face was red with suppressed laughter, while the others turned discreetly away. Irritated, Alex looked back down at the disheveled maid.

"I am weary of your wicked tongue, my lady. Cease, or

I will tie you facedown over the back of a horse and see how well you can rail with your head bouncing off its belly."

Unrepentant and not a bit subdued, she glared up at him with all the spitting fury of a wet cat. "I will not allow you to touch me, you vile . . . odious . . . *Scot!*"

"If 'tis your virtue that concerns you, there is no need for worry. I will not bed an Englishwoman."

Alex signaled for one of the men to help her up, then turned on his heel and stalked away. Robbie handed him the reins to his mount, still not looking at him, though his broad shoulders shook a bit with stifled amusement.

"What do you intend to do with her, Alex?" he asked in Gaelic that was shaky with suppressed laughter.

"What do you think? 'Twas you who recognized her and pointed out her importance. I will hold her to barter with Warfield for Jamie's release." Alex led his mount forward, ignoring the chill press of wind against his wet garments. "We have lingered too long so near the keep. Unless we wish to sup with the earl in his dungeon this eve, we had best leave England behind quickly."

"Aye." Robbie looked up at him at last, his eyes dancing with mirth. "Do you think you can hold the lass, or shall I fetch a length of stout rope?"

"Nay, I am too tempted to drag her behind the horse to chance using a rope. We needs ride swift and hard for the border, so I will hold her in front of me."

But actually holding the squirming maid was another proposition, Alex learned to his grim displeasure. She wriggled like a fish on a hook, panting curses that no gentle lady should know, much less spew like a fishwife.

"I would be fascinated to know where you received your base education, madam," he muttered at one point, when the echoes of an epithet concerning his manhood—or lack of it—had barely faded. "Your command of the English language is a bit daunting."

"And what would you know of proper language, when you slur your words as if you have a mouthful of rocks?" She pushed futilely at the arm he kept hard around her waist, sounding a little breathless but no less furious than she had an hour before. The hard rhythm of the horse's pace lent an odd, clipped accent to her words. "I do not know what you hope to gain by this foolish act, but my father and brothers will see your heads on pikes at the castle walls before the day is done."

" 'Tis doubtful they even know you are yet gone. If you are in the habit of wandering the countryside unattended, I do not think you will be missed for a time. Long enough for us to be well back into Scotland."

She grew quiet at that comment, and another shiver coursed through her body. Alex realized with grim surprise that she was much more terrified than she feigned. Her loud fury masked the fear that no doubt engulfed her, and for the first time, he felt a spurt of pity that she, too, had been caught up in this bloody conflict. At least Jamie had chosen his course; this maid had hers thrust upon her. Yea, he could well feel compassion for her plight, though he would not risk Jamie's life by freeing her in a moment of compassion.

Leaning forward so that his mouth grazed the wet tangle of hair behind her ear, he said softly, "We mean you no harm. Your father has taken my brother prisoner, and we seek to barter you in exchange for him."

Another tremor ran through her slight form, and she twisted slightly so that he could see her fragile profile. "You are fool indeed, sir, if you think any act you may inflict upon me will alter my father's actions. He is not a man to be swayed from his course by sentiment."

"Strange words coming from a loving daughter."

Her laugh was short and strangled, and he glimpsed the brief quiver of her lower lip before she turned her head away. "Strange, indeed, but 'tis the way of it. I know him. If 'tis to his advantage, he will bargain with you. If it is not—I will rot in whatever prison you make for me before he meets your terms."

The horse stumbled in a rut on the narrow, hard track they followed, and Alex brought him upright with a steady hold on the reins. His arm tightened around his captive to keep her seated. It was most likely that she only sought to further her cause by casting doubt on the situation, for no father would refuse to bargain for his daughter's release. It was not so very much to ask, the exchange of two rebellious Scots for a lovely English flower. No, Warfield would bargain, despite what this maid might say to dissuade Alex from his course.

"What is your given name, lass?"

She did not reply for a moment. Then, grudgingly, she muttered, "Lady Catherine."

"Catherine. . . ." After a pause, he murmured, "You put me in mind of another Catherine—"

"And you, sir, put me in mind of a mannerless cur!"

He laughed softly. "Pull in your claws, little cat."

"Do not call me that."

"Catherine? Or Cat . . . or perhaps I should refer to you as her ladyship?"

"I would prefer you not speak to me at all, but if you must, Lady Catherine will do."

"You sing a weary song, Lady Catherine. Be still now, before you unsettle my horse so that we are both thrown onto the hard road."

After the first warmth of the day, the capricious fall weather began to change. The clouds scudding overhead were stacked one atop the other and darkened ominously. The wind grew cold again, and the smell of rain was in the brisk currents that whipped the horses' manes and the men's loose plaids into flapping banners. Tree limbs bent and swayed, littering the narrow track through Kielder Forest with small branches and leaves.

As daylight faded into gray afternoon, then deep dusk, Catherine huddled miserably in front of the Scot who held her captive in his rough embrace. She'd heard his companion call him Alex. Putting a name to her abductor did not allay her growing fear, nor lessen the dread that she may never see her home again.

Would her father bargain with this rogue Scot who had dared abduct her from beneath his very nose? Or would the earl consider her abduction the price she must pay for disobeying his edicts and leaving Warfield without an escort? No doubt, he would be inclined to do so, and it was ironic to think that the only thing that might keep him from refusing this Scot's ultimatum was her upcoming nuptials to Bothwick's heir.

That, she mused, would be all that would matter to him. The earl had made it quite plain that he had no use for her save as a pawn for increasing his coffers and position. It still rankled, still hurt that he thought so little of the fact that she was his child. Even her mother did not consider her wishes, but in light of her own circumstances that could be forgiven more easily. Why would a mother have reason to think it should be any different for her daughter than it had been for her?

A gust of cold, wet wind summoned a shiver from her, and Catherine wished for what must have been the thousandth time since she had been plucked so rudely from the stream that she had played the obedient daughter for once. Oh, why had she not heeded her mother's warnings about leaving the castle without an escort? Since this dreadful conflict with the rebel Robert Bruce had worsened, times had grown more precarious than ever before. No one was safe with marauding Scots roaming honest English lands, looting, killing, abducting. . . .

"Here, lass." The rough voice was accompanied by a length of surprisingly dry plaid draped over her shoulders. "It grows cold."

He pronounced it "cauld," his words formed with an odd cadence that was curiously melodic. Catherine wanted to refuse, to fling off the warm wool and announce disdainfully that she had no need of anything Scottish. Yet her hands were shaking violently from the chill, and the wind found every little rip in her wet garments with icy fingers. She stiffened, but did not acknowledge his courtesy as she allowed the plaid to remain over her shoulders.

An enigma, this Scottish rogue, polite one moment, frightening the next. Even his appearance was contradictory; the features of an archangel marred by a wicked scar on one cheek, a thin white crescent that stitched from the edge of a dark eyebrow to the corner of his mouth. Yet despite the blemish he was comely, with a masculine symmetry of wide brow, thick-lashed gray eyes, straight nose, and defined lips above a strong, square chin. He wore no beard, though a dark shadow presaged the thick growth along the line of his jaw and around his mouth. It was an intriguing face, where expressions of savagery and humor seemed equally comfortable.

Catherine shivered despite the welcome warmth of the wool, and the object of her thoughts tightened his arms around her. "Still cold, catkin?" When she did not reply, he laughed softly. "You might well grow used to it, for 'tis a long way to where we go."

It was on the tip of her tongue to demand their destination, but she did not ask. What did it matter? Far or close, she would never know how to find her way home. While she might have oft wandered fields and fens in England, making her way through this hostile land would be far different from the idle roaming of a child in safe, familiar territory. No, she was more alone than she had ever been before.

Closing her eyes, Catherine prayed fervently that God would deliver her from danger, or at the least, forgive her sins should she die. She silently recited the rosary, mentally ticking off the beads of each decade as she offered the appropriate prayers. With every jolting step along the rutted track that wound through forests and over rugged slopes, she besieged God with penitence and pleas, yet the numbing journey did not cease. They rode into the night, and the jangle of harness and thunder of hooves was an incessant noise in her ears that finally lulled her to fitful slumber.

When she woke, the pitch-black of night had given way to a misty gray glow that made nightmarish silhouettes of bare tree limbs and rocky ridges. She ached all over, and her muscles were stiff and sore when she tried to shift position.

"Hold, lass," the now-familiar voice muttered in her ear. "We are almost there."

"Where?" Her sleepy mumble was ignored, and she blinked slumber-haze from her eyes as she strained to focus. As the sky grew lighter, she could see that thick mist shrouded the land in an eerie, suffocating blanket. No one spoke. Not even the horses made any sound, save an occasional wheeze of exhaustion or scrabble of hooves on rock.

Gradually, Catherine became aware that they were ascending a steep grade, winding between the bare, twisted limbs of bushes and stunted trees. The Scotsman's body was a solid, heated presence, and his arms were still tight around her. For the first time, she was grateful he held her so closely. The brief glimpses she caught of sheer rock walls falling away from the rutted track they rode were enough to instill terror. Holy Mother of Mercy, where was he taking her? To some mountain cave?

By the time the mist lifted, the sun was rising behind a towering crag that loomed upward like a giant's fist thrust from the center of the earth. At the very summit sprawled a sharply angled line of curtain walls, and behind them could be seen the unmistakable turrets of a stone fortress. Clouds snagged on the topmost tower, obscuring the identifying pennant, but the Scot named it for her:

"Castle Rock. . . ." He shifted in the hard saddle and said in a harsh tone, "And I will allow no Englishmen to take it away again."

"I cannot imagine any sane Englishmen wanting it," she returned tartly. Instead of being angered by her observation as she half expected, he laughed.

"I do not doubt that. I have yet to meet an Englishman with a dram of good sense."

"And yet you Scots still have not managed to best the English army . . . surprising, in light of the fact that you think we English are incompetent."

"Nay, lass, I did not say the English are incompetent. Just foolish. There is a difference, though you may not think it. You, for instance, seem intelligent enough. Yet you mercilessly tweak the nose of the captor who holds you. Would you consider that brave or foolish?"

Behind his light words lurked a wealth of innuendos that she did not care to examine too closely, and she drew in a deep breath of damp air that smelled of gorse.

"Diverting," she replied tersely, and his laughter rumbled past her ear.

"You have a quick tongue, lass."

"Too quick, I have been told."

"I do not doubt it for a moment."

There were moments his accent seemed dense, and at others, it disappeared almost completely. Catherine half turned to glance back at him. His beard had grown thicker during the night and he looked tired. Long dark hair gleamed with moisture, tiny droplets like diamonds clinging to the sleek strands that brushed his shoulders. Yet he sat erect, and his grip on her had not once slipped, even while she slept in his folded arms.

One of the other men called out, and Alex turned his head to answer, replying in the same incomprehensible language. Gaelic, of course. These men would speak it as their native tongue. It had a certain melodic pattern to it, but she did not understand a single word, and could only guess by their gestures and intonations what was said.

The group parted, several men splitting off from the main band to ride over a rocky crag and disappear; others stayed with the main party as they passed through a small village, then rode up the steep slope toward the fortress. Fatigue sapped Catherine's strength but not her fear, and the nearer they drew to the curtain walls that enclosed the keep, the more fearful she grew. What would happen to her once they arrived? There had been no time for more than cursory threats on the hasty flight from England, but once they were safely inside, what would this dark Scotsman do? Beneath his outward geniality, she had glimpsed ruthless purpose, and it was not a comforting thought.

Catherine concentrated on remaining calm when they paused at last before the gates and the drawbridge was lowered to allow them inside. The weary horses picked up speed, their hooves clattering over the wood-planked bridge as they passed beneath the iron teeth of the portcullis. Twin gatehouses flanked the drawbridge, and once the party was inside the thick walls, the portcullis was lowered behind the last rider in a shrieking rattle of chains. Torches lit a long, narrow passage that was lined with guardrooms and bent sharply at the far end. Men leaning in some of the doorways called out as they rode by, and Alex answered easily, as if his return with a bedraggled female draped from his saddle was commonplace. Perhaps it was, she thought, and felt the terror well again.

Resolutely, she swallowed her fear and stiffened her spine. None would see her quail as if she were a terrified goose. Nor would she lose her dignity again as she had when he first came upon her. She was, after all, Lady Catherine of Warfield, and she would be treated with respect.

Taking furtive stock of the keep, she recognized with dismay that it was well fortified; indeed, precautions had obviously been taken to withstand even a lengthy siege. She smothered a bubble of panicked laughter at the thought. What army would be hardy enough to climb this precarious hill to camp outside the walls and lay siege?

"What think you, my lady, of Castle Rock?"

Staring straight ahead, she managed a disdainful shrug at his query. " 'Tis obvious far too much coin was spent to make it so dark and forbidding."

"Yea, so it was. I rebuilt it well. Not even my father would recognize it now."

That gave her pause. So 'twas *he* who had done all this? He was lord of this keep? This time she turned to look at him. "You must be very quarrelsome if you need a keep this well fortified."

White teeth flashed in a grin that lent his features a disarmingly youthful expression. "Aye, some say I am exceedingly quarrelsome. And some say that I am a man who lets no insult pass without reprisal."

"Men who live peacefully would not need to spend all their coin on soldiers and battlements."

"Such as Lord Warfield? Would you say he is a peaceful man, my lady?"

Catherine was silent. There was no point in attempting to reply to that question. All knew of the earl's violent nature. Even the most vicious rumor about him had a basis in fact, she feared.

When they emerged from the passage into the light again, Catherine squinted at the sudden brightness. The clouds had dissipated, so that sunlight filled the open bailey and glittered on the stone. Gardens stretched along one wall, bordered by stables at one end and thatch-roofed storehouses at the other. A most impressive—and formidable—fortress.

Despair rose inside her, and Catherine steeled herself. What would the earl say when this border rogue approached him with a proposition to exchange hostages? 'Twas doubtful her father would agree. After all, any hostages he held would no doubt be valuable to him—suddenly she recalled the two Scots just brought to Warfield, the younger clad in a plaid very like the length of wool wound about her now. She half turned to look sharply at the man behind her. "Is your brother older than you?"

"He is a stripling, younger by near fifteen years, but old enough to be taken hostage by English brigands."

Catherine stiffened. "My brother is no brigand."

"Your brother?" He looked startled, and reined in his mount by a flight of stone steps leading up to the towering keep. "I was told the earl is your father."

"Yea, he is, but 'twas not my father who captured the prisoners you want. 'Twas my brother."

"Then mayhap I should conduct my negotiations with him instead of the earl."

" 'Twill do you no good. My father is his overlord and

has the final word in the matter. It is he who holds their lives in the balance."

Catherine's hard-won control wavered, but her voice was steady. It was true. The two Scottish captives were plum prizes, Nicholas had told her, and King Edward would be most pleased by their capture. For her father to release them would be a miracle that she did not expect.

The Scot gave her a thoughtful glance as he dismounted and pulled her down from the saddle to set her on her feet. Immediately, her knees crumpled and she would have sprawled gracelessly on the ground had he not caught her. A faint smile crooked one corner of his mouth as he held her up with his hands beneath her elbows.

Embarrassed, Catherine snapped, " 'Tis difficult to stand after so many hours spent on horseback."

"Yet I manage it well enough." Before she could form another retort, Alex bent slightly and scooped her into his arms, cradling her against his chest as if she weighed no more than a child as he mounted the steep stairs with irritating energy.

Catherine bit her lower lip to hold back sharp words. It would never do to be dropped on a staircase this steep, and she certainly did not trust this Scot not to do it if she angered him. When they reached the top of the stairs, he strode through wide double doors and into a great hall that smelled of stale smoke, foul rushes, and the residue of a hundred past meals. Gnawed bones were scattered atop tables and benches were overturned. Empty ale pitchers lent a pungent scent to air already befouled with the taint of unruly hounds and spilled ale, ample evidence of the lack of a goodwife to oversee the servants' duties.

Alex muttered under his breath, then swung her to her feet again, this time keeping one hand on her arm in a clasp that was light but firm. "Hold, my lady. I shall rouse the servants to ready a chamber for you."

Sweeping the hall with a derisive glance, Catherine asked caustically, "Do you mean for me to sleep in this uncivilized hovel? It has the stench of a stable."

His jaw tightened, and a muscle leaped beneath the beard-shadow. "Aye, my fine lady, I do indeed mean for you to sleep in my home. If 'tis not civilized enough for you, take comfort in the fact that you may soon be back where you find the lodgings more to your liking. Unless, of course, your father replies with typical English civility, and then you may well end your days in this hovel."

A veiled threat lurked beneath his words. Catherine said nothing as he stalked away from her, calling in Gaelic for his servants. She stood where he'd left her, gazing in dismay at her surroundings. Torn banners hung awry on the smoke-blackened walls, and in the rafters overhead perched birds of prey. Droppings added to the foul mess of filthy straw on the stone floor, and there was an air of general disorder about the hall that would have sent Lady Warfield into a swoon.

A little stiffly, she moved to stand beside a tall candle rack, where the tallow tapers had guttered. Her hands knotted into painful fists, and she stared blindly at the congealed tallow wax lumped on the candle stand. For the first time, she truly feared that she would never see her home again. Shuddering, she murmured the first words that came to mind: "*Júdica me, Deus, et discérne causum meam de gente non sancta—*"

"*. . . ab hómine iniquo et dolóso érue me,*" a rough male voice finished behind her, and she turned sharply to look up at her captor. His mouth quirked into a mocking smile that did not reach his eyes.

"Do you think the English are the only men who pray in Latin? I know that prayer as well, my lady—'Give judgment for me, O God, and decide my cause against an unholy people—from unjust and deceitful men deliver me.' Fitting, I think, that I should give voice to those last words, do you not agree?"

"I . . . I do not know what you mean," she managed to get out weakly.

"Yea, lady, I think you do. When next you pray, mayhap you had best ask God to deliver us all from deceitful men, for if your father fails me, he fails you as well."

Catherine could not reply. All hope that she might find mercy in this man dwindled away, leaving only rising despair. If her father did not agree to his terms, she was doomed to end her days in the barbaric land of the Scots. . . .

4

It did not sweeten Alex's mood to find his hall in turmoil.
It should not matter to him what the maid thought of his
home, and it rankled that it did. A few well-placed kicks
and curses were enough to rouse the servants from
drunken stupors into clumsy efforts to right benches and
tables, mop up spilled ale, and scoop fallen food from the
stale rushes. Yet he had seen reflected in violet-blue eyes
the image of his home from a stranger's perspective, and
it was not a pleasing vision.

Nor was it pleasing to have her offering prayers for
deliverance from unholy men—meaning, of course, him.

Curtly, he beckoned a servant to his side and spoke to
her in Gaelic. "Take the lady to a chamber, Mairi, and
see that she is given all she needs. But do not let her out
of your sight, or give her a moment's freedom."

Mairi, an older woman with wise eyes and a tart
tongue, gave him an appraising stare before nodding. "It
is a black day when I am sent to guard an English prisoner."

"She is hostage against Jamie's return." Alex lifted a

brow when Mairi stood silently studying the young woman. "Do you have a quarrel with her presence, Mairi?"

"I have a quarrel with the presence of any Sassenach in Scotland."

Alex did not respond. Mairi's husband and only son had been killed by the English years before, and she still harbored hatred against them. Understandable, and one of the reasons she was so suitable to guard the fair English flower who still stood with silent dignity by a rack of guttered candles. Alex frowned. In the thin light that trickled through the tiny windows, he saw the utter weariness etched in the girl's face. Her eyes resembled nothing so much as huge purple bruises, dark against her ashen pallor. Such a fragile, well-defined face, her bone structure delicate and strong at the same time, with determination in the set of her jaw and the limpid gaze she lifted to him.

"You are to go with Mairi," he said to her in gruff English. "She will tend your needs."

The girl's eyes flicked to Mairi's resentful face. " 'Tis doubtful either of us will enjoy the alliance. Does she speak any English?"

"Enough. She is not meant to be a companion."

"Nay, I did not think so." Straightening her slender shoulders, she added quietly, "I would like to request the comfort of a priest."

"A priest! Do you think I intend to execute you, girl? I do not. You are far too valuable to me alive."

"Then you refuse my request?" Velvety soft eyes stared at him with steady contempt, and he shook his head angrily.

"Nay, I do not. If 'twill comfort you, I will send Father Michael to you when he returns."

Her cool nod of acceptance was reserved and relieved at the same time, and Alex felt another one of those irritating twinges of compassion that he tried to ignore. It was maddening, this feeling that he had erred when he knew he had not.

Pivoting, he stalked across the hall without glancing back at her. She was a hostage and no more. Once Jamie was returned to him, he would never see her again, nor would he want to. It would be enough just to have his brother back safe and alive.

He found Robbie in the bailey near the stables, leaning casually against a heavy oaken beam and chewing on a straw stalk. As he drew near him, Robbie lifted a tawny brow and grinned. "You look fit to kill, Alex lad. Has the wee lass got you vexed? She did not prick you with a blade, did she, or mayhap her claws again?"

Alex drew the back of one finger over the raw scratches on his cheek, wincing a little. "No more than seems usual for her. I vow, she swings like a pendulum between hissing cat and frightened kitten."

Robbie shrugged and spit out the straw stalk. "Like most females, I warrant. What do you intend to do?"

"Send a message to the earl offering an exchange of hostages. She can make her mark on't to convince him we have her."

"Aye, but will she?"

Alex scowled. "She will not be given a choice, Robbie. She will sign whatever she is told to sign, and I will send Warfield a lock of her hair to prove my intent."

"And would you, then?"

"Would I what?"

"Harm her if Warfield does not yield us Jamie."

Startled, Alex did not reply for a moment. It had not really occurred to him that Warfield would refuse. Rail and counter, perhaps, but not refuse. What man in his right mind would refuse to retrieve his own daughter from the enemy?

But even as the thought flitted through his head, Robbie reminded him in soft Gaelic, "Do not forget how the Sassenach bastards have treated the Bruce's womenfolk, Alex lad."

"Yea, 'tis true enough. And a bitter draught to swallow that Bruce's wife is still held prisoner, though her plight is better than that of his sister."

"Only a bloody Sassenach would hang women outside castle walls in wooden cages for nigh onto four years." Robbie drew in a deep breath, his face creased with harsh lines. "He did not even spare Bruce's twelve-year-old daughter until his own people grew outraged."

Alex sighed. "When Bruce's sister was caged on the castle walls of Berwick, no ransom offer he made swayed the English. While Edward yet holds Bruce's queen, her father is the Earl of Ulster and one of Edward's staunchest lieutenants. He is too powerful for Edward to risk offending him by treating her harshly. Will Warfield be as obstinate as King Edward?"

Robbie pushed away from the oak beam and put a hand on Alex's shoulder. "You may well have the lass for a long time, Alex. She is our only bargaining point. Do not forget what Bruce told you. . . ."

"How could I forget." Alex frowned. "Not that I blame him for it. He has lost so many to this bloody war that the fate of one rebellious lad cannot be allowed to matter."

"Aye, but the Bruce should be pleased that you have snatched the earl's daughter from under his very nose. But be forewarned—he might well want to hold her as security for the return of his own women."

Alex met Robbie's clear gaze steadily. "I do not think

Robert Bruce will begrudge me exchanging an English maid for my brother. He knows Jamie is my only family now."

Robbie shrugged. "I hope you are right. Now, I think we have earned a bit of hot food and pitchers of ale to wash away the taste of English dust from our throats."

" 'Twill take more than ale to wash away the bitter taste that haunts me."

Robbie's tawny brows lifted. "How can you be bitter when you have the earl's own daughter locked in yon tower chamber to await his reply? Few Sassenachs are willing to allow the hand of a Scotsman to sully their daughter. And 'tis a notion you had best plant firmly in Warfield's mind along with your offer to exchange for Jamie."

Amused, Alex agreed. "You have the torturous mind of a fiend, Robbie, but I commend you for it. 'Tis too bad you are not consulted as one of Bruce's advisers. We might well win back Scotland without a drop of bloodshed."

"Nay, lad, not if I was consulted." Robbie closed a fist around the hilt of the sword hanging at his side. "I find fighting the English far too entertaining to give it up for blather."

Alex accompanied Robbie to the hall and called for a pitcher of ale to be brought. It was several pitchers and much later when he thought of Lady Catherine again, ensconced in a chamber in the east tower and safely under lock and key. On the morrow, he would have her make her mark on a letter for Warfield.

A fire blazed in the central hearth, huge logs sending up showers of sparks and emanating warmth in a small circle beyond the blaze. He stretched out his long legs toward the heat, eyes half-closed, a bit bemused with ale and a heavy heart. Jamie . . . far too young to be at the mercy of the English, though his own impulsiveness had caused his plight. But he was the only family left to Alex now. All the others had gone through the years, most slain in battle—save his mother, who had succumbed to childbed fever.

Frowning into his cup, Alex tried to summon his mother's face from memory. It was so vague, a blur of red-gold hair and light eyes that evoked feelings of warmth without solid image. He had not been much older than Jamie was now when she had borne the babe, dying of it before Alex returned from a skirmish with English border troops. So long ago, yet he still felt the emptiness and anguish at her loss, still recalled the mix of emotions at the birth that had claimed his mother and left behind a healthy, squalling infant. His first resentment of Jamie had long since faded, replaced by a fierce desire to keep alive and safe the last reminder of Catriona Fraser.

Oddly, the captive in the tower reminded him in some way of his mother. Perhaps it was the unusual shade of hair they shared, that coppery glow like sunlit bronze that caught the eye. Or perhaps it was that Lady Catherine's name was the English form of Catriona. Another similarity that was both striking and disconcerting. Yet the differences were just as obvious, as this Lady Catherine had a more prickly nature than his mother's sweet temperament. Ah, God, how he missed her, even after all these years. Her death had dealt him a harsh blow.

So long ago now, even before the Fraser estates had been deseisined by Edward I, before his father had died in another attempt to reclaim them from the English. It was a bitter fact that he had been not long dead when his son had finally managed to wrest their lands back from English hands. But he would hold them this time, though the ancient title that had once been his heritage was now worn by one of Edward's nobles. It was galling, that the enemy used that which was rightfully his. . . .

"Whsst, Alex lad, where have you gone? You put me in mind of a lost puppy with that long face."

Alex smiled, and he looked up at Robbie with a shrug. "I *feel* much like a lost puppy at the moment, Robbie. I had hoped to bring Jamie back with us."

"Aye, but we have the next best thing in Warfield's bonny lass. If the Border Lion can be brought to his knees, she should do it. Of course, there are those who say Lord Warfield has no fondness for anything other than English dirt and stone, unless 'tis his gold."

That was what Alex feared—that the earl would prefer the value of Scottish hostages to the value of his daughter. After all, King Edward would pay well in coin and favor for Robert Bruce's cousin, and if a worthless Scottish youth happened to be part of the prize, then so much the better. It was not a pleasant thought.

Nor was it a pleasant confrontation when he approached Catherine the following morning. She stood silent and pale in the chamber, the brightness of her hair a vivid contrast to her colorless face as he spread the parchment on a table and held out a quill.

"Make your mark at the bottom of the parchment, so your father will know you are alive and well."

"Unless I pen words to that effect, he will still know nothing more than he does at this moment," she snapped.

Alex stared at her with rising irritation. His head hurt. His eyes were scratchy from lack of sleep. He had lain awake all night planning his strategy. Now she refused his request, another irritation, albeit minor.

" 'Tis of no difference to me if you will not put your mark on this parchment, but it might very well ease your father's mind. Do you not care for his repose?"

"No more than do you." Her brows lifted slightly when he swore at her. "I daresay my father will lose no sleep over this. He will do what he thinks right, as he has always done, and trouble himself no more over the matter. It is a trait of his that I have often admired, and more often abhorred. But it is the way of it, sir."

"What of your mother? Does the countess feel as he does? Or would she like reassurance that you are alive, do you think?"

Her lower lip quivered slightly, but she shrugged. "My mother will think what my father tells her to think."

"Will she? Lord Warfield is a most formidable man, if he is able to govern the thoughts of another person."

"Yea, he is indeed most formidable, as you will soon discover to your regret."

"That remains to be seen." Curse her, she defied him to the teeth. Frowning, he slowly drew his fingers along the sleek length of the goose quill. "I have been known to be formidable myself when crossed, my lady. If you value your skin, you will make your mark on this parchment and be done with it."

"I refuse to be a willing accomplice to my own imprisonment." Though the telltale quiver of her lower lip betrayed apprehension, her chin jutted out with defiance.

Goaded, Alex tossed aside the quill and closed the narrow space between them in a single stride, drawing a *sgian dhu* from his boot top as he did. He grabbed her by one wrist and swung her around when she would have turned away, holding the sharp dirk up so that she could see it.

"Nay, lass—if you will not sign, I must have some way of assuring your father that I do indeed have you."

Her eyes widened, soaking up light from the window slit behind them. She flicked a glance at the gleaming blade of the dirk, then back at him. "Will you send him my head? 'Twill hardly convince him that you mean me no harm."

"Nay, but 'twould convince him he had best agree to my offer if he desires to see the rest of you." His grip tightened when she tried to twist away, and he muttered under his breath, "Hold, you silly goose. Would I slay my only advantage? I am not so foolish."

Using his weight as leverage, he pinned her against the edge of the table. She leaned back and away from him, her breasts straining against the tattered velvet gown. He briefly glimpsed creamy skin, and he lifted his gaze from the tempting sight with determined indifference. He raised a silky loop of her bright hair in one hand, then deftly sliced it free with his dirk. She did not move as he held up the dangling lock of hair.

"A token for your father, my lady. Pray he accepts my offer."

He stepped back from the table and looked down at her. She half sprawled on the table, palms behind her to prop herself up, her face a study of defiant fear. "I pray only for my deliverance from unholy men," she whispered huskily.

Insult battled with anger as Alex stared down at her. Curse her, she wore a face like a martyred saint! Did she think him so crude as to defile her? To send her back with a Scots bairn in her belly? Yet, leaning backward half atop the table as she was, her body draped almost seductively over the wooden surface, he found her infinitely enticing—and dangerous.

He gestured with his dirk. "Now, my lady, perhaps you will be so good as to remove your garments for me."

Her ashen face paled even more. "I will not."

"Yea, you will, whether it be willing or no. 'Tis up to you if you do it, or I do it for you. But I warn you—I will not be gentle."

"I do not doubt that." Her lower lip quivered slightly and quickly thinned to a harsh, straight line. "Yet I have no intention of disrobing for you, or for any other man."

A sardonic smile touched the corners of his mouth. "I have told you, my fine lady, that I would not soil myself with your virgin's blood, and I meant it. Do not fear that I mean to ravish you. I find your garments of much more value than I do your maidenhead."

Outrage flashed in her eyes, turning them from light violet to a deep purple. "If you mean to insult me, you are far from the mark. I would sooner die than allow a vile Scots savage to put his hands upon me, and you are the—"

Before she could finish, he put a harsh hand on her shoulder. " 'Tis best for your continued good health that you leave your opinions of me unspoken. I want only your garments. Disrobe before I begin to think your protests are just coy flirtations."

There was another moment's tension, then she twisted free of his hold and rolled gracefully from the table to stand beside it and gaze at him with disdain.

"Very well. If 'tis my humiliation you think to gain, however, you will be disappointed."

"I think to gain only your garments." Impatient, he indicated the gown with a raking sweep of his dirk. " 'Tis of no matter to me if they are intact or in ribbons, so do you set to work before I do."

She bent her head, and the coppery fall of gleaming hair fell forward to hide her face from him. Alex smothered an involuntary spurt of sympathy. Her hands were slender and fine-boned, the fingers long and well mani-

cured, trembling as she fumbled with the side laces of
her gown. The outer garment was loose over her tighter
undergown, the scooped neck embroidered with gilt
thread that was now frayed. She gave a quick yank, and
the tangled side laces parted. As the blue velvet crumpled to a puddle at her feet, her fingers curled into the
thinner undergarment. It was made of flimsy stuff, fitting
closer to her body. The torn bodice was unraveled, with
loose threads of pale blue lying in a linen web against her
breast. Without looking up at him, Catherine unfastened
the ties that bound it around her, and he glimpsed a
silken shift beneath. His mouth twisted. Well-guarded
maiden, armored with layers of clothing against masculine intrusion. . . .

"All of it," he said gruffly when she hesitated, and her
head flung up in an angry shimmer of loose hair.

"Yea, Sir Blackguard, so you have said."

He watched dispassionately as she twisted out of the
undergarment and flung it to the floor atop the velvet.
She stood there before him garbed in only the thin silken
shift that reached to mid-thigh. He waited until he saw in
her widening eyes that she at last understood what he
wanted.

"If you think the sight of my shift will move my father
to agreement," she said through stiff lips, "you are much
mistaken. 'Twill only anger him."

Alex shrugged. "I do not care what moves him to
come to your aid, only that he does."

Her laugh was strangled. "Yea, and I would not give
you odds that 'twill be to your satisfaction."

"The shift, my lady. Your maidenly protests and delays
bore me, and I grow weary of the wait."

It was a lie, he knew as he said it, for the sight of her
creamy skin and shivering innocence was more enticing

than he had anticipated. Indeed, his body had already betrayed him, and he was glad he was garbed in braies and loose trews instead of a more revealing tunic.

More gruffly than he intended, he again ordered her to disrobe. "Lest you have grown fond of Castle Rock, mayhap, milady?"

His mocking taunt brought an angry flush to her cheeks, and the quick retort: "Nay, no more fond than I would be of any sty, I warrant." In a graceful movement of her slender body, she shrugged out of the silken shift and tossed it contemptuously to the discarded pile of clothing at her feet.

If he had thought to humble her, he quickly realized his mistake. She stood proudly before him, her chin lifted with aloof disdain. Her arms were held rigidly at her sides as she looked past him to the narrow window slit that filtered gray light into the chamber. Alex stood still, suddenly aware that if he moved at all, it would be to caress the tempting curves before him. Saint Jerome, but she was a beauty, temptation painted in cream and rose, high firm breasts with up-tilted nipples knotted into tight rosettes, a tiny waist that needed no stays or binding, slender hips, and thighs with a nest of red-gold curls at the juncture—despite the chill in the air, heated blood pulsed through his veins with thundering urgency.

Chagrined, he knew that 'twas he who was humbled, not this pale creature who was his brother's only hope. With difficulty, he bent to retrieve her discarded garments, wadding them into a bundle beneath his arm as he finally met her icy gaze.

"If I were as unholy as you seem to think, no pleas or prayers would save you. Remember that, milady, when next you pray for your deliverance."

Violet eyes regarded him with unblinking animosity. "It has been said that the devil garbs himself in the guise of a man at times, feigning kindness to the unwary. I do not intend to waver in my prayers for deliverance."

"Then we both pray for the same thing, for as I said before, the earl's answer may deliver us all."

Jaw tight, Alex left the chamber without another glance at her, slamming the door behind him.

As the echo of the slamming door faded, Catherine's legs buckled and she crumpled to her knees on the cold stone floor. She was shaking, her hands trembling as if with the ague. For a moment she had thought he would take her atop the table with the utter disregard of a man taking a field whore. Another shudder racked her body.

It had taken all her strength not to curl into a ball in front of him, modesty shrieking at her to hide herself from his intrusive gaze. But it was what he expected from an Englishwoman, and she would not give him that satisfaction. Nay, she would give him nothing but contempt, even if he killed her for it.

Still shivering, she pushed herself to her feet and moved to the narrow cot against the far wall. The blanket was thin but big enough to cover her, and she draped it around herself as a cloak. Bare toes curled up from the chill of the stone floor, and she thought of her fine-woven hose and soft slippers, left by the banks of the stream beyond the hedgerows. What would they think when they found them? When they received the Scotsman's demands?

It was easy to imagine her father's fury, her mother's tight-lipped acceptance, even her brothers' vows of retribution. More difficult was imagining the earl's acquiescence to any proposal from the enemy. He hated the Scottish with a passion that bordered on insanity, in her opinion. Usually her mother sent her from the table when he began one of his diatribes against the savages to the north, but not before she'd gleaned enough to know how he felt about them.

As the uncontrollable shivering eased, weariness seeped into her limbs. She sagged into the hard mattress and buried her face in her open palms. Why was she now so exhausted? Despite her fear and the cold chamber she occupied, she had slipped into a deep, dreamless sleep the night before. She had not wanted to wake. If not for the cheerless servant named Mairi, she would have pulled the rough wool blankets up over her head and stayed in the narrow cot all day.

But Mairi had forced her to rise before the sky was more than a pale gray, to wash her face with cold water from a cracked pitcher and bowl, then eat a morning meal of oat pottage. Surprisingly, she had found it tasty, though she was reminded of her brother's wry assertion that Scots ate more oats than did all the horses in the entire kingdom.

Now the long day stretched endlessly ahead of her like the promise of eternity. Catherine willed herself to motion. She could not lie abed all day. It was not her nature to be idle. Always, she found something to do, whether sneaking dusty volumes of ancient books from her father's library, or simply talking in the kitchen with Cook, she could not be inactive. Was she now doomed to stare at four walls all day, with nothing to do but dwell on her hopeless situation?

Her chamber was unadorned by any tapestries to ward off drafts. The narrow cot was the only furniture other than a table and a three-legged stool. A scattering of rushes were strewn about the floor, and a meager supply of wood was stacked beside a shallow hearth. Only embers glowed to lend warmth to the chamber, and wind whistled through chinks between the stones. Clearly not a prized chamber.

She rose from the cot and studied the rough hemp sheet stretched over the thin mattress. It would be rough against her skin, but better than remaining naked beneath the wool blanket over her shoulders, and she set about fashioning a crude garment. It took ingenuity but at last she had ample covering, save for her feet. Her toes bent up from the cold stones as she moved to the window ledge set deep into one wall. It was narrow and recessed, a portal to the world that allowed in little more than a hazy glow. Peering out, she could see only thin slices of life below, and hear only faint, muffled sounds of people going about their daily duties. A loud creaking of winch chains cut through the murmur of voices as the drawbridge was lowered, and she thought then of her brother Nicholas, and how that sound had often meant a sweet homecoming.

Ah, sweet Mother of Mercy, what would he say when he knew she had been abducted? Would he mourn for her? Would he be angry? And more importantly—would he come for her?

Almost desperately, Catherine held to that hope. Even if the earl would not come for her, Nicholas would. He would not allow her to languish in an alien land, at the mercy of men like this Scottish brigand who had so rudely snatched her from her own lands. Yea, Nicholas would come for her.

Catherine leaned her cheek against the rough stone of the wall. She would wait patiently. She had little choice but to do so. Waiting might teach her patience, a virtue she had always lacked. Many were the times Father de Crecy admonished her for impatience. Now she would learn to cultivate it, to embrace it.

Yet as time wore on, Catherine found herself pacing the confines of the bedchamber relentlessly. She had counted the stones in the wall time and again. There were eight hundred forty-two between the cot and the far wall. Was it her imagination, or were the walls closing in around her?

By the time Mairi returned, she was even glad to see the dour-faced woman, and greeted her with barely restrained impatience. "I thought you would never come back."

"Aye, and 'tis no' like I wanted tae, ye know." Mairi squinted slightly at her, her thin lips pursed in dislike. "But the laird expects it of me, so here I am, coddling ye like ye were a bairn. Here is yer evening meal. Dinna waste it."

"Wait—" Catherine put out a hand then quickly withdrew it when Mairi glared fiercely at her. "What manner of food have you brought?"

"Wha' does it matter tae ye? 'Tis food. Eat it. 'Twill put some meat on your skinny bones."

Catherine peered at the contents of the tray Mairi had brought, and frowned slightly. "Is that my bread?"

"Aye, wha' else d'ye think it is?"

" 'Tis brown bread instead of manchet—"

"Aye, manchet and pandemain is for the laird o' the keep, no' a prisoner." Mairi bristled when Catherine's eyes narrowed at her tone. "And ye dinna need tae be looking at me like tha', either. Ye are no more than a captive, so dinna be putting on airs tha' ye be better than me."

"No, I was not *putting on airs,* as you so provincially refer to it. 'Tis just that I am not accustomed to eating brown bread."

Her cool reply earned another glare from the older woman. "Then ye ha' best get used tae it, for 'tis all ye will get from me, your *ladyship.*"

With effort, Catherine refrained from a reply that

would only make matters worse. She had not expected such animosity from this quarter. From her captor, yes, but not from this stout older woman who reminded her of Old Nurse, who had cared for her until she was ten.

The wooden platter was slammed to the table with unnecessary force. Catherine turned away and moved to the window to gaze out, too near tears of frustration and despair to risk another confrontation with the servant. She stood there until she heard the door slam behind Mairi, followed by the grating of a key in the lock. Then her shoulders slumped and she pressed her cheek against the cold stone window facing.

Had it been only the day before she had wished for an escape from her forthcoming nuptials to Ronald of Bothwick? Not in her wildest dreams had she thought an answer to that prayer would come so quickly, or take such a deadly direction.

A wry smile twisted her mouth. Never would she allow her Scots captor to know just how much he frightened her. To show weakness to an enemy—and he was by his own words an enemy—would be fatal. It seemed he waited and watched for her to err, to reveal a chink in the armor she tried so hard to keep intact. The strain was excruciating.

Summoning her courage, she picked at the unappetizing food on the tray. Cold meat graced the hard trencher of brown bread, and a hunk of cheese nestled in the midst of dried peas that looked flavorless. Catherine gazed glumly at her evening meal. If this was the best fare her captors could offer, 'twas no wonder they coveted English lands. How could people survive on such meager repast?

Yet, to refuse sustenance would render her weak, and she could not risk that. So she picked gingerly at her food, grimacing a little at the tough, stringy meat that was near unrecognizable. Mutton? Pork? Or beef from a scrawny cow? It could be rat for all she knew, but she managed to swallow several bites, followed by a hard crust of the bread and a bite or two of cheese. Watery ale in a small earthenware jug washed it down, and Catherine thought longingly of Cook and the delicious meals brought to Warfield's hall.

Closing her eyes, she envisioned a recent feast at her father's table, conjuring up images of roast pigeons, chickens, quail, oxen, and duck, visualized even the steam rising from hot venison pies and baked tarts. Her stomach rumbled at the enticing memories of savory preserves of nuts, fruits, and spices, and she opened her eyes. 'Twas sheer torture to think on what was not available, nor likely to be. Pottage seemed her more likely fare in this dismal stone keep so far from civilized food and friendly faces.

Gamely, she finished every bite of food. If she was to keep up her strength, she must force herself to eat despite how unappealing she found the victuals. After the unsatisfying meal, there was little left to occupy her time, save feeding the last piece of wood to the fire and dreamless sleep.

Dusk had come to plunge the room into near darkness before she heard the sound of a key in the lock again. Sitting upright on the edge of the cot, Catherine lifted her head to stare toward the door. Not even a fire dispelled the gloom of the chamber, now lit by only a weak ray of light from the narrow window slit. She blinked against the bright ellipse of candle glow as Mairi shuffled into the chamber.

"Here be light fer ye," came the gruff comment, followed by the clatter of a wooden candlestick atop the table. The candle flickered, then steadied to cast a rosy pool of light. A rustling sound of cloth accompanied

Mairi's terse explanation that the laird had sent up warm clothing and more blankets. "No' tha' ye ha' need of 'em, tucked away as ye are in a room out of the wind."

Catherine did not reply. She was far too grateful, and far too stubborn to show it. She sat still until the surly maidservant shot her a sullen look and left with an echoing slam of the door. When she heard the metallic click of key and lock, she rose stiffly to her feet.

With cold, shaking hands, she lifted a length of warm wool. It was a simple gown such as peasants wore, with no overgarment or decoration, only a leather girdle to lace beneath her breasts. As the gown fell around her shoulders and settled over her hips, comforting warmth enveloped her. Wool stockings and a pair of shapeless shoes were quickly donned, covering skin prickled with cold. Tremors of chill eased as she plucked a pair of wool gloves from the pile and tugged them over her slender fingers. They were rough and scratchy, nothing at all like the soft gloves she usually wore, but that mattered little now. Her priorities were confined to survival.

She held tightly to that determination in the following days when hours stretched into an endless blur of defiance occasionally broken by moments of stark despair. The Scotsman did not come to her tower room again, and dour Mairi was her only link with the world outside her small round chamber.

She felt herself diminishing, becoming as colorless and blank as the stones that formed the walls, and had the fanciful notion that if her captor did return, he would not be able to see her. She would be invisible to him, just one of the gray stones that were indistinguishable one from the other—like a spirit trapped in the trunk of an oak, a timeless face peering out at the world and slowly fading into time before memory . . . soon, no one would remember her.

5

Storm clouds bunched over Warfield keep in ominous shades of gray and black. A brisk wind blew over the bailey and the two men standing alone in the muddy center. Nicholas Worth, Lord Devlin and heir to the earldom of Warfield, swore harshly at the crumpled parchment he held in one fist.

"Damn that Scottish bastard!" He looked up to meet his father's steely eyes. "We can stop scouring villages and fields for Catherine. Alex Fraser, laird of Castle Rock, has taken her. He offers an exchange of hostages—one for two. His brother and de Brus for Catherine."

"Does he. How vexing." Lord Warfield did not flinch from his son's suddenly narrowed gaze, but stared back calmly. "I cannot do that, of course. He will have to offer different terms."

Nicholas held up a shorn curl of coppery hair. The silky strands wound around his fingers as if seeking comfort, so soft and satiny smooth, reminding him of all the times he had affectionately ruffled his sister's hair. "This time it is a lock of hair. Next time, it may be her head."

"Do not be so dramatic. Do you think even an ignorant Scot would so quickly harm a valuable hostage? He will not."

"Dare we risk it?" Nicholas's hand closed on the lock of hair. "He has her. Even if he does not kill her, there are worse fates for a maid in the enemy's camp."

Lord Warfield blew out a heavy breath of irritation. "We must be discreet. Curse her, she has managed to jeopardize her betrothal to Ronald of Bothwick with this trick."

"Is that all you care about?" Nicholas stared at his father with rising anger and disgust. "She is your daughter, for Christ's holy sake! Can you not spare a bit of honest concern for her?"

"Aye, I could if she had not been so foolish as to leave the castle unguarded. She is no longer a child, yet behaves as the most foolish infant. Now she has endangered a merger with Bothwick, from a fit of pique and absurd notions of chivalry and romantic love." The earl snorted. " 'Tis the very reason I forbade her access to the library and discouraged her ability to read, yet she defied me on that score as well. Nay, my concern lies now with how it will be explained to Bothwick. His envoy will not long be fobbed off with that ridiculous tale of maidenly modesty and a pilgrimage to a nunnery as the reason she has not appeared. We must be prudent."

Drawing in a deep breath to curb the vicious words he wanted to fling at his father, Nicholas said only, "I wish to reply in person to this bastard Scot. Perhaps I can persuade him that he has chosen the wrong way to gain the freedom of his brother and countryman."

"There will be no freedom for de Brus or the boy. They will be sent to King Edward when he desires it, and he will decide their fate. I have already sent a messenger to inform him of their capture."

"And Catherine?"

"If her capture is kept secret, I will offer a hefty ransom—but only if she is yet undefiled. I can hardly wed her to Bothwick if she has been well used by Scottish vermin." He stroked his chin with a thoughtful gesture, then shrugged. "Though perhaps it might be done if she is wise enough to pretend intact virtue."

Bile rose in Nicholas's throat. There were moments he hated his father, despised him as a coldhearted bastard, but this was not the time to bring up old resentments. Stiffly, Nicholas persisted: "I will go to Castle Rock and offer whatever it will take to free her."

"Not yet. Wait until I have consulted—"

"No!" The single word burst out so furiously that Lord Warfield halted and stared at his eldest son with narrowed eyes. Nicholas struggled for composure. "She is my sister. I am overly fond of her, and will not risk her life or her virtue any longer than is necessary. To protect her I will keep her situation quiet, but I go to Scotland for her, whether you will it or no."

" 'Tis not too late to name Robert my heir instead of you," the earl replied softly. "He is more malleable, and able to see sense."

"And also a lazy coward, too fond of soft ways to bestir himself to battle or stewardship. His estates are in ruin, and he has had them less than a year. Yea, name Robert heir if that is what you wish, and all that you hold dear will no doubt be speaking Gaelic as their native tongue before you are dead a year."

Nicholas's retort silenced the earl's objections, but it was plain that his father was not pleased.

"Oft, 'tis better to lose the hand than the entire arm, Nicholas. You might well remember that."

"Yea, so I will, but if the hand can be saved, then it should be done."

"Go then, but do not attempt to take de Brus or the Scots brat with you. They stay. Stall Fraser if you can. Tell him that you must see Catherine to ascertain that 'tis truly my daughter he has . . . your brothers will accompany you, and while you barter with the Scot, they can peruse Castle Rock to determine its strength and weakness."

"I prefer to go alone. Robert and Geoffrey will only be in the way."

"Yea, go alone and you may linger alone. Take a show of force with you, or you may end your days in a Scottish sty. You will do as I tell you. You are worth much more as a hostage than is your sister."

It was the best he could hope for, and as Nicholas made plans for the journey north, he wondered grimly how such a man could be his sire. Harshness in war was one thing. To care so little for the fate of his own child was another. Perhaps that was why Nicholas had grown so fond of Catherine, recognizing in his sister a spirit of fire and rebellion that he had oft felt as a boy. His defiance had been curbed with harsh beatings and rigid discipline, but Catherine's spirit was being slowly stifled beneath the weight of indifference. Both methods were equally lethal.

"Miles." He beckoned his captain of the guards to him. "Mount a troop. We ride north before the day is done."

Looking startled, Miles nodded. "Yea, m'lord. Do we take just Devlin men, or do the earl's soldiers go with us?"

Nicholas thought of his father's soldiers, well armed and trained, but loyal only to the earl, and shook his head. "Nay, we take only our own this time, Miles."

He would not risk Catherine with more duplicity. She would need all the loyalty he could muster to save her from a cruel fate. Tucking the lock of her hair into his sherte, he moved swiftly across the muddy bailey toward the stables. There was yet much to be done.

Catherine heard him coming down the corridor. She knew it was not Mairi, for the footsteps were heavy and assured, not the shuffling gait of the older woman. Tensing, she folded her hands in front of her and turned to face the door, keeping the window behind her so that her expression would be shadowed.

A key turned loudly in the lock and the door swung open with a harsh creaking of hinges. The Scot ducked slightly to enter, his height greater than the doorway. He surveyed her coolly with his light eyes, his expression unreadable. Her heart lurched, and a thousand thoughts streaked through her mind, a thousand different fears.

To her surprise, he bowed slightly, a gesture of courtesy she did not expect, and said, "Good morn, milady."

Cautiously, she inclined her head in the barest of acknowledgments. "Good morn, sir."

A faint smile curved his mouth. "It has come to my attention that you find your visit here lacks excitement."

She stiffened. "Nay, what I said to Father Michael was that I find your household wearisome. But then, I would prefer boredom to certain notions of entertainment."

"No doubt. Since Father Michael reports your spirits to be withering without proper company, I thought to relieve your tedium."

"With *your* company?"

"If I choose." His cool reply was guarded, and she noted a small flicker in his eyes that betrayed his chagrin at her derision. So, he was not as immune to insult as she had begun to think. It was a worthwhile bit of information to file away for future use.

"Perhaps your company is better than dying slowly of

tedium, but I prefer a slow, uncertain fate to a swift, certain one."

Leaning back against the oak portal, he crossed his arms over his chest and regarded her without smiling. "Do not be so sure of that, milady, until you are faced with the choice."

Silence stretched awkwardly, and Catherine studied him with a slightly lowered gaze. His trews were faded, his sherte of fine quality linen that showed age, and his knee-high boots were scuffed and muddy. A sword was strapped around his waist, dangling with lethal promise at his side.

Impatience edged his words as he said, "I see my long absence has not improved your opinion of me. 'Tis of little consequence to me if you languish here alone. I came only to offer you relief from your solitude, but if you prefer—"

"Pray, pardon my sharp tongue, sir." She said it quickly as he pushed away from the door with the obvious intention of departing, desperation overcoming her natural aversion. "Since Father Michael can no longer come, I find the days overlong and unbearable without some task to fill them. I can weave, if you care to have a loom brought to me. I can spin wool into yarn, or knit garments . . . I am not accustomed to being idle for so long."

Pausing with one hand on the door latch, he looked at her for a long moment, his gray eyes serious and considering as if calculating her sincerity. "I was told you read."

His abrupt comment startled her, but she nodded. "Yea, 'tis true."

"Do I have your word of honor that you will not attempt escape if I allow you from this chamber?"

Hope flared, but she gave him a cautious reply. "Am I so feared a captive then?"

"Nay, but none here have the inclination to waste time dragging you back should you attempt flight." A flicker of impatience knit his dark brows into a frown. "I am not a tolerant man, milady. Do you give me the answer I seek, or linger here with only your own company to fill your days. 'Tis your choice."

"With so gracious an invitation, I can do naught but accede to your request. Of course you have my word that I will not attempt escape. Where would I go? I am in an alien land peopled by the enemy."

"See that you keep that in mind." He stood back and gestured for her to precede him. After the briefest of hesitations, she crossed the chamber and moved through the door. Even knowing she was still a hostage, freedom from the tiny circular chamber was cheering.

The corridor was short, but with long windows that allowed in light on each side. Shutters were opened on the gray day, and a brisk wind carried in the smell of rain as they traversed the hallway to the stairwell. It spiraled down in a tight coil, narrow steps and dank closeness lit only by oil lamps in small niches. Light flickered and wavered over the stone steps as she made her way down cautiously, ever aware of the towering presence just behind her.

Silently, he guided her down another corridor off the stairwell, to a heavy door. Reaching past her, he pushed it open and it swung noiselessly into a large, airy chamber. Catherine stepped inside, trepidation melding into astonished delight.

"Oh, what a lovely room this is!"

"My father had it built." Alex stepped around her to the windows, shoving one open to allow fresh air. Lit candles danced in candle stands, and a horn lamp burned steadily beside a bolstered chair obviously meant to welcome an occupant. Shelves lined one wall from floor to ceiling, holding volumes of leather and wood-bound books.

"May I?" Catherine indicated the books with an up-lifted hand.

He shrugged. "You did say you could read, I think. Choose a volume that interests you."

There was an undisguised challenge in his tone, and she understood immediately that this was a test of some kind. She had pleaded for rescue from her boredom, and this was his answer.

Catherine did not deign to reply verbally to his challenge, but moved instead to the bookcase. The inevitable Greek tragedies were there, with treatises in Latin and French. After studying several dozen titles, she chose a slim volume of French poetry. She could feel him watching her as she flipped it open to peruse the lettered pages. It was beautifully copied, with flowing script and intricate drawings on the thick pages.

"Pray, read to me, milady. It has been some time since I have heard a woman read poetry."

She looked up at him with a cool lift of her brows. "I do not care to read aloud."

"No doubt." A cynical twist of his mouth accompanied his advance toward her. "Humor me, if you please. If for no other reason than because I have temporarily freed you from your chamber."

"Very well. Shall I read in French, or translate it for you?"

"A translation would be satisfactory."

"If you insist." She riffled the pages a moment, both resentful and amused by his skepticism of her ability to read, then cleared her throat and began to translate:
" 'The story I shall tell today Was taken from a Breton lay Called *Laustic* in Brittany, Which, in proper French would be *Rossignol*. They'd call the tale In English lands

The Nightingale.' " She felt his eyes on her, but kept her gaze firmly fixed on the stiff pages of the book as she read further. " 'There was, near Saint Malo, a town Of some importance and renown. . . .' " He remained silent as she read more, unmoving until she reached the lines, " 'They were much happier than before And would have asked for nothing more But lovers can't be satisfied When love's true pleasure is denied—' "

"Enough."

Catherine halted and looked up. He was staring at her with a strange expression. She shrugged carelessly. "There is much more to read, sir."

"I know that. I am familiar with this particular ballad. 'Twas composed by Marie de France, I believe."

"Yea, so it was." She closed the volume with a crisp snap, and held the leather-bound book to her chest. "I admit I am surprised that a man such as yourself would read this kind of verse."

"No more surprised than I am to find a woman who reads it so eloquently, I should think."

"Or one who reads at all, I infer."

A faint smile flickered. "Aye, 'tis true enough, I vow. I did not expect to harbor an educated female."

"Not exactly educated, but not ignorant, either." She ran a fingertip over the closed volume's edges. "Men are said to be illiterate if capable of reading in only one or two languages. For a female to read at all is a vaunted skill and quite useless, I have been told."

"And who would be so ignorant as to say that?"

"My father." She smiled wryly. "He shares the opinion of many men, who think a female should use her skill for the creation of children and tapestries, and little else."

"I cannot say I completely disagree with that opinion, though 'tis not likely that I would agree with Lord Warfield on much else. I would prefer meeting him on a battlefield to a bargaining table." Clasping his hands behind him, he moved across the room in strides as loose and easy as a large cat to stand in front of the windows, staring out.

Catherine watched from beneath her lashes, more than a little curious about a man who in one breath professed to read poetry, and in the next spoke casually of war. There were depths to him she had not considered. Was it possible he was not just the crude, savage Scot she had first thought him? If he was civilized, there may yet be hope for her.

"Of course, my father also said that Scots are vicious, untaught barbarians prone to devouring their own children if their larders are empty," she commented, still watching him from beneath her lowered lashes.

Alex turned sharply, and his dark brows crowded his eyes in a scowl. "I have no doubt Warfield would make such a remark, but am surprised that you dare repeat it to me."

"Are you? I beg your pardon. I thought we were being candid."

"Candor is for the captor, not the captured."

"I see. Honesty avails only those holding the sword, is that right, sir?"

"Usually." His mouth quirked into a tight smile. "It has been my experience that prudence is more useful to those beneath the blade."

"Yet the Scots still defy their rightful king. Would not prudence be of more use to you than arms?"

"Not if it involves yielding one hide of land to a king who has stolen the crown with lies and deceit." Crossing the room to the hearth, where a fire burned brightly, he leaned one arm on the stone mantel and regarded her with a brooding expression. "You are a cheeky maid, to speak so boldly to the man who holds your life in his hands."

She looked up at him, lifting her brows in feigned astonishment. "Again, you must forgive me. I was under the impression that my life was in my father's hands."

"No. Your fate is in your father's hands. Your life, I hold."

"Of which fact you relish reminding me." She placed the book on a table, feeling his eyes follow her as she crossed the chamber. Candle glow brightened the meager gray light streaming through the tall windows. Tiny rainbows danced across the floor in wavering patterns. The opened window allowed in cool air that smelled of imminent rain and distant freedom.

Alex laughed softly. "Next, I suppose you will claim that your father is a noble human being with the morals of a saint."

"I am not a fool, sir." Catherine clutched the back of a chair with both hands, the dark wood smooth beneath her fingers as she held it tightly. "Nor am I blind. I am well aware of my father's faults, as I have told you. But at least he did not sneak like a thief into your home to take your brother. Your brother, youthful as he may be, chose to engage in violent conflict. Do you deny it?"

"Nay. Jamie chose to leave the protection of his home, where you did not. But if I can save him from certain death, I mean to do it, whether you agree or no."

She wanted to say that her father would not kill his young brother, but did not. It was a lie, and he would know it. Instead, she chose another tactic. She would see how far she could go with this man.

"Truthfully, sir, Robert Bruce is to blame for your brother's capture."

Irony marked his expression. "Is he? 'Twould greatly interest me to hear how you reached that conclusion. Pray, share with me your reasoning, my lady."

"Very well." She traced a carved vine with one finger, watching him to gauge his reaction. "If Scotland were to be reasonable and acknowledge Edward as their true and rightful king, none of this conflict would be necessary. The Earl of Carrick would retain his lands and peace would reign. Instead, Robert Bruce has lost his earldom and will soon lose his life, along with the lives of countless men, women, and children who have fallen victim to his ruthless depredations."

Silence fell. Rain pattered softly against the glazed windowpanes, and the fire hissed in the grate. His face had not changed, but remained as if chiseled from stone as he studied her so long her nerves began to fray under his cold stare. Finally, he pushed away from the mantel and moved to stand in front of her, dark and tall and intimidating, with only the chair between them.

"You have been wildly misinformed, my lady." His tone was soft, but the words were clipped and hard. "Are you so ill-taught that you do not know the truth? Or is it that the English prefer to ignore the facts, and invent their own tales to justify their deceit?"

"Nothing of the kind." She steadied the nervous quiver of her hands on the chairback. "Is it not true that after the Scots King Alexander died and his granddaughter was declared the new queen, King Edward signed a treaty granting conditions for Scotland's independence? But when little Queen Margaret died soon after, the Scots who had signed that treaty treacherously declared John Balliol king of Scotland instead of following the terms of the agreement—which would have given Edward the right to the Scottish throne."

"Those facts are far too bare, madam." The thin white scar on his cheek tightened. "The Scots who signed that treaty with Edward were little more than minions of the English crown, intent upon their own ends rather than the wishes of most of Scotland. 'Twas crafty Edward who had these Scots make Balliol king. And after Edward had this puppet king declare the signed treaty null and void—thus releasing Edward from his promises of Scottish independence—John Balliol was discarded like a broken jug. Nay, Edward is not a man to be trusted."

A wintry smile curled his lips as she stared up at him with uneasiness. "Do I see uncertainty in your eyes, my lady? Perhaps if you think on't a time, you will see the truth for yourself."

"That still does not justify Robert of Bruce's claim to the throne." Her protest sounded lame and uninformed, even to her own ears. Was it possible that all she had managed to learn was wrong? But how could it be? No, these Scots were masters of manipulation, as her brother had once angrily remarked. And this man was the most adept at it, despite the kernel of reason he injected into his explanation.

"Bruce's claim is valid. He is directly descended from King David on his father's side, and because of this, in 1238 his grandfather was named heir presumptive by King Alexander II. When the king remarried, however, his son Alexander was born and became his heir and king. But the Bruces have never forgotten their royal blood or favor."

Catherine did not deny that there was a ring of truth to what he said, but it had been ingrained in her to believe in Edward's claim to the throne of Scotland. There must be a reasonable explanation, an argument for all the issues he raised. If only she could think clearly, but the days spent in solitude had rendered her mind near numb with endless monotony and apprehension.

With a lift of her shoulders, she said at last, "Yet the Bruce family aligned with the English at one time."

"Aye, but only to fulfill their oath of obligation. The Bruces never paid homage to John Balliol as crowned king of Scotland, nor recognized his coronation. They kept faith with the allegiance they had sworn to Edward, and in turn, he promised them the crown of Scotland once Balliol was deposed. Again, Longshanks lied. And that was his undoing, for by it, he freed Robert Bruce to seek that which should be his."

Catherine frowned at the curved back of the chair she held, anything to avert her gaze from the tall man staring down at her so dispassionately. "You seem to have an answer for everything. Yet 'tis true that since I was a small child, followers of Wallace and Bruce have swept down into England to burn monasteries and even infants. Just a year ago, Bruce crossed the Solway with his army and sacked Lanercost Priory, scarcely six leagues from Warfield. He ravaged Hexham and Corbridge, looting and taking hostages, then moved to Durham to fall upon those hapless merchants just as they were putting up stalls on market day. He burned the town to ashes, killing rampantly."

"Yea, I know well what happened. I was with him." A faint smile curled his mouth. "And I was with James Douglas at Hartlepool, when he ransacked the town and took wealthy burgesses and their wives as ransom."

"Then you do not deny the depredations that have been visited upon innocent citizens!"

"Yea, lady, I do deny it. Bruce does not kill the innocent, as does your Edward. Those who do not resist are spared, and women and children are not slaughtered."

"Fie on you, sir, for telling such tales! Next you shall say William Wallace and his men did not burn alive a school full of children or attack villages. . . ."

"War is war. And much is attributed to Bruce and William Wallace that never happened. How else could Edward raise an army to fight men who want only their freedom if he does not convince his soldiers of false atrocities?"

"For a crude Scot," she retorted in rising frustration, "you have a nimble tongue."

His countenance relaxed slightly, and the suggestion of a genuine smile tucked the corners of his mouth inward. "Aye, so I have been told before. But so do you, lass."

"I have not exactly come off the best in this war of words, I fear." Some of her tension eased as he grinned, and she looked away from him again. "I will think on what you have said, though I cannot help but suspect you have only twisted the facts to suit your purpose."

He shrugged. "I invite you to listen and learn. 'Tis the only way to glean the truth."

"Perhaps, but 'tis my thought that how truthful a man is depends on which country he is in when he voices his opinion."

"By that reasoning, milady, should your father happen to be in Scotland, he would be branded a liar if he swore that Edward is Scotland's rightful king. Is that right?"

"You name him liar now, when he is yet in England." Curse him, must he stand so close? She could not think, could not breathe with him standing over her, and she gripped the chair back more tightly. "I am certain my father would give you point for point his reasons why Edward is king, just as you can give reasons for Bruce's claim. There are truths, and in the end, God will decide who is right."

"It has been said that God is always on the side of the biggest army."

"Then 'tis certain Edward will be victor, for his army numbers many more than the Scots."

"Do you think so?" There was an odd note in his voice, and she looked up at him then, struck by the intensity of his tone. "Edward may have more soldiers, but Scotland's army is made up of its people, and numbers far more than the foreign mercenaries King Edward hires to wage war against a country they care nothing about. In the end, no man will risk all just for coin. 'Tis only men who have nothing left to lose but their lives who will risk all. I suggest you remember that when you begin to doubt the outcome, milady."

Silenced not just by his argument but by his tension, she watched him warily as he prowled the room like a great cat, predatory and dangerous in his dark mood. She kept the chair in front of her as if to shield herself from him, a flimsy barrier, in truth, should he choose to pounce. Finally he turned toward her, pivoting on his boot heels to stare at her intently, but his words were civil.

"I am just returned, and still wearing mud from my journey. You may linger here as long as you like, but call for an escort ere you return to your chamber."

"Of course. May I take a book with me?"

Some of his tension eased, and he nodded. "Aye, take what you like. 'Tis certain no one else here has the time to read them."

Catherine bit back a scathing remark on her wasted hours, forcing herself to nod graciously as he took his leave of her. With the closing of the door, relief flooded her, and she sank into the comfort of the chair that had supported her.

If he was not right, he certainly believed he was. And

that, she had observed, made a man dangerous. Did not her father believe himself right? Yea, and he was most dangerous.

Her hands trembled slightly, and she tucked them into her lap to still the quiver. She felt as if she were standing at the edge of Castle Rock's highest parapet, precariously balanced over sharp crags below. A single misstep and she would go plummeting to her doom. . . .

6

— ❦ —

"Any answer from the earl?"

Alex glanced up at Robbie and shook his head. "No, as you well know."

"It has been a fortnight since you sent our offer."

Sliding his foot all the way into his boot, Alex gave an irritated grunt that Robbie chose to ignore.

"What do you think the bloody earl intends, Alex?"

"If I knew that, I would no doubt also know the mystery of life. Give over, Robbie. I am in no mood to ponder questions with no answers."

Robbie slouched against the carved chest at the foot of Alex's bed, regarding his companion with eyes narrowed in thought. "There are answers," he muttered after a moment, "but mayhap not the ones we want to hear."

"I do not doubt that for a moment." Alex pulled a clean sherte over his head. It smelled of fresh air and heather sprigs. His nose wrinkled. "How many times must I tell Mairi not to allow the gillies to salt my garments with flowers?"

A soft hoot of laughter greeted his muttered complaint. "You must smell sweet for the ladies, Alex lad."

"I have no time for the ladies."

"Not even for the one in yon tower?" Robbie's sly question earned him a fierce glare, but he gave an undaunted chuckle. "Did you think I would not notice how you look at her? I saw it in your eyes that first day. 'Twas not to scare her that you kissed her but to satisfy your own want."

"I kissed her because she behaved as if I was too dirty to touch her, not for any other reason."

Robbie's eloquent shrug disagreed, but he did not argue the point. "What did the Bruce have to say about you taking her hostage?"

"That it was a waste of time and effort." Alex slung a wide leather belt around his waist and buckled it before looking up at Robbie again. "He has dealt with Warfield before and has no high opinion of him."

"Aye, so I feared." Robbie scrubbed a hand over the light beard bristling on his jaw. "Are we to join Bruce soon?"

"I have until January to do what I can for Jamie. Then we are to join James Douglas in subduing the Lothian province and take as many castles as possible before the cursed battle we shall be forced to wage against the English on midsummer's day."

Nodding, Robbie said, "A pox upon Edward Bruce for committing not only his brother, but all of us to that battle. If he had not grown weary of laying siege to Stirling Castle and accepted the crafty terms of the English commander's offer—"

" 'Twas an ill mind that prompted him to that oath," Alex interrupted, frowning. "The English know well 'tis the Bruce's policy not to risk pitched battle with their greater numbers. But when Lord Mowbray offered to freely yield Stirling Castle to the Scots unless King Edward rescues them by midsummer's day, he was only setting the date for a confrontation. Edward will never let Stirling Castle go without a fight, as it is vital to the English defenses." Alex shrugged with irritation and muttered, "As the Bruce's brother should have foreseen, instead of allowing Mowbray to Cozen him into such damaging terms."

Silence fell between them, both men lost in grave contemplation of the past as well as the future. It was Alex who broke their preoccupation by announcing that he was famished.

"It was a hard ride to Bruce's camp and back here. While we eat, you can tell me what transpired here while I was gone."

Shrugging, Robbie accompanied him from his chamber and into the hallway, relating events of minor squabbles and a feud over the ownership of a pig. "The sow is set to farrow, and William of Kinnison claims she be his, while his dead brother's wife swears the sow belongs to her."

"Did you settle it?"

"Aye." Robbie nodded in satisfaction. "You now have a new sow until she farrows, then lots are to be cast to divide the grice."

"Neatly done." Smiling, Alex glanced up as they rounded a corner, then stopped. Accompanied by a sullen Mairi, Lady Catherine approached, several books tucked under her arm. When she saw him, she jerked to a halt under the flickering light of a wall torch, looking a bit uncertain.

"As you see, sir, I am being escorted, though she is most unwilling."

"So I see." Alex regarded Mairi with grim amusement, and asked in Gaelic if his orders had been followed regarding the lady's chamber. When Mairi shook her head, he frowned and said, "You may go."

Mairi jerked her head in assent, then stomped away, leaving Catherine staring after her. "If I offended her," she muttered, "please tell me how so that I can repeat the offense the next time she wakes me before first light."

Alex grinned. "Mairi believes one should not stay abed once the sun has risen."

"A remarkable policy, but detestable when one has not slept soundly."

"We go down to the hall to sup, milady, if you would care to join us." He didn't know why he offered, save that she looked so lost at the moment, so vulnerable with her load of books and ill-fitting garments. Her hair was tucked into small coils above her ears, but loose tendrils had escaped to dangle against her cheek and the nape of her neck.

Obvious surprise lit her eyes, but she nodded her acceptance. "I grow weary of my chamber, and would welcome company for my evening meal."

Aware of Robbie's sidelong glance, Alex ignored him as he took the books from her and gave them to a servant along with instructions in Gaelic. Then he held out his arm, and after only the briefest of hesitations, she tucked her slender fingers into the crook of his elbow, the pressure light but firm as she accompanied him.

The hall was filled with soldiers and servants, loud and raucous as they entered. As they crossed the rushes to the high table, Catherine's clasp on his arm tightened as if for protection. The hostile glances had not gone unnoticed, but Alex steered her to the table without acknowledging them. If there were any who had objection to her presence, they could voice complaint to him. None, of course, would do so openly.

Still, constraint was apparent as they took their seats, and several glanced away uneasily when he bent a cold stare in their direction. He would not be rebuked in his own hall, by God, no matter the sentiment against his English hostage.

Catherine leaned close to murmur, "Mayhap your kind invitation is an ill-favored idea, sir. There are those here who seem to take my presence amiss."

"Do you fear them?"

Her delicate brows dipped over her nose. "No, of course I do not."

"Then pay them no heed. These people sup in my hall at my sufferance, and if they are displeased by my choice of company, they are at liberty to seek sustenance at another lodging."

He had deliberately made his words loud enough to be heard at the other tables, and after a moment, several men rose and quit the hall. Others exchanged glances, then resumed eating, and very shortly it was as if there had been no interruption. Alex beckoned a page forward with a platter of meats, and another quickly followed with a large tray of breads such as manchet and wastel, baked with fine white flour. Cheese and dried fruits were brought to the table, pitchers of ale and wine were refilled, and jellies and comfits were added to the repast.

Alex watched Lady Catherine, noting her hesitation. He leaned close. "Do you fear illness if you sample our fare? 'Tis not what you are accustomed to, no doubt, but 'tis filling."

A faint smile curved her lips. "As 'tis much better than the fare I am usually served here, I have no complaint. Neither do I have a dining knife or spoon."

"Ah. An oversight." He held out his eating dagger, a small implement with a jeweled hilt, fit for the table and little else. "You may use *sgian dhu* if you like."

She stared at him. "Skawn—"

"*Sgian dhu—skean du,* if you will. My dirk, or dagger. It once belonged to a lady, and should easily fit your small hand."

Accepting it, she looked at him curiously. "You do not seem the kind of man prone to using feminine cutlery."

He shrugged. "You may find this hard to believe, but 'tis for sentiment's sake that I use it. It was my mother's once, and I cherish it for that reason."

Her brows lifted slightly, and color flushed her cheeks with a rosy glow. Alex regarded her more closely. Aye, she was a true beauty, even garbed in the plain wool gown of a housewife. The leather girdle was laced snugly beneath her bosom, accenting her small waist and the swell of her breasts. The gown's faded color was flattering, a soft yellow that somehow complemented her skin and hair. Gleaming red-gold curls softened aristocratic features: a high forehead and elegant cheekbones, the straight line of her nose, full mouth that always looked as if it had just been kissed, with a sultry tumble of lower lip that was inviting and seductive. Yet it was her eyes that intrigued him most, violet-blue and large beneath a luxuriant sweep of dark lashes, filled with mystery and shadows, bewitching and aloof at the same time, leaving him with the feeling that she held the key to all the secrets of life.

A little nonplussed by the direction of his thoughts, Alex nodded curtly when she smiled at him and murmured her gratitude. "I am most honored that thou wouldst share such a treasure with me, sir."

"You must eat. I want it back when you are done." He sounded churlish and he knew it, and was not surprised when her smile faded and she retreated into silence again.

He ate without speaking to her, directing his comments in Gaelic to Robbie on his other side. Yet he was all too aware of the maid, of her dainty motions as she speared her meat with his mother's dagger, her open mouth and graceful sips of wine from a pewter goblet. Her slender fingers delicately stripped the meat from a chicken leg, tucked chunks of thick white bread into her mouth, and sopped up gravy from her trencher.

It grew increasingly difficult to keep his mind on the direction of Robbie's conversation, a fact he could not long hide. "Your mind is elsewhere," Robbie said in Gaelic. His brows lifted with amusement. "Shall I hazard a guess to the direction?"

"Devil take you." Alex took a long draught of ale. His trencher was still full of roast pork and partridge. "It has been a long day and a long ride, 'tis all."

Robbie's gaze strayed to the maid, then back to Alex. "You did not send her garments with the message to the earl. Is there a reason?"

Shrugging, Alex toyed with the sculpted stem of his pewter goblet. "I did not wish to use all my weapons in one blow. A lock of her hair should suffice to convince them we have her."

"Ah, and her shift will be further proof of what may happen should they refuse our offer." Robbie nodded slowly. "Canny enough."

Alex did not respond. It would sound foolish to say that he had found himself reluctant to imply violation of her. It would be a last resort, one used only if all else failed. Somehow, even the pretense of violation would seem all too real—too close to his true desires.

Silence fell between them, and he was uncomfortably aware of Robbie's considering gaze as he toyed with his trencher of food. The arrival of musicians was a relief, welcomed with an approving nod and a promise of a full purse. Pipes and flutes were presented, and the ready melody of a rousing ballad swirled over the hum of casual conversation. Slyly, Robbie translated the lyrics into English.

Alex listened politely, the words of the Battle of Stirling Bridge well known to him. At his side, he felt Lady Catherine shift, and slanted her a quick glance.

"Does the song distress you, milady?"

She cast him a burning look from beneath her lashes. "It would be impolite to disagree with my . . . host . . . on his choice of entertainment."

"Yea, but you will humor me this time."

Her mouth thinned, and she lifted her shoulders. "As it is rather one-sided in favor of the Scots, you must know I find the ballad disagreeable."

"Aye, but 'tis true that King Edward was defeated at Stirling Bridge. Or were you told otherwise?"

"I am aware of Stirling Bridge. And also Falkirk, in case you have forgotten that outcome."

Her stiff reminder of Scottish defeat amused him, and he signaled to the musicians. The minstrel gave him an appalled stare when he suggested they play another tune.

"Another tune, my lord? Do you have a preference?"

"Aye. Sing of the Battle of Largs. In English."

"The Battle of Largs. . . ." The minstrel drew in a deep breath and bowed slightly. "Aye, my lord. As you wish."

Beside him, Robbie laughed softly. "A prudent choice."

Alex shifted his attention back to the lady. "As the Battle of Largs involved Norway and Scotland, I trust this meets with your approval."

"If they must sing of battles, it will suffice."

"And what would you have them sing? Love songs?"

Her beautiful eyes met and held his gaze. "Is that so

very bad? Can there not be more love and less hate in this world?"

"You ask the wrong person, my lady. 'Twas not my father who created this situation."

Her slender shoulders lifted in another shrug. "I meant the war between Scotland and England, not this dispute you have with my father."

"Dispute is a rather mild term for what he has caused by taking my brother prisoner without hope of ransom."

For a long moment she searched his face with shadowed eyes, then shook her head sadly. "It does no good to argue the point. Sing what you will. Say what you will. I am at your mercy, as you so readily informed me earlier."

"But you have opinions, my lady."

"None you respect." Her mouth twisted wryly. "If I voice them, you counter with your own view of the same, and we end in debate. If I must remain here, I prefer peace, or what passes for peace in this land."

As Alex stared at her with a frown, the pipes wheezed loudly, and the first strains of the ballad rose into the air. *"Stately stepp'd he east the wall. And stately stepp'd he west; Full seventy years he now had seen; With scarce seven years of rest. . . ."*

Leaning forward, he said softly, "Peace reigned in Scotland for near two score years, until Longshanks grew greedy and coveted the Scottish crown as well as English. . . ."

"He lived when Britons' breach of faith Wrought Scotland meikle wae; And aye his sword tauld, to their cost, He was their deadly fae. . . ."

"Perhaps because Scotland has shown itself incapable of ruling its own people," she shot back, her voice rising to be heard over the pipes and minstrel. "It is a country divided against itself, and though Bruce may call himself leader and king, only a handful of Scots acknowledge him."

Anger sparked her eyes and flushed her cheeks, and Alex was suddenly aware that the pipes had wheezed to a halt and silence had fallen. He looked down the length of the hall, recognizing animosity on the faces staring up at them, and decided it was best she retreated to the safety of her chamber. Even those who did not understand English could understand the contempt in her voice.

He rose to his feet and put out a hand. "My lady, it is time you retire for the evening."

Rising gracefully, she said coolly, "I find the evening's entertainment much too merry for my tastes, and will be glad to seek my peace."

Without acknowledging the hostile glances directed toward her, she allowed him to lead her down the hall past the now silent tables, up the winding curve of stairs to the tower. She was silent, her back rigid, and Alex had the dark thought that he should never have yielded to the impulse to allow her in the hall. Even the most innocent of actions went awry with this maid.

When they reached the chamber she occupied, he swung open the door and stepped inside. His gaze flickered over the interior, noting that the changes he had commanded were now done. Tapestries hung on the cheerless walls, warming the cold stone and blocking some of the draft, and a generous supply of wood was stacked on the hearth. A new mattress stuffed with heather and feathers graced the rope bed, and a branch of candles flickered brightly in the center of the table, shedding rosy light over the stack of books she had chosen. Bolsters cushioned the chair, and a wooden frame and needlework stood near the window.

Lady Catherine made a small, inarticulate sound when

she saw the changes, then turned toward him with a strange expression. "Have you received word from my father?"

Startled, he shook his head. "I still wait. Why do you tarry until now to ask?"

Indicating the room with a sweep of her arm, she murmured, "Outfitting my prison after a fortnight, I thought you had received a refusal from him."

"It was my understanding that this had already been done. I did not know until today that your comfort was so lacking. You are a hostage, not a prisoner."

It was true. He had been appalled to see the bleak, cold room where she languished, bereft of any comfort or activity to while away her time. If he had not ridden to counsel with Bruce so soon after bringing her here, he would already have ascertained that his commands were not followed.

A faint smile played on her lips, and she lifted a book, hefting it in her hands a moment before looking up at him. "I wouldst be most intrigued to hear your definition of hostage, sir. It seems to differ from mine."

" 'Tis simple enough. A hostage is a person held to fulfill a pledge, or until certain terms are met."

"And a prisoner?"

His mouth hardened. "A captive, deprived of freedom, action, and expression. Sometimes—life."

"Then as a hostage, I am free to roam?"

He scowled. "No. You must suffer my whims, I fear. Did you not sense the mood of the men in my hall tonight? To allow you freedom may endanger you."

"I thought you were master of this hall, the lord of the castle."

Her mockery was obvious, and his anger rose. "I can school men's actions, but not their thoughts, milady. For that feat, you must look to your father."

"Odd, that you admit an Englishman can do what a Scot cannot."

"Not cannot—will not. In Scotland, there is not the great distinction between the classes that exists in England. Here, even the lowest man is free. He chooses to follow his heart and conscience, not who his overlord commands him to follow."

"That explains the rampant switching of loyalties, then."

He shrugged. "Men are free here to choose their leader, and that oft breeds ambivalence. 'Tis a two-edged sword."

She stepped close to him, looking up at him with shadowed eyes. "Then can you not change loyalties if 'twill free your brother?"

"I could not change loyalties if it would save my own life," he said softly, "and will not do so even for Jamie."

A brittle laugh escaped her, sounding hopeless. "Then we are all doomed, for neither will my father change his stand."

"You do not know that."

"Oh, yes." She shivered as if chilled. "I know it to be the truth. I will die here ere he meets your demands."

In the thick silence that fell, a sudden gust of wind rattled the wooden shutters closed over the window and made the branch of candles dance. Alex studied her desolate face, frustration rising. This was no game she played, but her conviction. What if she was right? It was unbearable to think so . . . that Jamie would be delivered to Edward and a grisly, cruel fate. He thought of William Wallace and a dozen other supporters of Robert Bruce. All had died horribly, meant to be a lesson and discouragement to anyone who dared to defy the English king. That many of the condemned had never sworn to Edward and could not legally be viewed as traitors was ignored. They were hung, drawn, and quartered, their heads placed on pikes to warn those who would follow them.

Yet Bruce still fought, still commanded men, still risked all to gain Scotland's independence.

Alex was still contemplating the grim reality of his position when Robbie appeared at the open door of the chamber. His eyes were alight, excitement sharpening his features. "We have word that English riders approach," he said in Gaelic, and Alex's hope renewed.

His gaze swept back to Catherine, who had tensed as if understanding the import if not the meaning of Robbie's announcement. "If you are still inclined to pray, my lady," Alex said as he turned toward the door, "do so now."

7

Catherine waited fretfully. She had pushed open the shutters over the window and peered out, but could see little in the dark rainy night but badly flickering torches in the bailey below. Riders had come, she thought, but she knew not how many. Her father? Her brother? Or only another Scot come with information from Robert Bruce? She paced the floor restlessly, knotting and unknotting her hands.

Candles lit the chamber with steady light, good tapers that did not smoke or gutter easily, made of beeswax and not tallow, more expensive than even those her father used. A faint smile grazed her lips. She had found it touching that Alex Fraser had seen to her comfort. He was a complex man, with emotions she had not guessed he would possess.

Her hand slid downward to the small eating dagger he had lent her. It had been forgotten, and she pulled it from the folds of her gown to gaze at it now. *Sgian dhu.* Tiny jewels adorned the hilt, and the blade was still sharp, though the tip of the dagger had been broken. His mother's dagger, cherished and kept close, a prized memento of a woman gone from this world. Yea, a most complex man.

As her life had been spent listening to scraps of information about these primitive barbarians to the north, she had not expected to find civilized emotions in any of them. It was surprising and disturbing to realize that not everything she had learned was true. Her first impression of the Scotsman who held her hostage had undeniably altered, and that in itself was cause for alarm.

That first day he had been every bit the savage she had long feared, the embodiment of the lullabies of her childhood that promised a terrible fate to the child who wandered from home . . . yet tonight he had been garbed as the finest gentleman, a man who would be welcomed into any English manor. His clean white linen sherte, dark trews, and high boots of a country gentleman were casual yet elegant. A supple leather weskit snugly fit his broad chest, belted by an ornate strip of leather studded with brass and adorned with the jeweled dagger she now held. Beautiful and lethal, tall and lean, more like a weapon than a man, Alex Fraser was a contradiction to all her preconceived knowledge about the Scots.

Frowning, she toyed with the dagger. Was it his courtly manner that she had not expected, ingrained behind the stringent demands he imposed upon himself as well as those around him? She had taken note of the way he held himself in check, betrayed by an occasional tension in his jaw or flash in his eyes. Yet he had not relinquished control of his temper as her father would have done, no matter how she had pricked him.

Except for that first day, in the face of her frightened contempt, when he had held her hard against him and forced a kiss on her. His attempt to subdue and humiliate her had been more effective than she would ever acknowledge to him. And yet he had been affected by her as well, for she had seen it in his eyes, the same glitter that she had seen in the eyes of courtiers in her father's home, young men smitten by the earl's daughter but too wary to betray it. Only one young man had ever been reckless enough to attempt wooing her, and his fate had been swift and harsh when her father discovered it.

Catherine's hands quivered slightly on the dagger's hilt, and she closed her eyes. She had been young, barely thirteen and still discovering her maturing femininity, still foolish enough to cast soft glances at a fair face and think a flirtation innocent. Young David's admiration had been heady, his poems and songs flattering, and the fragrant blossoms proffered to her tucked away in her carved chest as keepsakes. Perhaps the flirtation would have faded of its own accord in time, but David had made the fatal mistake of kissing her cheek, an act seen by a servant who swiftly reported it to the earl.

Retribution had been horrifyingly complete. A public flogging in the center of the bailey had near crippled the young man, and only his kinship to a powerful family saved his life. As it was, he had been sent from Warfield broken in body, a warning to any who would attempt the same.

Since David, no man had been dauntless enough to court her with even a casual word. It was strange to think that her first real kiss had been given her by the man who took her hostage, a kiss given out of anger instead of affection.

The memory of that kiss had haunted her dreams, intruding into her slumber to leave her restless and yearning for answers to the unfamiliar sensations that invaded her body. It was not that she was ignorant of what happened between a man and a woman, for life in a castle was hardly private. Couplings were oft glimpsed in shadowed alcoves and beneath stairwells, the rough intercourse between knights and serving wenches commonplace. More than once she had stumbled across one of her brothers in just such a situation, incidents both embarrassing and amusing. For men, it was expected. Yet for a daughter of the earl, even a simple flirtation was disastrous. No, she was not ignorant, only inexperienced.

Perhaps that was why her heartbeat quickened when the Scot came near her, watching her through his black lashes, a half smile on his face as if he were remembering what she looked like without her shift. And that particular memory had the power to scald her, to bring a hot flush to her cheeks and leave her teeming with vague emotions. Pride had been all that kept her upright then, kept her from sinking to her knees at his feet and pleading for mercy. Had he not been so detached, perhaps she would have cowered, but his cool acceptance of her nakedness had saved her some humiliation.

Just as unnerving were the other occasional wanderings of her thoughts, the recollection of the press of his lips against hers and the water rushing around them, the power of his embrace as he had held her so tightly against him, the evidence of his desire a hard pressure against her wet thighs. Oh, yes, she had known of his need, had been terrified by it. And yet now, in the chaste bower of her prison, she could not help but wonder how it would feel to have him hold her with tenderness instead of anger, his strong hands gentle on her bare skin, his mouth a heady invitation instead of harsh punishment. And perhaps that was the greatest shame of all, that she even considered allowing the touch of the enemy.

Dragging in a deep breath that smelled of rain through the open shutters, Catherine moved again to the window ledge and peered out. The rain had eased a bit, but still the torches below sputtered and flickered, giving off scant light in the shadowed bailey. Across the broad yard she could see lamps lit in the stables, and knew that the horses were being tended. Who were the visitors? Oh, God, let it be her brother who had come for her, for she was certain there would be no rescue from any other quarter.

Pressing her flushed cheek against the cold stone of the window facing, Catherine delved into her meager reserves of patience and waited.

Nicholas, Lord Devlin, waited tensely for the Scots bastard to arrive in the antechamber to which he had been escorted. His men were without, under guard in the bailey but promised safe conduct from Castle Rock once his interview with Fraser was done. Anger simmered beneath his carefully blank expression as he was kept waiting much longer than he deemed necessary. A familiar tactic, and one he had oft employed himself, but irritating nonetheless.

At last Fraser arrived, pausing in the arched doorway to survey Nicholas with a cool gaze. "My negotiation is with the earl, not a rank upstart."

Despite his awareness that the taunt was another method of putting him on the defensive, Nicholas flushed angrily. "Did you really expect the earl himself to deal with a paltry Scot?"

"Yea, if he wishes to see his daughter again." Fraser entered the chamber calmly, and it did not escape Devlin's notice that he wore a sword at his side, though his own weapons had been taken at the gatehouse. The Scot moved to stand at the grate where a fire burned smartly. Smoke curled upward into a chimney that looked to be new, an addition to the original structure. Nicholas waited, and after a pause, Fraser indicated a chair with a wave of one hand. "Be seated and state your terms for the exchange of hostages, Lord Devlin."

It was the moment he had dreaded, coming more quickly than he'd hoped, not giving him time to gauge his opponent. He took a deep breath, stalling as he slowly seated himself in the proffered chair and leaned against the high back to regard Fraser with hooded eyes.

"Before I state our terms, I would see for myself that my sister is alive and unharmed."

"You will have to accept my assurances."

The cool reply provoked a hot retort: "Not if you wish to see your brother alive again."

"Did you bring him with you?" A cocked brow indicated that he already knew the answer to that question. "I thought not. Why should I give you further proof when I have none? 'Tis more than possible that Jamie is already dead, or delivered up to Edward for execution."

"He is alive and in Warfield's cellar. How long he remains alive, depends upon your actions. Release my sister and I can promise the earl will not kill him."

A sardonic smile curved the Scot's mouth. "If I were to be foolish enough to release my hostage, Jamie would be swinging from the king's gallows before nightfall. I am not so foolish to believe English promises."

Nicholas rose to his feet. "Then we have nothing more to discuss. I came for my sister, and cannot return to Warfield without proof that she is yet alive. If you wish to barter for your brother's life, you will provide me with evidence that you have her, and that she is unharmed."

A log in the fire popped loudly, and sparks spit onto the stone hearth at the Scot's feet. He returned Devlin's gaze for a long moment, then called a servant to him and gave instructions in Gaelic.

Turning back to Nicholas, he said softly, "You will have your proof that I have her, since a lock of her hair is not enough to convince you."

Nicholas shrugged. "There are many with hair that bright hue, though none as beauteous as Catherine."

Fraser returned the cold stare, animosity in his face and rigid stance—the way he stood with his feet apart and legs braced, his hands at his side as if ready at any moment to draw his weapon. Nicholas wished fervently he had his own sword at his side instead of only the small eating dagger that would be of little help should the Scot renege on his promise of safe conduct.

Tension between them mounted with the silence, and when the servant returned with a smallish casket in his hands, Nicholas felt a spurt of dread. Without thinking, his hand moved to the hilt of the small dagger on his belt, and he stared at the casket as the Scot placed it atop the table and opened the curved lid. At first he did not comprehend what he was shown, frowning at the length of blue velvet. Then he recalled Catherine as last he had seen her, garbed in a flowing blue velvet gown, a pearl-encrusted crispinette over her bright hair as she moved across the bailey toward the postern gate. 'Twas what pricked him most, that he had seen her flight and not stopped her. He should have, but he had known how raw she must feel after the cruel interview with their father. And so he had not prevented her escape, but thought instead that she needed some solitude.

He moved to the table and lifted the length of blue velvet, twisting it between his fingers. "This could belong to any woman from your village. I have no assurance that 'tis my sister's gown."

His ploy was for naught. Fraser reached under the folded velvet and drew out another garment. He held it up, and the firelight gleamed on a silken shift, reflecting in the glossy threads with a brilliant shimmer. In a quick flick of his wrist, he tossed it in the air.

"Women of Kinnison village do not wear impractical silk instead of warm wool under their gowns."

Catching his sister's shift, Nicholas strove hard to control his temper and his outrage. The silk was rent on one shoulder, evidence of a struggle, and his belly knotted at the thought of Catherine being mauled by this man. It took a moment, but when he at last spoke, his voice was calm.

"If my sister has been violated, there will be no salvation for your brother, I can promise you that." He looked up to meet the Scot's flinty gaze. "And that is an English promise you can be certain will be kept."

"Dogs oft bay loudest before turning tail and fleeing. If my brother is harmed, 'tis doubtful you will e'er see your fair English flower again. In my grief and anger, I may yet do the worst."

Nicholas drew in a deep breath, and his hands knotted fiercely in the torn silk shift. "I must know if Lady Catherine is as unsoiled as the day you took her."

" 'Tis typical English that would think the worst vengeance I could inflict would be to put a Scots bairn in her belly before giving her back to you. Yet nothing is thought of dangling a Scottish noblewoman from English walls to be displayed as if in a menagerie."

"Answer me." Rising fury sickened him, and it was all he could do not to spring at the taunting Scot and plunge his dagger into that black heart. "Has my sister been disgraced?"

Fraser's lip curled. "Not unless you consider her father's actions her own disgrace. Nay, I have not taken her to my bed if that is what you ask. But I offer no promise as to the morrow should my terms be refused. Even were she as plain as a wattle fence, 'twould be vengeance indeed to return her to you with my babe inside her. Think on't before you relate my terms to the earl—my brother and de Brus in exchange for an unspoiled English flower."

"Should one hair on her head be harmed—"

"Do not make threats you are in no position to enforce, my lord Devlin. Your men are under guard and you are unarmed. Go, and inform Warfield that I await his answer within a sennight."

"Too soon." Nicholas played for time, knowing his father's mood and now this cursed Scot's intent. "We must have a month, as the earl will needs consult the king before he acts."

"A fortnight. No more."

"Do you give safe conduct to any envoy we send to Castle Rock?"

"Yea, as long as my envoys are guaranteed the same surety. And, Devlin—" Fraser put out a hand to indicate the opened casket and spill of blue velvet. "Advise your father that I am not a patient man, and as the winter days grow shorter, I find his daughter more comely with each passing hour."

There was nothing Nicholas wanted to reply to that taunt that would not end in violence, and he turned hard on his heel and stalked from the antechamber. Hatred burned as hot and high in him as a lightning bolt, and when he reached the bailey he bellowed for his men to saddle their horses. His mood was savage, his temper raw, and he pushed past the Scottish sentries with unnecessary force. Angry mutters rumbled after him, but one of the Scots quieted the others with a few short words in Gaelic as Nicholas strode toward the stables.

Miles looked pained as he met him in the driving rain that pelted the ground into thick mud. "Are we not to linger the night in dry shelter, my lord?"

"I will not dwell a night under the roof of so base an enemy, not if I am able to spend it in good English rain." Ignoring the grumbling from his men, he began to saddle his horse. Steam rose from the cooling hide that was still damp from the weight of the saddle. But he did not intend to spend a single night in Scotland, and certainly not in the reluctant hospitality of the man who held his sister.

No man dared protest, but led their weary horses from the dry comfort of the stables and mounted them. At the gatehouse, their weapons were returned as the creaking of winch chains heralded the rising portcullis. Hoofbeats were muffled by mud and rain as they rode toward the lowered drawbridge and out into the dark, wet night. Yet the chill did nothing to cool Nicholas's temper, and the desire for vengeance burned hot in his throat. Worse, was the nagging fear that his father would yet refuse Fraser's demands. And God only knew what would befall Catherine then. . . .

8

—— ❦ ——

"Change, as I see, is ever the world's way—Loud windy weather turning warm and soft, And even the great moon changing day by day, And humblest things thrown by degrees aloft; Hideous War, with all his armor doffed, Grown Peace: unchanging, though, Love's cautious pride And willful cold. And so I am denied."

Catherine marked the page and closed the book, placing it atop the table, too restless to be comforted by words that somehow echoed her own fears. She moved again to the window, unsurprised by the rivulets of rain streaking the ledge and shutters. It was always this way during the gray days of winter. The calends of December was not so distant, and she thought then of Warfield, and the celebrations of Christmas. It was the one time of year that the castle was festive, for then even her grim father relaxed enough to allow merriment to reign. There were feasting and games, dances and minstrels, and the halls were festooned with greenery that spiced the air with the scent of pine and fir.

Would her family celebrate without her? Or would she be home for Advent, as she hoped. . . .

Nay, she thought bitterly, she doubted she would be home even for Saint Stephen's Day, for no word had yet come that her father had agreed to terms that would release her from her prison. Poor Nicholas. Even from her high tower, she had recognized the fury in his voice as he shouted for his men to mount, had watched in dismay as the gates were opened and they rode over the lowered wooden bridge in a clatter of hooves to disappear into the night.

Despair had briefly convulsed her, before she reasoned that of course there would be details to concede, terms to set and negotiations for an exchange. That Nicholas had come at all was heartening. So she strengthened her spirits with the self-made assurances that all would be well, that at least her father was considering rescuing her. It was more than she had expected.

And apparently, insufficient for the Scotsman.

His footfall was easily discerned as he approached her chamber, and as he swung open the door, his expression was unreadable. Rising to meet him, Catherine felt the familiar hammer of her heart, the tension in her stomach a hard knot as he ducked to enter the doorway.

He repeated no details of their meeting, only a dry recital of her brother's request for a delay. Watching her, he added flatly, "You had best pray he does not play me false, my lady, for I am in no mood to haggle the finer points of a truce. Time runs swiftly, and my patience lags far behind."

It did not seem the time to disagree, and she made no comment. After a short sizzling silence, he left, shutting the door behind him with a decisive snap.

But later, thinking on his veiled threat, she grew incensed. It was bad enough that she was being held hostage, a mere pawn in this struggle between two powerful men involved in their own schemes, but to be made to suffer terror and apprehension through no fault of her own added insult to the injury. Yea, he had best think again if he thought to cow her with vague threats of dreadful fates, for she was too near the breaking point to endure much more.

As if he sensed how close she was to rampant defiance, he did not come to her chamber again, leaving her to stew in her misery for an entire fortnight. Only Mairi came, her dour presence blessedly short as she confined herself to bringing meals or supervising the delivery of a tub and water for baths, often muttering what Catherine was sure were vile imprecations in Gaelic so she could not understand them. Other times, she would have preferred Mairi did not speak English, for the older woman was most provoking.

"Daft notion, tae sit in a bucket o' hot water as if a hen in th' soup pot," the older woman muttered after Catherine first insisted on a bath. "Next ye'll be demandin' silks an' satins in place o' gude warm wool gowns."

"Not as long as I must remain in this drafty hole," Catherine retorted, and Mairi stomped away.

But the round wooden tub was brought up, and buckets of hot water were poured into it until she deemed it enough. A rather threadbare towel accompanied a small jar of soap, and Catherine placed them on a stool by the tub, then dismissed the gawky young servant who had lugged the heavy buckets of water up several flights of stairs.

"Thank you, Thomas."

He scooped his bonnet from his head and flushed. "Tam, milady," he said in clumsy English. "Thomas wa' me da'."

"Excuse me. I misunderstood." When he did not

move to the door, she said, "I wish I had coin for you, but you must know I do not."

A rather shy grin squared his mouth. "Och, 'tis no' expected, milady. We are tae tak' care o' ye, his lordship said, an' see tha' ye ha' all ye need."

"Except my freedom of course." She smiled when his grin broadened and he nodded.

"Aye, I darena think o' th' skelpin' I wa'd get were I tae let ye escape."

"Unless you have a rope ladder in your sherte, there is no fear of that. I am here at your master's sufference, and will remain so until an agreement is reached. But it is not so bad, for I have books to read that pass the time."

His gaze strayed to the tall stack of volumes atop the table. A thatch of unruly black hair covered his head and hung down his neck; his garments were patched in places, the gathered tunic around his waist threadbare, but his eyes were lively and bright, and intelligence shone in his features. "Me mam taught me some letters, but tha' wa' long ago. I can put down me name, but no' much else."

"If it is allowed, I would be glad to help you with your letters. Once learned, it is easy enough to read."

Blue eyes gleamed at her brightly. "I wa'd laik tha', I wa'd, milady. Shall I ask?"

"It would be best. And now, perhaps I should make good use of this water before it cools."

His gaze flicked to the water, then to her bare feet, and his pale cheeks reddened again as he backed toward the door. "If ye need more, send for me an' I will bring it tae ye."

"I will, Tam."

When he had gone, Catherine moved the table in front of the door, a flimsy barrier, but enough to give her time to cover herself should someone come. Quickly, she removed the rough wool dress and leather girdle, and stepped into the tub. The heat of the water against her legs was luxurious, and she slid down as far as possible in the rather shallow bath. Hot water rose to barely cover the tips of her breasts, flushing her pale skin a deep rose. Her legs were bent at the knees, ivory islands thrust up from the water and gleaming in the light of fire and candles. Tilting back her head, she rested it against the edge of the tub and reached for the soap.

Though it did not lather well, it was fragrant, spiced with musky scents that were more masculine than feminine. Yet it was deliciously sumptuous, a banquet for the senses, a lavish delight as she soaped her arms, then her legs. She wiggled her toes, then scrubbed between them.

Sighing, she sank lower in the tub, bending her knees more so that she could wet her hair. It floated around her in dark tendrils, tickling her face and breasts, absorbing the water until it grew heavy. Now the water covered her ears, and she could hear the pulsing flow of blood as her heart beat, pushing through her veins in a rhythmic melody, a mysteriously soothing sound. The wash of warm water on her bare skin, the spicy scent of the soap, the beat of her heart, had a curious effect on her. Her body felt suddenly weighted, alien to her, oddly vulnerable and powerful at the same time. Slowly, as if drawn by invisible cords, her hands moved to touch herself, to slide her fingers over the wet warm flesh of her breasts, stomach, and thighs. The pulse of life beat stronger now, pooling between her legs with a searing excitement that made her breath come faster. She pressed her thighs tightly together to stem the surge of sensation, but it only made it worse.

Flushed with distress, she curled her fingers into fists atop her thighs. Sinful, to caress herself there, to even acknowledge that sensitive, unfamiliar part of her body—

she had been taught to ignore any strange urgings she may have, to pray for forgiveness should she accidentally and unwillingly touch the part of her that God had declared sacred. Yet if it was sacred, why did her mother allow her father to violate that sacrosanct part of her body? Was it sacred only until marriage? Those were questions that had earned her sharp rebukes and severe punishments when she was younger, and had never been answered to her satisfaction.

But was it a sin? Was it so wicked?

Softly, with her eyes half-closed, Catherine scrubbed her palms over her thighs, then back up over her belly to her breasts. Her nipples were hard like small pebbles from the river, puckered against the cool air. She covered them with her hands, feeling wicked and carnal, yet unable to stop. The peculiar throbbing was between her legs again; it reminded her of the way she had felt when Alex Fraser had kissed her, and again when she was forced to disrobe for him. She pressed her thighs more tightly together, but that only intensified the aching pulse. Tentatively, she raked her palms over her nipples, and was startled by the piercing tremor that rippled through the center of her. The ache grew sharp, contracting the muscles of her stomach and igniting a fire between her legs, and she sat up with a jerk, her breath coming in harsh little gasps for air as she grabbed at the sides of the tub.

She felt so flushed, her entire body aflame with quivering sensation and shame. What was the matter with her? Never had she done such a thing, the strictures she had been taught so deeply ingrained that it had not occurred to her to flout them. Yet now, here, with thoughts of the gray-eyed Scot in her mind, she had touched herself in impure ways. It was said that Scotland was a heathen land, and she was certain it was true. A heathen land with a heathen host, and she was falling prey to its influence.

Shaking, her hair a heavy wet cloak dripping down her back, molded to her spine, she stepped from the tub and reached for the towel. Her hands were trembling as she wrapped it around her. Puddles of water pooled on the stones at her feet, spreading wider when she did not move.

Finally, slowly, she let the towel fall to the floor and reached for the clean gown Mairi had brought her. It was warm and dry, rough against her skin, eliciting more strange shudders as it rubbed over her sensitive nipples. The wool clung to her wet skin in damp patches, made worse by the dripping weight of her hair. She clubbed her hair into a single thick strand and twisted it to wring out the water, then pushed it over her shoulder to dangle down her back. Her movements were clumsy as she pulled the leather girdle around her ribs, fingers fumbling with the laces that tied it beneath her breasts. This gown was bigger, the scooped neck lower, and she adjusted it by tucking extra material beneath the girdle, bunching it so it would hold.

Then she used the cooling bathwater to wash the other gown, dunking it into the sudsy water and scrubbing it vigorously against the sides of the tub to dislodge dirt and any small creatures that may have taken up residence. She thought of the fuller's earth her mother used, and the sweet-scented soap and preparations for cleaning garments. All that she had taken for granted, never dreaming that one day she would wish for just such drudgery. How amused her mother would be to hear it.

She was draping the wet gown over a chair before the fire when she heard the scrape of boots in the corridor outside the chamber and looked up, her heartbeat quickening. The key was in the lock and the door was opening before she could move the table, and with a sudden push, it toppled over in a resounding crash.

Alex Fraser filled the doorway, scowling at her. "Do you think a puny table could keep me out, milady?"

Calmly, she said, "It was not meant to keep you out, but to give me warning should I have an unexpected audience for my bath."

His gaze shifted to the puddles of water on the floor and the wooden tub, and his taut stance relaxed. He stepped into the chamber and closed the door behind him, seeming to fill the room with his presence. His black hair was tousled as if by the wind, and he smelled fresh and clean. A cloak was slung over his shoulders, reaching to his boot tops in the back and open in the front. He wore trews and a white sherte, and a padded leather vest that was belted around his middle. She glimpsed a sword hilt at his side.

"Your father sent news," he said abruptly, and her gaze shifted to his face. He was staring at her through slightly narrowed eyes. "His envoy is delayed and will be here in a fortnight to conduct negotiations."

"Then he has agreed to your terms?"

"He has agreed to nothing. He thinks to play me like a harp, delaying as long as possible."

She shifted from one bare foot to the other. Her wet hair hung heavily against her back, dampening the wool gown beneath it. She shivered a little as a cool draft chilled skin still damp from her bath, and turned her back to the fire for warmth and to dry her hair. The smell of wet wool rose around her, vying with the musky fragrance of the soap she had used.

Alex's gaze dropped, and a shadow darkened his face and eyes, his lashes lowering slightly as he stared at her. Her throat tightened. She stifled the impulse to cross her arms over her chest as his gaze rested on her breasts.

There was a heated intensity to his scrutiny that puckered her nipples and left her feeling flushed and strangely weak. Mortified by her body's involuntary reaction, she reached up to bring her hair forward as if to comb her fingers through it, using the long strands to cover herself. The hair was cold and damp against skin left bare by the scooped neck of her gown, wetting the wool bodice where she draped it over her breasts to conceal her reaction to him.

His faint smile told her he was aware of her ploy, but the heat in his eyes did not lessen. Softly, his voice a husky murmur, he said, "Are you aware that the fire behind you outlines your body perfectly through that thin wool gown, milady?"

She stared at him, her fingers stilling in her hair. "No." Her denial came out in a throaty whisper, forced from her lips only by great strength of will. She could not move, could not speak, could only watch with thrumming nerves and pounding heart as he moved toward her.

" 'Tis true." His voice was still so soft, languorous and heavy, a soothing purr like that of a great cat. "Yet I have seen your sweet form before, and 'tis not a sight to be soon forgotten."

Firelight danced over him in flickering patterns of red and gold, its reflection glittering in his eyes and turning them to molten silver, then glancing off his belt buckle and the cloak pin on his shoulder. Her limbs felt weighted and unable to move; her hands were still trapped in her hair. Gently, he untangled her fingers from the silky strands that snapped with static life of their own, and he lowered her arms to her sides. Her world was a mass of contradictions, vying sensations, with the heat of the fire behind her, her wet gown cold against her skin, and the damp weight of her hair brushing over her breasts. She did not struggle, did not protest as he touched her cheek, traced her quivering lips with his finger, curved his hand down over her throat to tilt back her head.

Dimly, she knew she should protest. This was the enemy, a man who did not respect her past or her present, who used her only for his own gain. But what else had she known in her life? She was a pawn, born into a world where she was of use only as a device to gain more wealth, more lands, more power. If she was returned to Warfield, she would be bartered to Ronald of Bothwick in exchange for greater lands, greater influence—her wishes discarded as only the naive tantrum of a child.

But if she gave herself to this Scot, there would be no marriage with Bothwick, and no profit for her father. Yet the earl delayed negotiations, stalling for time with no thought of his daughter, what she might be suffering, what she might fear. It was the final proof that she meant nothing to him. She was only a tool.

Warm lips pressed against the curve of her throat, the smooth underside of her chin, then against the single tear that traced her cheek. His breath was heated, but soft against her skin, and she closed her eyes in surrender. What had she left to lose?

His head lifted and his hand wound into the length of her hair to gently hold her still as his other hand began a teasing journey. Strong fingers curled into the edge of her bodice, pulling it down to free her breasts, their weight uplifted by the leather girdle beneath them. A thumb raked across her beaded nipple and she shuddered. It was so different from earlier, from her own timid explorations and from the flat of palms so much softer than his callused hand. And the sensations he elicited were stronger, sharper, more vivid as he rolled the taut bud between his thumb and finger.

Her entire body was quivering, the throbbing ache

between her legs a steady pulse that was mystifying and urgent. Her sensations were heightened, so that she felt the brush of the wool gown against the back of her thighs, the heat of the fire, the weight of her hair, and the tantalizing brush of his hands against her breasts, all at once. She wanted to open her eyes but did not dare, afraid that she would see her own wickedness reflected in his gaze.

Then her eyes flew open and her back arched with shock as he took her nipple into his mouth. He suckled first one, then the other, his mouth wet and hot, lips tugging on her with strong motions that summoned the most exquisite pain between her thighs. Her eyes shut tightly again. Her entire body was as taut as a strung bow; she felt as if the least pressure would make her snap.

Somehow she was clinging to him now, her fingers clutching the voluminous folds of his cloak, her body bent backward and supported by his arm behind her waist. His dark hair tickled the bare skin of her throat, smelling of wind and fresh air, a masculine fragrance that filled her nostrils. He pulled her hips against him; his belt buckle pressed into the soft swell of her belly, sharp and hard through the thin wool. The muscles in his arm flexed behind her, and his hand spread over her buttocks, fingers digging into her soft skin. He was bent over her like a dark hawk, the winged folds of his cloak enclosing them, his body a lean pressure against her willing softness.

A trembling moan filled the air, vibrating between them, a wordless plea and surrender suspended in time and mind and memory. Catherine felt herself falling, her body being cradled in strong arms and a great dark veil being pulled down, blotting out everything but the beautiful, scarred face above her, the fierce gray eyes and hard intensity that seared her to the soul. She was lost, and she felt a liberating, swooping joy in it. . . .

9

He burned for her. Agony, to cradle her supple body in his arms and not take her; torture, to deny himself the release he craved by plumbing her depths until they were both satiated with it.

But he had given his oath.

Ah, Christ have mercy, he had sworn to deliver her to the earl unspoiled, and by all that was holy, he could not risk Jamie's life by yielding to the clamoring demands of his body. Not now. Not when success was yet a possibility.

He throbbed with urgency, his body tight with arousal to the point of pain. And she was willing . . . he had seen it in her eyes when she looked up at him from before the hearth, had seen her trembling lips and tightened nipples against the thin wool gown, seen surrender and confusion and need, and he had known before she did that she would yield. It had undone him.

From the beginning, he had recognized his desire for her but rejected it because he had no other option. To yield to it would make him no better than the earl, promising one thing while doing another. What he had not expected was this sudden, complete capitulation from her. It had been much easier when she feared and hated him, made it simple to keep his own hunger at bay.

Now the barriers were gone, her defenses giving way to this heated surrender that left him dangerously susceptible.

The muscles in his belly tightened. So beautiful, this fair English flower, tousled and still damp from her bath, gleaming skin rosy in the firelight, her small, perfect breasts impudent and teasing.

If he had any control, he would leave now, before his body outvoted his mind. But he knew, even before the thought faded, that he was going to stay, to hold her, to touch her and ease the need that thundered through him like a storm.

Lifting her, he carried her the short distance to the narrow cot against the wall and lowered her gently to the mattress. The fresh fragrance of heather surrounded them as he knelt beside her. She was staring up at him now, her eyes hazy beneath half-lowered lashes.

"Close your eyes, catkin," he murmured, and smiled a little when she wordlessly obeyed. Fine time for her to become pliant. Now, when she was in danger of being deflowered by the enemy, she should be fighting him tooth and claw.

And, oddly, he found himself curiously at a loss. Kissing her had been impulsive, a temporary yielding to the need she'd provoked in him. Now that she was acquiescent, he felt strangely reluctant. Insanity, to continue, and torture to stop. But he had gone too far. . . .

He unfastened the clasp at his throat and shed his cloak, letting it fall to the floor beside the bed. Raking a hand through his hair, he gazed down at her, at the gentle rise and fall of her breasts with each breath she took, her flushed skin and parted lips . . . bending, he kissed her on the mouth, teasing her lower lip with his teeth until he heard her breath quicken.

When his own breath came in harsh pants, he sat back to regain control, a little rueful at how easily his restraint weakened with this fair maid. Her eyes were still closed, dark brown lashes shadowing her cheeks. Delicate eyebrows like graceful wings puckered slightly as he traced the sculptured line of her mouth with his fingers, the elegant curve of her cheek and jaw, and the arch of her throat. His hand moved lower, fingers dipping into the hollow of her collarbone. A small pulse beat there, rapid as the flutter of a frightened bird.

His body throbbed. He knew he was going to regret this, knew that he would suffer for it, yet he wanted her with a ferocity that shocked him. Nothing would ease the hard ache in him but the feel of her closing around him, the deliciously tight bliss of plunging his body into hers and hearing her soft moans in his ear.

When her tongue came out to wet her mouth in a quick slide over the exquisite tumble of her lower lip, heat exploded in his belly. His fingers paused on her damp skin, his large, brown hand a vivid contrast against her white softness.

He unlaced his leather jerkin and unbuckled his belt, tossing them atop his cloak. His white linen sherte followed, and cool air filtered over his heated skin as he leaned over her. He took her hand and pressed her palm against the bare muscles on his chest, watching her lashes flutter at the contact. Slowly, he dragged her splayed fingers down the length of his torso in a light, erotic glide. The fire in his belly burned higher and hotter when he reached his waist and the band of his trews. Her hand was cool and quivering against him. He tightened his grip, and with his other hand, untied the cord that held his trews closed. Her long lashes flickered again, and he watched, fascinated, as the tip of her tongue swept over her lips.

"Open your eyes now, catkin."

His hoarse murmur pried open her eyes, and she peered at him from beneath her lashes. Color mounted in her cheeks and her hand jerked as if to pull away. He held it tight.

"I will not hurt you, pretty kitten. Lie still for me." On his knees with his legs spread over hers, he held her gaze as he tugged at his trews. The fabric fell silently away, and he released his clasp on her wrist when she snatched her hand back. He did not move, but waited. His chest hurt. His breath was constricted and tight. And he throbbed with a fierce need.

She was so small, so delicate and fragile, as innocent and naive as a newborn lamb when all around her was so harsh. It was amazing that such a creature had been produced by a man like Warfield. He would have expected someone more like Devlin, bristling with hard edges and words, hatred and animosity running unrelentingly deep.

A shudder ran through him when she reached out again, her touch tentative and light, a butterfly brush of her fingertips against his taut belly. Virginal curiosity glittered in her eyes, untutored passion making them shine. She had no idea what she did, or what to do. He tensed, but did not move as she began to lightly explore him, stroking over the tight bands of muscle on his belly with fluttering caresses that made the blood converge between his thighs. He swallowed a groan each time the back of her hand grazed the rough, bulging fabric that barely covered his rampant sex.

When he could stand it no longer, he caught her hand and held it tightly, pressing it against his stomach.

" 'Tis my turn again, catkin."

His voice sounded all wrong, hoarse and agitated instead of calm. He took another deep breath.

"I want to look at you, sweet maid."

She did not answer, but lay still as he began to untie the laces binding her leather girdle. He felt clumsy instead of certain, silently cursing his awkwardness as he tugged the stubborn laces free. The wool gown was easier, slipping over her head in a single twist. He sat back on his heels and sucked in his breath at the sight of her lying in the nest of her unbound hair, the red-gold mass spread beneath her naked body in a silken cape.

A feast for the eyes, a veritable banquet for his senses, the sight and smell and feel of her, the delicious hunger that was exquisitely painful and magnificent at the same time. It was all he could do not to spread her legs and plunge inside her, bury himself hilt deep in her body and ease his hunger. He felt his control slipping, and reined it in tightly.

Bending, he spread his fingers and cradled her jaw in his palm, holding her gently as he kissed the ivory skin above the edge of his open hand. Her warm breath fluttered against his cheek. He moved to her mouth, coaxing open her lips with his tongue to explore lightly at first, then with deepening thrusts that mimicked the sex act, the friction of his tongue against hers an erotic torment. A low moan vibrated in her throat, and he left off kissing her to catch his breath.

He stretched out beside her, one leg bent half over her thighs in a light weight. Resting on his angled elbow, he watched her as his fingers began to ply her flesh in soft, teasing strokes. She shivered when he caught her nipple between his thumb and finger, and he smiled wickedly and leaned to kiss her again. Still kissing her, he moved his hand to her other breast, tugging with light fingers at the beaded rosette. She moved restlessly, her body shuddering and her hips arching a little in awkward entreaty. Untried, unlearned in passion, yet her body was eager, trembling and striving against him.

He closed his eyes and thought of his first time, so long ago now, yet vivid in his memory. Sweet patience and gentle instruction had eased him from novice to skillful lover in time, and he had been ever grateful to the pretty kitchen maid who had ushered him into manhood. Her generosity had elevated the act from mindless coupling to a sharing of more than bodies, an introduction to sex most men did not get.

Catherine twisted beneath his ministering hand, then gasped softly when he moved his fingers lower, walking them lightly over the flat expanse of her stomach to the pale red and gold curls at the juncture of her thighs. He raised his head, watching her through narrowed eyes as he plucked softly at the silken threads on her mound. She quivered, and a crimson color rose in her cheeks.

"I do not think I—"

"Shh, catkin." He bent to kiss her again, pressing tiny kisses around her lips until she quieted. Her body was moving under the relentless caress of his fingers, her hips twisting in an enticing blend of invitation and denial that was all the more arousing. He slid his hand lower and smothered a groan at the deliciously soft, slick skin in the cleft between her thighs. Moving his hand in circular strokes, he gently pushed her legs slightly apart. Her muffled cry was swallowed by his mouth over hers, and he kissed her fiercely now, an unrelenting pressure and piercing sweetness that drove him closer to the edge.

Madness to touch her like this, the temptation to default on his sworn oath an ever-present lure. But he was no green youth unable to marshal his lust, and he could keep to the letter of his pledge while yet satisfying them both. It was a fine line between honor and disgrace, and a true test of his resolve.

He broke off the kiss, breathing in short, harsh pants. Curse her, why must she have yielded . . . why had she stood as she had, with the firelight behind her silhouetting her supple curves, the tight knot of her nipples an open invitation, and her eyes wide and hungry . . . inevitable, this driving need to take her, to fill the aching desire in her eyes and body. And inevitable, too, the disastrous results if he should lose the shaky vestige of control he still claimed.

He might have stopped then as reason intruded into the haze of lust that drove him, but with a little female whimper that was so lovely and so erotic, she arched her hips upward into the pressure of his hand between her legs. The white skin of her breasts and throat was flushed with abandon, her thighs quivering with strain as her heels dug into the wool blankets spread over the mattress.

Slipping his hand lower, he delved into the tight, hot recess, his fingers sliding on feminine moisture as he explored innocent flesh. Ah, God, she was so tight, so alluring, her movements so artless and utterly female, and he forgot for the moment everything but the compelling need that drove them both.

Covering her breast with his mouth, he tugged at the nipple with fierce suction, rolling it with his tongue as she clutched at him with both hands, her fingers tangling in his hair to hold his head, her slim hips driving upward against the stroking pressure of his hand. His fingers slid deeper inside her, until he encountered the intact feminine barrier against intrusion. The proof of her virginity ignited a ferocious desire to possess her completely, to go where none had gone before and make her his.

He sat up, kneeling between her parted legs. His free hand moved downward to his trews and pushed aside the woolen restriction that held him. Freed, he arched his hips, replacing his fingers with hard male flesh and sliding over her with slow, sizzling strokes. Grasping her thigh, he pulled her closer as he angled his body into the vee of her legs. With her thighs pressed against his folded legs, he shifted to clasp her around the waist and lean forward, pressing the first tiny bit into her. Deliciously hot, insanely inviting, she opened her legs for him, rocking her hips to take him.

Alex paused. His fingers dug into her hips as he held her still, and he closed his eyes and clenched his teeth. It was so tempting to push harder into her, to sheathe his turgid length inside her . . . but he was bound by an oath to leave her virgin, a technical point that he chose to interpret in his own way. He would leave her an unbroached maiden, but not a virgin in the strictest sense.

It was vengeance and justification, but more than that, alleviation of his need for her.

With great restraint, he rocked forward again, withdrawing from her to slide his hard body across the sweet, damp center of her. She moaned, arching upward, and he began to move his hips in a rhythmic pressure that sent tremors through him. His hands shifted to her legs, and he lifted them and pushed her thighs together in a vise around his length, his movements growing faster as he felt the culmination gather. She was gasping beneath him, muttering his name in throaty moans, her hips meeting his every thrust as he slid across her wet cleft in erotic, seething strokes.

A strangling sob caught in her throat, and her head moved from side to side, her lower lip caught between her teeth as she clutched at him frantically. He watched her through narrowed eyes, holding tight to his control until he felt her buck beneath him with growing frenzy. With gritted teeth, he waited until he recognized the signs inherent in female ecstasy, then surrendered to the driving need to seek his own release. As she sobbed incoherently in his ear he leaned over her, raking his sensitive length over her tight crevice with rough motions that brought him quickly to release. A shudder racked him, then another, and he held her tightly in his embrace, burying his face into the curve of her cheek and shoulder, dragging in deep breaths that smelled of freshly soaped hair. It tickled his jaw, and after a moment he lifted his head.

Her eyes were shut, tear tracks on her cheeks. Her lips looked bruised and swollen, and he rested his weight on one elbow to trace them with his fingertip. "Are you all right, catkin?"

Another shudder rippled through her body. He was still trapped between her clenched thighs, a torment and pleasure. "Yea," she answered, but it was a soft, unconvinced whisper.

Sighing, he held her without speaking until her trembling ceased. Then he brushed the damp hair back from her forehead and gently kissed her brow, her closed eyes, the tip of her nose, and her mouth.

"Are you sorry?" he asked when she finally opened her eyes to look up at him, and wondered even as he asked why he bothered. Being female, she would blame him for her yielding, and truthfully, he deserved blame for taking advantage of her innocence. If she had not known the consequences of her actions, he certainly did.

But she surprised him.

"No," she answered after a moment of thoughtful silence. "Not sorry. Overwhelmed, perhaps. Embarrassed."

"Embarrassed?" He shook his head. "You have no reason to be embarrassed, catkin. You are lovely, and far sweeter than any man deserves."

He was faintly surprised to realize he meant it. In spite of her initial contempt and rebellion, she had since acted with honest dignity. If anything, she had shamed him with her example.

Her laugh was soft and quavering. "And now I am ruined for any other man. I do not complain. 'Tis what I sought, after all."

Shifting to one side, he reached down to work the wool blanket free and up over her flushed, misty body. She gripped it tightly with both hands and covered her bare breasts.

"You are not ruined unless you wish to be," he said flatly. "I did not pierce your maidenhead."

She went still. Another tremor shook her. Then her head turned to look him full in the face. Her eyes were wide and searching, points of uncertain light flickering in the dark pupils. "I am not unaware of the details of what passes between a man and a woman."

"If you think I broke your maidenhead, you are." He could not help a small, amused smile at her stare of disbelief. "We were intimate, my sweet, but not fully so. You are still a virgin."

"Damn you!" she whispered, then burst into tears.

Alex stared at her in astonishment. It was not at all the reaction he had expected. Suddenly he knew with a swift certainty what she wanted—to avenge her father's insult of refusing to ransom her, and in the way she knew would prick him most. He should be offended, but strangely, he was not. It was just the sort of thing he might have done were he in her position, and he began to laugh.

She glanced up at him crossly, her brows drawing

down over her teary eyes. "Do not dare to laugh at me, sir!"

"Forgive me, catkin, but you are the most winsome maid to ever insult my manhood by using me thusly. I admire your tactics, if not your deceit."

"Deceit? I never pretended I wanted you for yourself."

"No?" He smiled as he drew a hand lightly over the wool-covered mound of her breasts. She shivered, and his smile deepened. "I think you deceive yourself with that lie, catkin."

She looked away, and he gazed at her profile with growing respect. This maid with the haunted eyes and luscious body was more than he had bargained for when he'd scooped her off that rock. And he wondered who would be bested in this game of wits, for 'twas certain she did not observe the customary rules.

It should, he thought, be a most entertaining contest.

10

Lord Warfield drummed his fingers against the table's surface with obvious irritation. Nicholas was unmoved. He stared at his father coldly.

"If you refuse, Catherine's fate is sealed. She is your daughter, for Christ's holy sake!"

"Do not blaspheme, Nicholas. You are not too grown a man to escape my fist."

"Nay, but I am too grown a man to allow my sister to be raped while I debate her value in coin." He surged to his feet, his frustration spilling over. "Are two villainous Scots worth more to you than your only daughter?"

"Nay, but one of them is Bruce's cousin, and he is worth all to the king. Edward's favor I do value above all else."

"Curse you!" Nicholas did not try to avoid it when his father rose sharply from his chair and drew back his fist, nor did he flinch when the blow fell. He was rocked back on his feet by it, and felt blood spurt from a cut lip.

"Curse me, do you!" The earl glared at him, his height

and broad shoulders blocking out a view of the ante-chamber behind him. "You would curse me for certain were you to be spending your days in a dark cell instead of walking free. Do you think I have not given up much to be where I am? To have the king's ear and vast tribute?" He held up his hands, scarred and coarse from years spent on the battlefield. "These hands have wrested gold and lands from those too weak to keep them, and these hands have been clasped by kings in gratitude for my service. Nay, you would not be so quick to lay blame were you to know what it has cost me to rise to this position, you arrogant young whelp. Do not speak to me of value, for you do not know the meaning of the word."

Nicholas glared at him, not bothering to wipe the blood away from his mouth. His hands clenched furiously at his sides. "Yet Catherine is not gold or land, but flesh and blood. Your flesh and blood."

"Yea, and she chose to flout my authority by leaving the safety of Warfield to roam the woods unattended by guard or even a handmaiden." The earl's eyes narrowed slightly. "I was told you saw her go and did not stop her."

He drew in a deep breath. " 'Tis true."

"And yet you blame me for not rushing to her rescue." He gave a sharp bark of laughter. "If you had your wits about you, she would even now be safely here instead of in the Scotsman's lair. Should harm come to her, you might look no further than yourself to lay blame. Now go, and do not belabor me further about my decision."

Nicholas did not move. "I would know what you intend."

"Would you." His lip curled. "I intend to petition the king to hang those murderous Scots on a gallows along the road to Dundee. That should be a good enough answer for Sir Alex Fraser."

"You condemn Catherine."

"She made the choice when she left my protection to go wandering in the fields like a common harlot. Now you know my intentions. Go and be content that you have had your say in the matter."

When the earl moved to a side table and poured wine into a goblet, Nicholas spun on his heels and left the chamber, pushing past his brother Geoffrey in the doorway. His brother scowled, but after a single glance at his expression, did not attempt to delay him.

He was before the doors of the guardroom when he heard his mother call him. He paused, waiting for her. A muscle flexed in his cheek as he turned, and he prayed his mother would not scour his already raw temper.

Lady Warfield drew near, beckoning to him to follow her, and he did so reluctantly. She went to an alcove hung with heavy draperies that shifted slightly in a draft. For a moment she said nothing, but stood where the light came through oiled skins stretching over the window to play across her face. Her skin was still unlined, smooth and pale as new-fallen snow. She wore her usual barbette atop her head, the headdress securing the woven crispinette of gilt and semiprecious stones that held her hair. Her gown was encrusted with rich embroidery, and bore a long train.

"You have spoken with your father," she said after a moment, her French soft and precise.

"Yes."

"He has reached a decision."

Again, her precise words were a statement instead of a question. Nicholas nodded.

"I see." Her hands twisted together in the only indication that she was gravely disturbed. A ring of keys jingled from a strap on her wrist. "I presume that he has decided against yielding up his prisoners to retrieve Catherine."

"So he says, madam."

She drew in a deep breath and looked away. The unlined surface of her face seemed to crumple slightly, but when she turned to face him again, there was no sign of distress. "You are bleeding, Nicholas."

He scrubbed the back of his hand over his cut lip. "A token of displeasure from my father."

"Why do you torment yourself by disagreeing with him? You must know you cannot win."

Again that flat, calm tone, unemotional and serene. He cocked a brow at her. "I beg your pardon, madam, but that is not the truth."

"Oh?" Her eyes widened slightly, the only reaction she allowed to show on features chiseled as if from marble. "Am I to understand that your wishes have swayed him to your view, then."

"No. But that was not my goal. I am no longer a child to be commanded to think as he does. I am a man now, with my own convictions."

"Yet you are as dependent upon his whims as are we."

"I have my own lands."

"At his sufferance."

"Again, madam, I must disagree. My lands are my own, to hold as I see fit, part of the dowry you brought with your marriage. If my father disinherits me, he still cannot take back what was not his to give. And if he should try," he added softly, "I will fight him to the death."

She stared at him for a long moment, while a slight draft rustled the heavy draperies and dust motes rode the scattered shafts of light. "You speak boldly, Nicholas. It is easy for a man to be defiant. But not so easy for a woman."

"Perhaps not." He felt a twinge of pity for his mother for the first time. Despite her closed expression, she seemed suddenly vulnerable. "Madam, are you worried about Catherine?"

"She is my daughter. Her fate concerns me."

Again, no emotion colored her words. He frowned. "If it is any consolation to you, I do not intend to allow her to languish at the mercy of a man like Alex Fraser."

"I do not see what you can possibly do to alleviate her situation."

"Frankly, madam, neither do I at the moment. But I will find a way."

Silence fell again, in which Lady Warfield studied her eldest son gravely. A faint jingle accompanied her movement as she turned away—the household keys on her wrist clinking softly on their metal ring. "I shall pray for your success, Nicholas."

And then she was gone, gliding away like some fey forest creature, elusive and enigmatic as always. He stood in the alcove a moment longer. His mother was right. What could he do to rescue Catherine? Even had he enough men to mount a sizable army, Castle Rock was near impregnable. A siege could last months. And during that time, anything could happen to Catherine.

If it had not already. . . .

Catherine smoothed the page of the book and started reading again, trying to make sense of the printed words that danced crazily in front of her eyes like chicken tracks in snow. Her valiant effort ended with the slamming shut of the book and its return to the esteemed place of honor on the table. It was no use. She could not keep her mind on the lengthy French poem long enough to grasp the gist of it.

Her own fault.

Now that she had descended into venial sin, it seemed

she had a taste for it. How many times since she had lain naked on that cot with Alex Fraser had she relived it in her mind? Too many to count, and each memory summoned fresh details and shivering reactions.

Yet she felt no regret. She should. It went against everything she had been taught. There should be better reasons for yielding to—nay, *encouraging*—a man's illicit touch. But she had none. Vengeance, perhaps. A blow against her father. Pitiful excuses. And yet . . . and yet, there had been a sweet triumph in the act, a glorious feeling of power when Alex Fraser had trembled beneath her exploring hand. An expression of near pain had darkened his handsome features at her light touch, his ragged breathing harsh and labored when she slid her fingers over the taut, heated ridge of muscles on his flat belly. Each time her hand had grazed the swollen wool that hid his arousal, he'd groaned. Yea, 'twas a most powerful feeling, knowing that she could make him shudder just by caressing him.

Now, oddly, she no longer felt quite so helpless. There was a sense of control that she could affect a man with so paltry a device as her touch. And though Alex had not relinquished command of the moment, she knew that her acts had defined his. If she had resisted, pushed him away and rejected him, his sense of honor would not have allowed him to persist. He was a contradiction, a Scottish barbarian with principles. An enigma.

Restless with her thoughts, she paced the floor of her chamber, then moved to the small slitted window to peer out. A cold wind blew, howling around the tower at times, keening wails like a doomed soul that made her shiver. She closed the shutters again and lit another candle to brighten the gloom, then sat in a chair by the table. She was still a prisoner, of course, despite what had passed two nights before. Not that she had expected anything different. Her situation as Alex Fraser's hostage was achingly similar to her position as Warfield's only daughter—a pawn in a game between powerful men.

And what of Alex Fraser? He was no earl, yet he wielded great influence with the Scots king. Enough, perhaps, to affect her release? It was a thought. If Robert Bruce brought his mighty force to bear upon Warfield keep, it was yet possible that she would be returned to her father. In light of recent events, a most unpleasant prospect. There were few options for her, though it had at last come to her in the dark hours of the night that there was still a way she might gain freedom without losing all. If she pled violation, she could achieve entrance to a nunnery. It would be a twofold vengeance, for the earl would be bereft of a marriageable daughter as well as the lands that were her dowry, all in a single stroke.

And she would gain independence. . . .

The now-familiar rattle of a key in the lock of her door drew her attention, and she sat up straight in the chair, heart pounding with a mixture of hope and dread. What would she say when she saw him again? What would he say? It would be so awkward, after their intimacy.

Yet her visitor was not Alex Fraser, but a man she knew only as Robbie. He paused in the doorway as if reluctant to enter. His burr was so thick, the English words sounded strange to her ears. "Ye are wanted downstairs, milady. I am tae escort ye."

She stood up, smoothing the skirt of her plain wool gown with nervous gestures. "Why am I needed so early in the day? Has word come from my father?"

He shrugged. " 'Tis more likely ye are tae get those answers frae the laird."

With trepidation, she accompanied Robbie from her chamber and down the winding, narrow stairs to the entrance of the hall. Smoke curled upward from a huge fire, and there were several men gathered around it. Her heart thumped erratically. An envoy from the earl?

As she entered the crowded chamber at Robbie's side, she felt people turn to look at her. She could not stop the heated flush on her cheeks, but kept her head held high. They probably knew, of course. Servants gossiped, and there would be at least one who had noted that their lord lingered overlong in the tower with his hostage. Mairi hated her, and was probably relishing the fact that the English maiden had yielded to their lord. It took great strength of will to cross that vast hall without betraying by word or gesture that she noticed the stares.

Alex detached from the group of men and strode toward her. Her heart hammered painfully against her ribs as he approached. Must he affect her so? Perhaps he was not the most beautiful knight she had seen, but the burnished black of his hair was striking in contrast with his dark skin and smoky eyes, almost exotic. Not even the wicked scar on his cheek detracted from his appeal.

He wore a plaid wound round his waist, the vivid scarlet and blue wool bright against the duller colors around him. His long white sherte was full-sleeved, blousing at his wrists, and he wore a dirk tucked into the wide belt that bound his plaid. An impressive sight, with his lean height and graceful stride, a man who projected assurance and power.

And yet when she looked at him she thought of the man who had lain next to her on a mattress of heather, the man who had held her naked body in his arms and caressed her intimately, and felt the heat rise anew in her face.

When he paused in front of her, a faint smile touched the corners of his mouth as he held out his arm for her to take. "I trust you slept well last night, milady."

She drew in a deep breath and nodded. "Yea, sir, I slept as well as possible under the circumstances."

His eyes glittered with laughter, but his expression was solemn. "I am most pleased to hear it, milady."

She curled her fingers over his proffered arm and walked with him to the high table set up beyond the center fire. Cushions bolstered her chair, and a dainty spoon with a carved handle was placed on the table. He pulled out her chair for her and waited. She looked up at him, baffled by this unexpected display of courtesy in front of all.

"Am I to be executed, sir?"

His brow rose. "Do you deserve execution?"

"That answer lies in one's personal viewpoint, I would think."

"True." He grinned. "Shall I ask Mairi for her opinion?"

"Not unless you have the gallows already built."

"Too much effort, I fear. A block and sharp sword would be easier and more merciful. Do you be seated, milady. We have hungry guests who wait impatiently for their dinner to be served."

Were these guests the reason she had not seen him the night before? She glanced toward the men, then took her seat, feeling a little conspicuous at the head table. It was so confusing, that she would be treated as an honored guest when she was so obviously a prisoner. No noble's daughter should publicly appear garbed in a rough wool gown and leather girdle instead of embroidered velvet or cloth of gold. No wimple or even crispinette covered her bare head. Now she wished she had taken special care with her hair instead of coiling it above her ears so carelessly that a few strands escaped to dangle against her cheeks.

It was awkward, not knowing her position, but she would cheerfully bite her tongue before asking if she was to play hostess. Not that she was unsuited. After all, she had learned proper etiquette just out of swaddling; on occasion, she had substituted for her mother when the countess was ill. Surely, she could manage easily enough in a Scot's crude hall.

The men she had seen earlier were seated in places of honor at the high table. For the most part they were older men, with the cares of their years marking their faces. A few of the names she gleaned were known to her: Sir Robert Boyd, Sir Neil Campbell, and David Barclay—close adherents of Robert Bruce. The others she did not recognize, and one man's name was not mentioned.

Laughing easily with Robbie, he stood apart from the others, and it was his unusual appearance that caught her eye. Black hair framed a face of naturally pale hue, and he wore a dark green and blue plaid that made his skin look even paler. His eyes were intense and bright, his movements quick.

When he glanced up suddenly, he caught her gaze and grinned, his mobile features taking on a mischievous expression. She found herself smiling back at him, taken with his boyish charm. Perhaps not all the Scots were dour, cheerless men.

Alex took a seat beside her, and noticed the small play. Stretching out his long legs in front of him, he indicated the Scot with a nod of his head. "You have not been introduced to all our guests, milady."

"No, I have not, though I recognize some of the names in passing."

Alex laughed softly. "I imagine you do. They are well known to those who fear justice. Sir Robert Boyd, for instance, a more doughty warrior you will not find in England or Scotland. 'Tis said that the Bruce depends as much upon his strong arm as his quick wit."

The man in question looked up with a smile. "You are too kind, Fraser," he replied in the same English used by his host. "Do you expect compliments in return?"

"Yea, if you can put down your cup long enough to voice them."

Sir Robert laughed, and lifted his cup. "In tribute to a worthy warrior and stout heart—who has shared his ale and meat with our empty bellies. May God smile on our cause and our king."

This was met with raised cups and a rousing cheer from the assemblage in the hall, and Catherine lifted her own cup but did not drink. She felt the gazes on her, but stubbornly refused to relent.

Alex leaned closer to her. "Can you not drink the health of those who will be the victors, milady?"

"I beg pardon for my error. I thought we were drinking the health of Robert Bruce, not King Edward."

He only laughed, but when she glanced up again, she felt the steady gaze of the tall, dark-haired Scot resting on her thoughtfully. He was the only man not seated; he still stood by the fire, one foot resting on a low bench.

When he saw her watching him, he held his cup high. "If you will not drink to Robert Bruce, milady," he said in a lisping burr, "then drink instead to the Black Douglas."

"I will not." Her fingers tightened around the stem of her goblet. " 'Tis said that he is the devil, even more so than Robert Bruce."

Laughter greeted her remark, and beside her, Alex

said wryly, "Perhaps I should introduce you to our feckless friend, milady."

An awful suspicion ignited as Alex continued, "May I present Sir James Douglas, late of Castle Douglas, now lord of the realm—or destroyer of it, depending upon which view you believe."

A slight chill trickled down Catherine's spine, and she could not help another glance at the young man grinning at her so wickedly. This was the Black Douglas? The man who was said to hold most of northern England in terror just with the invocation of his name? And she had heard that very name whispered by nurses to frighten their young charges into good behavior. She shivered now with remembered tales of his daring exploits that had taken so many good Englishmen from this life, and yet she found it near impossible to believe that this boyish young man with the slight lisp could be the same. . . .

He swept her a courtly bow. "I am most privileged to meet the Earl of Warfield's daughter. Are you enjoying your visit to Castle Rock, milady?"

It was such an innocuous question, asked with such placid expectation, that she found herself smiling. "More than you would enjoy your visit to Warfield, Sir James."

He grinned. "I have no doubt of that. Though once I did chance to meet your father. I do not think he liked me very much."

"An understatement, I am certain."

"Doubtless. It was an awkward time for us both, as he was wroth over the mislaying of his kine . . . a wee failing of mine, that I oft forget to consult the owner before I move his beasties about."

Robbie MacLeod laughed softly. "Aye, yer reiving and spreaghs ha' led tae some merry fighting at times, I ken."

Unabashed, James Douglas shrugged. " 'Tis usually the way of it. If good fortune is with me."

Catherine stared at him in dismay. This young man with the open face and wicked eyes was not at all like the fiend she had always envisioned. Had he really committed such dark deeds?

She leaned forward, holding his gaze. "Sir James, I must ask you if 'tis true that you razed your own castle to the ground to spite the king."

A reckless light danced in his eyes. "Yea, milady. I did it to tweak Edward's nose. And to spare more English lives from being lost in trying to hold what is mine. Though I admit that I tire more from the inconvenience of killing such poor soldiers than the joy of doing it."

The cadence of his words softened the content, and she sat back again. She should be horrified and repulsed, yet somehow she was not. It was true then. This young man who was feared over the breadth and width of England and part of Scotland was no monster, no mythical warrior with powers of darkness, but a youngish, ordinary man—if it was possible to call a man ordinary who had managed the feats of war he had achieved.

And all she could think of in response was a soft "Why?"

"Why?" James Douglas shrugged again, a brief lift of his broad shoulders, a casual gesture. "Because I wouldst rather my ancestral home be naught but a pile of stones than a harbor for another night for ignorant men who seek to destroy that which they do not understand."

"What is there to understand? We are at war. You follow Robert Bruce's lead, while Edward rightfully demands your loyalty. It seems a simple enough position."

"Nothing is ever as simple as it seems." His lisping words had grown soft, but rather than seeming gentle, he now had the air of a predator poised to strike. "There is an old parable that explains it best, I think. Shall I tell it to you, milady?"

She shifted uneasily, aware of Alex's tension beside her, but after a moment, nodded. "Yea, if you will."

Douglas took a sip of his ale, eyeing her over the rim of the goblet for a long moment, then nodded. "Once, a fisherman built a small hut next to the river to keep watch on his nets. He had a bed, a fire, and a single door. It happened that one night when he left to check his nets, he was gone a long time. When he returned, he saw by the light of the fire that a fox had invaded his hut and was devouring a salmon. Stepping into the doorway, he drew his sword and cried, 'Traitor, thou must die!'

"Brother fox, fearful, saw that he was hemmed in by walls on every side. The only way out was through the door, but 'twas blocked by the man. Yet close by on the bed lay a woolen cloak. The fox seized it in his teeth and pulled it over the fire. When the fisherman saw his cloak burning he hurried to save it, so that the clever fox sprang through the door and escaped."

Douglas paused, his eyes riveted on her face as he added softly, "The Scots are the fox and the English the fisherman, and we shall escape as cleverly as did the fox in my tale, milady."

Silence hung heavily in the hall, broken only by the popping of burning logs in the fire and the sputtering of torches on the walls. Captivated as much by Douglas's intensity as his trenchant tale, she barely felt Alex shift beside her.

"As always, Sir James, you have commanded the rapt attention of the assemblage." There was a sharp edge to Alex's tone that penetrated Catherine's fascination with James Douglas, and she turned slightly to look at him in surprise. His mouth was slanted in a smile that looked all wrong as he regarded Douglas. "Pray, tell us the latest news of Edward's doings. Has he yet yielded up his foolish notion of relieving Stirling Castle?"

A brief pause, then Douglas shook his head, a sly grin squaring his mouth. "Nay, if anything, he is obsessively pursuing that end. All this last spring and summer, Prince Louis of France sought to achieve harmony between Edward and his barons, but Edward would not forgive Lancaster for his part in Piers Gaveston's death until his queen prevailed upon him to listen to her brother Louis. Last month Edward relented and accepted a humble apology from Lancaster and his followers for daring to slay his favorite. Now, think they that the odds are in their favor, for 'tis true that they number more than do we." A shrug expressed his disdain for that fact. "Since we are committed to do battle in June, we must whittle away the English hold on our lands to lessen their advantage. And," he added with a gleam in his eyes, "I have a plan to effect just that end."

"Ah, I have no doubt of that." Alex's words held an undertone of satisfaction. "Mayhap we can discuss this plan at our leisure after dinner."

" 'Twas my hope, Sir Alex." Douglas swept a gallant bow in Catherine's direction, then he moved to a table to allow a squire to offer a ewer of scented water and a cloth to wash his hands.

Catherine watched him go with a sense of relief. James Douglas was fascinating, but she found him fascinating in the same way a viper was—threatening and lethal, and much too frightening to endure for long. Alex Fraser was dangerous, but there was a difference, a more controlled menace to him than that which emanated from just beneath the charming surface of the Black Douglas. Sir James would surely be more reckless, would risk too much, and if he failed, would lose all. To her mind, such danger was too engulfing to bear.

She looked down at her still full goblet, frowning. Why had she been invited to the hall? Was there some hidden motive behind Alex Fraser's courtesy? Her head throbbed with anxiety and confusion, and she barely looked up when a dish was placed before her. Pottage filled carved pewter bowls, and white bread and cheese garnished large wooden platters in the middle of the table. Roast meat lent a heady aroma to the array of victuals prepared for the guests.

"Are you not hungry, milady, or have you lost the dirk you were lent?"

Alex's soft query lifted her head and summoned a faint smile from her. "I yet have the dagger, sir. You said it was precious to you, and as I do not have a belt to wear it and did not want to chance its loss, it is in my chamber."

"Your sense of obligation is impressive."

There was an edge of scorn to his words that sharply brought her attention to him. "You mock me, sir."

His eyes rested on her face a moment, smoky with some emotion she could not fathom, then he looked away. "Nay. I mock myself, I think." Before she could ask what he meant by that cryptic remark, his gaze turned back to her, eyes half-hidden by his thick lashes. "What think you of Sir James Douglas, my lady?"

"His reputation is fearsome." She frowned slightly at his intense regard. "Is that what you mean, sir?"

"All have heard of the dangerous exploits of the Black Douglas. Yet despite his reputation, 'tis said that many women find him attractive."

She considered that, then nodded. "Yea, I can easily understand that."

"Can you? Do you find him attractive as well, milady?"

"Undeniably. But in the same way a sword is attractive, I think. Beautifully formed, yet dangerous and cruel."

His eyes rested on her for a long moment, but she

could read nothing in his expression. There was a strange tension between them that had not been there a few moments before, a wary regard in his attention that bewildered her. A tiny shiver trickled down her spine and lifted the hair on the nape of her neck.

Reaching out, he lightly touched a curl dangling in front of her ear. "Yet swords have their uses, milady."

"So they do." She drew back slightly and his hand fell away. "But I weary of instruments of war, and wouldst yet cleave to peace, if such a thing were to be found in Scotland."

"Have you met violence within these halls?"

"Nay, not as you may mean. But conflict does not have to be violent to be frightening."

A faint smile touched the corners of his mouth. "I had not thought you fearful of anything save mortal sin."

Heat scoured her throat and burned her eyes. "Yea," she whispered, "and I have courted damnation far too well of late."

"And regret it, I see."

A lie stuck in her throat. She wanted to fling his taunt back in his face, but could not. In truth, she did not regret it, and loathed herself for her weakness.

Alex studied her face for a few moments longer, and when she did not respond, sat back in his chair with a soft oath. After a moment, he turned away to speak to Sir Robert, and Catherine focused on the food before her to escape the measuring stares directed toward her from those in the hall.

Conversation flowed around her in a ceaseless tide, ebbing and flowing, much of it in Gaelic. Even when English was spoken, many of the idioms were too baffling to determine their meanings. Then Sir Neil Campbell leaned forward, his voice gruff as he said in English, "But what can we expect when even the barons are not honorable enough to keep their pledged oaths? Warfield is a prime example, and I would not be surprised to learn that he believes himself justified. Would you agree with me, Lady Catherine?"

Appalled, she looked up at Campbell. "I would not agree nor disagree, sir. My father never took me into his confidence."

"But surely you are aware of his tactics, his perfidy in swearing safe conduct, then slaying those whom he had sworn to protect."

Her hands trembled slightly on the carved handle of the spoon she held. "Again, sir, I must plead ignorance."

Sir Neil's brows lowered in a scowl. "Did you not live at Warfield keep? Did you not sup with the earl, and digest treachery along with your meat?"

The spoon clattered against the wooden side of her bowl as she dropped it. "Who is to say what is treachery and what is treason? Here, I have heard only of how you would defy your rightful king with sword and deception, yet you accuse my father of being duplicitous."

"Yea, and rightfully so, my lady." Sir Neil gazed at her coldly. " 'Twas my kinsman he slew so treacherously after promising him safe conduct across his lands."

"As was mentioned earlier, Sir Neil, this is war. I am certain your kinsman was made aware of the risks should he deal unfairly with my father."

"Unfairly?" Sir Neil's jaw hardened. "I do not consider escorting a sick wife and two small children across Warfield land to reach the Solway Firth unfair. Unwise, perhaps, in light of the earl's barbarous slaughter of them all, but not unfair. He sought only to return his wife to her family for proper care, as she had been held hostage near to the point of death. They were slain, my lady, along with two bairns not old enough to be out of swaddling."

Catherine's stomach knotted, and the food she had eaten felt like a heavy lump as she regarded Campbell with rising dismay and daunted heart. She did not want to believe that her father would do such a thing, yet knew it must be true. He had too often said that Scots were like a sickness on the land that must be destroyed at first sprout and not allowed to flower.

"Sir Neil," Alex said softly, "I do not think the lady should be made to bear the blame for her sire's actions. And neither do I think she was taken into his confidence either before or after his heinous deed."

Campbell drew in a deep breath. "Yea, I forget myself. Grant pardon, Sir Alex. It was rude of me to castigate another guest at your table for faults which are not hers."

" 'Tis not my pardon you need ask, Sir Neil, but the lady's."

Catherine shot Alex a quick glance of surprise. His words were soft, but his tone steely. Silence had fallen along the table, as all waited to see the reaction of this renowned warrior who answered to no one but Robert Bruce. After a moment, he bowed his head stiffly and looked at Catherine.

"Grant pardon, my lady, for my hasty words. My heart is still sore from my loss."

She hesitated. Grief marked Campbell's face, striations that cut deep into his features as if permanently etched there. An ache ignited in her, spreading outward until it felt as if her ribs were being squeezed.

In a whisper, she said, "If, indeed, it was my father who visited such loss upon your house, I am most shamed by his monstrous deed. 'Tis I who should beg your mercy for the wrongs that were done to your kinsman and his family, Sir Neil."

There was another moment of silence, then Sir Neil's ravaged face softened slightly, and he inclined his head toward her. "I should be shamed, my lady, for heaping abuse upon an innocent. Of all men, I should well know that one cannot force another to compensate for unearned sins."

It was scant balm to her tortured soul, and the knowledge that her father was regarded so widely as a man brutal beyond most was anguishing. Yet she could not quail before such watchful gazes, could not betray the depth of her shame before men who would relish her pain.

With as much dignity as she could muster when her throat felt raw and her breath was tight in her chest, she inclined her head gracefully. "Perhaps it would better serve us to speak of other things, Sir Neil."

It was Alex who agreed. "Aye, 'tis indeed time for us to converse more easily among ourselves. The hour for more direct discourse will be when we are joined by the others."

Others? Catherine wondered briefly if he meant more Scots would soon arrive. It seemed the hall was already full to bursting with armed knights and rough-looking men with various woolen swathes draped across chests and belted around their waists. There was the dull gleam of wicked weapons, huge double-edged axes and thick spears, and sheathed swords that clanked with soft menace against thighs and wooden benches. It was a room ready for war, and the thought chilled her to the marrow. Even in her father's hall, there had not been this air of barely leashed violence.

She yearned to retreat to the silent security of the tower chamber, where she could find solace in beautifully lettered volumes of poetry, or at least in mute prayers of entreaty for her salvation. But it was quickly evident that they were to linger in the hall, for musicians entered with harps and lutes, the more traditional instru-

ments of her experience, rather than the loud and raucous pipes that had serenaded them before.

Lively music filled the air, and there was laughter and
merriment as boisterous couples began to dance. Some
women were garbed in narrow lengths of bright-colored
wool as well, though it was worn as adornment, pinned at
one shoulder to flow over their backs to their waists. Occasionally, Catherine would catch their curious glances at
her, and wondered wryly what they thought of this hostage their laird had imprisoned. Mairi made no secret of
her opinion, but she was not the only woman who lived in
Castle Rock.

She thought of Bess, and how distressed the young
maid must be at her mistress's abduction. No doubt, Bess
would be one of the few who missed her. It had always
been difficult for Catherine to relate to the young women
who were fostered at Warwick, for she had so little in
common with them. While the others giggled and compared compliments from lovestruck swains, she had remained aloof, unwilling to admit that none dared pay her
court for fear of the earl's wrath. Only on occasion had
she joined them, and that when wandering troubadours
visited Warfield to sing songs of love and gallant cheva-
liers.

Then she had felt a rare kinship with others her age. If
she had been able to trust them, she would have read to
them from the volumes of poetry her brother possessed,
for she knew they enjoyed the romantic tales. But she
had learned at an early age that trust is a nebulous quality
oft betrayed for personal gain. It had not left her with an
enduring faith in most.

And so she had not taken the risk of her skill being
betrayed to the earl by one of her mother's handmaidens,
preferring instead to secrete herself in some shadowed

alcove to peruse the volumes filched from her brother's store. The only relief from her self-imposed loneliness was Nicholas. He was the only one who truly cared for her welfare and her happiness. And it was Nicholas she mourned most in her absence from Warfield.

The gaiety of the hall reminded her how he enjoyed the lively dancing and music of feast days, when the earl's strict rule grew lax enough to allow merriment. Then, her brother would seize her by both hands and dance her down into the midst of the revelers, until they were both breathless from laughter and exertion. It was at those times that she felt cherished. Almost content. But those moments were too few and too rare.

Drawing in a ragged breath, she let the music swirl around her now without notice, staring down at the clasped hands in her lap, praying that she could soon escape. Childish laughter broke her reverie and she looked up to see two small children approach the high table. A boy and a girl, about six and five years of age respectively, came to a halt before the table and made their courtesies, the boy bowing from the waist while the little girl managed a clumsy dip. Both were handsome children, dark-haired with rosy cheeks and glowing eyes. They were trailed by two young women, who paused in the center of the hall to watch the children.

Beside her, Alex stirred, and turned his attention to the children. He beckoned, and both came toward him with smiling faces and expectant eyes. He spoke to them in Gaelic and they answered, then each gravely acknowledged the greetings of the guests at the high table.

Catherine smiled when they glanced at her, then back to Alex, who said something to them in Gaelic. In English, he said to her, "This is Christian and Sarah. They speak a little English, if you care to greet them."

"Of course. Good morn, Christian, Sarah."

A little slowly, the young boy said in a rough burr, "Good morn, milady."

The little girl stared up with round eyes, her pursed lips slightly quivering. Then she said faintly, *"Ha neil Sassenach."*

"Yea, Sarah, you have English enough to say good morn," Alex said, then he must have repeated it in Gaelic, for the little girl took a deep breath and nodded.

"Gude morn, m'lady," she burst out, then beamed when Alex laughed approvingly.

After a short conversation in Gaelic, Alex beckoned to a servant, who brought the children a comfit. Then the two women still standing in the center of the hall came forward quickly. Halting, they bobbed in front of the table, then looked up expectantly. A servant placed small purses in their outstretched hands. Again, the two women bobbed courteously as their eager fingers closed around the jingling pouches.

Leaning back in his chair, Alex spoke to them and they replied animatedly, accompanying their comments with smiles and flirtatious glances at him. They were pretty women but obviously Kinnison villagers, and Catherine was surprised at how familiar Alex was with them in front of his guests. None of the men seemed to notice the exchange, however, speaking among themselves in low tones. After a few minutes, the women departed, ushering the children in front of them.

"What pretty children," Catherine said when she felt Alex looking at her, more from a desire to distract him than anything else. "And very well behaved."

"Yea, I insist upon it."

She looked at him curiously then. "I thought the people of Scotland were free to do as they please, and answer to their laird for naught but loyalty."

"Yea. 'Tis true."

"Then why do you insist upon good behavior from the children of your village? Is that not tyranny?"

She had meant to gently mock him, to seize upon an implied contradiction in his denunciation of King Edward, but he gazed at her with a faint smile curling his lips.

"Do not parents demand obedience from their children?"

"Of course, sir, but you are not parent to—" She halted abruptly, warned by the amused gleam in his eyes. Her composure began to unravel as he remained silent, and comprehension dawned. "Those are your children, I take it, sir."

"Yea, lady, they are."

"And which of the women is their mother?"

"Both." He shrugged lightly at her appalled gaze. "Do not tell me that in England there are no natural children born."

"Of course there are." She inhaled sharply to stifle words of censure. How could she berate him for deeds such as her own family had committed? For it was true that several babes had been born of Warfield blood without benefit of a priest. It was not uncommon, but she had never seen the children or the mothers paraded through the hall.

Something of her thoughts must have shown in her eyes, for he leaned forward to say softly, "They are my blood, and I will not deny them a place or my presence. They are innocent of all blame in their creation, and I would not have them shamed. While their mothers still live below in Kinnison, my children live here. I see to it that they are welcome in my hall, and are given all that their station in life can provide. None are allowed to slight them. Nor will I censure their mothers unless I care to censure myself, for 'twas of my own free will that I lay with them."

Catherine stared at him, feeling heat stain her cheeks scarlet. How had he guessed her thoughts? And how was she any different from those two women, save that he had not taken what she was willing to give?

And then, fleetingly, she had the awful thought that she envied them for their freedom in choosing their own destiny, in lying with a man without thought of reprisal other than perhaps the creation of a babe.

Oh, how much she had changed in the weeks since she had been brought to Castle Rock! For as she gazed into Alex Fraser's clear gray eyes, she knew that she longed to lie with him as completely as those women had done. . . .

11

Torches flickered on the stone walls, but beyond the bright pools of light loomed shadows black as pitch. Nicholas strode down the dank, narrow corridor behind a guard. Faint, desperate sounds infiltrated the murky halls, oppressing and furtive, like the dry rustling of rats in the walls.

"Do you know which cell?" His impatience penetrated the guard's silence, and the man turned with a jangle of keys to peer at the metal ring he held up in the wavering glow of a wall torch.

"Aye, m'lord. 'Tis this one." The guard's hand shook slightly as he rattled the keys, turning the ring to squint at the selection.

"By all that is holy, man, do you find the right key before I freeze in this cursed hole," Nicholas muttered in a snarl that earned him a frightened glance from the guard.

"Aye, m'lord. I do be hurrying."

Nicholas grimaced at the man's obvious fear. He put a hand on the burly guard's shoulder. " 'Tis too cold for us both in this damp hole. When you have let me in, seek warmth at the closest fire. I will call when I need you."

"Aye, m'lord." The guard gave him a quick glance as he slid the key into the hole, then ventured a warning. "Do you be careful, m'lord. I would not trust these Scots savages."

"They are chained. But I will heed your warning."

With a grinding grate of metal on metal, the key turned the tumblers in the lock and the heavy wood and iron door opened with a groan. The guard jammed a torch into a holder on the wall so that light filtered into the cell, then Nicholas dismissed him. A fetid odor greeted him as he stepped inside, the ordure of confined men stinging his eyes and nose. It took a moment for his eyes to adjust to the darkness that cloaked the cell.

Two pairs of eyes glittered in the fitful light, and chains clanked softly. "Welcome, my lord Devlin."

The Scottish burr grated on his temper, and Nicholas took several steps closer. Adam de Brus stared back at him, unblinking. There was no hint of surrender in that hot-eyed stare, only hate.

"I would ask how you find your lodgings, de Brus, but as 'tis much like the Scottish hovels you are used to, I doubt you would recognize the difference."

"What else have you English left us, but hovels? You burn field and forest, slaughter our women and spear our children, then think us ungrateful. Yea, 'tis true enough that I find little difference in this stinking hole and the devastation visited upon my homeland, but 'twill not be true for long."

"No? As intriguing as I find that comment, I shall not take you to task for it. I have come for another reason."

"More torture?" Chains rattled again, and there was the sound of shuffling straw as de Brus tried to rise. He managed it clumsily, as his wrists were manacled to rings in the wall and tethered by short links. "I am ready. Leave the lad alone this time . . . he has had more than his share."

Nicholas was startled. He had not thought torture would be used against them. But as light filtered across de Brus's face in unsteady shafts, he saw fresh scars and dried blood, cracked lips that looked well chewed. De Brus wore only a thin sherte with a ragged hem that barely covered his privates. A glance toward the boy revealed de Brus's dirty red plaid wrapped warmly around thin limbs. Young Fraser also showed evidence of harsh abuse, but he, too, struggled valiantly to his feet to face his tormentor, eyes blazing with a hatred far too adult for so tender an age.

Not for the first time, Nicholas felt a wave of shame at his father's actions. Adam de Brus was a man full-grown, but this lad could not be much more than thirteen or fourteen, too young to be much of a threat. Old enough to bear arms, perhaps, but immature enough to be bested easily by any man able to wield a sword. No, Fraser's brother should be sitting around a fire listening to tales of war, not enduring the hardships of torture and imprisonment. It was galling that Scotland's refusal to accept their rightful overlord led to its youth being slaughtered like helpless sheep.

He turned back to Robert Bruce's kinsman. "I want from you what no torture could extract, de Brus. Guidance."

Incredulous laughter greeted this comment as Adam de Brus stared at him in the capering light. "Guidance, my lord Devlin? What game do you play now, I wonder, to come and taunt me with such blather."

" 'Tis no game, de Brus." He moved closer, choking a little on the stench of filth and unwashed body. The straw at his feet was heavily soiled and matted in clumps.

When he kicked at one of the dirty mounds, it let out a squeal and scuttled away. De Brus laughed softly.

"You have annoyed my pet, Devlin. Or my dinner, should I be fortunate enough to snare the beastie."

Bile rose in his throat as Nicholas looked up to meet de Brus's ironic gaze. "Tell me what I need to hear and I can promise you better fare, de Brus."

"Can you promise our freedom?"

His brow lowered at the mocking reply and he shook his head. "Nay, I cannot. It would be a lie to say I could."

"What ho, an Englishman who is reluctant to lie? Can this be possible?"

"At times." His mouth quirked in a faint smile as he regarded de Brus. "As in Scotland, it depends upon the man."

For a moment de Brus stared at him. His hands opened and closed, and dull light glinted off the iron manacles around his wrists. Then he said tightly, "What advice do you seek, Sassenach?"

"Information about Alex Fraser."

The youth's head jerked up, and he snarled something fierce in Gaelic, but de Brus shook his head and replied in the same language. After a short, heated discussion, his eyes shifted back to Nicholas.

"Tell me what counsel you seek about Alex Fraser, and I will tell you if I can answer it."

"Fraser holds my sister hostage against the return of you and the boy. It is unlikely that the earl will agree to an exchange. I want to know what may persuade Fraser to release Lady Catherine unharmed."

Soft laughter greeted his words, and Nicholas waited without reaction. It was said de Brus was hot-tempered but had a fondness for children and women, and he prayed it was so. For no other reason would he have swallowed his pride to come here, defying his father's orders and his own belief in his king. But something must be done, for time was growing short and he feared for Catherine's welfare.

Again, the young Fraser growled something in Gaelic, and again de Brus replied. This time, it was Fraser who responded to Nicholas in a hoarse burr: "Alex willna gi' up tha' which he doesna want tae gi' up, Devlin. 'Twill do ye no good tae offer less than he demands. 'Tis a waste o' yer time tae try."

Nicholas drew in a deep breath that stank of despair and dampness. "I thought a letter from you might persuade him to consider ransoming the lady. I can do nothing about your freedom, but I can better your circumstances here."

The boy laughed. "Wha' more can we ask? We hae water, a roof o'er our heads, and fresh meat should one o' the rats come too close."

Beneath fierce bravado, a tremble lurked, and Nicholas recognized weakness. But he merely shrugged as he moved to the doorway and halted in the opening. "Mayhap you have forgotten what roasted mutton smells like. And hot bread, and flagons of ale. After I remind you, we will talk again."

He left then, the echo of the slamming cell door a hollow ring in his ears as he moved back down the narrow corridor. Such human misery, such squalid quarters—and he had never given it a thought while dining above with fine linen and endless courses of meats and breads. It moved him to pity, but not to surrender. Whatever it took, he would find a way to retrieve Catherine.

Once de Brus and young Fraser had ample time to breathe in the tempting aromas of roasted meat, bread, and stews, he would return and see if perhaps they were more agreeable. It would be another kind of torture, to see and smell the food placed just out of their reach, and perhaps harder to bear than that which the earl had visited upon them.

It occurred to him as he mounted the narrow winding staircase that led upward that he had more of his father in him than he would like to acknowledge. For he knew that he, too, would be ruthless in achieving his purpose.

"Checkmate, milady." Alex leaned back in his chair, gazing at Catherine with satisfaction. Her face was flushed pink where her palm rested against her cheek as she focused upon the chessboard. Long, slender fingers toyed with the carved playing piece, and her brows knit in a frown.

Then she sighed and looked up at him. "I concede."

He grinned. "Concede or no, the game is done. And now my prize."

Despite a mutinous set to her mouth, she took a deep breath and said firmly, "King Edward is a—"

"Caitiff and a bogle . . ." he supplied when she faltered.

"Caitiff, bogle, and skyte. And Robert Bruce—"

"King Robert."

She scowled at his interruption, but said, "King Robert is a braw. . . ."

"Callant." He grinned. "A pretty man, brave and stalwart and true. Say it."

Rebellion glittered in her eyes, and she muttered the words so quickly they came out as one. When he nodded with approval, a flicker of amusement tugged at her mouth.

"You are not easily pleased, sir."

"Nay, I am not. Nor am I easily beaten at chess. You are a lovely player, but a poor one, milady. You must learn patience and strategy before you can hope to win."

Lifting her cup, she took a sip of wine, gazing at him

over the rim. A branch of candles cast flickering light over her face. There was something softer about her of late, a new bearing that intrigued him. She still argued with him about the merits of English politics, but there was a difference. Somewhere in her deep violet eyes lurked a new respect for him. It was as intriguing as it was baffling.

And disturbing.

It had caught him off-guard, this new softness she presented, and the erratic tenderness that he had begun to feel for her. That was the most disturbing, that he found himself weak enough to be susceptible, to let her under the guard he had kept intact for twenty-nine years. Few had pierced his barriers and forced him to care, and those were kin to him by blood. For this one female—a daughter of the enemy—to manage it was daunting.

She sat back on the stool, rolling the pewter goblet between her fingers, still studying the chessboard. "It seems to me that you made an unwise move, sir. How did you yet win by giving up your bishop?"

"To win, one must be willing to sacrifice. Even the queen if necessary."

"But not the king."

He smiled. "Again, the victor must weigh all risks and advantages before making such decisions."

Her brow lifted. "Are we still speaking of chess, Sir Alex?"

"I am. But I sense your mind strays to other topics." She was so obvious at times, and yet he could not decipher her reasons for her actions. Female mystery and lucid honesty, a lethal combination.

"What of my father?" she asked softly. Her eyes caught his gaze and held it. "Has there been no word?"

"You know there has not." It was a sore subject with him. Near two months had passed without the arrival of an envoy, only a single message sent by courier to inform him that the earl still waited on his monarch's reply. He was left with the untenable option to either do as he had warned Devlin he would do, or accept defeat. Neither was tolerable.

A slight frown puckered her brow again, and she traced the goblet rim with a fingertip, slowly, studying the liquid inside the glazed cup as if it held a secret she wished to know. A log popped in the fire. Gray light barely lightened the glazed windows of the small chamber filled with books.

After a moment of silence, she gave a soft sigh. "On the morrow, 'twill be the feast day of Saint Nicholas."

"Yea. 'Tis not long now until the celebration of Christmas." He hesitated, thinking he knew what must distress her. " 'Tis customary to observe certain rituals, milady, which I am certain are familiar to you. There will be dancing, singing, feasts and merriment, and on the day of Christ's birth, a special mass said in the chapel by Father Michael or another visiting priest."

"Advent has begun," she murmured, and glanced up at him again. "But 'tis not that which pricks me, sir, though I am glad that there will be familiar festivities. On the morrow, it is my brother's feast day as well."

"Ah. Nicholas."

She nodded. "Yea. I realize you hold no fondness for him, but he has oft been the only light in my life. I miss him. This will be the first we have been apart on his feast day, save one year when he was still being fostered by the Earl of Hereford."

Alex's jaw tightened. "Hereford. The de Bohuns have been a thorn in Bruce's side for far too long. 'Tis to that family that Edward I gave Bruce's lands of Annandale and Carrick when he was deseisined and a hunted fugitive. Now that Edward's monstrous pup is king, he has given the Bruce domains in Essex to the de Bohun family, as well. They are accursed."

"Did you not say that ofttimes a queen must be sacrificed to yet win all? Perhaps this is the same."

He stared at her. There was no mockery in her tone or face. "Do you equate ancestral lands with chess, milady?"

"Nay, but I do compare strategy. It is the same, I think, with war. Am I right? Is not war just another, more deadly form of chess?"

She surprised him as much as she irritated him, and he rose from his chair. "Yea, lady, but with much larger stakes than an idle wager."

Restless, snared by his fierce desire to free Jamie and his fierce need for this woman, he was caught between the two. How did he reconcile the dual nature of his wanting? He could free Lady Catherine. And Jamie would die. Or he could hold her and pray that the earl would relent and consent to exchange hostages. And Jamie might still die.

Or he could ease the hunger she stirred in him, and nothing would be reconciled but his driving need. . . .

It was not that he had not considered it, for he had. Countless times had he gazed at her and felt the hot surge of desire in his loins prompting him to take her to his bed and taste her sweetness to the full. But he had not allowed himself to do more than touch her casually, a flick of his fingers against her cheek, a caress of her uncovered hair, a lingering stroke on her back as he guided her beside him. He had not trusted himself to use restraint the next time he was so unwise as to hold her naked, shivering body in his arms.

But was the need to bridle his desire still relevant? There had been no word from Warfield or Devlin, nothing but silence from the men who held his young brother's life in their thrall. . . .

Frustrated anger rose hot and high in him, and his hands clenched into fists at his side. Curse the impetuosity of a youth who had gone out after de Brus, and curse himself for making war seem grand and noble instead of teaching his young brother the reality of it, the stark horror of men dying and horses screaming, and all around there was the sound and smell and taste of death . . . but he had not told Jamie that. Nay, he had spoken of past exploits of his own and of Robert Bruce, of the Fraser men before them, fighting beside noblemen and kings; dying at times, but living on in tales of glory and valor. Yea, that much was true enough, but he had dwelled too long on the homage instead of the inhumanity one man did to another, and because of his failure, Jamie was now in a dark cell awaiting a cruel death. He should have told him the truth, told him how a man oft soiled himself in battle, and how when he died his bowels emptied—if he still had them. That might have dissuaded him from running after glory, from being so eager to follow the hotheaded de Brus into a skirmish with Warfield.

If he had only told him. . . .

"Sir Alex?" Catherine rose gracefully to her feet, and the fresh fragrance of lavender wafted over him. New soap, a gift to her from James Douglas before he had gone. How had Douglas known what would delight a woman when he had not? It had never occurred to him that scented soap would so please her, and it had not occurred to him how furious he would be that Douglas had thought of it first.

Nor had it pleased him that he had felt deficient in some way, and even a little guilty when he had seen the expression on her face at meeting his children. But by all that was holy, it was not a matter that had concerned him until them. Men lay with women, and women oft bore children from the encounters. It was a natural enough thing, and he saw to the well-being of them, so he saw no reason for her silent censure. But he felt it. And perhaps that was the difference in her now, the awareness of him as more than just her captor. He had presented her with new facets to his life, and she had observed them well.

Her fingers grazed his arm and he jerked, snapped from his reflection by her touch. A high flush colored her cheeks as she stared up at him.

"Are you well, sir?"

"Well enough." He returned her stare more coolly than he felt. Just her touch burned, the memory of her beneath him returning to scour him with heat.

She recoiled slightly. "Very well, sir. Perhaps you will excuse me to return to my tower chamber. It grows late and I wouldst rest."

"Would you." A mirthless smile tugged at his mouth. He did not dismiss her and did not know why, but stood staring down at her until she began to back away.

Uncertainty flickered in the eyes upturned to his, and she lifted her chin in a gesture of flustered defiance. "Yea, Sir Alex, I would. Do you give me leave to depart?"

He caught her wrist and pulled her slowly to him, turning her arm so that her palm was up. His thumb scrubbed gently over the soft pink skin and heel of her hand, then he pressed a light kiss in the cup of her palm.

She drew in a sharp breath and her fingers curled inward to hold his hand with artless trust. He held her still, looking into her eyes. The world veered sharply, giving him a glimpse of paradise, of what could be and should be, but was denied him by the vagaries of fate and war and the bestiality of men. Yet he could not help himself, though the reasons and the time were all wrong, and he knew he courted damnation.

"Yea, milady, you may withdraw, but I shall escort you to the tower."

"There is no need—"

"On the contrary." He pressed her hand against his chest, holding it as he held her gaze. "There is a great need."

12

Catherine stared up at him. Black lashes lowered over the smoky gleam in his gray eyes. He held her hand against the soft leather jerkin he wore. A shudder went through her. It was the intensity in his face that sent her heart thudding, the steely glitter in his eyes that made her pulse race.

She opened her mouth to offer a token protest against his arrogance, but it was too late. He was turning her with a hand under her elbow, guiding her to the open door and ushering her into the corridor. Lamps burned high on the walls here, safer than sputtering torches that sent showers of sparks down to singe clothing and skin.

A thousand thoughts passed through her mind as Alex escorted her up the narrow, winding staircase to the tower room she occupied, none of them comforting. In the month since word of her father's refusal to barter for her had come, she had been cautious. Not by word, or glance, or accidental brush of her hand had she betrayed herself to Alex Fraser.

Yet when she was near him—playing chess, or dining

in the hall, or once even dancing with him—it was difficult to restrain the inclination to lean closer to him, to look up at him through her lashes with the bold coquettishness of a burgher's daughter.

And now, O Lord have mercy, he had her by the arm with far too tight a hold, his heat a solid presence at her side as he took her to the private chamber where he had not been since the day they had lain together on that small bed. Her face was afire, yet she shivered as if chilled to the bone when they arrived at the tower room.

Leaning past her, he pushed open the heavy wooden door. It swung inward with a slight creak of the hinges. Catherine stepped inside and moved to the table. She focused on one of the stacks of books there, running her fingertips over the edges of a leather-bound volume. A low fire burned on the hearth, and a branch of candles flickered in the center of the table.

" 'Twas kind of you to escort me to my chamber, sir," she said softly, unable to look at him but fully aware that he stood inside the room, seeming to fill it with height and brooding presence.

The door shut with a solid click. "I did not do it to be kind, *demoiselle*."

Demoiselle . . . so formal, so French and aloof when he was looking at her with anything but indifference. She did not dare look at him, but knew the instant he moved. The intensity had sharpened in him, grown stronger the closer they drew to the tower, and she felt it now as a palpable thing, quivering in the chamber as if a large beast crouched against the wall.

To ease the tension, she lifted the volume of poetry and cradled it in her open palm. "Whatever your motives are, sir, I value your company."

"Do you?"

His soft query vibrated with focused need, and she

blindly flipped open the poetry volume with trembling fingers and held it up. "Wouldst thou like for me to read? 'Tis a roundelay. . . ." A slight quiver blurred the last word, and she steadied herself deliberately as she began to read aloud the verse that she had perused so often in the last weeks: " 'Laughing grey eyes, whose light in me I bear, Deep in my heart's remembrance and delight. Remembrance is so infinite delight Of your brightness, O soft eyes that I fear. . . .' "

She faltered, acutely aware of the import behind the verse she read, of Alex's gray eyes resting on her so intently, and her own shaky composure. Why had she chosen this verse? It was too true, too close to the way she felt about him . . . yet the volume had opened to this page as if by intent.

"Go on, milady." The husky timbre of his voice was so intimate, leaving her flustered.

"I . . . 'tis not necessary." She closed the book with a snap and set it gingerly atop the stack. "The hour grows late and I am more weary than I realized. Perhaps another time we will read."

A strange smile touched his mouth. "The hour is not late, milady. 'Tis still early. Vesper bells have not yet rung."

"Days are so short now . . . it is dark so much earlier, that it always seems later"—he stepped closer and she took a deep breath before finishing in a faint whisper—"than it is."

"Yea, lady. It is much later than it seems." He grazed the slope of her cheek with the backs of his fingers, a light stroke that summoned a shiver from her. She could not look up at him, but felt his gaze resting on her downturned face. Gently, he hooked a finger under her chin and lifted her head so that she had to look at him. His eyes were dark gray and veiled by black lashes. He bent, and his mouth brushed across her lips in a feathery caress.

Catherine felt light-headed. Her heart thudded painfully against her ribs. She wanted to push his hand away, wanted to retreat, but there was nowhere to go.

And then he was putting an arm behind her, pulling her against him with an inexorable strength that she could not have resisted had she the will left. There was something spellbinding in the way he held her, touched her, kissed her in such light, fluttering brushes of his mouth over hers. A slow, steady beat began in the pit of her stomach. His kiss deepened, his tongue slipping between her lips briefly, then withdrawing. He smelled of musk and leather. The palms of her hands moved to spread against his chest, against the supple leather jerkin he wore over his shirt. It felt cool under her palms, almost slick as her fingers curled into it in a convulsive motion.

Lifting his head, he stared down at her a long moment. His chest rose and fell evenly, but the beat of his heart was swift and hard against her palms. Somehow, the knowledge that he was affected gave her back a sense of power. It was heady, this profound awareness of her ability to command not only herself, but the very pulse of this powerful, enigmatic man.

Slowly, she slid her hands up the slick leather garment to skim her fingers through the hair brushing his shoulder. It was soft, thick, and straight save where a strand curled around her fingertips. His breathing grew harsh when she touched his cheek, tracing the thin line of the scar lightly, an exploring caress along the contoured plane of his face.

He caught her hand then and held it fiercely; a muscle flexed in his jaw. "Token of an English blade. Does it offend you?"

"Nay." Rising to her toes, she pressed a light kiss on the edge of his mouth and the scar, then another on his jaw. " 'Tis a badge of courage." A rough growth of beard tickled her lips as she moved them along the square line to his chin. His breath was warm against her face, with a faint aroma of the spiced wine they had been drinking earlier.

"Courage." His low laugh curled against her hair. "It was certainly not courage that earned me this mark, milady, but chaos. Unless you have ever seen a panicked rout, you would not know how desperate men can become."

Freeing her arms, she slid them around his neck and clasped him lightly. She looked up at him with a faint smile. "I find it most difficult to envision you in a panic, sir."

"If I had been in a panic, perhaps I would have been more cautious," he muttered as his arms circled her, holding her against him. "But 'twas one of your stalwart English knights who gave me this after he had surrendered to me at Loudon Hill."

"It gives you a wicked, dangerous air, sir—one that I find quite intriguing."

"Being English, I imagine you do like seeing the enemy marked by an English blade." His wry comment was accompanied by a sweeping caress with one hand, a slow, luxurious glide of his palm down her back to her hips. He held her against him, eyes half-lidded, a self-mocking smile curving his mouth. "I am reminded of that knight each time I see my scar. Perhaps, sweet catkin," he murmured huskily as he cupped her buttocks in his palm, "I should leave you with a mark to remember me by as well. . . ."

"And perhaps," she replied softly, "you already have."

"Have I?"

"Yea, though not where 'tis so easily noticed as the mark you bear." Taking his other hand, she placed it on her left breast, holding it close against her so that he could feel the thudding beat of her heart. "P'raps 'tis here that you have left your mark, Sir Alex, where none have done before."

It was true. Dizzily, she considered how she had changed in the past two months, how her view of this harsh Scotsman had altered from fear and contempt to respect and an emotion dangerously close to love. Was she not foolish to be so vulnerable? To allow this man— the enemy—to affect her so? Yea, no doubt. But if she was, it was the first time she had ever dared to be so.

Alex stared down at her without moving or speaking for several moments, his gaze locked on her face with an expression she could not read. Was he pleased? Angry? Or was it only one more vow of love from a casual tumble, such as the two village women who had borne his children? Had they, too, professed love for him? Or perhaps they had known their place in his life and accepted it, had known he would care for any children they may beget, and known, too, he would give them the honor due to the mothers of his offspring—but not his heart. Perhaps, for them, it was enough.

Lifting his hand from her hip, Alex wound his fingers into her loose hair and tugged gently, until her head was tilted back and she could look nowhere but into his eyes.

"Be careful, milady, that you do not confuse lust with love. Both are dangerous to the inexperienced."

She drew in a shaky breath. "As I have little experience with either emotion, I shall have to trust in you to guide me."

He looked stunned. Then he gave a soft, amazed laugh. "Is that not too like trusting the wolf in the sheep pen, milady?"

"Perhaps. But 'tis all I can do. . . ."

As her words trailed into a whisper, he shook his head. "You have undone me, my lady. I am confounded."

"Are you?" She dragged a fingertip across the smooth expanse of his lower lip. "Yet, you look like a man very certain, and very much in control."

His laugh was ragged, and a little bitter. "Ah, if you just knew how I waver at this moment . . . my firm resolve may be for naught."

Putting her palm over the hand he still held against her heart, she opened her mouth to say that she felt the same, but in a swift motion, he bent his head to cover her lips with his in a searing kiss that stole her breath and left her clinging to him weakly. As before, it consumed her.

All thought left her mind, leaving behind only formless impressions and an escalating cadence of blood through her veins. She felt light-headed. Dizzy. And more aware of her body than she had ever been before, of the thrumming pulse that blossomed between her thighs with insistent rhythm, of the touch of his hand against her breast, and the languid arch of her hips into his encroaching frame.

As the steamy depths of her haze alternated between excitement and lassitude, she felt a distant prick of conscience: this was wrong—wicked and carnal and all the things she had been told all her life would earn her damnation and the fires of hell. And she knew, with that small portion of her brain that was still capable of functioning lucidly, that she should resist with all her might. Nothing good would come of this.

But then, hard on the heels of that realization was the scorching memory of before, and how he had made her feel with his hands and his mouth, and she wavered again. Did it really matter if she gave him all? It would be her own choice, not a choice made for her by men who did not care, men whose only concern was power and wealth. Did she have the courage to make that choice for herself and accept the inevitable consequences?

In a strange way, it had been easier to have everything decided for her, for then she had little option but to do as she was bid . . . but this moment was hers alone, and she alone would bear the cost . . . it was too much. She was suddenly afraid, not of Alex Fraser, but of herself; of emotions too long denied and far too vulnerable to risk for transitory vengeance or to ease her loneliness. She should tell him that she was unwilling . . . she should look into his eyes and say that she could not do this.

But he was gazing down at her with molten silver eyes beneath winged brows, beautiful and scarred and oh so dangerous . . . terrifying and tempting beyond expectation.

She closed her eyes, and was suddenly weightless. There was a sweeping sensation, and then she felt the familiar cushion of heather mattress beneath her. It cradled her shoulders and hips in sweet scent and comfort, then dipped beneath his weight. He bent and kissed her again, tasting of spiced wine and heady excitement. His tongue licked at her lips, her chin, then laved her mouth in a slow, sensual exploration that left her shivering. She opened her mouth and he slipped inside it, heated wine, cinnamon, and cloves, all mingled with tumultuous desire.

A low moan vibrated in her throat. His hands were on the laces of her leather girdle, swift and sure with spare motion that divested her of the garment. Her breath came ragged and swift, almost painfully. There was a creaking groan of bed ropes as he shifted his weight to his knees and gathered her into him, his hands beneath her shoulders as he lifted her to press his mouth against the base of her throat. Then he moved to loosen the tidy coils of hair over her ears, freeing them so that the unbound plaits waved over her shoulders and down to the bedding.

In a soft, hoarse mutter, he said, "You are very beautiful, catkin."

Shyly, afraid of what she might see reflected in his gaze, she opened her eyes to look at him. Smoke and fire, a seductive curve of his mouth, heated promise and sensual assurance gazed back at her. She felt hot and cold at the same time, with the steady, surging insistence between her legs mortifying and exciting. What should she do? What should she say? Oh, if only she knew what she really wanted from him, if what she felt was only lust, as he had said, or love, as she had thought. Perhaps it was both, because the time she spent with him these past weeks was pure torment, watching him, his potent masculinity reminding her of how he had touched her that day, felt against her, his weight and power devastating and arousing. Yet she had also known that beneath his careless mockery, he was a man she could respect.

It was to that man that her mind and body answered as one.

"Alex," she whispered softly, desperately, and reached for him. Plucking at the laces of his leather jerkin, she freed them and spread her hands against his bare chest under his sherte. His skin was hot under her palms. She stared in fascination at the contrast of her white fingers over the dark muscled skin. His chest rose and fell in labored breaths as she lightly explored the sleek contours. Flat, dark brown nipples were partially hidden by the folds of his white sherte, and she could not resist touching them. His muscles contracted, and his hands tightened against her back, fingers digging into the skin

of her shoulders. Emboldened by the effect she had
upon him, she teased the hard nubs between thumbs and
fingers with soft pinches.

"Christ. . . ." His voice cracked. "You see . . . how
easy it is . . . for you to torture me, catkin. . . ." His
breathing was swift and irregular. His lashes half-closed
on the smoky glitter in his eyes, and his mouth curved
into a seductive smile. "I know I shall regret this, but I
can show you even more effective methods of torturing a
man, sweet cat."

"Can you?" Moving in slow, languid strokes, she slid
her hands downward, amazed at her own daring but
caught up in something beyond her control. She felt
powerful, brazen, and completely wanton. "Does this torment you, sir?" She pressed her hand against the hard
bulge outlining his trews and felt him throb beneath her
palm. "And . . . this?" Curving her fingers around him,
she measured his length with slow, careful massage,
shaping her hand to him, marveling at the rapid change
in his body. His hips moved forward into her palm as she
stroked him through the wool in steady motions that
drew a rough mutter from him.

"Jesus. . . ." It was a groan and a prayer, slipping into
the heated air with soft emphasis. His hands fell away
from her back and shifted to her shoulders, fingers cupping them in a tight clasp as she continued her rhythmic
strokes.

A flush warmed her face. She felt wicked and daring
and on the verge of a great discovery. Alex had swelled
beneath her attentive ministrations to a steely length that
pressed hard against the fabric of his trews. He was
breathing harshly now, looking down at her from beneath
lowered black lashes as he watched what she was doing.
His sherte gaped open where she had pushed it aside,

and his sculpted chest rose and fell with each deep breath he took.

It was exciting, knowing she could arouse him like this, and a queer agitation filled her as he pressed into her strokes, his hips bucking forward in a smooth, rolling motion. His hands fell away from her shoulders and to his sides, clenching into fists as his head tilted back and he groaned again. Light from the fire left half his face in shadow, lending his expression a mysterious cast.

Her own breath came more swiftly now, and a little raggedly. Sitting back on her heels, she put her hands to her face, a bit appalled at her audacity. Her entire body felt afire with excitement and embarrassment. As his hands went to the cords binding his trews around his waist, she knew she should look away, but did not. It was as if some invisible force held her, and she watched silently as he untied the cords and the fabric slipped away.

When he took her hand and brought it back to him, she resisted but he held her with gentle insistence. " 'Tis no' so very different from before, lass," he muttered in a thick burr, and placed her palm over him.

He held it there, and the throbbing pulse in his length matched the cadence of her heartbeat—rapid and strong.

"You are wrong," she whispered, "it is very different from before . . . so soft and yet so hard . . . and hot."

His laugh was slightly strangled. "Aye, 'tis hot enough to burn, I vow. And I am burning, catkin."

Flustered, she did not move her hand when his lifted away, but shaped him in light caresses that drew another moan from him. Shy curiosity became bold exploration, brushes of her fingers over his turgid length becoming an arrant discovery of texture and dimensions, of her new-found sensuality. It was frightening and exhilarating and wondrous.

Then he put his hand over hers again, and his voice was choked. "Enough. Ah, Christ above . . . enough, or I shall rush what should be slow." He drew in a deep breath. "Now 'tis my turn to enjoy you, catkin . . . here. Let me help you with this gown. . . ."

His hands removed any protest she may have made as he tugged at the wool, gathering it in his fists and up over her head to toss to the floor beside the bed. Still on their knees facing each other, he sat back for a moment to gaze at her. She flushed and looked down, wishing she could see herself as he saw her, wishing she knew if he found her as pleasing as she did him. . . .

"Beautiful," he murmured, "beautiful catkin . . . did you know your breasts are near perfect? Small and rounded—why do you blush? You should be proud. Poor catkin—has no one ever told you how lovely you are?"

"You know you are the first man to see me thus," she replied in a soft, quivering voice.

"Yea, I do not doubt that." His words and smile were tender. "But I cannot be your first admirer. What? No long poems of undying love and unrequited passion written to you in praise of your eyes, your lips, your hair . . . your breasts? What must the men in Warfield's hall be thinking. . . ."

It would do no good to tell him that none had dared even glance at her for fear of the earl, and she closed her eyes and shivered when he traced the tiny blue veins visible beneath the pale skin of her breasts with his finger. His touch was light and arousing as he skimmed over her flesh, lingering idly.

"Sweet catkin . . . so beautiful, with soft white skin the color of new milk . . . and your nipples remind me of rosebuds, all pink and shy and ready to flower . . . like that. Yea, like that, sweet girl. . . ." His thumb caressed the tightening bud into a hard knot, making the steady throb between her thighs beat faster. Cupping her other breast in his palm, he slowly rotated his thumb on that nipple as well, until she became breathless and agitated.

She looked up at him, and a faint, crooked smile curved his mouth. "You like that, I think, catkin. Good. I like seeing you blossom for me . . . beautiful English flower."

His head bent and he kissed each breast, then her throat, then up to her ear. His breath was heated, tickling her cheek and making her shiver, then he pressed his lips against her brow. It was a tender gesture that brought unexpected tears to her eyes, and she closed them so he would not see. But he must have, for he brushed a fingertip against her lashes.

"Tears? Open your eyes, catkin. Look at me."

She obeyed, but stared at his chin until he nudged up her chin with a bent finger so that she had to look into his eyes. "Why do you weep? Are you afraid?"

"Yes. Of you. Of me. Of . . . this. . . ." Her hand swept down to encompass her body. "I do not know what to do with all these feelings I have of late, and am afraid of what they mean."

Her soft whisper faded before he drew in a deep breath and shook his head. "You need not fear my touch. I will not hurt you."

Tears blurred her vision as she stared at him. "Yes. You will. You cannot help but hurt me. . . ."

An odd expression crossed his face. "Not willingly, little catkin. Never that."

It should matter that he did not deny it, did not swear never to do her harm, but strangely, she understood. Life was so uncertain, full of surprising twists and turns, that promises were too often made in vain.

And so she did not protest when he bent his head, his

mouth covering hers in a kiss that was salty with her own tears. He slid one hand into her waving hair, his fingers circling the whorls of her ear. She shivered at the soft contact.

"Beautiful catkin," he whispered against her ear, his breath a heated caress. His knees squeezed her thighs, wool rough against her bare skin. "Too lovely to resist . . . too sweet to deny. . . ."

His words trailed into silence as he slid a hand down the curve of her spine to her buttocks and held her. He made a small noise low in the back of his throat. Catherine could not move; her breathing was labored. He leaned over her, pushing her down against the mattress, a solid weight and steady pressure. Hooking his hands beneath her knees, he pulled her legs from under her to straddle his waist. It left her open to him, vulnerable and exposed, and with an inarticulate cry she moved her hands to cover herself.

He caught them, his smile lazy and heated. "No need for that, catkin. Not now. Is there? Nay, I did not think there was . . . be still a moment, my sweet. . . ."

The soft words and sensual tone penetrated her sudden shyness, and she allowed him to move her hands to her sides. He was still dressed, his wool trews open to reveal his rampant desire for her. It was so shocking and somehow arousing that he was clothed and she was not. He caressed her, his thumbs sliding over the center of her in a searing stroke that took away her breath and ignited a new heat. Pressing upward under his touch, she moaned softly.

Oh, mercy . . . sweet mother of mercy . . . it was so sinfully wanton, so exquisitely seductive, kindling an aching need in her that she knew he could quench. She parted for him when he pushed gently at her thighs. He leaned over her, and his weight spread her legs as he kissed her mouth, deep drugging kisses that left her breathless and yearning, her body arching into his with rising urgency. Still kissing her, he reached between their bodies to slide a finger inside her, a scorching intrusion that was exciting and frightening at the same time. Gently, he slid his tongue between her lips in light, teasing strokes as his hand moved between her thighs in parallel rhythm.

Tension rose in her, and she met his thrusts with her own, her tongue dueling his and her hips rising to accept his invasion. Then he paused and lifted himself off the bed. When she reached for him, blindly seeking, he returned to kiss her fiercely and caress that damp, throbbing ache between her legs. Then his hand moved, and in its place was a new intrusion, the heated length she had caressed before. It was hot and rigid against her softness, slipping on the moisture there, erotic strokes that brought another moan from her. He moved against her, his arms braced on each side of her on the mattress, his length driving forward to slide over that aching center of fire and need . . . she caught at his hips and was surprised that the wool trews were gone.

Then that thought slipped into the newer realization that something had changed as his body shifted to slide inside her, a hard, stinging pressure that made her catch her breath. He did not withdraw but pressed closer, heated flesh thrusting deeper inside, filling and stretching her to the point of pain—but not beyond. It was exquisitely erotic and dangerous.

Holding her breath, she looked up at him. She could see the tangled spill of his black hair and the taut curve of his splendid shoulders, but not his face. He had paused with his full width heavy inside her. Yet it did not assuage the ache, the throbbing urgency that drew her body taut as a bow string and left her quivering with agitated expectation. Restless at his delay, she squirmed beneath him, wanting more, wanting what he had given her before, that delicious ecstasy that was so elusive and so intense it left her shattered.

He lifted his face to look at her, his silver-gray eyes searing into her with fierce intensity. "Be still. . . ." It was said in a groaning mutter, and she could not help another small wiggle of her hips that made him close his eyes, his lashes darkening his cheeks. "For pity's sake, catkin. . . ."

"Alex . . . Alex, please . . . help me. . . ." She wasn't quite certain what she asked, but he knew. He had known before and he would know now. . . .

A shudder ran through him and his head lowered again. Then he glanced up at her as he slid forward, his male hardness stretching and filling her again until the pleasure turned to pain and she gasped. He paused at once and looked away. His body throbbed inside her with heated pressure that seemed all encompassing, filling her world as well as her body. She arched her hips upward, seeking release and the same euphoria she had experienced with him before.

He put his head down again and drew in a ragged breath. "Jesus. . . ."

She did not know if it was a prayer or exclamation this time, but then he shifted, and now he lunged forward in an unyielding invasion that was as shocking as it was complete. A startled cry burst from her and he swiftly covered her mouth with his own. But as swiftly as the pain had pierced her, it ended, leaving only an unfamiliar fullness in her, and the steady throbbing of his body. Welcome invasion, delightful sin . . . and this time, she knew she was no longer a virgin.

But then there was no time to think about that, only the slow, luxurious thrust and drag of his body inside her, the clamor of sensations that overrode one another and came together in a seamless tide. Caught up in the wash of desire that flowed over her, she was aware of him surging against her and into her, withdrawing only to drive forward with shuddering force. The faint scent of musky soap filled her nose, throaty mutters filled her ears, and his fiercely intent face hovered over her to blot out the rest of the world. He was her world . . . he filled it completely at this moment, his aggressive power and potent sensuality eclipsing everything else.

Driving all coherent thought from her mind once more, Alex thrust into her with a ruthless, burning friction. She ached for him, ached with the searing reality of his body's intrusion, and moved beyond it into that nebulous realm where release hovered just out of her reach. His breath was harsh against her cheek as he slipped his hand between them, scraping his thumb over the sweet nucleus of pleasure that made her shiver, his body a relentless force as he swept her with him up and up and past the pain into sweeping pleasure.

The first tremor rocked her and she clutched at him, crying out. His movement quickened and a fevered groan mingled with her soft cries, keening sounds like the sob of the wind at the shutters echoing in the chamber. It came in shattering clarity, an explosion of light and heated release. Wave after wave washed through her, intense and annihilating, draining her of tension and strength. And then he was thrusting deep in a quivering stroke that burst within her in harsh tremors, and he went still.

Shivering with reaction, Catherine held him as he relaxed atop her, his weight resting half on her, half on the mattress. One hand stroked back his hair in gentle movements as his head rested in the curve of her neck and shoulder. His breathing was ragged, but gradually began to slow. When he finally moved, he withdrew slowly and she could not stop a surprised gasp at the raw friction.

He lay next to her and propped himself on one elbow to gaze down at her. "Now you know the difference, catkin."

She smiled. "Yea, now I know the difference."

It was true. What had happened between them before was nothing compared to this . . . and she was suddenly, fiercely, glad. The little membrane that was so coveted was gone forever, and never again could she be made hostage of it. Her father could not use her as a prize to dangle before eager suitors more anxious for her dowry than they were her . . . no, she was free now to choose for herself.

She drew a finger over the light bristle of beard on Alex's jaw. "You are a braw callant, sir."

His brow rose at her Gaelic phrase, and a smile curved his mouth. He clasped her hand in his to kiss her fingertips. "Yea, milady, so I am. 'Tis kind of you to notice."

"I notice everything about you."

He grimaced. "I find that frightening. Here. You are chilled."

As he reached down to draw up the wool blanket over her shivering form, she took note of his naked body, magnificent and powerful. His dark skin was smooth, with only small scars from years of battle, and lean muscle banded his chest and belly. She flushed and looked away when he glanced back at her, grinning.

"Sly minx . . . if you continue to look at me like that, I shall begin to think you far too precocious for a virgin."

As the blanket settle around her in warm folds, she glimpsed a red stain on the wool. She pointed to it. "Your proof, sir—"

"Catkin, I was teasing you. God knows, you were virgin indeed." Leaning forward, he took her chin in his palm and kissed her mouth gently. Then he drew back a little and gazed at her as he held her face. He stared at her for a long moment, intense and enigmatic, until she began to frown with concern. Then he muttered awkwardly, "I hope that one day you will forgive me for this."

"Forgive you?" She lifted her shoulders in a gentle shrug. "You have saved me. My father wouldst barter my maidenhead to the highest bidder. This was done of my own free will. I shall never have to return now, for he will not have me back once I tell him that my worth as marriageable pawn is gone."

His mouth tightened. He raked a hand through his hair and looked away, then looked back at her with a strange light in his eyes. "Do you not want to return to Warfield?"

"Nay, not now." A little shyly, she reached for his hand, still too full of these new, scalding emotions to feel comfortable with them. Then he curled his fingers around her palm and held her, and she smiled. "But 'tis a moot point, as my father does not intend to meet your demands."

"So I have realized." He rubbed his thumb over the heel of her palm, frowning. Then he looked up at her through his tangled lashes. "Catherine, these are times that oft breed confusion in loyalties, and lead men to acts they would not consider in a sane and orderly world. I am as guilty as the next man of acting without reason at times."

Her hand clenched. "Have you heard from my father?"

"Nay, I told you earlier that I have not."

"But you know something." There was a somber intensity to him that alarmed her, and she studied his face for a long moment in the scant light afforded by fire and candle glow. "What is it?"

"Christ . . . there has been no word from your father or your brother. The terms of my offer were simple—you in exchange for my brother and de Brus. No effort has been made to satisfy these terms, or even alter them. . . ."

His voice trailed into silence, and she shook her head in confusion. "I know all this . . . why are you now disturbed?"

Coiling his lean body, he surged up from the bed, standing over it to stare down at her darkly. Conflicting emotions were evident on his face, chasing across features drawn tight with unspoken words. He raked a hand through his hair, and his tone was taut with frustration.

"Catkin, there are some things you do not know, that you might take amiss were you to—"

A sudden pounding on the door rattled it on the hinges, and the latch clanked as it swung slowly open. Before it had moved inward more than a small bit, Alex moved with swift agility to grab a wicked dagger from his boot on the floor. It was long and gleaming and sharp, reflecting light from the fire in glittering sparks as he stood poised in aggressive menace.

But it was no intruder who stood in the doorway. Mairi paused as if frozen, staring at Alex and then Catherine as color flooded her face. There was an awkward silence, then she began to speak in harsh Gaelic, gesturing toward the bed with wild motions that Alex curbed with a few sharp words. Tension and resentment vibrated in the air with chilling transparency. After a moment, the elderly maidservant snapped a few more words, then swung about and shut the door behind her with an echoing slam.

Alex turned to Catherine, and there was a grim set to his mouth. "It seems that your brother has arrived with an offer for your release, milady. Clothe yourself, and I will send you an escort to the hall so you may greet him."

13

Nicholas waited impatiently by the fire, slapping his leather gloves against his bare palm loudly. It was a devilish night, with cold rain and a wind strong enough to peel hair off a dog, and now that he was here, he did not want to be kept waiting. Where the devil was Fraser? He wanted to see him, not this glowering Scot with the face like a crumpled rag who had obviously been sent to guard him.

"Where is Fraser?" he demanded when the silence stretched too long.

The Scot's light brows lifted, and his shoulders moved in a careless shrug. "When he is no' busy, he will be doon tae see ye."

"If he values his brother as he says, he will make time to see me quick enough."

The Scot pushed away from the wall where he had been leaning and stepped forward, bristling with ill-concealed hatred. "Ye hae taken yer own sweet time aboot comin', so I wa'd no' be so quick tae make demands, Lord Devlin."

Nicholas eyed him with growing irritation. "I came as quickly as I could wrest an agreement from the earl, and I will not listen to censure from a Scots rogue about it."

It certainly did not help to know that the Scot had a valid point. The deadline was long past for an agreement, and even now, the offer he brought fell far short of what Alex Fraser demanded. Desperation alone bade him make the offer, but he knew with a sickening feeling of doom that he would be refused. Yet 'twas all he had, and he did not dare delay any longer before meeting with Fraser again. Already, he feared he was too late.

Laughing softly, the Scot let one hand fall to rest upon the hilt of a sword dangling from his belt. "Ye hae no' much choice aboot wha' ye will listen tae, milord. Ye are in Scotland now, and 'tis no' yer place tae be giving orders."

Because he was right, and because it was galling to admit it even to himself, Nicholas clenched his teeth tight to keep from spitting out the harsh words on the tip of his tongue. Curse them all, these ragtag Scots with cheerless stone fortresses and mighty swords—he would like to see them all slain upon the battlefield, ending the blight that scoured England from east to west and left her vulnerable to foreign enemies. But he had not come here to engage in verbal battle with this man. He wanted Alex Fraser, and more than that—Catherine.

Silence fell in the antechamber off the great hall where they stood, only the popping of logs in the fire breaking the tense stillness. Nicholas stared at the insolent Scot with mute fury.

Finally he heard someone approaching the open door, and flicked his gaze from his guard to the opening. Fraser strode into the antechamber and said something to the Scot in Gaelic. The rough-looking guard grinned and nodded, then gave Nicholas a last glance before he left.

"Charming company," Nicholas drawled, watching Fraser closely as he came toward him. "We had a lovely chat while I waited on you."

Fraser's dark brow rose, and a faint smile curved his mouth as he moved to a table bearing a pitcher and cups. "Robbie is loyal and fierce. A true Scots patriot."

"I gathered that. He looks capable enough of slitting throats in the night."

"He is quite adept at that, as long as they are English throats bared to his blade. Wine?" Fraser held out a brimming cup, and though he wanted to refuse, Nicholas took it to give himself time to assess the man's temper. Fraser lifted a cup to his lips, staring at him over the rim. "It is safe enough to drink, my lord Devlin, should you fear poison."

Nicholas shrugged. "I do not fear such treachery from you as long as we still hold your brother."

"Ah. So we dispense with the formalities and courtesies already. I approve, for I am a man who likes to come quickly to the point . . . what of my brother?"

"He is well. I bring you word from him."

"It is not words that I require, Lord Devlin."

Damn this insolent Scot, who stared at him as if he were the lowest churl . . . it made him suddenly aware of the mud streaking his boots and mantle and ruining the white surcoat he wore beneath. Fraser looked as immaculate as if he had just risen from a bath, garbed in a gilt-trimmed soutane with a long-sleeved sherte of fine linen beneath, and an intricately wrought gold girdle circling his hips, bearing a dagger sheath studded with jewels. His eyes narrowed slightly. The Frasers had held a title once, until King Edward I revoked it for treason— but this presumptuous Scot behaved as if he still had more than the lower rank of landed knight.

Stiffly, Nicholas said, "I have not yet seen for myself that my sister is alive and well. Do you expect more?"

"Yea, but 'tis plain that I am not dealing with men of honor, or my demands would have been answered in the time I allotted to you."

A chagrined flush heated his face as Nicholas returned the Scot's stare. "You were sent word of the reason for the delay."

"That was not enough." Fraser set his empty wine cup down on the table and moved to stand by the fire, propping a booted foot on the stone hearth. "You were given a fortnight to reply, and it has been thrice that."

Smarting from the truth and the choking feeling of impotence the earl's callous indifference for Catherine's return had caused him, Nicholas could not reply for a moment. Fraser would not like what he had to tell him, and he was determined to delay that moment as long as possible. He moved to set down his gloves and his full cup on the table, then turned to face his sister's captor.

"I am at your mercy, Sir Alex. There have been circumstances beyond my control, or I would have been here much sooner. As dear as your brother is to you, so is my sister dear to me. May I see her before we continue our negotiations?"

Something flickered in Fraser's eyes, but he nodded curtly. "Aye. I sent Robbie for her, and you will be able to see for yourself that she is alive and unharmed. Will I have the same assurance about Jamie?"

Nicholas drew in a deep breath. "I have brought you proof that he is alive and as well as can be expected."

Fraser's face changed, his features sharpening. "If he has been harmed—"

"I swear to you on my honor as a knight that he is alive, though hating his prison. I saw to his care myself, and he and de Brus are being fed well, with warm garments to ward off the cold." He slid a hand beneath the edge of his surcoat and drew out a small leather pouch. Weighing it in his palm, he studied Fraser for a long moment. Then he held out his hand, allowing the pouch to dangle by cords from his fingers. "This was hard-won. Your brother may be young, but his will is strong and he is slow to trust. He cost me days of delay."

As the pouch came to rest in Fraser's outstretched palm, he looked steadily at Nicholas. "This had best not be in lieu of Jamie's return."

Nicholas did not respond. There was no good answer he could make to satisfy Alex Fraser, nor even himself. So he stood quietly while the pouch was opened and the Scot examined the contents. He should have drunk the wine. It would ease this sudden inkling of disaster, the impending doom he felt looming ahead.

"Nicholas?"

The soft, familiar voice jerked his head around and he swung about to see Catherine in the doorway, her face wreathed with joy as she came toward him. He caught her up in his embrace, arms around her slender body as he buried his face in her unbound hair. She smelled of lavender. "Ah, sweet kitten . . . I thought never to see you again."

"Nor I you." Hot tears wet his neck above the edge of his mantle. "Oh, Nicky . . . I *have* missed you so!"

When he set her back on her feet, she clung to the loose edges of his mantle, her hands curled into the fabric with fierce tenacity. He held her close to him, and cupped a hand beneath her chin to lift her face so that he might see her better.

"Are you well, kitten? Unharmed?"

Color stained her cheeks a bright pink that contrasted with the misty violet of her eyes, and she lowered her lashes demurely and nodded. "Yea, Nicky, I am most well."

"Good." He held her a moment, then put her at arm's length, still clasping her hand. She was garbed in rough clothing, a yellow wool gown with a tan leather girdle tied under her breasts. The gown was short, revealing delicate ankles clad in thick hose, and shapeless slippers on her feet. Amused by the vast difference in her usual apparel, he looked up. "You look like a milk maid in that ugly garment. Have you learned to make butter since you have been here?"

He had meant it as a teasing jest to lighten the moment and ease the mood, but she shook her head. "Nay. I already knew how to make butter, and cheese, and all the other wifely tasks that I have been taught since I was still in leading strings. I have been allowed to read here . . . as much as I like. It has been most rewarding."

Nicholas frowned. There was a subtle difference to her now, something he could not quite determine. She had always been his little sister, someone he must protect and love and cherish. Yet now she seemed almost self-assured. Mature. Or had she always been this way and he had not noticed? It was disconcerting to think she had changed in only two months, but perhaps living in constant terror would cause such a difference. He glanced at Fraser, who stared back at him.

"May I speak to my sister privately, Sir Alex?"

Fraser's eyes narrowed. "This is a private chamber, my lord Devlin. Speak as you will."

"Do you think I will spirit her away from under your nose? I have no weapons. Even if I did, my men and I are shut up in your keep. What can I do but talk?"

"Yea, you do that readily enough." Fraser's glance slid toward Catherine and lingered, and she colored prettily under his gaze. A faint smile touched the corners of his mouth, and when the Scot looked back at him, Nicholas was suddenly confronted with a new suspicion. His heart began to thump furiously in his chest, so that he barely heard Fraser say, "While I read the message my brother sent I will leave you to yourselves in this chamber. Guards are posted at the door. You do not have long."

Focusing on Catherine, Nicholas waited until the Scot departed and closed the door behind him, then moved toward her. She looked up at him, a quick slide of her eyes in his direction before she looked away, and the suspicion became awful certainty. He grabbed her by the wrists, fingers digging into the tendons until she gasped in surprise.

"Nicky—what are you doing?"

"Tell me what has happened to you, Catherine." He didn't mean to sound so rough and angry, but his voice came out all wrong. "I asked if you had been harmed . . . tell me the truth of it."

"I have not been harmed." She twisted futilely in his tight hold. "Free me or I will scream."

"Will you? Does that mean the Scots bastard will come to your rescue? Would you set him against me?"

She looked miserable and turned her face away. "No."

"Then for the love of Christ, tell me the truth—has he touched you?" Silence fell, and Nicholas groaned. "O Lord have mercy . . . sweet kitten . . . say he has not hurt you."

Tears spangled her lashes, but her chin was lifted and she said with quiet dignity, "He did not hurt me, Nicholas. It was nothing like that. He was gentle—"

Releasing her hands with a shove, Nicholas turned away and pressed his face into his palms. He breathed in leather and bitter hatred, resentment rising hot and high in him as he struggled with this knowledge. Damn the Scot—he had sworn he would not despoil her—but he had also given warning of what would happen if his terms were not met. A feeling of nausea rose in his throat, and he could not look up at her, could not bear to see her and know that the Scot had put his filthy hands on her soft white skin. . . .

"Nicky?" She put a hand on his shoulder and he jerked away.

"Christ, Catherine. You could at least have had the decency to make him take what you so willingly gave."

"Damn you!" His head snapped up and he stared at her with narrowed eyes as she railed at him, using some of the phrases he had taught her long ago to amuse himself, French curses that still had the power to sting.

When she was through, glaring at him with wet angry eyes and flushed cheeks, he shrugged. "You have not forgot them, I see, but I vow I never thought you would use them against me."

"I use them where I see fit. How dare you suggest that it would be better for me to be raped than to yield!"

"Kitten—"

"Nay, do not pretend you did not say it, for I heard you most plainly. You may not like it, but he did not force me to do anything I did not want to do. Yea, you may well look shocked. But did it ever occur to you that I may have my own free will? My own choices? And do not think this the naive tantrum of a child, for what I did, I did for a reason." Her voice was quivering, but indignation lit her eyes. "I am not a child nor a fool. I am fully aware of the consequences of my actions, and I embrace them."

"Do you?" Nicholas's voice was tight. "Perhaps you have misjudged what the consequences will be. Do you think our father will allow this matter to be forgotten?"

"Nay, but I have not forgotten David of Linwood, though you may well have done so."

Baffled by her tirade and the astonishing depth of her pent-up emotions, Nicholas shook his head. "I have not forgotten David of Linwood, nor what happened to him. How does this affect us now?"

Catherine moved to the table and poured wine in a cup, then turned back to face him, her voice steady though her hand trembled. "David did naught but kiss my cheek, and was near beat to death for it. Since then, I have not dared to glance at another young man for fear of the same or worse happening again. And always, Papa reminded me how I have been a burden to him, how he cannot make an advantageous marriage when I am so rebellious a maid—he cares nothing for what I think or feel, only how much land or power I will bring to him." She lifted the cup, her eyes bright as she looked at him over the rim. "But now the precious barrier he protected so fiercely for his own gain has been yielded, and to a man he cannot intimidate."

"Aye, perhaps so, but he can have Fraser's young brother flayed alive, and there will be no family to protest the deed as Linwood had. Ah, I see that you had not thought of that. Christ above, Catherine, I have been turning myself inside out these past weeks trying to placate our father as well as Alex Fraser, and in one mindless act, you have managed to destroy us all." His laugh sounded hollow and hopeless, as indeed he felt at this moment. Shaking his head, he moved to brace his arms against the mantel over the fire, staring into the flames.

After a moment, he felt her come up behind him. She touched him lightly on the shoulder, but he only shook his head, sick with anger and grief. "Why, kitten? *Why?*"

"Nicholas . . . I cannot explain it when I am uncertain of all my reasons, but I can tell you this—he is not as I had feared. There is a kindness to him that—"

"Kindness!" The word was torn from him and he swung about, incredulous at how quickly Alex Fraser had managed to convert her from what she had known all her life to his own distorted convictions. "Christ have mercy, I suppose now you will tell me that Scotland should be independent and Fraser should be king."

Her mouth set into a mutinous line that he recognized and he just stared at her. There was nothing he could say that would change what had happened, and despite her naive foolishness, he still had to protect her. But how? It would not be easy.

"Nicholas," she said with a sigh, "I do not know how it happened or why, but I do know I feel a great attachment to Alex Fraser."

"Kitten, you fancy yourself in love with him because he is the first man to bed you." His bluntness widened her eyes but he pressed on. "It is common for a maid to feel the same about any man who takes her maidenhead, but especially a man who is gentle with her. Once you are away from him, you will see that I am right."

"Have you come to take me back to Warfield?"

He wanted to say yes; he wanted to take her with him and leave this accursed pile of stones before cock crow, but knew there was no likelihood of that. It was galling that her face reflected dismay at the thought.

Clasping his hands behind his back, he stared down at his sister and wondered if he'd ever really known her. He had thought so. Now she was alien to him, with her stubborn little chin slightly tilted, and the mutiny in her eyes a bright gleam.

"If I said I had come to take you with me, what would you say, kitten? Would you be glad?"

"No." She met his gaze steadily. "I would not be glad."

It was the answer he expected, but bitter nonetheless. "You fancy yourself in love with this Scottish brigand."

She laughed softly. "I once corrected him when he named you brigand, so I should do the same for you now. Yea, you are right, Nicholas. I fancy myself in love with him, but not perhaps as you mean it."

Scrubbing his hand over the back of his neck, he muttered with sweet irony, "I shall never understand the female mind, and I thank God for it."

"Do not be angry with me, Nicky. You should be happy that I have discovered even a brief moment of contentment."

"Not only do you expect me to accept this ridiculous fascination you have for a man who is our sworn enemy, now you want me to be happy about it." His jaw clenched. "I am not. Nor will I be content until you are back in England again. I would like nothing better than to see Sir Alex Fraser's head on a pike, if you must know the truth." He drew in a deep breath at the stark white pallor of her face and managed to say calmly, "But your happiness is important to me, kitten. Even if we do not agree on the source of it."

"Please, Nicholas, can you not do something to free the hostages you took? Will our father not listen to you at all?"

He had no intention of discussing with her his great difficulty in juggling both his father and Fraser, and so he shrugged. "Perhaps. It is—"

"Devlin." Fraser appeared in the doorway, swinging it wide to enter. A scowl creased his face as he held up a scrap of parchment that had been folded several times. "Is this all the proof you brought?"

"It is. Is it not sufficient to convince you that your brother and de Brus are alive?"

"Yea, but it does not satisfy the terms of my offer. I do not want written assurances, I want them in the flesh. Do you think I do not know they could have been executed before the ink was dry on this letter?" He held it in his fist, frustration showing in his dark features.

Nicholas said calmly, "I do not have the power to release them from their cells, but I do have the power to see they are not abused until I am able to exchange them for my sister."

"I was told 'twas you who captured them. Are they not then your prisoners instead of the earl's?"

"They were until I gave them into his safekeeping." His mouth twisted wryly. "Until you abducted Catherine, I had no reason not to promise them to the king as his hostages against further Scottish reprisals. It will take time to remind the king that they are mine to ransom as I see fit."

"Curse you for a liar and a fraud, Devlin. Do you think me fool enough to play this game any longer?"

Temper surged hotly in Nicholas, but he held it back with an effort. "Sir Alex, we must both play this game until we have achieved our ends to mutual satisfaction."

"I will not be satisfied until Jamie is back here at Castle Rock."

"Nor I until Lady Catherine is quit of Scotland and safe at home in England. As we have similar goals, we should strive together to meet them."

"How do you propose to do that when you have no power to release Jamie or de Brus? Christ above, man, you are in no better a position than my brother."

That rankled. Nicholas glared at him. "With an important exception—I have powerful friends and relatives."

Fraser laughed softly. "And a fat lot of good they seem to be doing you, Devlin. Where are they? I have had no missive from them. Or from you, for that matter. It is long past the date I set for a reply, and yet you arrive at my gates with demands and no answers."

"Are you acquainted with the Earl of Hereford?"

Fraser's eyes narrowed. "Aye. His name is well known to me."

"Hereford has influence with King Edward. I fostered in his household, and his nephew is my foster brother. He has agreed to assist me with this matter, but it takes time to affect—"

"Humphrey de Bohun is not a man who helps any but himself," Fraser said bluntly. "I do not look for aid from that direction."

"Nay, you should not," Nicholas said softly, letting his anger show, "but I can. He will heed my requests for the return of your brother and de Brus because I will ask it of him to keep my sister from being further dishonored. . . ."

It was more than he'd meant to say, and he saw at once from Fraser's harsh stare that the Scot was aware of the true meaning behind his words.

"Nicholas. . . ." Catherine's soft voice was appalled, and she stepped forward as if to come between them. He stopped her with an uplifted hand.

"Stay out of this, Catherine. 'Tis not your place to interfere."

"Then whose place is it? Yours? His? Whose life is most involved, pray tell me!" When he glanced at her with a frown she took his arm in a tight grip. " 'Tis my fate and his brother's life that are in jeopardy, not yours or de Bohun's or our father's—do not dare tell me not to interfere!"

"Your brother is right," Fraser growled. "You may be the most involved, but you are not in the position to make decisions. You have seen him and he has seen you. Return to your chamber, Lady Catherine."

Nicholas was tempted to protest the Scot's arrogant command, but knew that his sister's presence would only complicate any discussion, so remained silent. Her glance at him was one of utter disbelief and betrayal, and he placed his hand atop hers and pried up the fingers she had curled around his arm.

"Go to your chamber, kitten. You know I will do all in my power to see you safe and content."

"Nay, you will do all in your power to arrange matters to your own satisfaction, not mine."

He smiled bitterly. "I near killed my horse riding here to your rescue, and you accuse me of having hidden motives? You sorely wound me. Yet you are my sister, and as I hold you more dear than you avow, I will yet seek to right the wrong that has been done you. Now go, so that Sir Alex and I can deliberate what must be done."

"Nicholas—"

Alex Fraser reached for her, his hand coming down on her shoulder in a grip that was firm yet mild. "Robbie is at the door, Lady Catherine. Do you go with him."

It raked on his already raw temper as Nicholas observed the Scot's hand on his sister, but he held his tongue. It would avail him nothing to tweak this Scots rogue's nose more than had been done already by his father's refusal to release Jamie or de Brus.

Fraser called out and the ugly Scot appeared in the antechamber door as if he had been standing there listening. He stood back respectfully to allow Catherine to precede him. When she turned in the open doorway to look back at him, Nicholas did not betray the sudden wrench of his heart at her expression of pain.

"*Au revoir, mais sans adieu,*" he said softly, and her

face crumpled at his farewell. Then she was gone, sweeping from the antechamber to disappear from his sight.

When he looked back at Sir Alex, he was staring after her as well, an odd expression on his face. But the face he turned to Nicholas was empty of emotion.

"What can Hereford do to effect Jamie's release, my lord Devlin?"

"He has not only the king's ear, but my father's. If there is any man in this entire kingdom who can manage it, 'tis the Earl of Hereford."

"Yea, but will he?" Fraser's mouth twisted. "It has not been my experience that de Bohun exerts himself for any man's gain but his own."

"Perhaps not, but he happens to be in my debt in a certain matter." Nicholas paused, then chose his words most carefully. "Lady Catherine is young and naive, susceptible by her very inexperience to certain inducements. If my father should chance to hear that she is not as innocent as she should be, there will be no arbitration or exchange of hostages. Were she a widow or a burgher's daughter, no one would take it amiss. But she is an earl's daughter, and promised as a virgin in marriage to Ronald of Bothwick. Both our families have powerful friends, some who have not yet cast lots with either England or Scotland. A swaying to either side could mean a shift in the balance of power that could strike a lethal blow in either direction. Should you be foolish enough to attempt marriage with Catherine, it would end your brother's life more swiftly than any other act you could commit. A Scottish rebel in the family is a dishonor my father would not endure for a moment. If you seek to better your station—"

"Hold!" Fraser looked furious. "I may now be only a landed knight, but my lineage is as good—nay, better—than yours, my lord Devlin. Frasers have been in this land since the time of the Conqueror, and my kin are as noble as are yours. One of my kinsman, Sir Alexander Fraser, is Chamberlain of Scotland and privy to the king. 'Tis our common ancestor's name I bear as well, given me by my father who regarded him highly as a kinsman, warrior, and statesman. So do not set yourself above me in station, for you are not."

There was nothing Nicholas could say that would not exacerbate the tension, so again he held his tongue. Fraser stared at him coldly. "Should I choose to wed your sister, it would be an honor for her."

"My father would consider that an act of war, Sir Alex."

A frosty smile curled his mouth. "Do not tempt me, Lord Devlin. Few things would give me greater pleasure than to meet the Earl of Warfield on a battleground."

Nicholas reached for the leather gloves he had dropped on the table and pulled them on. "Do I have your safe conduct to leave?"

"You do. But hear this, Lord Devlin—the next time you arrive at my gates you had best have my brother and de Brus with you, or there will be no surety granted you. My patience is at an end."

"I expected no less from a Scottish rebel." Nicholas met his gaze steadily, and added softly, "Wed my sister and you seal your brother's fate. 'Tis your choice."

Once more, a weary Miles met Nicholas at the stables, but this time the loyal captain had the horses rested and ready to ride. As the bridge was lowered in a shrill creaking of winch chains and torches sputtered in the wet wind, Nicholas rode over the planked surface without looking back. He did not relish the inevitable interview with his father, for he would be forced to lie if he wanted to save Catherine. He almost laughed at the irony of it. The truth was far worse—she had no desire to be saved.

PART TWO

14

---　❧　---

February 1314

Winter winds howled fiercely about the towers of Castle
Rock, like the wail of a banshee. Alex stood on frozen
mud in the bailey, smiling a little as James Douglas
capered about, swinging his sword at imaginary enemies.

"Och, you should have been there, Alex Fraser. A fine
fight it was, with the English fleeing like demons from
hell were after them!"

"No doubt, 'tis what they thought when they saw your
bonny face."

Douglas grinned. Wind whipped at his hair with growing ferocity, and lifted the edge of his plaid to snap like a
banner. "Do you join us? We leave at cock's crow for
Roxburgh, to relieve the English garrison of their duties."

An answering grin spread over Alex's face. "Yea, you
know I do. It is time I did more than warm a bench in my
hall of an eve."

"And will your lady not protest if she learns you mean
to go fight the English?"

"She is not my lady. Lady Catherine is my hostage."
Alex eyed Douglas narrowly. "But do not think that gives

you leave to ply her with scented soap and dainty comfits, for my hospitality does not extend that far."

Douglas laughed. "A man can only straddle a fence for so long, Alex. But do not glower at me with so black a face, for I only dally with the lady. She is lovely, and I fancy her smile, I admit, but I would not want you for an enemy. You are too fierce."

Alex had to smile himself at that, for James Douglas had never been known to consider any opponent too fierce or too many; a failing or a strength, depending upon one's point of view. He took chances, but he was a brilliant tactician and only took the most calculated risks.

"How many men do you think we will need to bring down Roxburgh?" he asked as they strode across the bailey toward the keep. "I will lend my forces, though I need to leave men enough here to protect Castle Rock."

Douglas slanted him a sly smile. "I want only three score men."

Incredulous, Alex stared at him. "Sixty men? To take an entire garrison?"

"Yea. It can be done. I have a plan. And I have decided upon the men I want to take with me. You are one."

Alex thought about Catherine. He would have to leave her behind, but she would be well guarded by his men. Robbie was dependable and could be trusted to do what was necessary in case of attack. But Alex did not know what to expect, for there had been no word from Devlin or the earl since December 6, Saint Nicholas Eve. The celebration of Christmas had been bleak, save for another written message from Jamie and de Brus. At least they were still alive. Devlin had kept his word on that score.

It was doubtful Warfield knew of his daughter's true situation, or he would have lodged a formal protest and launched an assault on Castle Rock by now. Obviously, Devlin was keeping his silence, but Alex did not think it was to avoid such a battle.

As they entered the hall, Catherine looked up from her chair by the fire. A boy sat at her feet, an open book on his lap, his face screwed into a tortured expression of intense concentration. Tam again. Alex wondered cynically if Tam really wanted to learn to read and write English or just wanted to be close to the Lady Catherine. How quickly she had begun to fit in. Only Mairi still refused to relent in her hatred. She had not yet forgiven him for taking the "Sassenach bitch" to his bed. Understandable, if a bit awkward.

Rising to her feet, Catherine smiled at him as he and Douglas approached the fire. "Good morn, Sir Alex. Sir James."

Douglas looked around the hall with a lifted brow. "Is this the same hall I visited two months ago? Nay, it cannot be. There are tapestries on the walls, and clean rushes, and I do not see bird droppings on tables or even birds in the loft. Am I at Castle Rock? If so, I find it too greatly changed to recognize. Except for the beautiful lady. . . ."

In Gaelic, Alex said, "If you must charm someone, there is a winsome maid below in the village who may be prone to believe your blather. Do not waste your time here."

"But would it really be a waste? Should I not find encouragement, I would still enjoy the chase."

"Hunt elsewhere."

His bluntness only earned another grin from Douglas, but when James spoke to Catherine again it was about the boy she was instructing in his letters. Tam read aloud for them, halting words in clumsy English, but with an air of pride in his accomplishment.

Alex watched Catherine, her dainty movements that were so innately feminine as she leaned over to point out a letter and whisper something to Tam, the quick smile of encouragement she gave him, and thought that Douglas was wrong. She had changed even more than the appearance of his hall. Not just outwardly—though he had seen to it that she had clothes more befitting her station after Devlin's biting remarks about her looking like a milk maid—but where it was not so easily noticed.

With quiet authority, she had gone about directing the cleaning of the hall one day when Mairi was visiting in Kinnison and he had put Tam and two other servants at her disposal. It had not occurred to him that she would make such sweeping changes in such a very short time, but she had. He had been too surprised to take offense at her temerity.

Domestic skills were not something he normally thought about, but when the hall was refurbished, he was reminded of how it had looked when his mother was alive. She had taken pride in her smoothly running household, and with a few soft words and perhaps a smart slap or two, the affairs of the keep were maintained in perfect order.

Catherine, of course, had gone about her goal more quietly. Her position was precarious and she knew it. So she had depended upon the goodwill of a handful of servants to accomplish her aim. Bemused by the improvements, he had not reminded her that she was still hostage and only allowed certain freedoms.

Mairi had done that immediately upon her return, and the ensuing scene had put him right in the middle of a female squabble, an unenviable position for any man.

"The whey-faced bitch may be sleeping in your bed, but she is not the mistress here!" Mairi had railed at him in Gaelic. "I will not have her playing wife when she is only a leman. . . ."

Any attempt to placate Mairi was met with stubborn refusal, and in the end, Alex was forced to remind her that he was master of the keep and made the rules. "Do not berate me for my decision, because I will not allow it, Mairi. Now come, let her take some of the burden from your shoulders. It keeps her busy and lightens your load."

"Set her above your own, and you will rue the day, Alex Fraser, mark my words." Mairi had glared at him, then at Catherine. " 'Tis an evil day that saw her come here."

"Evil or not, she is here and will be here for a while yet to come. She is still hostage. 'Tis true she is not locked in a chamber, but she is not free to leave either."

Drawing herself up, Mairi said stiffly, "Yea, but I am free to leave. I will not come back until the Sassenach whore is gone."

As he'd watched her storm from the hall, she had looked more frail and older than he'd noticed before. It weighed on him that she so hated Catherine, but he would not relent. Now he must find another guard for Catherine when he went with Douglas, one that was suitable yet not caught up in her charm.

Lifting his head, he looked up to see Robbie watching him. Yea, Robbie MacLeod was loyal and fierce, and while he might jest with Alex about the maid, he would not be susceptible to her beauty or wiles should she choose to use them. Perhaps he was being too cynical, but if he was to err where Catherine was concerned, he intended it to be on the side of caution.

He beckoned to Robbie, and he came, moving across the hall with swift, certain strides. "You are to ride with the Black Douglas?" he asked his lord.

"Aye. We leave at cock crow tomorrow. Logan will be in charge of the men-at-arms, but 'tis you only that I trust with the care of the lady. See to her safety first, then her comfort."

Robbie looked surprised. "You do not need me to go with you, Alex?"

"Douglas is taking only a few men. I need you here more than I do with me this time. If I should not return, you know what to do."

"Och, do not fash yourself about the lady, nor summon ill fortune with thoughts of defeat. You will return, and the lady will be held safe here until you do."

Alex put a hand on Robbie's shoulder. "I can always depend upon you. Join us at the table. Perhaps Douglas has brought news from the Bruce."

Steaming venison pies and haunches of beef were served, and across the hall a piper played a lively skirl as they sat at table to eat. Laughter rose in occasional bursts, and castle hounds yapped for scraps and attention. Douglas sat on his right, with Catherine on his left and Robbie just beyond them.

As they ate, James Douglas told them what he had learned of Edward's movements. "On the side of good, Edward seems to be more humane to Bruce's queen than was his father. He has just granted her spacious lodgings at Rochester Castle, though she is still a prisoner there, and ordered that she is to have twenty shillings a week for expenses. 'Tis meet that female hostages be treated kindly, do you not agree, Lady Catherine?"

His sly glance at Alex earned him a scowl, and Douglas only laughed before he continued. "At the end of November, Edward wrote a letter to the Earl of Dunbar telling him he intends to bring an army north before midsummer. And just before Christmas, he sent out writs to eight earls and eighty-seven barons summoning them all to appear with their knights, arms, and soldiers at Berwick on June tenth. On the way here, I learned that he has confirmed to his Scottish supporters—curse the Comyns for fools!—that he fully intends to lead an army against Bruce. Rumor has it that he will make Pembroke the Viceroy of Scotland again."

"None of this is surprising," Alex pointed out with a shrug. "We have long been aware of Edward's intent to meet us in battle on midsummer's day. What of the Earls of Lancaster, Warwick, and Surrey? Have they yet answered his summons?"

Douglas shook his head, stripping off a juicy portion of beef and chewing it before he replied. "Nay. They are not like to reply until they see which way the wind blows. They will meet their feudal obligation, but still harbor too much resentment against him to ride to his standard."

Alex nodded thoughtfully. Then he asked, "And Warfield? Has he yet answered the summons?"

Douglas grinned. "Aye, 'tis said that he did not need a summons to send his vow of support for Edward. But we knew that he would do so, especially now."

Catherine's head had come up, but she bowed it again quickly, staring down at her trencher with a small frown. It was often in his thoughts that she had lingering loyalty to her father though she swore she did not, but he knew for certain how she felt about her brother. Despite their angry words, she loved him, and grieved that he had not sent word to her since she had last seen him on the eve of Saint Nicholas's feast day.

Later, when he found her alone in the chamber he now shared with her, he asked her the question foremost in his mind: "Where lies your loyalty, catkin? With your father and brother, or with your new home?"

She looked up at him, shadows darkening her eyes to deep purple. "Is this my new home? Are you then reconciled to losing your brother?"

"Nay, you know I am not. But he is yet alive, and if I am able, I will free him."

"How?"

The simple question took him aback, and he gazed at her with a frown. "God willing, I will manage it, but in truth, I do not know how. The earl is not willing to barter, and I have nothing else to offer that will sway him. If your brother fails . . ."

As the sentence trailed into silence, she laughed softly and turned away to stare out the window at the dark night beyond. "Yea, now you see how worthless I am as a hostage. You would have done better to take Nicholas, for my father values him."

He heard the bitterness, and went to her, turning her around to face him. Hooking a finger beneath her chin, he tilted up her face so that he could look into her eyes. "Do not allow your father's stubborn foolishness to convince you of a falsehood, catkin. You are not worthless."

Sighing, she rested her cheek against his chest, undoing him with the simple, trusting gesture. He put up a hand rather awkwardly to stroke her bright hair, letting the silken fibers flow over his fingers in a soft tangle. How did she do this to him? Turn him into a mass of confusion? It was not something he would ever admit to anyone, least of all her, but there were moments when he felt an overwhelming softness for her, an unfamiliar emotion that stirred and troubled him. It was unexpected. Lust he knew well, but not this surge of yearning for her that had nothing to do with her sweet, soft body and everything to do with the fierce desire to keep her safe at all costs.

When she drew back, tear tracks marred her pale

cheeks and he brushed them dry with his thumb, managing a smile. "Dinna greet, lass," he murmured in the familiar dialect that seemed natural with her now. It came easily to him, tripping off his tongue with tender sympathy. A woman's tears always undid him, but especially this woman, who wept so seldom when other females seemed to spill constant tears like Scotch mist.

Curling her fingers around his hand, she held it against her cheek and smiled. "I do not mean to weep, but it seems so hopeless at times. Are you going away?"

Her abrupt change of direction made him smile. "Aye. It will not be for long, unless Douglas finds that his perfect plan has gone awry. But that is unusual. He is unrivaled in concocting wild, implausible strategies that actually work."

A frown drew the delicate line of her brows over her eyes. "He is a man who takes too many risks. I would prefer that you stay, but I know from experience how useless it is to ask a man to be safe rather than retreat from certain danger and possible death."

A little surprised by her comments, he studied her for a moment. The change in their relationship had been dramatic since Saint Nicholas Eve. It was not a situation that was strange to him, for he had noticed in his relationships with women that once intimacy had been achieved, they tended to cling and worry. Perhaps that was why he had always kept his intimacies casual, as with the two village women who had borne his children. That was the only tie he had to them now, for both had married well due to the stipend he gave them as mothers of his offspring. There had never been vows of love between them, and if the women had felt other than physical pleasure or satisfaction that they would be granted regular purses, they did not reveal it to him by word or deed.

It was the way he preferred it. Until now.

By all accounts, he should keep Catherine of Warfield at arm's length. She meant trouble to him if he allowed her to matter. He knew that well. As badly as he wanted Jamie safely back, he loathed the necessity of returning Catherine to her father should they reach agreement. When had she become so important?

"Alex. . . ." She turned his hand and pressed a light kiss on his palm. "P'raps it seems odd to you that I fret for your safety, when in truth, you are my captor and little else, but 'tis not a thing I fully understand myself. I do know that I cannot help the way I feel, and if you should come to harm, I wouldst be distraught."

Lightly, he said, "Then I will remain unharmed so as not to cause you distress, milady."

"You jest, when I am most serious."

"Yea, but there is naught either of us can do but take each day as it comes, catkin. If I were to bog down in worry, then I would lose whatever edge I might have over my enemy."

"But—"

Bending his head, he kissed her to stifle any more protests or words of worry. After a moment, her lips grew soft under his, and parted to allow him entrance. Quickly, their discussion was gone from his mind as he concentrated on the sweet softness of her, the heady taste of her mouth, and the feel of her silky skin beneath his roaming hands.

He lifted her in his arms and carried her across the chamber to his bed, laying her on the mattress and following her with his weight atop her yielding form. Her breath wafted over his cheek when he drew back to gaze down at her with a smile, and her eyes were half-closed.

"You end every discussion you do not like this way," she murmured, twining her fingers in his hair.

"Complaints again, milady?"

"Nay, no complaints . . . just an observation. Kiss me."

He complied most willingly, brushing his lips over her mouth, the smooth curve of her cheek, then her eyelids before moving lower to press his mouth against the rapidly throbbing pulse in the hollow of her throat. She moaned softly, music to his ears, as stirring as the pipes playing a rousing battle tune. His blood beat faster in his veins and he lost himself in her fragrant flesh and yielding sweetness, forgot everything but the driving need to ease his growing sense of urgency.

His head moved lower to kiss the valley between her breasts through the soft velvet stretched over them. She responded with a little moan and restless arch of her body toward him. He smiled against the fabric, and nipped gently at the tight buds pressing against her bodice. Then he sat back on his folded legs and dragged his hands down her legs to her knees, bunching the velvet in his fists as he watched her. As the hem slid upward, his curled fingers brushed lightly over her calves, her knees, her pale thighs. She shivered beneath his touch.

Bending, he pushed the gown slowly up, kissing the skin of her inner thighs as he worked the fabric higher. A husky moan shimmered in the air between them, and he looked up at her. Her face was flushed with passion as she chewed at her bottom lip. Dragging his mouth over the soft flesh above her knee, he muttered, "You smell like lavender."

"Yes . . . yes . . . the soap. . . ."

He made a mental note to bring her a different scent, though it should not bother him that James Douglas had given her the soap. Another trivial reason for staying away from her, for he had never in his life felt the faintest twinge of jealousy about any woman. They were

there or they were not, and one was as good as another
when it came to sexual matters. Until now . . . Lord
have mercy, until now and this one woman, who of all in
Christendom, he should avoid as if she were a leper. Yet
he craved her, craved the sight and smell and feel of her,
craved her laughter and even her tears, and it tore him
apart that to save his brother, he would have to relin-
quish her. . . .

He slid his hands beneath her and lifted her, brushing
his face against the fragrant contours of her body and
breathing deeply of lavender and female. When he raked
his tongue over her she gasped and arched into him, a
lovely female sound of excitement that was arousing.

"Oh, Alex . . . what are you . . . doing?"

In answer, he cupped her buttocks in his palms and
pulled her closer, his tongue delving into her feminine
recess with steady rhythm that summoned gasps and
muffled cries from her as she pressed the backs of her
knuckles against her mouth. Through his lowered lashes,
he watched her face as he brought her to the brink of
ecstasy, stroking and kissing her until she curled her fingers in his hair and held him against her writhing form.

When her entire body trembled, he eased her down
to the mattress and stretched over her. With swift efficiency, he unlaced her gown and freed her breasts from
their prison of velvet. Shaping the small, firm mounds
with his hands, he kissed and fondled and suckled her
until she was panting and pleading for him, and only
then did he lift the edge of his tunic to press his arousal
between her damp thighs.

A flash of fire exploded deep in his belly, and he
paused, throbbing at the moist heat between her thighs,
his teeth clenched for control. Lord have mercy. . . .

Shuddering, she arched her hips, rotating them into
the hard pressure. Her hand crept between their bodies,

fingers finding and circling him, exploring the stiff swell with excruciating motions that drew a wordless groan from him. Unable to wait, he moved her hand aside and entered her, plunging deeply and moving with hot ferocity against her, unable to hold back, unable to think of anything but the heated urgency that drove him.

Clutching at him, Catherine flexed into his thrusts with matching fervor. Her back curved, heels digging into the mattress for leverage as she clung to him with both hands clasped around his neck, her soft cries echoing in the room until they were swallowed by shadows. Enveloped by heat and passion, he moved inside her with mindless strokes that sent shivers of anticipation down his spine. Sheer ecstasy, sweet torment, God he must be insane to so lose himself, but he was already lost, drowning in the honeyed depths without a prayer for rescue . . . and it did not matter. Nothing mattered but this moment, this woman, when all else could be forgotten for a little while. . . .

Then she was crying out, a soft keening wail of pleasure that triggered his own release, and the delicious friction shot him over the edge into that white-hot haze of oblivion that he sought. Panting for breath, he sagged against her, his face buried in the curve of her neck and shoulder. Lavender filled his nostrils and gratification loosened his muscles so that he held her that way while the fire burned low and candles guttered. It was enough to just hold her like this, to feel her damp heat around him and her breath soft against his face, to breathe her in and know that he was not alone.

Rain pelted them as they rode across the lowered bridge and away from Castle Rock. Douglas was whistling a merry tune that grated on his temper, but Alex said nothing. He forced his attention onto the coming assault and away from the lady he had left sleeping in his bed. As they rode on in the dark hours before dawn, the rhythmic pounding of the horse beneath him and the upcoming promise of battle began to lift his spirits. It had been overlong since he had been able to do something to ease his frustration. For the past four months, foul winter weather and circumstances had kept him bound with inactivity.

"Since all of Lothian province is seething with dissatisfaction these days," he said to Douglas as they rode, "it may be difficult to discern who is for Bruce and who is against."

"Yea, their situation is unhappy at best." Douglas shrugged, his words muffled by the edge of his plaid, wrapped over the bottom half of his face. "The people of the province are said to be within the King of England's peace, yet they receive no protection from him. Bruce regards them in the same manner as the northern counties of England and demands tribute or they suffer retribution." His laugh was whipped away by the wind, and after a moment, he spoke louder. "When the people of the province pay Bruce his tribute, the garrisons of the English-held castles raid their homes and shops and seize their goods and hold prisoners for ransom, all on the grounds they have been dealing with the enemy, of course. Devilish awkward position, do you not think?"

"To say the least. What of their feudal lord? Does the Earl of Dunbar not protect them?"

Douglas laughed. "Oh, aye, he protects them as best he can with his quill and parchment. Dunbar and the Lord Chief Justice, Adam Gordon, appealed to Edward with their pitiful plight, and he sent reprimands to the governors of his castles. Of course, the reprimands were duly noted and ignored, as any good Sassenach would do. The people are still oppressed, and have no one to turn to in their time of need."

"And we go to relieve them."

Even in the dim light afforded by the palest glimmer of the rising sun, Alex could see the glee reflected in James Douglas's eyes as he nodded. "Aye, Alex lad, that we do. We shall liberate loyal Scots and traitorous alike, some from their oppression and some from their lives of treachery."

"It is a bad position, to be forced to choose sides when your title and lands depend upon English law."

"Aye, but you did it quick enough." Douglas slanted him a curious glance. "You may have taken back your lands, but your family title is worn now by the enemy."

"Yea, I have my lands, but only because they are in Scotland instead of England. There are those who have lands in England who have lost all, or joined the English to keep from losing all."

"These are times that men must choose sides, and not ride the fence."

Alex did not answer for a moment, but rode silently over the narrow, muddy track. It was bitter cold even for February. Where the road was not mud, it was frozen to hard ruts. Ice crystals glittered in the furrows dug by wagon wheels and pounding hooves, reflecting chips of sunlight as dawn broke. In the distance a dog barked, and there was the smell of smoke in the air.

"Tell me," Alex said when they slowed to a trot to pass through a sleepy village, "what you think the chances are that Bruce will succeed."

"One in ten," Douglas said promptly, then laughed.

"But that is all that is needed. One chance. The nine are behind us now, and we have one chance to win all, as on the toss of the dice. Will we? Is that what you ask? If you ask Edward, he would say no. But if you ask Robert Bruce—aye, lad, we will win all. And my heart and my sword are with the Bruce, whether we win or no. And you, Alex Fraser? Where is your heart?"

"It has always been with the Bruce, since I was a lad of fifteen and he picked me up out of a bog and set me on my feet. I thought then that he was the finest warrior in all of Christendom, and I still do. When I was fifteen, I fought for my father and for my home. Since I met Bruce, I fight for my king."

"He has that effect on men." Douglas laughed softly. "And an even stronger effect on women."

"So I have observed. Women swoon at the sight of him, and are known to follow him from camp to camp in hopes of a kind word—or sleepless night."

Douglas grinned. "And 'tis plain you had your own sleepless night. Was the lady wroth that you left her warm bed for the cold?"

"The lady was too exhausted to do more than pull up her blankets when I left." He paused, thinking of her sleep-tousled hair and drowsy eyes, and how delicious she had looked lying there with the glow of a single candle washing over her ivory skin. He had not been able to resist waking her in the time-honored tradition men oft woke their lovers, and after her first sleepy protest, she had wakened enough to respond in a most satisfying manner. He would miss waking beside her of a morn, feeling her warm body curled into his with trusting innocence.

But he had no intention of letting James Douglas know how he felt, and shrugged off the teasing jests. There were other, more important concerns to deal with now. The problem of Catherine of Warfield would have to wait for his return.

For now, they must conquer the entire garrison of Roxburgh Castle with only sixty men. And here as well, the odds might be one in ten that it could be done.

15

—❦—

Catherine felt Robbie MacLeod's gaze on her, and her shoulders tensed. Finally she looked up at him. "Must you stare at me?"

"Aye. 'Tis my duty tae protect ye."

"For the love of all that is holy, do you think a band of villains is about to fall upon me here in the midst of the hall? 'Tis doubtful, though I am certain Sir Alex will greatly appreciate your loyalty and sense of duty."

Robbie did not respond, nor did he move from his position against the wall. He leaned back with his arms crossed over his chest, but remained in the same spot.

"Stubborn Scot," she muttered to herself, and looked back down at Tam. "You are doing excellently, Tam. Sir Alex will be proud when he returns."

And when would that be? She fretted with each passing day, and wondered if anyone would bother to tell her if they knew when he would return. Or if he would not . . . oh, Holy Mary, Mother of God, she could not start thinking such things or she would go mad.

To keep her mind from straying, she kept busy. Now

she worked with Tam. But later? What would keep her from dread visions of what might happen . . . not even the pleasure of reading was enough to divert her from the fears that plagued her when she thought of all the possibilities she now faced.

She was with the steward asking about the proper food for the approaching Lenten season when Robbie suddenly made a soft noise in the back of his throat and snapped to an upright position from the familiar slouch she had grown accustomed to seeing. Curious, she followed his gaze.

Across the hall, bearing down on them with grim purpose, was Mairi. The older woman was disheveled, her normally tidy gray hair in disarray and her clothing flapping about her body like a loose blanket. Catherine felt the steward take a step backward as Mairi reached them, but she held her ground.

Halting in front of Catherine, the woman's face was distorted with rage and hate. "I curse ye, whore of Babylon, for poisoning Sir Alex wi' yer witch's mind and body. . . ." Silence fell in the hall. Spittle laced Mairi's mouth, and her eyes were wild. "If no' for ye and yer wicked blasphemy, I wa'd no' hae been sent frae my place here!"

"I did nothing to you." Catherine's voice was calm despite the rapid thudding of her heart. "Nor did I ask to come here."

"A lie! Ye hae been sent here by the Sassenachs tae spy on us, and murther us all in our beds . . . I hae tried tae tell the laird, but he wa' bewitched by ye and wa'd no' listen tae me. . . ."

Robbie moved at last, coming to speak to Mairi in Gaelic, his voice rough and low. The woman shook her head vehemently, and glared at Catherine as she lifted a trembling arm to point at her. " 'Tis true . . . and ye know it well, ye scheming harlot . . . d'ye think the laird wa'd hae taken ye tae his bed otherwise? Nay, he wa'd no' do it, no' after he swore tae leave ye untouched. But I heard him tell tha' Sassenach lordling wha' ye call brother tha' he wa'd no' long leave ye virgin if there wa' no answer aboot Jamie, and ye maun hae known there wa'd be no answer . . . 'twas a trick tae hae him lie wi' ye, tae bewitch him so ye can open the gates o' a night tae let the murtherers in tae slaughter us all in our beds. . . ."

Robbie took her forcefully by the arm, speaking rapidly to her in Gaelic as he pulled her with him. He said something to those nearby, his voice sharp, and Catherine saw the fear and suspicion in the faces watching her. Even Tam looked askance, as if uncertain she could be trusted not to leap at them with a weapon.

She stood still, unmoving as Robbie evicted Mairi from the hall. She did not speak when he returned to her side and suggested she retire to her chamber, but accompanied him silently from the hall to the winding staircase that led up to the second floor. Echoes of Mairi's ravings seemed to resonate off the walls in eerie repetition, so that she heard over and over again that Alex had only taken her to his bed as vengeance against her father's delay.

It was not until she stood in the center of the chamber she shared with Alex—his chamber, with high bed and thick hangings, tapestries on the walls, and a constant fire with a decent chimney to draw the smoke—that she finally spoke.

Turning, she looked hard at Robbie. "Is what she said true, Robbie? Did Sir Alex tell my brother that if he did not soon receive an answer about Jamie he would take my virginity?"

Robbie glanced away. "I was no' in the room when

'twas said, milady, so I am no' the man to ask. Ask Sir Alex when he returns."

"Nay, that will not be necessary, for you have answered the question more completely than you know." Anguish made her hands tremble, but thankfully her voice was steady. "I would like to rest now. Please shut the door when you leave."

He hesitated, but something in her face must have convinced him, and he nodded. "Aye, but I will be outside the door should ye need me, milady."

It was not often he left his post, and she knew that he trusted few to relieve him, fearing perhaps that harm would come to her and he would be blamed. She watched mutely as he left, and waited until the solid door clicked with finality before she collapsed onto a low stool.

What a fool she was. She had hoped—thought—that Alex must feel some tenderness for her, or he would not be so attentive, would not have been so gentle. But now she knew it was not love, it was nothing more than lust that kept her in his chamber—it had never been anything but lust. He had warned her. She should have listened when he had said lust and love were equally dangerous. It was true. Oh, God, it was so true, and she had been so blind, so caught up in the unfamiliar emotions and physical urges that she had convinced herself he cared.

Yet the truth brought no real anger with it, only a grief as if someone she loved had died. There was a sense of pain along with it, that she could now see so clearly what she had blinded herself to before. But no anger. No self-righteous rage that he had lied to her, or at the least, not been entirely honest. She could not hate Mairi for telling the truth, and could not even hate herself for being deceived. It had been self-deception, after all, for he had not pretended to love her.

And perhaps that was the worst of it.

Pressing her fists to her mouth until she tasted blood, Catherine sat for a long time as shadows crawled across the room and squatted in corners like predatory beasts; the fire died and the candles guttered, plunging the elegant bedchamber with its silk hangings and embroidered tapestries into utter darkness. It felt right to sit where there was no light and no hope. It felt familiar.

A fluttering in her stomach kept her tense and on edge, but she betrayed nothing as she listened to Robbie MacLeod talk to the guard outside her door in Gaelic. He was leaving her with a new man as guard, a rare occurrence as Robbie had remained almost unfailingly at her side until now. Only on occasion would he leave her with another, and then for short periods of time.

But this was the moment she had been waiting for, been expecting for the past two weeks since Mairi had raved at her in the hall and shattered any illusions she held about Alex Fraser caring for her. After days of agonizing, she had finally accepted what she must do to end this anguish. She would leave Castle Rock. It would not be easy, and perhaps she would be caught, but she could not just linger here and wait for his return. It would be too painful to see him again, to look into his angel's face with the devil's own lie in his eyes. . . .

She had learned there was a nunnery close by; she would seek refuge there until she could enter a cloister in her own land. Her lands would be dowry to the church, and she would live out her days in relative independence and freedom. Now that she was no longer a virgin—in the eyes of the church and her father, an unwed woman with a past and no future—she would be accepted without debate about her eligibility. The church would be glad to receive her extensive dowry, and she would still be allowed to retain monies for her own use. She could travel if she wished, or linger in the sanctity and peace of the nunnery and devote her time to prayer and reading. It was a way of life free of the restrictions wives and daughters faced in the secular world.

And now the moment was at hand. She was prepared for it. Swiftly, she donned the garments she had hidden in a chest for this purpose, then slipped the velvet gown over her head and left it loosely tied at the sides. When she was certain Robbie had left, she waited a few more minutes, then opened the door.

"Guard . . . please . . . I am taken ill. . . ."

Disconcerted, the guard stared at her without response, and she wondered wildly if he spoke English. It was something she had not considered. Groaning, she clutched her stomach and bent double, then sagged to her knees. Alarmed, the guard knelt beside her, not touching her.

"Milady . . . be ye truly ill?"

His English was rough but intelligible, and she nodded before groaning louder. "Please . . . it is a female complaint that so ails me . . . I need a woman from the village . . . oh, Holy Mary, Mother of God. . . ."

Her last words were uttered in a moaning wail as if she were about to die, and the guard scrambled to his feet and looked around him in panic. It was obvious he was loath to leave his post, and she increased her moans, then went into shaking spasms that were not too difficult to mimic in her current state of agitation. She thought of a religious woman she had once seen, who had fallen to the ground in a fit of holy fervor and foamed at the mouth and thrashed about, and did her best to imitate the convulsions she had witnessed.

Apparently, she was very convincing, for after another glance and a few muttered words in Gaelic, the guard backed away, then sped down the hall with a clatter of sword and fervent prayer for his own safety. The echoes of the Latin prayer drifted back to her, and she kept her eyes half-closed in case he turned around. Lying in the open doorway of the chamber, she waited for what seemed an eternity before rising in a swift motion and stripping away her velvet gown. The rough servant's clothing she wore beneath was quickly covered with a long mantle she had pilfered from some hapless soul who had carelessly left it in the hall, and she slipped from the chamber into the empty corridor.

Below, she could hear voices, and in the bailey outside was the constant ebb and flow of normal activity. Accustomed by now to the back staircases, she used the one at the opposite end of the hall the guard had chosen, and quickly descended the tight, narrow spiral steps, blowing out the lamps in the niches to plunge the stairwell into darkness behind her. When she reached the bottom, she paused and, bending, scraped her hands over the dirty floor and rubbed it on her cheeks, forehead, and chin. She tucked her hair beneath a square of rough wool to hide it from view, knotting the corners together, then pulled the mantle's hood up to cover her head. She tugged on the wool gloves she had been given in her first days here, to cover hands that would betray her with their pale softness.

With pounding heart and a dry mouth, she made her way slowly across the small room toward the kitchens. No one paid her any mind as she moved with purpose to a bundle of rags tied with thin cord, and hefted it to sling over one shoulder. It was heavier than it looked and she staggered a bit under the weight, but did not pause.

She carried the makeshift burden as if it belonged to her. Sunlight and cold wind struck her forcibly as she stepped into the mud and clatter of the bailey, and she kept her head down as she moved along with the bundle of rags atop her back. No one seemed to notice her as she wove a path through the milling soldiers and various tradesmen. On the morrow, it would be Shrove Tuesday, the day before the Lenten season began and a time of festivity before the long season of fasting commenced. The keep was thus busier than usual.

When she reached the outer gates, open during the day to allow in tradesmen and those who had business here, she did not pause. Her heart was pounding so fiercely she felt as if her ribs would be bruised by its force. Posted guards oft stopped those entering, but generally did not detain those trying to leave. She found herself behind an old man with a load of woven baskets tied around his neck and across his back, and he began to quarrel with one of the guards.

Would he never cease his ranting in that querulous voice? If she were still within the keep when her absence was discovered and the cry went up, all would be for naught. This was her only chance. . . .

Finally the guard gave a disgusted grunt and a shove, and the old man moved along, still indignant about some slight he must have suffered, and she followed with her head low. She prayed to be invisible, for if she were forced to speak they would know instantly she was English.

But the guard stopped her with an arm stretched in front of her, his command rough Gaelic. She stopped, but shook her head mutely, keeping her eyes downcast. He said something else in a sharp tone, and she stood frozen in panic. What was he saying to her? He would quickly discover she did not understand his language, and all would be lost . . . but when she dared a glance upward, he was peering at her with narrowed eyes and she opened her mouth and made an incoherent sound, then pointed to her ears and shook her head. It was inspired.

At once, he shoved her forward, then looked at the man behind her and said something that must have been coarse, for they both laughed. It did not matter. She walked past him, bent under the bundle of rags, deaf indeed to all but the loud pounding of blood that filled her ears as she trod the narrow passage that led to freedom.

As she made her way across the bridge and down the steep hill toward Kinnison, she prayed that she would find the priory Tam had told her was only a few leagues distant. It was near Langholm, which was very close to the border. She just must remember to keep the rising sun on her left, and the setting sun on her right.

But it would be difficult, for even now clouds were scudding across the sky and the wind was growing sharp and colder. Without the sun to guide her, she may soon be lost, wandering with no one to help her in the country of the enemy. Never in her life had she felt more alone than she did now, and with each step, Catherine prayed for guidance.

16

❦

It was Shrove Tuesday, February 27, and the garrison of Roxburgh was celebrating the day before the beginning of Lent with a feast. Douglas, Alex, and a hand-picked group of men that numbered sixty in all approached the castle after dusk. Over their chain mail, they wore black cloaks that draped to the ground and blended them into the shadows. Silently, in single file and on their hands and knees, they moved along a narrow path as if they were cows or oxen that had been left in the fields for the night.

It was a brilliant plan—if it worked, Alex thought with grim amusement. He could barely make out the form of the man in front of him, shrouded by black wool with only an occasional clink of his sword along the rutted track to lend noise to the gloom. Stealthily, they made their way close to the castle walls, careful to appear aimless to any who may be watching. It was not until they were directly beneath the wall that they heard a sentry speak, his voice drifting over them in the quiet, cold night with crystal clarity.

"The local farmer must be making good cheer, for he has left out all his cattle."

Another man laughed softly and replied, "Good cheer tonight, but Douglas will have them tomorrow."

Laughing, the two men wandered along the stone ramparts until their voices faded.

Douglas beckoned, and his men came close to the foot of the wall, hooks and ladders in hand to scale the height. "Who drew the winning lot to go first, lads?" he whispered with a wild grin, and a man stepped forward eagerly.

"I am to go."

"Good man, Sim. Give us the signal when you have seen the lay of it."

Alex helped fit the iron hooks of the ladders to the top ledge of the castle wall, and Sim of Leadhouse swiftly scaled the ropes. They stood in the shadows and watched as he reached the edge of the parapet. There was a brief scuffle and grunt, and then Sim turned to look down with a reckless laugh, hissing, "All's well. Speed quickly."

With a muffled clump of boots against stone, they made their way up the hempen ladders and over the parapet to the sentry walk. A dead guard lay sprawled on the stones, stabbed in the heart to stop his warning. When they were all up, Douglas motioned and they separated into small groups, dispersing in different directions, keeping to the shadows and muffling the noise of their boots and swords.

Alex accompanied Douglas, and they moved along the sentry wall with silent purpose. When they rounded a corner, Douglas put up a hand to halt the small group, and Alex heard the soft sound of a woman singing. He peered through the gloom, and in the fitful light of a torch burning on a wall, he saw the figure of a woman seated on the edge of the parapet. Her back was to them and she was holding a baby and rocking back and forth, crooning a soft song.

In the dark, Douglas turned to him, and his teeth flashed white. "Listen. . . ."

Amused, Alex grinned back as the words to the song drifted into the night: "Hush ye, hush ye, little pet ye; Hush ye, hush ye, do not fret ye; The Black Douglas shall not get ye. . . ."

As she sang, Douglas approached her on silent cat's feet, and as the last words faded, he put a hand upon her shoulder and growled, "Do not be sure of that."

Turning, the woman's face crumpled in horror as the Black Douglas loomed over her, but he laughed softly at her terror. "Do not fear, good dame, for I will protect you this night. It is a holy eve. Go in safety, but remain hidden for protection from the fray."

Beckoning a man to him, he set him to guard her so she would not give the alarm, and they continued down the walk to the circular tower and winding stairs. Few men were about this night, but they could hear the noise in the great hall, where all were celebrating Shrove Tuesday with dancing and singing. Flanking the doors, they waited, and when Alex saw Douglas give the signal at last, he turned with the others and burst through the doors into the hall, bellowing the war cry of the Douglas. It rang through the hall, causing instant pandemonium.

Women screamed, dogs barked, and men shouted drunkenly as they grabbed clumsily at swords. Slashing fiercely about him, Alex cut down two men who came at him with uplifted weapons, pushing one free of his blade with his boot when the unfortunate man buckled over it. It was bloody work, intense and close in the hall, but the rout was quick as the English were taken completely by surprise.

Above the din, the governor of the garrison, William de Fiennes, managed to rally a few of his men around him and flee the hall. Alex pursued hotly, but de Fiennes made it to the safety of the keep and bolted the doors behind him. It soon became apparent that it made little difference, for the entire castle was in Scots hands. In triumph, they set about gathering prisoners and booty. Some of it would go to the Bruce for the royal coffers, but the rest would be split among them.

"Think you there will be enough to ransom your brother and de Brus?" Douglas wondered aloud as he lifted a handful of coins they had found in a chest and let it spill between his fingers in a bright metallic stream.

"Nay. All the gold in Scotland and England would not be enough to purchase Jamie's life, I fear." Alex hadn't meant to sound so bitter, but it had come to him over the weeks with slow, painful realization: Warfield would never yield.

Douglas looked at him thoughtfully. "There is another kind of currency that might yet purchase both Jamie and de Brus from a man like Warfield. Summon Lord Devlin to you again, but this time without promise of safe conduct. When he arrives—as he surely will—take him hostage in place of the lady. 'Tis my guess that Warfield will relent for his heir, if for nothing else."

"The idea has occurred to me. Yet if he does not? Do I then have two hostages?"

"If all is lost and Jamie is executed, send Warfield his son's head on a silver platter."

"That would not bring back Jamie."

"Nay, but 'twould convince Warfield of your intention with his daughter."

A moody smile set stiffly on his lips as Alex shrugged. "If I were to slay the lady's brother . . ." He let the sentence go unfinished, suddenly loath to allow Douglas to know his mind, but the other man quickly guessed.

"Aye, 'tis true she would vow never to forgive you for it. Yet I have observed that women are oft fickle in their emotions, and she may find that you are more important to her than her brother."

Alex did not reply. It seemed unlikely that Catherine would ever be fickle in her love for her brother. And he would not want her to be less than she was.

Then Douglas abandoned the subject, and slinging an arm around Alex's shoulders, accompanied him to the great hall where they joined others in enjoying the feast that had been deserted by the English. It was the first decent food he had eaten since they left Castle Rock a fortnight before, and Alex ate with gusto.

The next day, when the governor finally yielded after sustaining a serious arrow wound to his face, Alex waited impatiently for de Fiennes to be granted safe passage to England and quit the castle. He was suddenly filled with the need to see Catherine again, to assure himself that she was still well. If Devlin discovered his absence, it was likely that Warfield would join his son in an out-and-out attack in order to free his daughter and obviate the need to continue negotiations.

Finally, William de Fiennes yielded the keys and took his leave, his little caravan departing Roxburgh Castle to move toward England. Sim of Leadhouse was given the glad duty of relaying to Bruce the news of Roxburgh's capture and no doubt receiving a hefty reward for the happy tidings, and Roxburgh was left with enough men to safeguard it until it could be razed to the ground. Destroying any hope of enemy occupation was the only way to ensure that the English would not return. The method was drastic, but successful.

Restless, Alex mounted his horse and waited for Douglas on the road outside the castle. Sparse afternoon sunlight glittered from behind heavy dark clouds, muted and hazy as it trickled over the rolling hills and slopes. Douglas eyed him with a lifted brow as he halted his horse beside him.

"You do not join us."

"Nay. I must return. My keep is vulnerable, and I do not trust Warfield. Once I have ensured all is well, I have agreed to ride again with Moray."

"Ah, my comrade in arms . . . give Moray my regards when you see him—and be certain he hears of Roxburgh's capture."

Alex grinned. It was well known that Douglas and Thomas Randolph, Earl of Moray, had a friendly rivalry, ever since Douglas had captured Moray and held him prisoner until he swore loyalty to Bruce. Since that time, the two men—so different, with Douglas tall, thin, and darkly restless, and Randolph shorter, stocky, and fair-haired—had been close friends. Bruce himself had noted the important differences between them and used them well, each in their own capacity. Randolph was measured in manner and astute in statecraft, but oft competed with Douglas in feats of daring and drama.

"I will tell Moray of your success with Roxburgh, so that I may watch him try to equal it. 'Twill be a most entertaining diversion, I think."

A reckless grin split Douglas's face, and he laughed. "We will meet again soon. Fare thee well, Alex Fraser. And give the lovely lady a kiss from Black Douglas when you see her!"

Laughing, Douglas put spurs to horse and sped away, and Alex grinned as he turned his mount toward the southwest and Castle Rock. He followed the Teviot River for a ways, then skirted English-held Jedburgh. The movement of enemy troops was constant, and he circled the town to the northwest in the waning light of dusk. Dark fell early this time of year, and with it this night came high winds and spitting snow.

Reluctantly, he decided to seek shelter in Jedburgh Abbey for the night. If he left early and the weather held, he would be able to reach Castle Rock by dusk of the morrow. Much depended upon the presence of English troops in the area as well—the region was thick with them as news of Roxburgh's fall spread swiftly, and he might have to ride far out of his way to avoid them.

When he reached the doors of the abbey, none answered his heavy thuds. He yanked impatiently at the bell rope, and heard it clang inside the hallowed walls. A cold wind blew from the north, chilling him to the bone, so that by the time a cowled monk opened the small grilled window in the door, he found it hard to speak without chattering.

"I seek shelter."

"It is late on a holy eve, brother. Seek shelter elsewhere this night, for—"

"But I am here, newly come from Roxburgh and a victory for Robert Bruce," he growled in Gaelic. "Do you deny me?"

There was a moment's hesitation, then the face vanished from behind the grilled window, and the shutter closed on it. He lifted his fist to pound again, but heard a bolt draw back with a grating, heavy sound. The door swung inward, and Alex entered with his horse. The friar stepped aside, then swung the heavy doors shut behind them and slid the bolt. He held a lamp high so that light bobbed erratically over his portly frame, peering at Alex's mail and weapon. Then he beckoned, and while his horse was given into the care of another cowled monk, Alex was led down a vaulted corridor illuminated by horn lamps set along the wall. A grassy courtyard edged one side of the corridor. Spiny branches of rosebushes waved spindly arms in the night wind as they passed, reminding him of supplicating hands.

The friar paused in front of a door, then pushed it open and entered another corridor, leading Alex inside at last, into the smell of candles and incense. He followed the silent monk, his sword clanking slightly against the walls of stone and their footsteps echoing down the hall-way. They passed a set of double doors that gave into a vast chamber filled with tables and benches and brightly lit by candles.

"That is the refectory," the friar said in English. "We fast in honor of the holy day, but 'tis where we serve the evening meal for guests."

The abbey was larger than it appeared, and Alex was surprised by the maze of hallways and doors. Finally the monk paused again and turned to indicate a door set into a small alcove. "You may sleep here this night, my son. For a fee by which we may continue God's work, you may dine in the refectory with the others. If you so desire, you may join us in our evening prayers in the chapel."

Now he spoke in Gaelic, and Alex answered in the same language. "Robert Bruce needs all your prayers."

Nodding his tonsured head, his round face broke into a smile. "You can be certain he receives them, my brother." He moved to the door and opened it. "It is small, but offers shelter. A candle costs a ha'penny." He looked down and closed his fingers around it when Alex pressed a coin into his palm, then withdrew a tallow stub from beneath his robe. He smiled again. "You will hear the bell ring for supper."

Alex followed him into the room that was little more than a cell. It contained a hard bed with a neatly folded wool blanket at one end, and a table with a carved wooden candlestick. The friar lit the tallow candle from his lamp and jabbed it into the end of the candle holder. Then he left, and Alex felt the silence close in around him as the door shut.

The complete absence of sound was unnerving. Always at Castle Rock there was noise, whether distant or close; it was never quiet save at night, and even then there would be the whispered rustling of sentries or guards or servants creeping about their tasks. But here, insulated from the world in hallowed halls of prayer, it seemed as if he could hear the blood run through his veins and his heart beat in his chest.

Tempted to wrap himself up in the blanket and go right to sleep, Alex debated going to the main hall for supper. But his growling belly made the decision for him, and he stripped away his mail hauberk, swearing softly before he caught himself when one of the leather straps broke. A pitcher of water sat on the edge of a stone basin, and he broke the ice in it to pour a small amount out to wash his face and hands, scrubbing them dry with the edge of his plaid. The room was austere but immaculate. Not a spiderweb graced a corner, nor did dust lay upon the small table. He smiled slightly. A spartan life, to be certain.

It was not a choice he would make, but he could understand a man's desire to retreat from the world this way. Most of the time, it was a quiet, simple life spent in prayer and the growing of food, dispensing herbs and advice with generous hands, guiding the lost and abandoned. There were those orders and priests who abused their offices, but most he had met were decent men with high principles. As in all areas of life, some few could influence the rest to either direction.

Pulling a small packet from the folds of his plaid, Alex

placed it on the table. It was wrapped in a square of silk and tied with ribbons, a neat parcel that contained scented soap and exotic perfume. He had found it at Roxburgh and taken it as part of his spoils from the victory. Inside were also rich silk ribbons of purple the same shade as Catherine's eyes, and a comb for her hair wrought of gold and amethyst. No doubt, some English soldier had purchased these for his lady. Now they would go to another English lady.

A bell rang, chimes sounding deep and the call to supper resonating through the abbey. More bells would sound the call to prayer or mark the hour. Alex adjusted his plaid for warmth and left his small cell, moving down the echoing corridor to the refectory.

Others had already arrived and taken seats on benches at the tables, some refugees from the night like himself, he supposed. There were even a few women draped in the required veils or wimples to cover their hair. One of the brothers came around with a small wooden bowl, holding it out discreetly for coins. Alex dropped in his contribution with the rest, but his attention was snared by one of the other guests' soft exclamation of dismay.

In French, she murmured that she had no coin. The brother hesitated, frowning, and the lady shook her head, her face shrouded by the draping of her wool veil. "I am sorry. I did not know. . . ."

"I will pay her coin," Alex said, and the lady's head came up. He froze with the coin held out, staring directly into familiar violet eyes. They widened, pupils expanding until her eyes looked almost black as she stared at him in horror.

"Good eventide, Lady Catherine." His English was rough with surprised anger, and she made a small, wordless sound in the back of her throat.

Fury gripped him—fury and apprehension and an

overwhelming sense of betrayal. There could be only one explanation. She had escaped.

Curse her. And curse his own foolishness for thinking she could be trusted. For thinking that when she had yielded her body, she had also yielded her heart. . . .

17

—⚜—

Mortal terror struck her to the marrow. Catherine could neither move nor speak, she could only stare at Alex Fraser as he regarded her with an expression of fury she had never seen before. Her first instinct was flight, but she immediately realized how futile that would be. No, her only hope was to brazen it out, for she was in a house of God. No man could harm her on hallowed ground.

The cowled monk had moved to stand at Alex's side, and he jiggled the bowl a little impatiently. Alex dropped the coin into it with a brittle clink. She bent her head, and with a trembling hand reached for the bread she was offered. She must think. A bowl of barley pottage was placed in front of her, and she dipped the crust of bread into it without glancing up, afraid of meeting the eyes like steel swords staring at her from across the table.

She had gone the wrong way; she knew that now. She had gone east instead of west, and the nunnery Tam told her of had never appeared. Three days of hiding and fear had rendered her near senseless, and the happy relief of stumbling onto this abbey, so much further than her original goal, had been her salvation.

She had spoken French, careful not to betray herself with an English accent, even though the town was held by English. The kindly porter had allowed her inside. A woman alone . . . the abbot was horrified. Robbery? Ah, what was a widow from a good merchant family doing wandering the country when bands of brigands roamed mercilessly . . . it was well she had come here, for word of a nearby raid had reached them earlier in the day.

She had thought, briefly, that she was safe. With nearby Jedburgh in English hands, she would be able to get word to Nicholas that she had escaped. All for naught now, of course. Alex Fraser was here and he would never allow her to send word to anyone, nor allow her to leave save with him at her side. She had seen it in his eyes, the lethal promise and menacing fury of a man who has been thwarted.

Yet at the same time, she resented his anger, and the righteousness that obviously accompanied it. Had he not taken her maidenhead only to fulfill a threat? It did not matter that she had yielded it for reasons of her own. It was hers to yield. And because there was nothing more than that between them, she would of course attempt to escape him as soon as she could. She was English and he was Scots. They were sworn enemies even before she had been born, and would be so long after she died. It was the way of things. She had been foolish to ever dream it might be different.

With slightly shaky fingers, she ate slowly, forcing down bite after bite, knowing that when the meal ended, he would find a way to confront her. Why had he not done so already? If she delayed long enough, perhaps he would leave. Idle wishes, of course. She felt him across from her as if he were the only man in the room.

The pottage was gone from her bowl much too swiftly, and when others rose from the table and began to leave the hall, she dared a glance up at Alex. His bowl was still full and his bread untouched. He stared at her still, his gaze flinty. Unnerved, she looked back down at her empty bowl and tried desperately to think of a way out.

A polite cough finally drew her attention, and when she looked up, one of the friars stood beside her and she saw that the refectory was empty—save for Alex Fraser. He waited by the door, one shoulder leaning against the frame as if he had all the time in the world. Perhaps he did. The friar gestured, and she reluctantly handed him her bowl. Then she rose to her feet. There was no point in delaying the inevitable any longer. She would face him.

But it was hard, walking toward the door and knowing he waited for her there, knowing that the illusion of love and tenderness she had created was shattered beyond repair. It had been so brief, so fragile, she should have known it was not to be.

"Milady." Alex put out a hand when she reached the door, his arm barring her progress as he stretched it across the opening. She stared at it, noting the tensed muscles visible beneath the sleeve of his sherte, and the brownish stains on the fabric. "A moment of your time, please."

His silky murmur had all the assurance of a purring tiger, and she drew in a deep breath. In French, she said, "I go to prayer, sir."

His arm did not budge, but remained across the door. "No," he said softly. "Though God only knows you should. I think you know why I must insist that you spare me some of your time. Or are you about to suddenly depart the abbey?"

She looked up at him then, angered by his mockery. "If I try, you will be on me quick as a cat. No, I cannot leave until I have your promise of safe conduct."

He smiled, but it did not reach his eyes. They were silver smoke beneath black lashes, regarding her as if she were an enemy—or prey. "I shall conduct you safely, if that is what you mean. But come, we should not discuss this here in the refectory, but where we can speak privately."

When he reached for her, she drew back. "No. You have no power over me while I am in the abbey. This is hallowed ground, and I am safe."

"Are you?" The cold smile again, curving his lips into an expression that was more like a snarl. "You cannot stay here forever. This abbey is in Scotland, if you have not noticed, madam."

"Of course I noticed." She paused, aware of the curious glances they received from the friar who was cleaning the tables. He must wonder why they lingered so long when all the other guests had gone. "But Jedburgh is held by the English, or did you not know that?"

"Yea, but for how long? Do not be foolish. Once you leave this abbey, you are at the mercy of Scot or English soldiers."

A bell rang, and the whispering sound of footsteps in the corridors reached them as the call to vespers summoned both monks and laymen. The friar approached the door, and slowly, Alex drew back his arm and allowed them both to pass through. But she felt his eyes on her and knew that she was well and truly caught.

The quarters for female visitors were outside, across a grassy courtyard, and Catherine hesitated. If she went

alone, Alex was quite likely to intercept her. So she
turned, aware that he was still behind her as she moved
along the corridor into the chapel. She filed inside, genu-
flecting toward the altar, and moved to the ranks with the
others. There were no benches as there were in the
chapel at home, where the lord and his family had their
private seats at the front; here there were only places to
kneel on the cold stones for the service. Already, the
chapel was crowded, and she took a place next to another
woman.

The heady scent of burning candles and incense filled
the air, and the monks lifted their voices in melodic
chant that seemed to rise to the top of the vaulted ceiling. The beautiful Latin words momentarily drowned out
her fears as she knelt in prayer, resonating from gilded
beams and soaring walls to fill ears, and mind, and heart.

"Dominus vobiscum," a sonorous voice intoned, and
the deep masculine response of the friars' *"Et cum spir-
itu tuo"* filled the air with full-throated piety. There was a
sense of peace and continuity that pervaded the beautiful
chapel and lent her strength. She prayed it would be
enough to withstand Alex Fraser.

As she suspected, he was waiting for her when vespers
ended and she left the chapel. This time, he took her by
the arm before she had a chance to avoid him, and swept
her with him down the hall and into an alcove. She was
shivering, but not from the cold, though it was certainly
frigid in the unheated halls.

Curling his hand under her chin, Alex held her tight in
his grasp, staring down into her face with eyes as barren
as the winter skies. "I would hear how you came to be
here instead of near twenty miles away, where I left you,
madam. And I want to know why."

She put her hand on his wrist, but could not push his
arm away. It was like iron beneath her palm, solid and

unyielding. With his fingers pinching her jaw, she managed to reply. "I walked. And you must know why without me saying it aloud. Would you endure being prisoner if you could be free?"

"Christ above . . . have you been mistreated? Did anyone there hurt you?"

Her face must have reflected her outrage, for he drew back a little and his eyes narrowed. This time she succeeded in knocking his hand away from her face. "Hurt me! I was stolen from my home and my lands without regard for my wishes, oppressed and threatened, made to disrobe for a man who is my sworn enemy, and you dare to ask if I have been hurt by anyone? Nay, not by anyone—only by you."

"And you know the reason you were taken. I have dealt honorably with you. You ate in my hall and slept in comfort. What you did, you did of your own free will. I did not force myself on you, so do not claim violation—"

Stepping close to him, she looked up into his face and hissed furiously, "Caitiff! Do you think I do not know why you took the virginity you first claimed to decline? It was not your noble reluctance that bade you wait, but an oath you swore to return me untouched. And I know about the other oath you made, the vow that if your brother was not returned to you, I wouldst not be returned to my family a virgin. Ah, I see that you remember now."

The breath felt tight in her throat, squeezing her chest painfully. He did not reply for a moment, but stood gazing down at her as if he had never seen her before. Then he looked away, his jaw clenched so tightly a muscle leaped beneath the dark shadow of a half-grown beard.

"Does it really matter why I took you?" he asked at last, turning back to look at her. "You were not loath to accept me. Until later, of course, when thoughts of ven-

geance against your father faded and you were left with
the full knowledge that you had bedded the enemy. Then
I became the coarse Scot again, unworthy of your prize."

Her laugh was shrill and a little wild. "Yea, I wanted
vengeance, I freely admit it. But I thought . . . I
thought it meant more to you after you were so tender
. . . I did not know, of course, why you had first sworn
not to take me. I thought you—cared." It was out before
she could recall it, and she flushed that she sounded like
a petitioner for his affection. Clenching her jaws tightly,
she held her tongue before she betrayed herself again
with more unwise words.

There was a strange expression on his face, almost
pain as he looked at her, and he veiled his eyes with a
sulky droop of his lashes. "You said you regretted that
you had done it. Why would it matter to you if I cared?"

"I never said I regretted it."

"Did you not? No matter. But you should know that
men say what will have the most effect in times of crisis,
catkin. I am certain I made a lot of threats to your
brother about you and about many things. And I no
doubt meant them when I said them, as he meant what
he said. God." He raked a hand through his hair, looking
suddenly more weary than angry. "If every threat made
was put to the test, the world would have been burnt to
cinders long ago."

"So. . . ." She paused, watching him, uncertain. "So
you did not mean what you said to Nicholas?"

"Oh, aye, I meant every word. I could lie to you and
say that I did not consider taking you in retaliation, but I
did. I thought very long and hard about it. But in the
end, it was not thoughts of vengeance that made me want
you."

She held her breath. When he said nothing else, she
blew out her breath softly. There was a wealth of innu-

endo in what he had said and not said. Oh, Holy Mother, it was not as she had thought, as Mairi had said. Perhaps there were no vows of love or affection from him, but that he would say as much as he did—and if she had not flown from Castle Rock only to be snared, she may never have known it.

Then she said, "Robbie will be most upset with me, I fear."

Grimly, Alex muttered, "Robbie will not waste time being upset with you once I have hold of him."

"Oh, no . . . do not be angry with him. It was not his fault."

"Madam, when a man full-grown and well versed in the ways of war allows a slip of a maid to escape a castle so well built a rat cannot escape without my leave, he needs be chastised most heartily."

She smiled a little. "But you must know that I am more clever than most at finding ways to leave fortified castles for I have been doing so all my life."

"A most intriguing virtue, catkin."

Catkin . . . she loved the way he called her that, with an odd inflection almost like fondness in his tone. Strangely, she suddenly wanted to weep. Perhaps it was the aftermath of anger, the sudden release of tension that had held her in its grip for over a fortnight. Not again would she allow unproven accusations from another to so distress her.

She looked up at him where he leaned with a bent arm pressed against the wall over his head. "Are you still angry with me?"

"God, I should be. All of Scotland is crawling with enemy soldiers, and you wandering about like a lost goose. You are fortunate you are not now lying dead in some ditch."

"But the English are your enemies, not mine."

"Do you think that would matter? A troop of soldiers and a lone woman dressed like a peasant can have a very bad conclusion. You are in Scotland. Your speech would not save you if they preferred to think you the enemy and available for sport." He raked a hand across his face and heaved a sigh. "You were in danger from both armies, catkin. Men are men. Some are more brutal than others."

It was not very heartening, and she suppressed a shudder at the thought. "But now you are with me. I will be safe."

He stared down at her. "Pray God you are right, for we are still a long way from Castle Rock."

It had been a strangely quiet journey. They rode slowly for the most part, skirting villages and taking paths that wound through the edge of Wauchope Forest. Alex wore a heavy mantle over his mail, and wrapped it around her where she sat in front of him on the burdened horse. Leaning back, with his arms around her and the beat of his heart a steady rhythm in her ear, she did indeed feel safe. How odd, that a man who was her sworn enemy should make her feel secure when she had felt imperiled her entire life. Not physically imperiled, perhaps, but in jeopardy of losing that part of herself that she held dear, the small, intrinsic idea of freedom that meant so much.

She thought of the night before, of the odd timbre in his voice when he had admitted it was not vengeance that made him want her. Dare she hope for love? And if it was love, if he did want to keep her with him, how then would they manage it? Never would her father agree. Not that his blessing was necessary for a priest to say the vows, but there would be swift, horrible retribution against Alex's brother for the deed. She could not coun-

tenance that, could not bear to have it on her conscience
if her happiness purchased a young man's death.

Her fingers strayed to the small cloth bundle tucked
into the folds of her wool gown. Scented soap, heady
perfume, and a comb for her hair lay nestled among the
silk ribbons. Gifts from him, given to her this morning
with awkward gruffness that had endeared him to her
even more. After spending a restless night on a hard cot
in a small cell with two women whose snores had kept
her awake, she had not been able to form a proper reply,
but stood as a tongue-tied maid on the steps of the abbey
and smiled foolishly. He had seemed to understand, for
his answering smile was soft, with no trace of the anger
that had marked him before.

Drowsing a little with the jogging cadence of the horse
beneath her and its hooves a uniform clatter on the hard
frozen ground, she sagged into Alex's embrace. It was not
until a sudden jerk of motion woke her that she smelled
it. Blinking sleep from her eyes, she looked about, dazed
with slumber and a little confused by the billowing
clouds that seemed to fill the glen below. They were out
of the forest now, on a high, wide ridge looking over a
steeply descending slope festooned with crawling gray
ribbons. Fog? No, fog did not have that sharp, acrid
stench to it . . . her heart began to thump hard in her
chest, and she sat upright.

"Alex . . . smoke."

"Aye." His tone was flat. "I see it."

Ahead, she recognized the familiar stone towers of
Castle Rock visible through the drifting haze. Her mouth
went dry, and she clung tightly to the saddle as Alex
nudged the horse into a hard, driving canter.

Long before they reached Kinnison, she could smell
and hear the devastation. Keening wails rose to mingle

with the still crackling flames and thick black smoke that poured into the air, and men shouted as they hauled buckets of water to douse the fires. Spitting snow melted quickly in the heat. Everywhere she looked was death and despair, heart-wrenching as they rode down streets littered with bodies and awash with blood. Half-timbered houses and shops that had been neat and prosperous smoldered in charred ruins. Children screamed for lost parents, and parents screamed for lost children. The din was deafening.

Not even the village church had been spared. Rope still dangled from the roof where the steeple had been pulled down to topple on the ground. Bits of bright glass from shattered stained glass littered grass and stone, and some windows had been removed to leave empty sockets like dead eyes staring out at the destruction. A priest sprawled in his cassock at the foot of the stone steps, his drawn sword still clutched in his lifeless hand. She did not look to see if she knew him, but glanced away with rising nausea.

Behind her, Alex was silent, but she felt his rage in the taut muscles of his arms on each side of her, the clenched fists on the leather reins as the horse danced nervously along the frozen ruts of the street. Tears stung her eyes and a sob clogged her throat.

Then someone recognized him and cried out in Gaelic, a hoarse bellow of anguish. Alex halted and answered him, his tone curiously flat. The man's face was black with soot and streaked with tears that made odd patterns on his cheeks. His bleary gaze flicked to her, and he said something else, his voice harsh this time. Alex answered sharply, and the man looked away, gesturing to the pile of rubble that must once have been his shop and home. Shattered splinters of wood and blackened stones were all that was left of it, save a single tiny shoe lying amid the ruins. It was untouched by fire or water, lying in mute testimony of the small foot that had worn it.

Never had she envisioned such ruin, and Catherine felt suddenly as if she could not bear to look any longer. Turning her head into Alex, she buried her face in the folds of his wool cloak. He put an arm around her to hold her against him, a comforting gesture in the midst of what must be a distress much greater than hers.

Beneath her, the horse pranced restively, and Alex nudged it forward again, the pace swift. In a blur, she glimpsed scenes of grief and despair as they rode through the street, not toward the castle road, but to a narrow, twisted lane of burghers' shops. Or what had been burghers' shops. Now charred, smoking rubble remained. Alex reined in the horse before a building that was only half-burned, and she heard a familiar voice greet them.

She looked up to see Robbie approaching. Soot streaked his face and his light hair was nearly black. Despite the cold, he wore a sleeveless jerkin, and mail chains covered his legs. He spoke Gaelic in the same oddly flat tone that she had just heard from Alex, and gestured to blanket-shrouded forms lying on the ground nearby. Alex sucked in a harsh breath and dismounted swiftly, nearly unseating Catherine as he leaped from the horse to move to the still forms on the ground. She watched, clinging to the horse's neck as Robbie grabbed at the dangling reins.

Alex knelt and flipped back the edge of a blanket. She could not see the forms, but knew with sudden horror who must lie there when a hoarse cry was wrenched from him. Then she saw the small bare feet peeking from beneath the wool, smooth, childish toes curled toward pink soles.

Catherine pressed the back of her hand against her mouth, knuckles digging into her lips. Robbie stood stone-faced, and one of the women she recognized from the hall as the mother of Alex's child fell to her knees sobbing beside the bodies. Snow powdered her black hair in gauzy drifts.

"Ohon! Ohonari . . . !" she wailed over and over in a keening cry that pierced Catherine, the sounds of her grief a sharp blade that cut all within hearing.

With hot tears running unchecked down her face, Catherine began to murmur a prayer for the dead, the Latin familiar on her tongue: *"Agnus Dei, qui tollis peccáta mundi: dona eis réquiem . . . Agnus Dei, qui tollis peccáta mundi: dona eis réquiem sempi térnam. . . ."*

Robbie looked up at her with ravaged eyes. "Yea, pray God grants these wee bairns eternal peace and rest, for there willna be peace in this land until the bloody English are all driven frae Scotland."

She held his gaze, somehow knowing the answer but compelled to ask the question: "Who did this, Robbie?"

The single word spat like a curse confirmed her worst fears and extinguished the flame of hope that had flared so brightly and so briefly.

"Warfield."

Alex turned, and she saw in his face and eyes the awful promise of retribution. He lurched to his feet, and his voice was a harsh rasp, unashamed tears wetting his cheeks. "When I have buried my children and those of my village, I will avenge them, blood for blood, life for life."

The English words were directed to her, and there was nothing she could say. In truth, she did not lay blame for his vow. How could she? Knowing that her father was responsible for this? For the first time, she truly understood the ravages of war, the scope of loss, and it appalled her.

Sickened, and aware that there was nothing she could do or say to assuage his loss, she watched numbly as Alex bent to tenderly lift the lifeless bodies of his children and bear them away.

18

—⚜—

Robbie stared at the stone floor of the hall, his downbent head and taut posture evidence of his grief and misery. Yet Alex did not relent.

"How was it," he asked softly, "that a mere maid was able to so easily escape Castle Rock? And that my sentries did not see the approach of an entire bloody army?"

Anguished eyes glanced up at him beseechingly. "She tricked the relief guard when I had gone to the garderobe. By the time he found me, she was not to be seen. We closed the gates and searched, but she had already slipped away. I drew the sentries from their posts to look for her, then Tam came to say she had asked him about Langholm Priory. It made sense that 'twas where she would go, but we could not find her. We had not been back long when Warfield struck, just after first light. We barely had time to close the gates, and those that did not make it in time . . ."

His words drifted into helpless silence. Alex could visualize it, the frantic villagers fleeing to the gates before they closed, with Warfield's armed soldiers in hot pursuit.

Their screams of panic must have been agonizing to hear, their death cries devastating.

His anger dissipated abruptly. He did not blame Robbie. He blamed himself. Most of all, he blamed the Earl of Warfield and his devil's spawn, Lord Devlin. Curse them both to hell, he would not let them escape this act without harsh retribution.

Robbie made an aborted gesture with his hands, his voice choked. "The bairns had asked to go with Mairi to visit their mothers . . . I did not think of them fast enough when we returned from searching for the lady. It all happened so quick—by the time we were able to arm ourselves, Warfield was gone."

"Do not blame yourself, Robbie. What is done is done. It may well have happened had I been here."

"Nay, you would not have let the lady from your sight. I failed you, Alex." Robbie fell to his knees suddenly, despair wracking his shoulders in harsh shudders. "Now they are dead and I am to blame for it. . . ."

Firelight flickered over Robbie's light hair. It still bore black streaks of soot, and his arms were raw and red from burns he had received in fighting the fires. But Alex could not offer Robbie more comfort when his own sorrow sat so near the surface, ready at the first crack to break through and unman him. He looked away from his comrade's awful grief, his jaw tight with emotion and his tone flat.

"Siusan still lives, though grievously wounded while trying to protect the children. She asks for Christian." A tight band constricted his chest as if a merciless hand were squeezing his heart, and for a moment, he could not finish his words. Never again would he see his bright-eyed son and daughter, hear their childish giggles, and feel their chubby arms around his neck. It was a pain to exceed even the grief of losing his parents, for the two innocents had been shorn of life before it began for them. Clearing his throat, he said hoarsely, "I cannot tell Siusan that he is dead, as is her husband. See that her father does so if he thinks she can bear the truth. On the day after the morrow, we will bury the children and Mairi in consecrated ground." He did not look up to see if he were acknowledged, unable to bear Robbie's despair as well as his own. "Pay the customary deid-dole to the beggars from my coffers. I will gather the deid-claes to clothe them for burial."

Robbie's words were thick. "And the wake? Grant that I may sit with them and keep the candles lit 'round the biers."

Alex nodded. "Aye, you may sit with them when I do not. After the burial, I will take all the men that can be spared with me to harry what of England I can compass. 'Tis your choice, Robbie. If you wish to stay here and hold the keep, I will leave you in command. If you wish to ride with me, you will ride at my side."

For a moment Robbie did not speak or look up. Another shudder trembled through him, then finally he tilted back his head. "I failed you the first time, but I will not fail you again, Alex. I will guard the lady and hold Castle Rock 'til the death."

Alex put a hand on his friend's shoulder and held it tight, his fingers digging into strained muscle until he felt Robbie relax beneath his grip. Then he withdrew, leaving the hall and Robbie as he moved to the steps that led to the second floor. There were those who would blame Robbie for their losses, and those who would blame him as laird. But most, he had already seen in the faces around him, blamed Catherine.

When he opened the door to his chamber, he saw her at once. She sat stiffly on the edge of a chair, her hands folded in her lap as she stared blankly at the far wall. He shut the door, and she did not move.

"Catkin. . . ." Slowly, her head turned to him, and he saw his own grief mirrored in her eyes. He halted warily, unable to bear it if she wept.

But she did not, though her voice was strangely tight. "Alex, 'tis my fault this happened."

He almost smiled. "You will have to fight Robbie and me for the privilege of bearing the blame, I fear."

As if she had not heard him, she said in the same taut tone, "It was my temper. My own foolish vanity that I was being made fool that pricked me to unwise action. It is a grievous fault of mine that I allow others to provoke me when I know better." Silence fell. Candles danced in the growing darkness, pinpricks of light in a world of gloom. "Had I remained, Robbie would not have been unprepared. If there is to be vengeance, let it be on me."

His brow rose. "Was it your arm that held the sword? I did not think so. 'Tis Warfield and Devlin who must bear the blame." He drew in a deep breath. "I am not without blame myself, catkin. How many villages have I burned? Slain the men and beasts, and pulled castles to the ground? As many, no doubt, as your father. Though God strike me if I lie, I have never killed a woman or child, nor would I allow my men to do so. 'Tis enough to slay fighting men without visiting war upon women and children."

"Alex?" Her lower lip quivered as she looked at him, and he steeled himself for what he knew she would ask. "If you have the chance, would you kill my brother?"

"Yea, milady, without a doubt." He did not flinch from her soft cry, though it sorrowed him to see her grief. "It is war, catkin. Devlin would be the first to agree."

Burying her face in her palms, she did not speak for a

moment, but sat in the lengthening gloom with her back bent in anguish. He did not go to her. There was nothing he could say that would ease the truth. For if he had the smallest opportunity, he would run his sword through Devlin and send him to hell. It would be small penance for the work he had done in Kinnison this day.

A large banner snapped so briskly in the wind that its red lion appeared to be dancing on the field of white. Held high, Warfield's standard was visible before his father hove into sight, and Nicholas reined in his mount to wait. The earl came into view moments later, leading an armed troop over the Lyne River. Snow lay in sodden drifts along the banks, frosting grass and trees.

Nicholas spurred his horse across the field and rode to meet them at the bridge. He drew alongside the earl as he rode up the riverbank. Without preamble, he said, "I am told you rode to Castle Rock."

"Yea, my cockerel, so I have." The earl met his gaze with an ironic twist of his mouth. "Fraser will not soon forget my visit, I vow, though he seems to forget yours soon enough."

Nicholas scanned the mass of soldiers and said softly, "Yet I do not see my sister with you. If you have been so successful, where is she?"

"My notion of success is the annihilation of the enemy. You prate of negotiation and give Fraser command of the situation, while I take command from him."

"Yet I do not see Catherine or even Fraser with you—did you breach Castle Rock? Rescue Catherine? Slay Fraser? Or did you strike down those who cannot fight back, and name it victory. . . ."

"Curse you for an impudent dog. The difference between you and me, Nicholas, is that I am not told what to do by my inferiors—if they dare challenge me, I destroy them."

"Pray God that is not the only difference between you and me, for I could not stomach knowing we are like in much else." Rage made his voice harsh, and the earl's eyes narrowed hotly at his words.

"Do not think to lesson me in front of my own men, or I swear I shall strike you down! If you had the courage for it, you would have gone with me."

"It does not take courage to slaughter the defenseless. It takes vanity and arrogance, as well as a willingness to risk damnation."

Answering fury leaped in his father's eyes, and he lashed out, but Nicholas easily avoided the blow. There was the clink of chain mail and his sword against his horse's side as he jerked back and the earl's fist met empty air. His horse snorted in alarm, and Nicholas grated through clenched teeth, "As a sworn knight, I took an oath not to be struck without striking back. You are my father and my overlord, but I will not take your fist again."

"Insolent pup! Get thee hence from my sight and do not darken my hall until you come to me on bended knees and beg my pardon for your audacity."

"Do not look for me soon. And a word of warning, lest you think yourself safe from reprisal—unless you killed him, Alex Fraser will be here soon enough."

Sawing on his reins, Nicholas pulled his horse's head around and set his spurs to him. Hooves pounded over spongy turf as he rode away without looking back. It was true then. Warfield had massacred Fraser's village, destroying hope for Catherine. All his careful plans, his negotiations and appeals to the Earl of Hereford, his petition to the king—for naught. For if he knew his man,

Alex Fraser would not tolerate the earl's assault without brutal retaliation.

Now he must ride swiftly to fortify his holdings, for it would not be long until the Scotsman avenged the wrong done him by the earl. And as Warfield's son and heir, it would surely extend to him, for there was certainly no love lost between them.

That there was no love lost between father and son would not matter.

In truth, though he detested the cause for it, he was fiercely glad of this opportunity to meet Alex Fraser on the field of battle. As much as he hated to admit it, his father was right when he said negotiations were futile. Nothing had been settled nor even come near being settled. Yet that was as much the earl's fault as anything else, for he would not yield on the matter of the hostages.

In desperation, Nicholas had even considered exchanging the hostages without his father's consent, and suffering the consequences once Catherine was safely home. But if he had failed, his one chance would be lost forever. As now. . . .

Bitterly, he reflected on the vagaries of war that oft left a man reeling from unexpected blows. It was the fatal surprises that always caught him off-guard. As with sweet Catherine.

He thought of her and wondered if she fared well, and if she still fancied herself in love with the Scot. No doubt, by now her belly was swollen with a Scottish brat. Had she watched the carnage in the village and known then the full horror of war? Ah, he had tried to keep her sheltered from it, for her gentle nature had been lent more to dreaming of sweet illusions than the harsh realities that afflicted the world. It had always amused him that despite their shared parentage, he knew only too well how the world worked while she seemed to have visions only of impossible achievements. She was the sole love and softness he had known in his life, and the thought of losing her forever struck him as hard as a physical blow.

Swearing softly, he considered his options. There was still the chance he could save her, but it would involve the Earl of Hereford. Pulling his lathered mount to a halt on the muddy road that led to his estates, Nicholas deliberated briefly, then turned away from Devlin. If Hereford would lend his ear and his support, Nicholas might yet sway the king to his side, for Hereford's wife was Edward's sister. Yea, but 'twould be his final gamble, for now Fraser would be looking for him as well as his father, and if he fell into either of their hands, Catherine would be lost.

19

The fair winds of April blew soft over Castle Rock, and the hills beyond were bursting with new green and splashes of color from wildflowers. Catherine stood on the ramparts and let the wind blow her hair back from her face, thinking of another time she had stood on castle walls to wait for a returning warrior. It seemed so long ago that she had stood on Warfield's parapet, waiting for Nicholas, but always in her mind it was the turning point of her life. For when she had run down to meet him in the bailey, she had seen the two captives who set into motion the train of events that changed everything.

Were they still alive, she wondered. No word had come, and if Alex knew, he had not mentioned it to her. It was a piece of his life that he kept apart from her. She had learned not to ask questions when he returned from one of his long absences, usually muddy and stained with blood, a grim light in his eyes and often new scars on his body. It grieved her that they could not commiserate, but he was right when he told her she could not bear to hear of the things that were done.

Ah, sweet Mary, she was such a coward. How did men endure the doing and the knowing, the death all around them? She was weak. But one promise she had wrung from him, and that was his oath that if he met with her brother, he would tell her. Good or bad, that much she would have to know. It was the first question she always asked of him.

Restless, she turned away from the parapet wall and saw Robbie. Her shadow, her constant companion. He was fiercely intent upon guarding her, never far from her side. This time, she did not mind. Oddly enough, she felt indebted to him. For of all of them, she thought Robbie had suffered most. Not just with grief, but guilt. It ate at him, gnawed him with continuous worry so that if she was gone from his sight for more than a moment, he set up a roar. She could not blame him for it.

"Be ye ready, milady?"

Coldly polite, deadly courteous, he kept her at arm's length. Perhaps he had never truly been a companion, but neither had he regarded her with such austere hostility.

Frowning, she ran a fingertip over the jagged stone of the parapet. "Will you ever forgive me, Robbie?"

He shrugged. " 'Tis no' my place tae forgive ye or no', milady. I am just set tae watch ye, and tha' I hae sworn tae do."

She sighed. "Would it help if I explained to you why I felt I must escape?"

He straightened from his slouch against the wall. " 'Tis no' my affair, milady. Be ye ready?"

She crossed the battlement, but paused to stare through a narrow crenel built into the high wall. In the distance beyond the walls, soldiers of the garrison practiced their marksmanship by firing arrows against a huge butt. Others staged mock combat, all training for war.

Much of Kinnison had been rebuilt, but there were still blackened timbers that pointed skyward from ruins. A cross rose high above the houses and shops, gracing the new church steeple. Inside the chapel beneath a small crypt lay the two bodies of Alex's children, side by side as they had oft been in life. Mairi rested nearby, peaceful at last in death.

Robbie had come up behind her, and Catherine turned abruptly, surprising him. He backed away a step, but she moved closer. "I do not apologize for what I did, but I do entreat you to understand that 'twas not to do harm to you or anyone at Castle Rock that I left. It was my own vain pride that pricked me, the shame at thinking I was being made a fool that kindled my escape."

For a long moment he stared at her, then looked away. New lines creased his weathered face, and his features were sharper than before, more angular. " 'Twas Mairi who set ye tae flight. I knew it even then. I should hae told ye better."

"Told me better? What do you mean?"

His gaze moved back to her, studying her. "He is no' the kind of man tae do wha' Mairi said he did. Oh, I grant ye he wa'd think aboot it, but he held his own mother too dear tae ever take from a woman wha' she isna willing tae give—or take it for the wrong reason. 'Tis no' in him. I hae seen Alex Fraser fight three men at a time and bring them all down, but he isna a man tae harm those who dinna warrant it. He wa'd never hae taken ye tae his bed if he didna want ye there, milady. No' tae spite the earl, or even King Edward." He looked away again. "I should hae told ye, but I didna think a little humility would do ye any harm. And that is my sin, for I knew how ye took wha' Mairi said tha' day."

Catherine scraped her hand over the rough stone. The smell of smoke was in the air, reminding her of that awful day, a holy week to everyone but her father. It was not something she would ever forget. She looked up, and saw him watching her.

"I understand, Robbie. Perhaps I would have done the same as you did in remaining silent. And for the same reason."

He nodded, and she left the battlements with him, descending the spiraling stairs to the great hall. The light evening meal was served, and the hall was noisy with soldiers and laughter, and then the inevitable music from the pipes. She had grown used to them, though at first she had hated the wild, primitive music produced by a squeezed bladder of air and a mouthpiece that resembled a flute. Now, she actually enjoyed the gay music that filled the hall of a night.

It was just past dark when a cry came up from the walls, and there was a stir at the doors of the keep. Catherine's heart beat faster, for none but someone well known to the garrison would be allowed into the castle grounds after dark.

When Alex entered the hall, she did not move, but watched him cross the rushes with his long, familiar strides. Each time she saw him anew, he never failed to set her pulse racing. As he approached, he stopped several times to talk to knights and foot soldiers alike, and she studied him intently. He seemed whole, though muddy, of course, his head bare and his mantle draped carelessly over one shoulder. He wore his chain mail and a surcoat, and there was something different about him than she had seen before, an underlying intensity bordering on excitement.

Then he looked up at her from the middle of the hall, and her heart skipped a beat. His mouth curved slightly upward on one side, then his attention was once more claimed by one of the men. It took him much longer than she would have liked to reach her, and now the entire hall was stirring with ill-kept excitement. Could it be—? Was the long struggle between Scotland and England finally over? Was that the cause of this elation in the faces of these men lining the hall? Her lack of Gaelic had never been missed more sorely, and she waited with growing impatience for Alex to come to her.

Finally he was there, smelling of peat fires and damp wool, but beside her at last. She tried to curb the desire to fling herself at him, still very much aware of the resentment of the people of Kinnison and Castle Rock.

"Milady." He lifted her hand to his lips, grinning a little at her disgruntled expression. "You are more lovely than even the last time I saw you."

"And your tongue is more agile. Have you news for me?"

He squeezed her hand. "It was told to me that Lord Devlin has joined Edward in Berwick, in the company of the Earl of Hereford."

Relief flooded her, and she nodded. So, they had not met in battle. God willing, they never would. "Wilt thou be with us long this time, Sir Alex?"

The courtesies were observed, though she knew that later, when they were alone in the chamber she shared with him, he would dismiss all pretense of formality.

A squire brought an ewer of water and a dry cloth, and Alex washed his hands and dried them before he took his seat beside her. She felt his gaze on her, and slanted him a glance from beneath her lashes.

"Milady, I have other news for you, some of which I have already shared with the men of Castle Rock." His eyes remained on her face, and she felt the first inkling of dismay at what he may say.

"Pray, share then with me this news. . . ." He was gazing at her so intently, his gray eyes shadowed by his lashes, and she could not help another dread feeling of premonition.

"All expeditions have ceased, and Edward Bruce and his men have been recalled from Cumberland. There have been summons sent throughout the kingdom calling up men for military service. Bruce is in Torwood Forest, and we are to join him there."

Searching his face, she held her breath. No, the war was not over at all . . . it was about to begin. Oh, sweet Mary and all the saints, she feared for the future. For their future.

"When will you leave?" she asked calmly, though her heart was pounding so furiously in her chest that she could barely breathe. "Will it be soon?"

"Aye. We wait only long enough to call up the rest of my men who owe military service. I leave in two days."

He was watching her closely, but she struggled to hide the despair that was sweeping through her. No, she could not betray her pain, not before all the assemblage who watched and waited for her to stumble. So she held her head up, clinging tightly to her composure, and said softly, "I wish you all Godspeed, sir."

A faint smile flickered on his mouth, and he leaned close, his voice a low murmur. "Perhaps later, you can wish me more than that, catkin."

An erratic pulse began to beat, and she flushed at the heated glitter in his eyes. "If you like, sir."

Her demure reply made him laugh softly and sit back in his chair. "I like, milady. Oh, I like."

Now a blush stained her cheeks hotly, and she looked away from him. The ebb and flow of conversation wafted around her, and she heard Alex speak to Robbie in Gaelic as was his wont. More food was brought to serve the laird, and he ate sparingly, his discussion with Robbie conducted in a low tone. Bruce's name was oft mentioned, and she knew with rising despair that they discussed the coming battle. There was a general air of excitement throughout the hall, with men jubilant at the prospect of leaving Castle Rock to fight the English.

Of course, they would want vengeance for the vile depredation her father had visited upon Kinnison, shaming the garrison that was intended to protect it. Yet in war, even she knew that villages were often left defenseless when the castle closed its gates to invaders. It was one of the most horrifying aspects of the constant conflicts.

And it had gone on so long . . . would it never end? Now there was to be more war, another great battle fought, and yet she thought with sinking despair that it would not end the strife either. The brutal reality of war had been brought home to her with sickening clarity when she had seen the ruined village and shattered lives. Nothing had been the same since. People who had been cordial to her before, even friendly, looked at her now as if she were the devil's handmaiden. Even Tam avoided her. His brother had been one of the men slain in the assault on Kinnison.

The men in the hall began to celebrate, singing loudly, while the pipers were brought in to play deafening ballads, rousing tunes that stirred the blood. Alex leaned close to her when she winced at a particularly shrill tune, and murmured that it lent men courage to hear of heroes.

"No doubt, but 'tis my thought that the wine lends them more than a fair share of that unwise bravery." She'd spoken tartly, and his brow rose as he studied her.

"Does the knowledge that we go to fight the English so distress you, Lady Catherine?"

Lady Catherine . . . his usage of her proper name meant he was displeased, and she sighed. How could she possibly tell him that it was not so much the thought of his fighting her own countrymen that distressed her, but the thought of his being wounded or killed? Nay, she could not. To admit such a thing when he had spoken no words of love would leave her open to him, and she could not. Looking away, she shook her head.

"Nay, 'tis the knowledge that this war is yet dragging on that distresses me. Does it surprise you? I have yet to meet a woman who appreciates war, yet men rush out to embrace death with an alacrity that still astonishes me."

An amused smile touched the corners of his mouth, as she had meant it to. He regarded her view of war as quaint and very female. He placed a hand atop hers where it lay on the table, and pressed lightly.

"You have a tender heart, catkin, as do most women. It is not fitting that such gentle natures enjoy war."

She held her tongue, though she wanted to tell him quite sharply that it was even less fitting for women to watch the men they loved ride off with such witless enthusiasm to slaughter one another. But she had engaged in these conversations before with Nicholas, and knew the futility of attempting to dissuade men from the notion that war was great sport. Even when they endured losses, such as the devastating ruin of Kinnison, their only thought was to go out and visit such loss on others. It baffled her, and not for the first time she thought that surely she must have been meant to spend her days in a nunnery rather than the brutal reality of the secular world.

And yet . . . and yet, there was the constant whisper in the back of her mind that reminded her of how it felt when Alex touched her, when his lips met hers and he filled her world with all that was so precious to her. . . .

Tilting her head to one side, she looked up at him and smiled, unwilling to concede but more unwilling to disagree. The harsh jangle of pipes and lute clashed, and men roared loudly with battle song and drink, and yet she could think only of this one man, this beautiful, brutal man with the scarred face and clear eyes like polished silver. And she knew then that she was truly lost.

The music finished with a flourish, and the piper stood breathless and red-faced from his exertions, waiting for the laird to indicate his appreciation. Alex turned his attention to him, and made a comment in Gaelic that must have pleased the piper, for he grinned broadly and nodded. The hall had grown more noisy than usual with the celebration, exceeding even the tumult of the Christmas festivity, and Catherine heard shouts of laughter rise above the chaos.

A feminine voice rose even higher to cut through the clamor, and she turned curiously. Coming through the crowd was a young woman who looked vaguely familiar to her. She had seen her before, but could not quite place where. It was a teasing memory . . . but when the young woman drew near the dais and called out to Alex in a tortured voice, it came to Catherine where she had seen that face and dark hair, and she tensed. In Kinnison, kneeling beside the body of her dead son, this young woman had cried loudly in her grief.

Alex rose to his feet and spoke sharply in their native tongue to the young woman. She answered him just as sharply, and with a trembling arm, pointed an accusing finger at Catherine. A spate of words flowed from her, among them a Gaelic term, *a'mhuirt*. Catherine knew what that meant, for it had been directed at her before, and Robbie had always quickly remonstrated with those who said it. He had translated it for her when she demanded to know what was being said.

Murder . . . murderer. . . .

Blood drained from Catherine's face and she sat stiff

and still as the young woman railed and wept, huge choking sobs that sounded as if they had been torn from her very soul. The hall had grown quiet except for the shrieks of the grieving mother, and Catherine felt hostile gazes bent in her direction from those watching and listening. Frozen, she tried to ignore them, tried to have compassion for the young mother, for in truth, she understood her grief.

These people would never believe that, would never believe that she had grieved for all the dead and the futility of their fates.

Again, Alex spoke sharply, and this time he beckoned someone forward who came to the mother's side to take her arm. It was an older man who tried to draw her away, but the woman pulled free and lunged at the table, throwing herself at Catherine. Her open mouth was spewing Gaelic venom, spittle flying over Catherine's hands.

Shocked, she did not retreat, but stared into the wet, red-rimmed eyes so close to her own. Not long ago, she had been very pretty, dark-haired and lively, with brown eyes that flirted with Alex, but now her face was thin and wan and ravaged with grief. Catherine thought of her as she had looked then, and wanted to weep as well.

Soldiers rushed forward at Alex's command, and took the woman by the arms, although not unkindly. They pulled her from the table and the dais. Then the older man took her again, and tears tracked his face. Sobbing, the girl collapsed in his arms as if suddenly boneless and allowed him to prop her against him. As he led her away, she looked up again at Catherine, and though she did not understand the words, she certainly understood the deadly threat in them.

Another harsh word from Alex, and finally she ceased her torrent of hate and rage, slumping into the man's embrace as they left the hall. People moved aside silently to allow them to pass, and Catherine could feel the censure directed at her, the hatred and resentment and something else: a sense of danger. In only a few hours' time, her father had managed to undo all the progress she had made in four months. Never would these people accept her, even if Alex did.

Unable to look up at him, she sat stiffly in her seat and stared at the ruined table, feeling the world move around her in a haze of jumbled impressions. Alex spoke to her, taking her hand in his and lifting her to her feet; faces stared at her as he walked her from the dais through the hall and to the winding staircase that led up to peace and seclusion . . . torches burned in holders on the wall and spit sparks that singed her clothing and burned her bare skin, the vivid scent of wax candles permeated it all and then Alex spoke gently to her though his words were a low incomprehensible blur.

Something clogged her throat, and she could not answer or make any sound, even when he gripped her hands tightly. His face swam into view, but was blurred by something wet that puzzled her until she realized it was her own tears.

Slowly, she put up a hand to touch his cheek, her fingers tracing the familiar, beloved line of the scar that curved from his brow to his mouth, and then she leaned forward to press her face against his chest and weep. Never had she wept like she did now, harsh racking sobs that shook her until she could not breathe, rattled her entire frame with paroxysms of grief so brutal she could not stop. She wept with all the abandoned surrender of a child, yielding herself to raw emotion and uncomplicated sorrow.

And through it all she was aware of Alex Fraser holding her against him, cradling her in his arms as if she were indeed just a child, rocking her back and forth as no one had done since she was still in the nursery. It was purging and liberating. It was the moment she finally knew that he loved her.

20

—❧—

fear. She

"Take her with us?" Robbie stared at him as if he had gone mad. "We go to fight, Alex, not tat lace."

"Christ above, do you think I do not know that?" His fierce retort silenced Robbie, and he drew in a deep breath to calm his temper. "I cannot leave her here. You heard Siusan. If I leave Catherine behind, she will be dead before Kinnison is out of our sight."

"Och, Alex, idle threats from a grieving mother." But Robbie stirred uneasily, and frowned as he stared across the hall. A fire burned in the hearth, and a dog barked lazily.

"Nay, Robbie, you know better than that. Mairi poisoned Siusan's mind against Catherine even before Warfield's attack on Kinnison. That only sealed it. Did you look at those faces, Robbie? Not a man there that did not agree with every word Siusan said, every blame she laid at Catherine's feet. It was as if 'twas not Warfield who burned and sacked the village, but Catherine herself."

To his surprise, Robbie agreed. "Aye, you are right, I

fear. She is in danger if we leave her behind, and I cannot guarantee any man here would protect her. But what the devil will we do with her on a cursed battlefield?"

"Bruce is camped in Torwood Forest. Not far from there is a hamlet where she can stay. It should be safe enough for a time, with all the surrounding area save Stirling now in our hands."

A gleeful smile broke across Robbie's face, one of the few genuine smiles since Warfield's assault, and he shook his head. "Aye, with Roxburgh and Edinburgh Castle both taken, the English hold is weak. Does Black Douglas know Moray matched his feat so well?"

Alex grinned. "He does. It was a stroke of brilliance that yielded Moray the fall of Edinburgh Castle."

"And men adept at climbing sheer stone walls, I vow." Robbie laughed softly. "I wish I had been there to see the pride of Edinburgh captured by a band of thirty Scots. It must have been humbling for the English."

"The real humility will come soon, when we take back our country from them." Alex's grin faded, and he thought of the odds against it. They could not lose now, not after all that had brought them this far. Too much had been risked and too much lost. He thought then of Jamie, and of his children who had not been allowed to choose their fates either.

The loss of the last still grieved him sorely, but their deaths had been avenged.

Warfield keep was too well fortified, but not the outlying villages that belonged to it, and he had ravaged them with a thorough viciousness that rivaled the earl's brutality. It sickened him when he thought of the misery and death he had inflicted, and the open screaming mouths of terrified children as they fled the swords and burning brands. None had he slain, nor the women, remembering only too well his own dead. But the men who stood to fight were cut down with ruthless efficiency, all but the one man he wanted most: Robert Worth, Earl of Warfield.

When Warfield was plundered, he moved to harry Devlin's estates with the same merciless intensity, burning fields and storehouses, firing villages, killing the men who defied him. Though soldiers garrisoned Devlin's keep, the baron was not there. He had pulled down the fortress and left it a pile of smoking rubble for Devlin to find when he returned. It gave him small satisfaction, though it did not ease the vengeance that burned in him.

And his dead children were still dead. . . .

Curling his hand into a fist, Alex raked it across his jaw and looked up at Robbie again. "We leave on the morrow. See that all is in readiness."

"And the lady?"

"I go now to tell her to make ready."

Robbie nodded, and Alex moved toward the staircase. It would not be easy taking her with him, but he dared not risk leaving her behind. Not only would she be in danger from Siusan or others at Castle Rock or Kinnison, but if Warfield or Devlin learned that she had been left virtually undefended in a castle with only a small garrison, he would be risking Jamie as well.

It was a miracle that Jamie and de Brus were still alive and in Warfield keep, for he had been certain they would either be dead or delivered to King Edward by now. Yet word had come from de Brus that they still lived, urging him to come to terms with the earl as soon as possible. The message had been delivered by one of Devlin's men, another amazement. Perhaps there was truth to the rumor that there had been disagreement between the earl and his heir, and they were at odds. If so, it explained why they had not yet banded together against him.

As he reached the top of the stairs, he saw a faint

shadow flicker and disappear in the corridor, and he paused. All his warrior's instincts sensed danger, and he moved quietly around the corner, keeping to the wall. The echo of footsteps faded, and below, he heard the distant slamming of a door. Too late. He frowned. Why would anyone feel the need to slink about unseen? Yet there had been an air of stealth that raised his suspicions and his hackles.

When he entered the chamber he shared with Catherine he did not see her. Candles eased the gloom and cast light into the shadows. He stopped in the center of the room. She had not left the chamber since Siusan had confronted her, but remained here closed into herself like a hermit. Ah, she had even talked of going into a nunnery, but he had immediately disabused her of that notion. She had not argued with him, only smiled and turned away.

That she was not here now worried him, and he called for her. She answered at once, coming from behind the wall that hid the garderobe, her face a little pale.

"I fear me, sir, that the egg you sent me was bad. It had a vile taste that—"

"What egg?"

Her brow furrowed. "The lovely decorated egg that you just sent for my—"

"I sent no egg. Who brought it to you?"

"It was just a servant . . . I did not know him, nor have I seen him before, I think . . . Alex. Why?"

He strode to her and gripped her by the jaw, his fingers prising open her mouth. There was a faint aroma of bitter almonds, and he swore softly. "Did you eat it? Ah, Holy Christ—tell me!"

"No . . . I told you, it tasted vile. I spit it out." Crossly, she knocked his hand away from her face. "If you did not send it, who did?"

Relief swept through him, and he did not answer for a moment. Yea, he was making the right decision to take her with him, for it was apparent that she was in graver danger than he had thought. If he were not leaving in the morn, he would have routed the entire castle and village to find the culprit, though there would be many to suspect.

Instead, he pulled her to him and insisted that she wash out her mouth with wine, then took the cup when she was through. He cradled her chin in his palm and lifted her face so that he could gaze into her eyes. Lovely catkin, with beautiful eyes like violets, fresh ivory skin, and such trembling innocence despite all. So sweet and young . . . yet so much older than her tender years. This lovely English maid gazed up at him with the wisdom of the ages in her soft eyes. Grievous, that life should be so deuced full of hard lessons that aged the soul.

A coppery curl strayed from beneath the gauzy cloth covering her hair, bound by a thinly wrought circlet of gold around her forehead. He brushed her cheek with his thumb and smiled.

"Sweet catkin, I made a vow to protect you."

"Yea, so I am aware." She covered his hand with hers and held it against her cheek. "And I am well and whole."

"Despite your best efforts."

His jest made her laugh. "Yea, lord, despite my best efforts. Do you now regret being so diligent?"

"Nay. You must know I do not." He frowned slightly, then said with blunt resolution, "You will go with us when we leave at cock crow on the morrow."

Her eyes widened, reflecting light from the branch of candles that burned on the table behind him. "Go—to war?"

An unwilling smile tugged at his mouth and he shook his head. "I am not issuing you a sword and ax, no. But you are to go with us to meet the Bruce. I find myself reluctant to leave you here where my protection may be lessened by those who seek vengeance."

Again her eyes widened, seeming to fill her face as she stared up at him. "Ah. The egg. You think it poisoned."

"Do you still have it?"

"Nay, I threw it down the garderobe." She drew in a shaky breath. "Perhaps I suspected foul play, for normally I would not have noticed the strange taste. Everything in Scotland tastes strange to me."

He laughed and pulled her to him, unwilling to let her see the surge of affection that filled him at her calm acceptance of what had to be terrifying. He may be used to men trying to kill him, but even so he would dislike facing stealth instead of the blunt challenge of a sword. He preferred to see his enemies.

A tremor rippled through her body, and after a moment he lifted her in his arms and moved with her to the wide bed. Brushing aside the hangings, he placed her on the mattress and sat beside her.

"It will not be elegant, catkin, but there is a hamlet nearby the Bruce's camp that will be safe enough. I will be close so that I can see you often, though we will be devoting our time to training those who are untutored or undisciplined in the ways of battle." He looked away when she did not reply, recognizing the glimmer of fear in her eyes. In a taut growl, he said, "God knows, I should have returned you to your father by now, but I had hoped—"

"Nay!" Her fierce denial startled him, and he lifted a brow at the intensity of her tone. "I do not want to go back to him, but if it will save your brother's life, I will. Yet hear this, Alex Fraser, for I mean it truly—once 'tis done and he is safe with you, I will do all in my power to leave Warfield keep. Should you . . . want me . . . I will return. If not, I intend to spend my days in a nunnery, for I will not be at the mercy of my father ever again."

"Catkin. . . ." He stared at her helplessly. Want her? He dreamed of long summer days spent with her, lying in sunlit fields amid the heather, having her near him and knowing they would always be together. But he was too pragmatic to believe in illusions, and that was what 'twould be to think they could ever live in happiness and peace. Even if the Bruce succeeded in wresting Scottish independence from King Edward, there would be years of strife to follow, with both sides struggling to regain or hold power. His life expectancy had already exceeded that of many in this war, and was not likely to extend much further. What could he give her? He had not even a title or lands left to him, only the castle he had managed to wrest back from English hands with great loss and struggle. If not for the citizens of Kinnison who had risen to his defense with pitchforks and scythes, perhaps he would not have even that.

A muffled sob caught in Catherine's throat, and he bent to kiss her, anguished that he could not offer assurance and comfort, torn between what he wanted and what he knew would be. Her lips parted under his, and he tasted the salt of her tears on his tongue. It undid him. His resolve began to fray into tangled threads of apprehension that he would hurt her more by promising the impossible just to ease her sorrow.

So he kissed her more fiercely, grinding his mouth on hers in a kind of desperation. He tried to convey to her the words he could not say, emotions that would likely never be uttered aloud but were so strong at times he felt unmanned by them. Perhaps, one day when he was gone and she thought of him, she would remember how he had touched her, how she had made him tremble with her caress, and she would think kindly of him. It was all he had to hope for in this uncertain, precarious world in which he lived.

When she was trembling beneath him and her hands were moving restlessly from his shoulders to his arms and back, he sat back and gazed down at her. Her face was flushed, lips swollen from his kiss, her eyes fever-bright with passion. Gently, he removed the gold circlet that held the gauzy cloth to her head and pulled them both away to free her hair.

"I love your hair . . . so soft, like silk . . . gold in the candlelight, yet red when the sun shines on it . . ." He drew in an unsteady breath, feeling awkward and clumsy as he undid her plaits to pull the strands free around her shoulders. It waved over the feather-stuffed pillow beneath her head and around her face, framing features like fine porcelain. She was so delicate and fragile in appearance, with a resilience that continually amazed him.

He thought of her at the Jedburgh Abbey, the miles she had walked alone through deep forest and over rocky hills, determination and pure courage driving her on, and it humbled him. Christ. He would make himself crazy like this.

Bending, he kissed her again, softly this time, his mouth moving lightly over hers in the barest of brushes across her lips as he unlaced the side fastenings of her gown. He undressed her slowly, savoring each new revelation of her body as the garments were peeled away, then sat back on his bent legs to gaze at her with admiration and anguish. She lay quietly, her arms bent and her hands nesting in the wealth of hair spread over the pillow beneath her head.

Almost reverently, he drew a hand over the pale mound of her breast, fingers tracing a feathery pattern on her soft skin that made her inhale so sharply her breast quivered. It shuddered beneath his touch, cream and rose beauty beckoning to him, and he bent to rake his tongue over the taut nipple in a slow, heated glide that earned him another gasp of appreciation. Cupping both her breasts in his palms, he lavished first one and then the other with attention until her nipples were tightly beaded and her skin was flushed. Tiny blue veins marbled the lucent flesh with delicate tracery, and he sketched each one with his finger as if trying to memorize them. Perhaps he was.

Her lips parted and the tip of her tongue wet them; a pang of desire bolted through him with riveting intensity. "Alex. . . ."

Soft, wistful, his name on her lips was sweet agony to him, and he kissed her again. Then he stood up beside the bed and shed his garments, not bothering with laces but ripping them free, tossing jerkin, sherte, trews, and boots carelessly to the floor. He throbbed, and the crisp air on his bare skin did nothing to cool his ardor.

The mattress cushioned his weight as he moved over her and into her uplifted arms. Her hands stroked his bare shoulders, the muscles in his arms as he braced himself with a hand pressing into the bed on each side of her, and he slowly lowered to kiss her again. He straddled her body with a knee on each side of her, her pale thighs pressing against his inner legs with arousing contact. As he kissed her, she moved her hands between them to slide over his belly, and his muscles contracted involuntarily at her touch. With light, teasing caresses, she explored the ridge of his ribs and then his belly again, palms slipping over his skin with flagrant eroticism that grazed his tumescent sex and sent a shock wave through him. He groaned against her lips and she circled him with cool fingers that tightened, then relaxed again in erratic convulsions that made him shudder.

"God . . . catkin. . . ." His murmured fervor faded into a wordless groan.

It was quiet in the chamber, where the noise from the bailey outside could be heard only dimly, the faint clatter of horses and clang of weapons, an occasional shout that rose and then receded, a fusion of sounds that meant nothing and everything, the ramifications unspoken and indisputable: Life is fragile and uncertain.

Catherine shivered under the renewed contact of Alex's body against hers as he pressed himself into the welcoming embrace of her thighs. Her hand fell away when he pushed into her body with a fierce thrust. She arched to meet him. His breath was harsh and swift, rasping into the close air between them as he took her with long shuddering strokes that made her cry out. Braced with his hands on each side of her, his arms trembled with the strain as he rocked against her in unbridled turbulence.

On a half sob, Catherine whispered, "I love you. . . ." Then her words were swallowed by the rising emotion that filled her heart and throat as she clung to him, shivering under the raw, almost violent friction of their bodies, striving for the release that seemed to hover just out of her reach . . . it felt as if she were in the midst of a storm, buffeted by emotion and the hard, driving rhythm of his body as he filled her with deep thrusts that brought her ever closer to the edge.

Yet still she did not feel close enough to him, even with his weight a tangible pressure and his hard body inside her . . . she yearned for the evidence that he cared, something that would truly fill the emptiness inside her. It eluded her, leaving her despairing and famished for the words that would ease her soul.

So, too, did physical release evade her, lost in the torment of her fears and the ache in her heart, so that when he reached his own pleasure she just clung to him with her face pressed tight against his damp skin. He held her, his breath a harsh rasp against her ear, then rolled to his side and pulled her with him, his hand on her hip. Slowly, his breathing returned to normal. She could feel him staring at her in the murky gloom of candle glow and shadows, but would not look up.

"Catkin. . . ." When she pressed her face harder against him, he hooked a finger beneath her chin and tilted her face up to him. "What is it?"

How could she tell him? How could she say that she had hoped he would say he loved her too when she had finally drummed up the courage to say it first? Was her conviction that he loved her wrong? Had she only deceived herself?

So to hide her disappointment, she swallowed hard and murmured a lie. "I am afraid to go with you."

Curving his arm, he brought her against him so that her body welded to his from breast to thigh. "Is that what frets you? I will see that you are kept safe, catkin. If you like, I will escort you to Jedburgh Abbey, for the town is still held by the English. Perhaps that would be best, for if I cannot return for you . . ."

She shuddered and shook her head. "Nay, it would be too dangerous. And it is too far out of your way."

He nodded, and stroked a hand through her hair, his fingers threading the loose strands like a comb. He held her in the muscular bend of his arm, idly caressing her, pressing an occasional kiss on her cheek or forehead, murmuring that he would keep her safe, until finally his hand stilled in her hair and on her hip, and his muscles relaxed as he drifted into slumber.

Catherine lay awake long into the night, battling the demons of her soul that tormented her with doubts and fears. But like the legends that told of soldiers springing forth from dragon teeth sown in a fertile field, new doubts sprang up to plague her, so that she was still awake when the candle guttered and the fire died.

21

Torchlight stung her eyes, smelling strongly of pitch. Catherine blinked against it. Despite a lack of sleep, she was tense and wide-awake, her nerves thrumming as she perched atop her mount in the midst of the bailey. Around her was the tumult of men with weapons and fresh horses eager for the coming journey. It was still dark, though the days had grown longer. Soon it would be May, and then the weather would be soft and night would not long linger on the land.

It should be a time to celebrate the passing of the bleak, cold days of winter, but instead it was a time of preparation. Fields lay fallow, the men who tilled them conscripted into the service of the Bruce. Husbands left wives behind, sons their mothers, and women stood weeping as they had done since time began and the first men had gone to war, some never to return.

Her throat tightened, and Catherine looked away when a young woman clung weeping to a soldier. She felt very much like doing the same. Yet she could not, even if she had the right to weep for Alex, for the daughter of an earl did not betray such emotion before all. Despite her situation, she knew her station, and would not shame herself or Alex.

He came to her, striding across the bailey with a reckless grin on his face, his eyes alight with pleasure, and she wanted to cry out with frustration. Did he not care that he may die in this war? Ah, God, what would she do if he did, for she did not think she could bear it.

But she said none of that when he reached her, only nodded calmly when he said she would ride beside him.

"Robbie leaves when the last of the men summoned join him here, and they will catch up to us on the road." He glanced around him. "John Elliot has arrived with a score of men, and we take a score. Robbie will bring near two hundred when he comes. When we all arrive at Torwood Forest, there will be enough men under our standard to make the Bruce proud, and fulfill Douglas's requirements."

"Sir James?" She was surprised, for she had not heard Alex mention that he was to fight with him. He looked back up at her with a slight frown.

"Yea, Black Douglas himself. We will form a division under his command. He summons the men from Lanark, Renfrew, and the Borders to him, and our roll call should be great, though not as numerous as the English."

Every word had the ringing tones of a death knell to her, another reminder of the perils that faced them. Her hands tightened on the reins, her gloves slipping slightly on the leather. She looked down at the palfrey she had been given to ride, a burnished sorrel with a gentle nature.

"It will be good to see him again," she said for lack of any other coherent comment that would hide her fears, and Alex put a hand upon her knee.

"Yea, milady, so it will." He drew in a harsh breath

between his teeth and curled his mailed fist into the cloak covering her. "If aught should happen to me, 'tis to Douglas that you should go. He will see you safely away from danger and Scotland." He looked up at her then from beneath his lashes, a strangely intense gaze that reflected torchlight in the smoky gleam of his eyes as he said softly, "I demand a promise from you, Catherine."

He sounded so serious, and her heart jumped a little at the low significance of his tone. "Demand, sir?" she said with a shaky little laugh. " 'Tis not oft you make demands of me."

"Aye. But this is one I expect you to obey. If it should happen that we are attacked before we reach the Bruce, you will obey me instantly and hide yourself. Should I be the victor, all will be well. But should I fall—nay, do not argue," he cut in harshly when she began to protest, "for I will not be gainsaid in this. Should I fall, you are to throw yourself on the mercy of the English and say that you have been my hostage. Once they learn your father is the Earl of Warfield, they will know the rest of it quick enough and see that you are returned to him. Do not try to aid me, or show yourself, but remain hidden where I put you, or so help me, if I still live, I will take great pleasure in treating you as a husband treats his errant wife and beat you until you are unable to sit or lie in comfort. Now swear to me that you will obey."

Irate, she glared at him. "I was not in the habit of obeying my father, sir, so I see no reason why you wouldst think I will obey you. But"—she put up a hand to ward off his angry interruption—"as it will no doubt distract you in a fight to think I might come to harm if I do not remain hidden, I will do so—at your *request*."

Outrage was reflected in his eyes and his mouth thinned into a taut slash. "By all that is holy, Lady Catherine, if you do not swear to me that—"

"Hold." She tightened the reins and her palfrey gave a skittish jump that removed Alex's hand from her knee. She stared down at him coolly. "Do not make idle threats, Alex Fraser, for I do not stomach them well." Pent-up anger and frustration burned her, and she returned hot stare for hot stare until he swore softly beneath his breath.

"Christ above . . . if 'tis what 'twill take to wrest an oath from you, I will respectfully *request* that you swear to me you will do as I bid you do."

She smiled sweetly. "On my honor as Lady Catherine of Warfield and subject of King Edward, I do swear to you, sir, that I will obey your commands should we be attacked."

Resentment simmered in his eyes and tone. "If you find it that easy, I see no need for your delay."

"Sir, I see no need for your demand, when all that was required from you was courtesy."

He drew in another harsh breath, but an unwilling smile touched the corners of his mouth. "Check?"

An answering smile curved her lips upward. "Aye, and checkmate, sir."

He laughed then, shaking his head. "You sorely try my patience, catkin, but I find it difficult to remain angry with your impertinence."

Their argument had relieved some of her tension, and Catherine sat silently as Alex mounted his huge destrier and spoke to his men in Gaelic. They rode from Castle Rock just as the sun broke from beneath an outcropping of jagged rocks, splinters of light piercing the sky and staining it crimson and gold. A crisp breeze blew, carrying on the currents the scent of morning fires and fresh bread, and as they rode through the narrow, twisting streets of Kinnison, she wondered if she would ever see the village again.

No doubt, many of the men with them wondered the same, for they rode quietly along the rutted track that led north to Torwood Forest, where the Bruce waited with a growing army. The clatter of hooves against hard-packed dirt and muck was constant, and the metallic clank of weapons and jangle of horse harness announced their progress through small villages and quiet wood. Sunlight flirted with clouds and shadows chased them over broad fields and steep rocky crags.

When they forded the Esk River, Catherine's horse shied at the rushing water, and Alex leaned from his huge destrier to grasp the bridle and tug the palfrey forward. The water was unexpectedly shallow, yet the gentle mare blew and snorted nervously as they crossed. Clambering up on the opposite bank, the horse stood trembling when Alex released the bridle. Then his destrier swung its great head, snapping at the mare savagely, and Alex jerked his reins to curb the beast.

Catherine thought of Nicholas and his frequent warnings to be 'ware of a warhorse's temper, and she pulled her mare away from the destrier's reach. "I fear your horse is sadly lacking in proper manners with a lady, sir," she said when Alex cast her a sidelong glance. "My beast is gentle and fearful."

"Unlike her rider." Alex grinned when she lifted her brows at him. "I feared earlier that you would savage me if I did not heed your rebuke."

"I might have." She nudged her palfrey into a trot and away from Alex, saying over her shoulder, "I still may."

He laughed, and she fought the sudden wave of love that overpowered her at times, making her yearn to tell him of her heart's desire. There would be a time, if God and fate were kind, that she could say again what was in her heart. Next time, it would not be in the throes of passion, but with unfettered clarity, and he would have no choice but to listen—and to answer. It was the last thing that she both feared and yearned for, for any answer was better than uncertainty.

Nicholas, Lord Devlin, strode the ramparts of Berwick impatiently. Curse them, what was the delay? He was ready to leave, weary of marshaling foodstuffs rather than men. An embargo had been put on the export of food, and over two hundred four-horse and eight-oxen carts had been drafted from various sheriffdoms to make up the wagon train that would provision the king's army. To his chagrin, he had been put in charge of procuring the supplies.

But as reward, Hereford had managed to obtain for him the king's promise that when the coming battle was over, he would grant him the lands of Castle Rock and Kinnison. King Edward grew expansive as he lingered at Berwick to await the coming conflict, and dealt out the patrimonies of Scottish gentry that he expected to soon gain. Already, the king had allotted the vast lands of Thomas Randolph, Earl of Moray, to the son of his close adviser, Hugh Despenser the younger, and other plum prizes to those of his followers who pleased him. This optimism was shared by most of the knights and barons, many of whom had brought with them household furnishings such as tapestries, furniture, and even baronial plate to refurbish the houses Edward had already promised them.

Despite a fierce desire to have Castle Rock just for the pleasure of razing it to a pile of rubble, Nicholas was uneasy at the confidence of the English army. It worried him, for none of them seemed to remember how viciously the Scots could fight. He did. It was sharply etched on his mind with every skirmish, every savage fray he had survived. There were times he was certain he would be killed, and in truth, he did not know why he yet lived.

Possibly to right the wrong that had been done his sister.

His sword scraped loudly against the wall of the tower staircase as he descended the steps to the bailey, his stride swift and determined. He saw Beakin waiting for him at the gate. A fine mist settled on his bare head and face as he beckoned for the man to come with him, and they moved to a sheltered arch beneath the wall.

"Fraser rides at last, my lord." Beakin's sharp eyes peered at him from beneath the metal noseguard of his helmet. "He has an army with him, and they ride north."

"Is she with him?"

"Yea, my lord. You were right. He did not leave her behind."

No, he would not, not after the last time he had left Castle Rock and the earl had attacked. Fraser was too smart to leave temptation behind in a poorly guarded fortress. He looked back at Beakin and nodded curtly.

"Tell me the route they use, and where we can meet the men you left to follow them."

"They crossed the Esk, so will most like try to skirt the Pentland Hills and go by way of Moffat, Lanark, and Motherwell. To my mind, an ambush could be laid between Moffat and Lanark. Too close to Motherwell, and you run the risk of falling into a nest of Scots."

"Will I have time to get there?"

Beakin hesitated. "Mayhap, milord. If your horses are swift and the Scots few."

Nicholas nodded grimly. The anticipation of action eased the constant irritation he had suffered of late, and he gladly put a heavy purse in Beakin's outstretched palm. "The rest you will get when we intercept Alex Fraser."

Beakin grinned, showing a row of blackened teeth. "Aye, milord. But do not be surprised if he is caught, trussed up and ready for you when we find them, for the men I left are in no mood to dally."

"As long as my sister is unharmed, I do not care what they do to Fraser." He thought a moment, then added in a soft voice that earned him a wary glance from Beakin, "But I hope he is still alive when I get to him, for I intend to lesson him on what it means to goad me."

"Aye, milord. Do we ride?"

"Yea, I have been waiting on your report. All is in readiness."

It occurred to him as he went to inform Hereford of his absence that he was taking a great chance in riding so deep into enemy territory. But it may well be the only chance he had for retrieving Catherine and killing Alex Fraser, and he did not intend to let it pass. Not now. Not after all these frustrating months of delay and careful negotiation. He was done with that.

And if he succeeded in recovering his sister, he fully intended to attend the executions of Adam de Brus and James Fraser, for it would be little enough recompense for what had been done to his lands. For de Brus, he had no regret, for the man was full-grown and knew the risks. But with the youth, there was a certain amount of reluctance, for Jamie Fraser had been too young to realize the perils of war. He had his brother to thank for that, he supposed, for it was what Scots ate along with their meat—hatred and vengeance. It would not be pleasant to visit such a fate on young Fraser, but he would not be the first innocent to die in this strife between Scotland and England. Nor would he be the last.

Nicholas waited tensely for the Scots to pass, motioning to the men behind him to remain silent. They hid in a thick copse of trees in the valley of the Clyde east of Biggar, watching the road below and the steady stream of Scottish soldiers. He began to wonder if any of the king's barons realized just how many Scots were answering Bruce's call to arms. A few were just peasants armed with crude weapons, but most were landed knights and barons who brought with them well-armed men and trained soldiers instead of the ill-fitted rabble they had been led to expect.

Still, it would be surprising if Bruce's army numbered even one-half of King Edward's, for a host of knights from Brittany, France, Poitou, Guinenne, and Germany swelled the ranks of their force. While the earls of Lancaster, Warwick, Surrey, and Arundel had not answered Edward's summons in person, they would each send their feudal obligations of a quota of cavalry and footmen. Also along with the veterans of King Edward I's campaigns was a knight oft described as the third best champion in all of Christendom. It was said that Edward II had ransomed Sir Giles d'Argentan from the Emperor of Byzantium, who held him prisoner, for an enormous sum. A surprising number of Scots arrayed on Edward's side as well, among them the expected John Comyn, son of the "Red" Comyn whom Bruce had murdered, and the former Scottish guardian Ingram de Umfraville and his brother the Earl of Angus. An impressive array, indeed, and more than enough to annihilate the Scots in battle.

Yet the Scots going to meet Bruce near Stirling made travel perilous for Devlin and his men, and slowed them so that he fretted he would not reach Fraser before Beakin's men set up the ambush. He wanted to be there, and would have been there now had Hereford not balked. Curse him. The earl had also dallied far too long in conducting a petition to the king to ransom Catherine, and so had let slip away any chance she might have had. For when Alex Fraser began to so ruthlessly harry northern England, the king refused to consider any clemency for his brother. It was a miracle de Brus and young Fraser were still alive, and a credit to him instead of Hereford that he had managed to convince the king to stay their executions until after the coming battle.

Hereford's laughter after the unpleasant interview with Edward had been unkind and nasty. "Had you not such a pretty face, my lord Devlin, you would not have gained concession."

It angered him, but he needed Hereford's favor and did not let it show. Shrugging, he had replied that for whatever reason, he was glad. "To execute them now would invite a dire fate for Lady Catherine."

"Do you think so?" Hereford's brow had lifted with languid amusement. "A Scots bastard in her belly, perhaps. You and your sister are both too pretty to suffer too dire a fate. Ah, do not look so harshly at me, Devlin, for 'tis the truth. The king was most taken with you." He'd paused, then laughed again. "Yea, a dire fate indeed, I vow, for we have all seen what happens to the king's favorites."

Nicholas still smarted from that conversation. He needed no reminders of the fate of Piers Gaveston, the king's murdered favorite. It was said Edward still harbored a fierce grudge against the Earl of Lancaster for the deed, and only bided his time to retaliate. For now, Lancaster's quota of cavalry and footmen were sorely needed.

"M'lord." Beakin snared his attention, pointing to the road below. " 'Tis clear. Shall we ride?"

"Yea, for we have wasted much time already waiting

on Scots to pass. Curse them. By the time we reach the troop following Fraser, they will no doubt be done and gone, and I will not be cheated of my satisfaction."

Putting spurs to horses, the troop rode from the wooded copse and into the valley of the Clyde River that wound through green hills and rugged slopes. Not far distant was a keep loyal to the English, one that had been held by Edward since 1311. There, Nicholas was certain, he could leave Catherine safely until he was able to escort her to England himself. Once this was all over, he would see that she was allowed to retire to a nunnery as she had once wished to do. It would be the best resolution, for now she would never be able to make a proper marriage, and the earl would never forgive her.

But still, his heart was heavy at the prospect, and he was bitter at the vagaries of fate.

22

Rain fell softly, pattering on leaves and ground, making mud of the narrow road they traveled. Alex turned to glance behind him. Catherine huddled in her cloak like a little wren with feathers fluffed against the wet gusts that blew through the valley. She bore the travails well, not complaining when the rain slashed down on them or they slept on the ground. There was no time to erect tents or travel comfortably, for the English waited for the unwary.

They followed the Tweed River north, crossing hills and fording near Broughton on their way to Biggar. Beyond, the land dipped into the lush, verdant valley of the Clyde that still showed traces of the ravages of both armies. English and Scot alike fought for the ground, tugging it back and forth like a dog with a bone.

Most of the English were gone now, save for a few scattered strongholds that had managed to resist or recapture their keeps. Some of these barons were loyal to Edward, many because of long feuds with the Bruce or one of his nobles, others because of extensive holdings in England.

As daylight waned, the weary horses were halted in a thick wood riddled with caves. They sought shelter there rather than risk alerting villages or towns to their presence. With less than fifty men in his company, Alex had no intention of attracting unwanted notice. He had thought Robbie and the others would catch up to them by now, and worried at their delay, as did John Elliot.

Fires were lit inside the mouths of the caves, small ones that would not signal their location. Catherine crouched by a tidy blaze and held out her hands to warm her palms, rubbing them together and looking up with a smile when he approached her.

"Good eventide, Sir Alex. Do we rise with the birds again in the morn, or linger in our blankets like slugs?"

He grinned. "If I choose to linger in my blankets, 'twill not be to play the slug, milady. I could think of more entertaining sport."

"No doubt." A faint flush pinked her cheeks, shaded by the edge of the hood drawn over her hair. Her fingers wiggled against the fire's heat. "But 'tis not private enough for the sport you prefer. I do not care to have two score onlookers observe our intimacy."

"No? Odd little catkin." He knelt on one knee beside her, his voice low and intimate. "What if I told you we could find privacy nearby? Wouldst thou then consider a bit of sport with me, milady?"

She looked at him askance, though he could see by the heightened flush in her face and gleam in her eyes that she was intrigued. It was one more thing that endeared her to him, this natural, open reception instead of coy delay and protests. What had been only an idle jest became earnest, and his blood quickened when she gave him a small, secret smile and nodded.

"Aye, if you can find any privacy in this wild land, I will be pleased to join you, sir."

He glanced around. Finding privacy should be simple enough, but avoiding the notice of his men would be more difficult. Many still resented Catherine, and he was careful not to present her to them in less than a noble capacity. He had kept his distance from her lest it remind them of what had passed, for any respect they felt for her status as an earl's daughter would be diluted then, and make her seem too accessible. It was a fine line he walked, made doubly difficult by the fact that all knew he had taken her to his bed. But he would not tolerate insults directed at her, and it would only cause trouble if he were forced to punish any man who dared. So to avoid conflict with men who needed to keep their minds on the coming battle instead of on past confrontations, he had to be discreet. Very discreet.

"Do you not feel the need for personal privacy, catkin?"

Immediately, she grasped his meaning and nodded. "Yea, 'tis true that I am in need of some privacy, sir. Which way do you think I should go?"

"Perhaps a little east, as I saw a secluded ravine not far away that is blooming with small yellow flowers and thick vines beneath an oak. A most inviting site."

Putting her hands on her knees, she nodded, and the edge of her hood slipped slightly so that loose curls fell free to dangle against her cheek. They glowed like copper silk in the firelight. A faint smile tucked one corner of her mouth inward, and she rose slowly to her feet to gaze down at him where he knelt looking up at her.

"If you will excuse me, Sir Alex, I must depart your company for now."

He stood and gave her a courtly bow. "You have my leave to depart, milady."

Moving away with slow grace, she passed through the mouth of the cave to the shadowed glen beyond. Some of the men's heads turned to watch her pass, then glanced back at him, ever wary of his watchful eye. They were quick, furtive glances, and he ignored them. He kept his gaze on the dancing tongues of fire, low-burning flames that slowly consumed the slender sticks of wood.

When enough time had passed, he moved in the opposite direction of the thicket where Catherine waited, and spoke to John Elliot about the sentries he had posted around the perimeter of the camp. Slowly, he made his way around the men in caves and rolled in blankets on the ground, until he had achieved a half circle. Then he moved down the same path she had trod, into the deep, quiet greenness of the wood around them.

It closed around him like a favorite soft glove, holding him in the palm of silent expectation, and he felt both comforted and excited. The gloom was darker beneath the spreading arms of oak and birch, with his steps muffled by thick layers of fallen leaves. She waited for him at the bower he had described, standing beneath a spray of yellow flowers that looped over her hair like chips of sunlight. He paused, and she smiled.

"Can you smell them?"

"Yea." He moved to her, and she looked up from beneath the cap of dainty blossoms. Pollen dusted her hair in a lacy froth. She wore it loose now, as he liked it, curving around her face in wisps. Reaching out, he touched a dangling tendril with his fingertip, and a delicate bloom drifted free at his touch. "The flowers smell sweet in your hair," he murmured as the scent wafted toward him. "As do you."

She smiled, a slow, languorous curve of her mouth into a seductive agreement. The days were longer now, and fading light graced her face with faint shadows as she studied him in the gloaming. The hood of her cloak was folded on her shoulders, and a carved gold pin held the garment closed at her throat. He lifted his arm to unfasten the pin, but she caught his hand, her voice a low murmur.

"Let me, sir."

Smiling a little, his hand fell away as he watched her. Her slender fingers were pale against the dark wool of the cloak, working to unfasten the pin. Then the edges of the cloak parted, and he drew in a sharp breath of surprise and instant arousal.

Beneath the cloak, she wore only her pride, and he stood in stunned silence and admiration for what seemed an eternity. Outlined against the black fabric, her body seemed to shimmer with ivory enchantment. Gauzy shafts of ephemeral light trickled through the canopy of trees and gleamed with final fading beauty on her skin and in her hair. Her breasts were alabaster crowned with rose, her waist a feminine curve to slender thighs and a silky nest of copper curls. His mouth went dry, and he moved at last with a jerky step forward.

"You are beautiful, catkin . . . so bloody beautiful . . . I do not think I can . . . God, do you know how you look standing there like that, with your hair unbound and your body open to me?" A groan came from deep within his chest, and he felt a peculiar ache begin to spread and grow. "A pagan goddess. Like the ancients . . . they would build a temple to honor you."

"Alex. . . ."

It was soft, a little shaky, but filled with an emotion he tried not to hear, and he knew suddenly that he could not listen or he would be destroyed. If he let her say it, he would become too distracted from his purpose to be of use to the Bruce, and all would be lost. If she loved him, he would be too loath to leave her as he knew he must do.

So he moved to her and slid his arms around her,

crushing her to him and slamming his mouth down over hers with a desperate ferocity that abolished everything but the moment. The fragrance of sweet flowers filled the air, and her skin was soft as velvet beneath his hands. He lifted her, pushing her against the broad trunk of the tree behind her, reveling in the little sound of shock and pleasure she made. Then he leaned into her, pulling her legs around his waist and lifting the edge of his plaid. He plunged into her with a powerful thrust, and she gasped.

It was madness, exultation, arrant sensuality as he held her astride him, her back cushioned by the cloak behind her, the tree a solid brace for his thrusts. Her breath grew faster against his ear, her cries muffled by his sherte, and she bucked into his pounding lunges. His arms cradled her thighs, and her ankles were locked behind his waist as she strained against him. Swiftly, fiercely, they reached the end at the same moment, his back arching as he hammered into her in one final convulsive thrust, and dimly heard her sobbing cry as she clutched him.

Panting, he leaned his head forward into the fragrant mass of hair and spring flowers, using the sturdy oak to hold himself up. She still clung to him, her legs quivering around his waist, her breath gradually slowing.

Then, with a soft little laugh, she said into his ear, "Now I know why you enterprising Scots wear nothing beneath your plaids. . . ."

Helplessly, he began to laugh with her, holding her close to his heart, drained of passion but not tenderness. It did not ease him to know that he would miss her most in the days to come. No one had ever touched the part of him that she did, and he was baffled and chagrined that the woman who finally mattered to him was the daughter of his worst enemy. Fate was perverse, and he could see no future for them.

Pulling back, he eased her down, tugging the edges of the cloak around her and pressing his lips to her forehead. "What folly, to lie in wait for me this way, catkin. What if another had come upon you here?"

"I would not have opened my cloak, sir."

Her prim retort made him laugh again, and he nuzzled the top of her hair with his chin. "Catkin, ah, God, catkin." It came out in a sigh, and he could not speak for several moments at the surge of emotion that filled him. Then he murmured as he lay his cheek against the crown of her head, "Did you know that a catkin is the carnal member of a plant, my sweet? Within it lie all the special powers to bloom, to flower and share the beauty that will renew life. As do you."

Her voice was muffled against his sherte. "I am not certain 'tis flattering to be regarded so, but I do know that I have blossomed since meeting you." She shifted so that her head tilted back, and looked into his eyes. Her hand came up to touch his face, fingers light against the scar that curved along his cheekbone. "You are everything I should fear, yet I do not. With you, I feel whole. Rare. None other has ever made me feel this way, or ever will."

Intense yearning swept over him, and he longed to tell her how he felt, longed to take her into his arms and say they would never be apart, but he could not. It would be cruel, and it would be wrong. So he just held her and said nothing, his arms around her as if he would never let her go. The serenity of the forest enveloped them in the soft sound of wind through the treetops and the quiet murmur of birds. Nearby a small burn trickled through the ravine that cut a path through fern and moss, and the light tinkling of water was sweet serenade as he held her and wished for what would never be.

Shadows lengthened and grew dark, yet they remained in the fragrant bower together, clasped in each other's embrace, cushioned by the spongy layer of moss that grew in the small hollow beneath the oak and vines. Seated with his back against the trunk of the tree, he held her to him in contentment and gratitude for this brief moment of solace. God knew, there was little enough of it in his world.

He must have dozed. No other reason would there be for his lack of attention when the distant muted shouts finally penetrated to jerk him to alarm. Shoving Catherine aside, he leaped to his feet, cursing beneath his breath at his folly. He knew better than to relax his vigilance for even a moment, yet he had allowed himself to be distracted by the sweet softness of the maid and his own powerful urges.

Shaking her, he hissed, "Stay here. Dress yourself, and hide beneath the vines. Do not move until I come for you."

Blinking sleepily, her hand clutched him in the dense blackness where no light penetrated. "Alex—what is wrong?"

"Remember your oath to me." He hugged her fiercely, then shoved her into the tangled web of thick vines and yellow flowers and grabbed his sword. "Stay hidden, as you promised me."

Without waiting to see that she obeyed, he spun around and left, moving toward the source of the din that was now discernible in chilling clarity. Swords met swords with brittle clashes, and men shouted in the familiar language of savage battle. There was no time for regrets, no time for misgivings, only the rushing surge of blood and battle fever that carried him into the fray.

It became quickly apparent that they were outnumbered and taken by surprise, but still they fought, not giving quarter, not relenting, for to do so would be to die.

The English overpowered them, scattering men and horses into the inky depths of the wood. A few escaped, following John Elliot. Alex saw them flee as he fought viciously, thrusting and parrying with his sword like a man possessed, filled with anger and anguish that he had not been ready for their attack.

But finally they were beaten back, the pitiful remnants of his men bloodied and few, panting in the fitful light of campfires. Alex stood with his gory sword in hand, knowing they were surrounded and beaten, cursing himself for it.

One of the English came forward, grinning a little in the feeble light. "Aye, ye do not look so brave now, Scots bastard!"

Alex did not move or reply, but stood numbly when his sword was taken from him and his arms bound behind him with rough rope. The leader beckoned, and he was dragged to him to stand in the light of a rekindled fire. Flames danced and grew higher, and Alex tensed as he saw the metal rod laid upon a small stone to heat.

Noting his glance, the man grinned. " 'Tis a small persuasion should it be needed. Where is the maid?"

Alex did not blink, but it came to him in a bitter rush of hatred that Warfield was behind this ambush. "What maid do you mean?"

"Do not play the fool, Fraser. I know who you are, and you must know who sent me after you. We wouldst take the maid back, though why his lordship wants her after she has been tainted by Scots scum is beyond my ken." He reached up to sweep off his metal helmet, then turned back to Alex with a light shrug when he remained silent. "It makes no difference to me if you tell us now or after we have applied the iron, but 'twill be easier on you if you yield her up. We will have her anyway, and return her in much the same shape as we find her." His laugh was nasty. "A little more used, perhaps, but that should not matter to a woman who has lain with Scots."

Any inclination he may have had to put Catherine into her father's hands instantly faded. Not through this man. He prayed that she would not listen to him this time, that she would not throw herself on the mercy of the English as he had bade her do.

"If I had the lady," he said after a moment, watching as a man knelt by the fire to turn the metal rod in the flames until it glowed bright red, "I would give her to you. I do not."

"You lie. We know you have her, for we saw her only two days past in your company. Where is she?"

The last was said with soft menace, and Alex swallowed hard as the metal rod was drawn from the flames and held up. The end of it radiated heat. He looked back at the leader.

"I do not know. She escaped into the woods yesterday, and we could not find her."

His lie was not believed, as he had known it would not be. The leader laughed softly, and ripped open Alex's sherte to bare his chest. "Fool."

Tensing, he kept his eyes on the leader as the other man approached with the hot iron. Fear coiled in his belly, sickening and weakening, and he wanted to open his mouth and blurt the truth. But he did not. Not even when the searing pain of the iron across his taut muscles arched his body and he clenched his teeth to keep from giving them the satisfaction of crying out. Twice the brutal iron scored his chest, and he did not yield.

Panting, he watched with crawling dread as the iron was placed into the flames again to reheat. His tormentor reached out to grasp him by the hair and jerk back his head.

"Where is the maid of Warfield?"

His guts tightened, instinctively reacting to the menace in the demand. His hands twisted against the ropes tightly binding his wrists, and he shook his head as he wished he were somewhere—anywhere—else.

"The maid is gone, I told you."

His voice sounded hoarse and all wrong, and the world around him was perceived only through a haze of pain; his men dead on the ground, English moving about in black silhouette against the light of fires, laughter and boasting of victory . . . but above it all, the knowledge that he could not yield up Catherine to these men.

Yet when the iron was drawn across his shrinking flesh and the agony blazed a trail over his belly, he feared he would tell all and bit down on his lip until blood ran warm down his jaw and neck to mingle with the raw wounds on his chest. He could stand it. He had to. But he had not thought his life would end like this, with the ignominy of torture making of him a cringing, writhing creature instead of a man.

No, no . . . ah, Lord have mercy on me and release me. . . .

It became a fervent prayer, held tight behind lips pressed closed as his body moved involuntarily away from the licking tongue of the hot iron. Through the blur of torment, he heard one of the men say that the Scot would not tell them. His chief tormentor laughed harshly.

"He will confess her whereabouts. Once I do this. . . ."

To his horror, Alex felt the edge of his plaid lifted and the cool night air whisk over his bare thighs and groin, and he knew what was intended. With a cruel smile, the leader grabbed him hard and held him in his palm, squeezing until the world dimmed around him. Just behind him loomed the red-hot iron, waiting.

"Now, me hearty, you will tell us what we want to know, by God."

Lord have mercy . . . Christ have mercy . . . I will tell . . . I will tell all. . . .

23

--- ⚜ ---

Huddled amid the tangle of vines and flowers beneath the oak, Catherine waited. The noise had long since ceased. Yet Alex did not come for her. Terrified, more for him than for herself, she crouched in the dark that clothed her like sable velvet and prayed. If he did not come, what should she do? He had told her to remain there until he came for her, and if he did not, she was to throw herself on the mercy of her country-men.

Yet she debated. It was impossible that he might be defeated. Alex was strong, invincible, a mighty warrior with a stout heart. He would not be vanquished.

As the night wore on and she remained hidden and miserable in what was becoming a prison of fragrant flowers and soft moss, Catherine knew she could no longer delay the inevitable. If nothing else, she must see for herself the results of the terrible noise she had heard, the shouts and screams and dying cries of men.

Rising to her feet, she stood on trembling legs for a moment as the blood rushed back into veins and muscles too long cramped. She brushed away leaves from the blue velvet nap of the gown Alex had given her as a replacement for her own, then tied the cloak more tightly around her throat. The cloak pin was lost, tumbled among the upthrust tree roots and vines when she had unfastened it earlier. Pulling the hood over her head, she moved toward the camp she had left behind what seemed an eternity before.

She had not gone far when out of the dark thicket a man suddenly loomed to grab her by the arm. Swallowing a terrified squeak of alarm, she immediately brushed aside his hand and said in her haughtiest tone, "Release me, knave! I will not be handled."

Though she expected him to grab her again, he did not, but peered at her in the dark shadows. "What is your name, milady?"

"Lady Catherine of Warfield. I demand to see your commander at once."

He laughed softly, and grinned at her in the gloom. "Aye, milady, and he will be most glad to see you. Come with me."

Her fear heightened with every step, for the man was English and therefore the outcome of the battle could not be good. Yet she held her head high and forced confidence into her step as she moved with him through the night, her heart pounding painfully in her chest.

A group of men stood by a blazing fire, their backs to her as they clustered in a tight circle. She glanced at them, then away as a familiar voice cried out.

"Catherine! Ah, God, kitten, is it you?"

Blinking, she turned toward the man approaching her, disbelief rising in her as Nicholas strode across the battle-littered ground to sweep her against him. He pressed her face tightly into his chest, and his voice was rough with emotion.

"Ah, sweet kitten, I thought never to see you again. Are you well? Unharmed? How did you free yourself?"

Confused by his appearance, and most of all consumed with terror for Alex, she pulled away from him. "I am most well, Nicky, but what are you doing here? Where is Alex?"

"It has taken me longer than it should have, for I only just arrived, but I was finally able to get here. Fraser is being . . . questioned, but now that you are here safe and alive, there is no more need for that. He can meet the fate I have longed to—"

"Nay!" Her fierce, agonized cry rose high into the air and turned heads toward them. "Where is he? God help you if you have harmed him, for I will see your blood spilled for it!"

Nicholas stared down at her in white-lipped fury. His blue eyes were almost black with rage and disgust. "So you still have not come to your senses. I had thought by now you would see the kind of man he is."

"Yea, I see it well, which is why I ask for him. Where is he, Nicholas?"

He did not reply, but there was no need as her glance swept past him to the group of men by the fire and she saw a familiar plaid. The blood rushed from her face to pool in her stomach, and she thought she would be sick as she saw the evidence of what had been done to Alex in the crimson and black streaks across his bare chest. Unconscious, he sagged in the tight grip of two men holding him up, and as her gaze lowered and she saw the plaid awry over his thighs, a new horror gripped her and she cried out with anguish.

Nicholas grabbed her arm and leaned close to hiss in her ear, "One word of betrayal before my men and so help me God he will die before another word passes your lips."

She believed him. Instantly, she hushed, but quivered so badly he had to hold her up. Softly, she said, "Release him."

"Nay, sweet sister, I will not do that even for you."

"Nicky. . . ." The broken plea stilled on her lips as his fingers tightened painfully around her arm. Summoning a strength she did not know she possessed, she looked up at her beloved brother, a man she thought she knew, and said with quiet promise, "If you do not cease this torment of him, I will tell one and all that I lay in his arms with a willing heart and naked body, and I will shout from the rooftops of every town from Berwick to London that I love Sir Alex Fraser with every fiber of my being. How will your pride bear that?"

It was evident from his taut features that he would not bear it well, and he confirmed it with a short jerk of his head. "His torment will cease for now, but you cannot alter his fate, Catherine. Do not try."

She drew in a deep, quivering breath. It was all she could hope for at the moment. Nicholas released her arm, and she stood still and sick as he strode to the men by the fire and Alex was freed to sprawl upon the ground. She wanted to go to him, but feared that Nicholas would prevent it and that such an act would make things worse for Alex. She waited, and when finally her brother came back to her, she went silently with him across torn earth that was stained with blood in places. Dead Scots were shoved aside, and she could not bear to look at them. Had it been only a few hours before that these men had laughed and jested with one another? Now they were dead, and she was the cause of that as well.

When Nicholas bade her be seated on a small flat rock just inside the mouth of a cave, she did so without murmur, but fastened her gaze on him as he came to stand by the untended fire. He clasped his hands behind him to stare at her with a brooding expression.

"Why, kitten?" He sounded baffled more than angry now, and she felt a stirring of hope. "Did he bewitch you? Put a potion in your wine?"

"I do not know." She paused as she recognized the opening he offered her. "Perhaps. It is as if I have been in a dream since I left Warfield." *So true, a wonderful dream. . . .*

"I would not put it past the bastard to drug you with something. They say the Scots have access to such knowledge and do not hesitate to use it." He looked at her more closely. "Did your food taste strangely?"

"Yea," she answered with all honesty, "it did. Do you think he used magic on me?"

"Not the magic you may mean, but various enchantments can be effected by certain potions." His jaw tightened. "He should be put to the sword for that alone."

Catherine remained silent, but her hands twisted in her lap. She thought of her mother, and how the countess never betrayed emotion, keeping her expression smooth and unlined despite whatever she might have felt. She would have to be more like her, would have to train herself to keep her thoughts better hidden, or she would be ruined. And Alex would die.

Without inflection, she mused aloud, "I am not one to suffer well the torment of any creature, man or beast. 'Tis my nature, but the past days have been torment for me. Do you think I will recover, if what you say is true, Nicky?"

Conflicting emotion chased across his face for a moment as he regarded her, and she thought perhaps she had erred. But then he shrugged, and there was a soft relief in his tone as he assured her that no doubt she would.

"If 'tis true that you were given herbs to render you susceptible to his will, then no doubt you will completely recover in a few days' time. It has been known to happen. The Turks are adept with such potions, and many were brought back from the Crusades to be used against honest people."

Bending her head, Catherine nodded. A thousand different ideas flew at her like bats in the night, all swiftly considered and rejected. Whatever she did, she would have to proceed with caution, or she would ruin all. It was painful to think she must deceive Nicholas, when all he had done was love her, but where Alex Fraser was concerned he would not yield. Therefore, she must do what it took to save Alex. This time there was no other choice for her.

Ahead rose the bannered turrets of Bothwell keep, thrusting into the bright sky like a fist. Catherine perched atop a sorrel palfrey that she had been given to ride, staring straight ahead as they neared the fortress. Nicholas studied her silently. He would like to believe that she would willingly abandon the Scotsman, but could not quite convince himself that it was true. Perhaps it was an attempt to save herself more humiliation now that she was taken, or it could be an attempt to save Fraser. Whichever, he would neither challenge her nor trust her.

A soft wind blew, belling out the hood of her cloak so that her bright hair spilled over her breasts. She had not bound it as usual, but left it free. It tangled in the breeze, but absorbed sunlight to glow like copper silk. She was so lovely, her pale face reflecting nothing of her thoughts or ordeal. If he did not know it to be false, he would think her just a maid out for an afternoon's ride over wooded slopes.

Not by word or gesture had she betrayed any thought

of Alex Fraser, though she had looked away when he had been put still unconscious over the back of a horse to be taken with them. Nor had Fraser yet regained consciousness, though at times he uttered a miserable moan.

Nicholas flinched a little from what had been done to him, but he did not regret it. Fraser should pay, not only for what he had done to Catherine, but what he had done to Devlin lands. Villages had been burnt to the ground, and while it may be true that no man was killed who did not offer armed resistance, it was insupportable that his crops had been ravaged, his livestock driven away, and his people left homeless. It was not the first time, for Robert Bruce had come through his lands two years before and laid waste as well; but the Scots king's act had been an act of war.

Alex Fraser's destruction was personal.

And now he had him at last. He just hoped Fraser lived long enough to face the executioner's grim justice. It would be sweet vengeance to execute both Frasers and de Brus at the same time. That act he would not miss, as he had missed the battle that saw Alex Fraser captured. He had arrived only when it was over, and Beakin's man Percy was already administering hot torment in an effort to discover Catherine's whereabouts.

He shuddered. God help him, he had almost felt sorry for Fraser then as the hot iron was applied. Yet even when being most brutally ravaged by the iron, he had not yielded up the information. At that moment, Nicholas had felt an unwilling admiration for the man's resistance to such cruel persuasion.

But it had done Fraser no good to try to protect her, for Catherine had still been found. It troubled Nicholas, for she had seemed truly horrified when she first saw what had been done to Fraser, then seemed to forget it. Yet she had always been far more tenderhearted than anyone of his acquaintance. That was one reason he had so often sought to keep her sheltered from the harsh truths of the world.

Yet life oft intruded in the most unkind fashion. He glanced at her again, frowning a little as she rode in serene silence, her face like that of a Madonna.

Bothwell loomed ahead, stone ramparts chewing at the sky, and he spurred his mount to a faster pace. His objective was in sight. Once Sir Alex Fraser was incarcerated in Bothwell's dungeons, he would escort Catherine safely away. Nor would he let her out of his sight until he had her back at Warfield, for despite his feud with his father, he knew that she would be safe in that formidable fortress. Only then would he return to see justice done, bringing with him to Edward's court the three prisoners that had so long been coveted.

Unlike his father, it was not power that he wanted, but vengeance. Blood recompense for the wrongs that had been done him by Fraser and the Scots that had ravaged his lands for so long. God willing, he would soon have it.

A challenge was issued by the sentries on the wall of the gatehouse, and when it was answered, the bridge was slowly lowered to allow them entrance. Hooves clattered on thick wooden planks as they crossed, and the grinding of the metal gate being lifted was loud. They passed beneath the jagged teeth of the gate and into a bailey, where their horses were taken.

Nicholas moved to help Catherine, but before he could reach her she had dismounted with dainty grace and stood silently. His hand fell to his side, and he frowned. The castellan of Bothwell Castle, Sir Walter FitzGilbert, came to greet him. A Scot loyal to the English, he gave the orders for the disposal of Devlin's prisoners.

Gesturing toward Alex Fraser, who was half-conscious

now and suspended between two burly men-at-arms, Nicholas said, "Take special care with that one. I want him alive for a while longer."

Grinning, Sir Walter nodded. "Aye, milord. He will be given our best chamber. Double chains?"

"Yea, wrists and ankles. Tether him well, for King Edward will greatly appreciate his presence at an execution soon."

Sir Walter laughed. "There will be many to join him ere long, milord. Once we have finally taken Scotland back from these rebels, every tree will have fresh fruit dangling from ropes."

Nicholas smiled at the jest and moved to take Catherine with him into the keep. Beakin would see to the placement of his men. The man was efficient and conscientious in his duty, a true value to him of late. Not many were left after the depredations visited upon Devlin, but it was Beakin who had rallied what he could of the garrison and gotten them to safety after seeing how it would end. And it was Beakin who had managed to track Alex Fraser and arrange the ambush that netted him the Scot as well as Catherine.

Yet as he escorted his sister up the stone steps to the forework of the keep, he could not help but think that she was not as docile and accepting as she seemed, for there was a taut set to her jaw and an occasional glitter in her eyes that forebode mutiny. He had seen it too often not to recognize it now. Yea, she would have to be closely watched or Alex Fraser might still cheat King Edward's executioner.

24

It hurt to move. It hurt to think. Alex wished sleep would come again, so he could escape the constant torment. At times it felt as if the iron were searing his skin anew, but 'twas only the reopening of a lesion that pained him.

Shifting when the pain grew too bad in one position, the clank of heavy metal chains rattled against the wall next to his ear. Iron manacles circled his wrists and his ankles, with a length of chain stretched between them and fastened to a huge metal ring in the wall behind him. He could move his arms to rest them on the floor, but could not reach his legs below the knee. The stone wall was cold and damp, the straw filthy. Sharp stalks jabbed into his legs in tiny annoying pricks, and occasionally found a raw welt or open abrasion.

While he regretted his capture and the loss of good men, he worried most about Catherine. Despite the assurance of a slow death, if he had to be taken, he was glad it was by Lord Devlin, and that he had come upon them before it was too late. Devlin would ensure that his sister was safe, and that was the best possible fate left for her now. He was as good as dead, and so were Jamie and certainly Adam de Brus. He dreaded the death that awaited him, for it would be the same grisly end as had been visited upon William Wallace, three of Robert Bruce's brothers, and countless Scots earls and barons. He would much prefer dying in battle than for the entertainment of kings, nobles, and common crowds.

But the choice was no longer his. There would be no quarter given. No regrets asked.

And yet, and yet . . . he could not stop a deep stab of regret that he had not told Catherine how he felt about her. It would be foolish to have done so, for he had always known how it would end, but there would be a certain solace in saying the words aloud to her. Too late now, of course.

Had she seen what they did to him? He hoped not. Though he had not cried out, clenching his teeth until his tongue was too swollen to use anyway, it was a shaming thing to have lost the battle and been rendered so helpless. It was not the way he would have her remember him—fainting from the agony of the hot iron on tender flesh. If Devlin had not arrived when he did, no doubt Percy would have unmanned him ere long.

Resting his head against the wall behind him, he stared up at the gloom of the ceiling. Faint light streamed through bars high up on the wall, and in the bailey outside his cell he heard the distant sounds of voices and laughter. He was alone. None of his men were near, and he wondered if he was the only survivor or if the others had already been executed. This slow, agonizing wait was worse than ten deaths.

Ah, Christ above, would Catherine come to see him executed? He prayed she would not. He would like to see her just one more time, to tell her that he loved her. And if she loved him, he would ask her to grant him the mercy of refusing to watch him die. But that was impossible. She would never be allowed so close to him.

The bars of light crawled across the cell floor as the sun rose higher, until they slanted over his face and he blinked against them. It was the only time of day that he felt, even for a brief moment, the warmth of the sun. Too swiftly, it would leave and he would be in darkness again. There was a comparison to his life somewhere in that gloomy thought, he mused wryly. Infrequent splashes of warmth all too swiftly taken away: his mother and father. Jamie. Christian and Sarah. Catherine . . . not, perhaps, as the others had been taken away, but gone to him just as finally.

Footsteps sounded in the corridor outside his cell and he turned his head toward the door, always expecting the key in the lock that would signal the beginning of the end. Food came once a day, just after first light, but never any visitors, so the days were long as he waited for the moment when he would be taken out to his death. His muscles tensed painfully as the steps drew near, then paused outside his door. A knot formed in his belly, icy cold and hot at the same time, and when he heard the metallic click of the lock's tumblers, he knew that his wait was at an end.

But when the door opened, no jailer or soldiers stood there to drag him up, but a cloaked figure in sweeping finery and smelling of flowers. He blinked, and the sunlight blinded him as he turned his head slightly to better view the visitor. But the moment she moved inside, he knew.

Catherine. . . .

Chagrin filled him, that she should see him like this, filthy in a bed of straw with his body befouled and stinking from his ordeal. Even worse, she smelled so fresh and clean even from the doorway, and her garments were new and immaculate as she swept into the cell in a rustle of velvet slippers over matted clumps of straw. She was holding a lace ball to her nose, and it was that he smelled as she moved toward him—a pomander such as those sold at the fairs, perfumed for ladies and gentlemen to ward off the foul odors of the city.

"Hold, milady," the guard said gruffly when she drew close to him. "I got me orders, and there is to be no familiarity with the prisoner."

Pushing back the hood to her cloak, Catherine turned to the guard and smiled sweetly. "Yea, sir, so I understand. Do you really think I want to be familiar with this . . . thing?"

The last was said with such loathing and contempt that it hit Alex hard, as if the words were a blow to the belly. The fierce rush of gladness he'd felt at seeing her altered to a wary tension as she laughed.

"La, sir, I but came to see the fierce Scots prisoner who has so abused many good English, as I told you. If you fear, perhaps more coin will ease your fright?"

The guard flushed angrily. "Nay, milady, 'tis not for coin that I fear, but that he might harm you."

"With you standing here? I would not fear ten of him as long as I knew you were there with your sword, sir. You do seem to be a man most capable of dealing with the enemy. Are you not?"

Some of the guard's anger eased, and he shrugged as he slid a glance toward Alex. "I could get into much trouble were it known that I allowed you to badger me into coming here. Lord Devlin gave strict orders you were to be watched closely at all times."

Catherine pressed the pomander to her nose and breathed deeply. "And so you shall watch me, sir. I do not want to be left alone with this man, for it would frighten me, after all that I have already endured." She turned slightly to face Alex, and said softly, "I only came to tell this man how much I detest him, how I abhor all things Scottish, and most of all—how I hate him."

Some of the light falling across his face shifted as he turned his head, watching her carefully. The words were of hate, but the look in her eyes was love. He did not mistake it. Could not mistake it. She had never been able to hide it from him, though he had not wanted to acknowledge what she felt. He wanted to smile, to return that love and sympathy, and to offer overwhelming gratitude that she had come to say her farewell in the only way open to her. If only he could tell her what he felt— but it would undo her efforts if he did. It was his last gift to her, this mute acceptance of the love she gave him.

So he remained silent while she insulted and reviled him until the guard was grinning and shaking his head, and all the while she was telling him with beseeching eyes and open heart that she loved him. The bars of light moved lower, striping his bare legs, and she faltered as her gaze dropped, then rose again. She turned away as if overwrought with anger, but he had seen the slight quiver of her lip and the shudder that ran through her.

Looking at the guard, she said, "The man is despicable. He is to die soon, is he not? Yea, so I thought. I would show him what an English noblewoman thinks of a man like him, a savage beast not fit to lick the boots of the most common English churl. . . ."

As she talked, she walked toward him, and Alex tensed. Had she gone mad? The guard would never allow her so close, but even as he had the thought, she came to him swiftly, bending in a graceful movement that smelled of perfume to slap him hard across the face. His head jerked to the side from shock and the force of the blow.

Then she was straightening, and exclaiming in vexation that she had dropped her pomander . . . "Ah,

there it is, in this filthy straw . . . I have it, Saunders."
Scooping it up, her hand grazed his fist and he felt the
cold press of metal.

His fingers instantly closed around it, and he felt the
unmistakable outline of a key pressed into his palm. The
back of his fingers brushed against something else she
had dropped there, and from one corner of his eye, he
caught the faint wink of jewels on the hilt of a dirk amid
the straw. His mother's dirk. . . .

Remaining still, he did not speak as Catherine sailed
across the cell to the door and the waiting guard. Pressing the pomander against her nose, she said in a faint
voice, "I feel so weak . . . wouldst thou assist me, Saunders? 'Tis the stench of Scot in this cell that has me in a
swoon . . . I vow it will be midnight before I recover,
and I do not want to miss the celebration in the hall this
eve . . . wilt thou accompany me to my chamber? I still
get lost, and cannot even find the east gate without help."

Saunders was helping her from the cell with an arm
around her shoulders, and Alex noted from the intense
set of his mouth that he was paying attention only to
Catherine's soft loose hair and intoxicating scent. No
doubt, it was the closest he had ever gotten to such a
beautiful woman, and an earl's daughter to boot.

When the cell door closed with a solid thud and the
key turned in the lock, Alex leaned his head back against
the wall and sighed. She had tried so hard, but still he
saw no hope. A key to his shackles would only free him
within the cell, and his mother's dirk would hardly hold
off a brace of armed soldiers if he did manage to escape
this hole. Even if he could disarm his guard and take his
weapon, then pray that he could leave the cellars unnoticed . . . he would be killed before he made it to the
wall. Or worse—recaptured.

Poor catkin. No doubt she had spent the last three

days concocting this plan and badgering the guard. But
he continued to think about it. Why disappoint her? At
worst, he would be caught or killed, and where was he
now? At the best—he drew in a deep breath. His hands
clenched convulsively around the key.

Yea, and her idle chatter was no idle chatter. A feast
meant food and drink, and distracted guards . . . "*I
vow it will be midnight before I recover, and I do not
want to miss the celebration in the hall this eve . . . will
thou accompany me to my chamber? I still get lost, and
cannot even find the east gate without help.*"

It was worth a try. After all, he had only his life left to
lose now.

Music from horns, harps, and flutes filled the hall, and
the castellan smiled benignly upon the revelers. On the
morrow, it would be May first, a day of celebration to
welcome the new season. In England, it was oft cele-
brated with decorated poles in the village, garlands of
flowers, and much laughter, singing, and dancing. But
this was Scotland and a time of war, when a hostile popu-
lace surrounded them. The only concession to the usual
festivities was a merry feast with music and dancing.

Catherine sat quietly beside her brother. She dared
not look at him, for fear he would somehow know what
she had done. Tense, she curled her hand tightly around
the stem of her goblet and sipped her wine. Her trencher
lay half-full, the meat untouched. Nicholas leaned close.

"Is the wild boar not to your liking?"

She set down her wine, "Yea, 'tis succulent, but I am
not very hungry."

"You must eat, kitten, and be strong enough to ride. I
have delayed too long already, but we leave the day after
the morrow to meet Hereford."

Frowning a little, she gave him a curious look. "Why is he to meet with us?"

"I have arranged it. When we leave here, we will rendezvous at the abbey near Jedburgh. It should be safe enough there, as we have matters to discuss. This meeting cannot be held in Berwick, but when it is done we will continue there before I take you to Warfield." He frowned. "I had not planned to take you with me, but this cannot be helped. I dare not trust you to anyone else."

Putting her hand on his sleeve, she said softly, "You love me well, I think."

He met her gaze, and in his bright blue eyes she saw the love and affection she had never received from another. Until Alex Fraser.

Nicholas nodded. "Yea, kitten, I love you well. You must know I do, or I would not have gone to so much trouble to see you safe. God knows, it would have been much simpler to let Fraser have you, but I could not." He looked down at her hand on his arm, and put his own over it. "I have defied even our father to keep you safe, Catherine."

She smiled. "You have defied even me to keep me safe."

"Yea, so I have." He grinned. "I would sooner face our father, I think. Now here, cut your meat before you eat, for it is a large piece. Where is your dagger?"

"It . . . was not mine. I gave it away, for it had too many memories with it."

Sobering, he nodded. "Poor kitten. You have suffered. I hope that you will soon be eased."

"Yea, so do I." A little sob caught in her throat, and she swallowed it. Why must he be so sweet and understanding now, when she had marked her course? He would never forgive her for what she had done, but she prayed that it would work even if he hated her for it. "Nicky . . . you know how I love you, do you not?"

"Yea, kitten, I do. Though you have a strange way of showing that love at times, I do know your sweet nature and gentle heart." He slanted her a glance, and reached to cut her meat with his own dagger. "Are you well?"

She looked down, watching as he sliced off a portion of meat with his dagger, a swift, clean stroke as if he were cutting butter. "Nay. Oh, not anything terrible, but . . . but I find I weary easily. Would you be distressed if I left early to go to my chamber? I will stay if you prefer—"

Instantly solicitous, he shook his head. "Of course I will not be distressed. Percy will escort—"

"No!" She drew in a deep breath at his narrowed glance. "Not Percy. Another man, but not Percy." *Not the man who held a hot iron to Alex.* . . .

She felt his eyes linger on her a moment, but then he shrugged. "Morgan will do, then. He is Welsh and a little rough, but stout. Shall I come to see you before I retire?"

"Yea, if you like." What else could she say? If she refused, it would arouse his suspicion, but she prayed that he would decide not to, or find feminine company to fill his hours. There was a flaxen-haired maid who had been flirting with Nicholas since their arrival, and she had seen him smiling at her as well. Yea, that would be perfect, if only he would be diverted.

It was quiet in the chamber she had been given, and she was grateful. All were below in the hall, attending the May Eve festivities. Since her arrival, she had had no privacy, not even for a moment. When one of the male guards was not following her every move, one of the female attendants or ladies of the castle was set to watch her.

The man tonight was a new guard, and she wished fretfully that Saunders had been given the post again. He was Sir Walter's man and more lenient than the others, or she would never have been able to convince him to allow her into the dungeon. That it was managed at all was no doubt due to the fact that Sir Walter was Scottish himself, though he avowed loyalty to the English. Perhaps his men felt sympathy for Alex Fraser.

Her heart lurched. Alex . . . he had watched her with his beautiful eyes veiled by his lashes at first, but when he looked up, she had seen in them something of her own heart. It had near undone her. Worse, seeing close evidence of his grievous injuries had made her forget what she needed to convey to him, so that she had stumbled about and put it so badly he may not have grasped her meaning. Would he? Had he been able to free himself from those hideous chains and flee the cell?

There had been no alarm raised, and she prayed it was because his escape had not yet been discovered. The grim alternative was insupportable. Oh, it was so faulty a plan, but she was desperate. Nicholas may love her, but he was not a blind fool, and she knew he did not trust her.

Twisting her hands together, she paced the floor, moving from the fire to the window, then back. It was dark outside, the curfew keeping all quiet. But Bothwell was very well guarded, and what if she had misread the message? Or the messenger? Though she had recognized John Elliot as one of the men who had ridden with them from Castle Rock, he had not appeared to trust her. Indeed, he had stood stiff and tense when she saw him carrying a load of faggots in the bailey, and she knew he thought she would betray him.

Instead, she had managed to convey her relief that he was there, and signal that she was willing to converse. It had been understandably brief under the watchful eyes of her guard, a passing comment that Alex was in the dungeon and needed their help. Elliot had swept a low bow as if in obeisance to her station, and murmured that he would leave her a message beneath the garden bench the next morn.

That was all, but it was enough to give her hope. She had plucked the crudely lettered message from beneath the stone bench in the bailey garden the next morn, and taken it to the garderobe to read in privacy. Tears filled her eyes when she saw the clumsy, familiar lettering in English: *Robie wil hav a hors at est gate midnit of the morrow. Tam.*

25

"Thou art a fine man, milord," the flaxen-haired beauty whispered close to his ear, and Nicholas smiled slowly at her over the rim of his wine cup. They were alone beneath a shadowed alcove, heavy draperies hiding them from the sight of those who passed, but the muffled sound of revelry from the hall was easily heard. A stone seat was cushioned with bolsters, and the narrow window was open to allow in the night air. Light filtered through cracks in shifting slices as the draperies moved in the soft currents of breeze.

Heat from the wine and desire swept through him, and he dipped a finger into his cup and spread a wine path over the maid's mouth. Her little pink tongue flicked out to smooth the drops over her lips, and his blood quickened.

Leaning forward, he tasted the wine from her mouth with his tongue, and hers came out to meet it. A bolt of desire shot through him at the contact. His breath came swift and harsh, and he grew impatient. She had been flirting with him since he had arrived at Bothwell, and his need had grown apace with the denial of it.

"Sweet Mary," he murmured, and she smiled at him with open invitation.

He set the wine cup on the window ledge and leaned over her, using his weight to press her back on the cushions. Mary sighed softly as he kissed her again, and arched into him so that her breasts grazed his chest. He looked down where her bodice gaped, perusing the luscious swells and valley that beckoned with erotic invitation. Then he leaned away from her, and put his hands on her breasts with bold intent. She did not protest, but smiled up at him, and he knew then she did not coyly tease, but would yield all.

Curling his fingers into the scooped edge of her bodice he pulled it down to bare the full, firm mounds. Her skin was tawny, and the nipples were large and brown. She gasped a little when he scraped his thumbs across the peaks, and they tightened instantly. He smiled. Gathering both large breasts in his palms, he pushed them together and bent his head to take the beaded nipples into his mouth. Another moan emanated from her, and she arched upward as he suckled her with strong pulls that increased his desire. Her soft little cries in his ear encouraged him to greater effort, and she began to writhe beneath him with almost frantic motions.

Finally he paused, flicking a glance up to her flushed face and open mouth as his hands moved to the laces of his breeches. "Mary, are you untried?"

"Milord . . . ?"

She sounded confused and breathless, but he would not be caught in a tender trap by a virgin who would later claim he had violated her and demand recompense.

"Are you virgin, girl? I would know now. . . ."

An indecisive expression flickered over her face, and

when she whispered, "Yea, m'lord," he slid his hand beneath her gown and up her thigh to test for himself. Slipping his fingers into her damp, heated recess, he met no barrier, and smiled at her lie. She whimpered as he moved his hand and raked his thumb over the source of pleasure that always brought female ecstasy. Gasping, she pressed into his hand.

Freeing himself from the tight constraint of his breeches, he began to kiss Mary again, coaxing her from passive acceptance to eager participation. She reached between them to curl her hand around him, and he groaned. Inspired by his response, she flexed her hand in the age-old motions that brought him to full erection.

Muttering encouragement against her mouth, her eyes, then her throat, Nicholas felt everything slip away but the driving need for release, for the *petit mort* that would, for one delicious moment, take him to the realm of oblivion and shuddering bliss. It hovered just out of his reach, until finally he moved aside her hand and slid into the welcoming heat of her body. She closed around him in damp fervor, and he felt the world go dim with each contraction.

Her thighs clamped around his waist, her feet dug into the bolsters for leverage, and she arched into his thrusts with eager response; the exquisite friction brought her quickly to panting release and female cries of pleasure that he smothered with his mouth. When she calmed, he began again the slow ascension to that pinnacle he sought, this time with a mounting ferocity that escalated with each driving stab of his body into hers. Enclosed by her damp heat and the musky scent that emanated from her, he lost himself to the motion and the seeking until he was aware only of her moans and his, the rhythmic slap of flesh against flesh, and the approach of his own release.

Sobs of fervor grew louder in his ear as she clung to him with her arms around his neck, drowning out the faint roar of tumult beyond, and everything was a haze of sound and smell and sensation that abruptly coalesced into wave after wave of climactic finality. Panting, his lungs working for air as the blood still pounded through his body, he hung over her braced on his arms, suspended still between that ecstasy and the slow dissipation of the haze that enveloped him.

Then the tumult began to penetrate his satiated mist, and he lifted his head. Through the open window, he heard the unmistakable sounds of battle, of swords clashing and men shouting, and he jerked away from Mary with a curse.

Dazed, she stared up at him with frightened eyes as he leaned to the window to confirm his suspicions, then she reached for him. He pushed her hand aside. "Hide yourself, Mary. We are attacked."

He rolled from the bolsters in a swift motion, cursing himself for being distracted as he tied his breeches, then yanked open the heavy draperies and bolted from the alcove.

He met Beakin at the far end of the corridor. "Give me your sword. Ah, Christ Almighty, who dares assault us?"

"There is no identifying pennant, milord, and 'tis too dark to see. Scots, of course." Beakin slid his sword free of the sheath and held it out.

"Of course." Nicholas slanted a swift glance at him and wished that Miles were here instead. His grizzled captain of the guards was better in a hand-to-hand fight than any man he knew, though Beakin was adept at the kind of fighting the Scots used, the strike and flee method that had visited such devastation upon the land.

"Arm yourself, and meet me in the bailey. Where do they strike?"

"The west gate . . . Milord—to my mind, 'tis unusual for the Scots to be so foolish as to storm a locked gate with such noise. They prefer stealth and cutthroat tactics. Do you think it could be a diversion for something else?"

Nicholas paused, and his mind went immediately to his sister. "Oh, God—Catherine!" He broke into a run, not toward the west gate, but toward Catherine's chamber.

Catherine was standing at the window when the noise erupted. Exultation was immediately mixed with panic. They had planned a diversion to aid Alex—but had he been able to free himself? Oh, God, what if he had not? She whirled around to look at the closed door. On the other side was the Welsh guard, a brutish man with little English and a sullen expression at missing the feast.

Had she not dealt for the past seven months with suspicious Scots whose language she did not speak? Yea, and yet she had somehow managed to communicate. Now, when it was so important, surely she could manage it again.

When she opened the door, the Welshman immediately snapped to attention, turning to look at her with a hand upon the hilt of his sword. She gave him an inquiring glance to disguise her swift assessment, and saw that he was tense and nervous. For some reason, she thought of Bess, and the Welsh maidservant's unreasonable fear of fairies and spirits in the night. Was it not Beltane eve? Yea, and she could well recall Bess's terror of the spirit night when 'twas said dark spirits freely roamed. . . .

Lowering her voice, a hand to her throat, she said

softly, " 'Tis the Tylwyth Teg that howls tonight? Is it not Vsbrydnos, the spirit night, and the witching hour when 'tis most dangerous?"

If the Welshman understood little, he definitely recognized the Welsh words for the Dark Ones, and crossed himself quickly, muttering in Welsh. His eyes darted to the window visible through the open door. The din drifted in through shutters left ajar. To Catherine, it was the unmistakable sound of battle. But to the Welsh soldier, although he must have heard it often enough, her suggestion and too much wine overrode his perception and plunged him into abject fear of the otherworldly spirits that were more fearsome than even armed Scots.

She stepped toward him, and saw the whites of his eyes roll in terror. He smelled strongly of the wine he had imbibed earlier, and she played upon his weakness without shame. "What is that? Do you hear it?"

He stared at her blankly, his hands clenched tight around the hilt of his sword, more unnerved by the sepulchre tone of her voice than words he did not fully comprehend, and she knew it. She moved even closer, and suddenly clapped a hand over her mouth to stifle a scream as she pointed down the hall as if seeing a wraith.

Drawing his sword, the Welshman whirled around to face the invisible enemy, and Catherine began to pray in Latin, words he would know and understand as she beseeched God for mercy on her soul.

"In nomine Patris . . ."

The soldier took a faltering step forward, gripped by fear yet mindful of his duty as he stared hard down the empty corridor. She took a step backward, easing along the wall.

"Confiteor Deo omnipoténti. . . ."

Another step back, then two, and the Welsh soldier

still advanced on an enemy he did not see but believed was there.

". . . *beátae María semper Vírgini.* . . ."

And she was gone, turning to flee down the hallway to the spiral steps that led below, desperate to find Alex.

The bailey was in chaos. Men scurried back and forth, buckling on swords and armor, some still half-dressed, some reeling from the effects of too much drink and celebration. She stood in indecision for a moment. The east gate . . . in the dark lit only by sputtering torches, she could not get her bearings. Beyond the bailey at the far end, she saw soldiers clustered on the walls and at the gates, some firing arrows, others readying pots of hot water to pour down on the heads of the invaders. If the diversion was at one end, then the east gate must be at the other. . . .

Turning, she moved quickly toward the opposite side of the bailey and the gate manned by only a few guards. She kept to the shadows, heart pounding furiously as she made her way over rough stone paths and hard ground. No one seemed to notice her, and she was almost to the gate when a dark figure suddenly loomed before her to block her path.

Startled, she let out a rush of air, and the man laughed softly. "Where do you go so quickly, milady? Does your lord brother know you are fleeing him?"

Percy. . . . , Hatred for this man welled in her, this man who had so enjoyed torturing Alex, but she kept her voice cool. "You are a fool, sir, if you think I flee from him. I seek shelter, and you bar my progress. Move aside."

"Nay, milady." He stepped adroitly in front of her as she again tried to pass. "We are well fortified here, and there is little danger from Scots. I will escort you."

Frustrated, and worried more for Alex than herself, she tried to evade his grasp, but Percy clamped a hand down on her arm and jerked her harshly to him. To her horror, he put a rough hand on her breast and squeezed painfully.

"Ah, do not look so outraged, milady, for any leman of a Scot's should not mind the touch of a real man."

Repulsed, and truly frightened now, Catherine twisted in an effort to free herself but he held her cruelly. White-hot pain shot through her as he gripped her breast in his huge hand. Gasping, she went still to ease the agony.

"Fool . . . my brother will kill you for this!"

"Nay, milady, he will thank me for halting your flight from him. Do you think he will believe you once I tell him how you sought to escape him yet again? Nay, he will not."

Though she struggled, Percy dragged her into the deepest shadows along the wall, ignoring her threats and cries that seemed to mingle with the general tumult to be swallowed unheard. She fought him, scratching his face with her nails, clawing at him in mindless desperation as he bore her down, slamming her hard against the dirt. As he leaned over her, fumbling under his jerkin to untie his laces, she jerked her knee upward, but he caught her leg and shoved it roughly to the side, then cuffed her a blow that rattled her teeth.

"Vicious bint . . . 'tis what you deserve . . . Devlin must be blind not to see what a whore you are . . . rutting with Scots and then weeping for their fate . . . be still, bitch!"

Salty tears streamed from her eyes to wet her ears and the hair at her temples as he curved a hand over her throat to hold her. One of her arms was bent behind and beneath her, and he ignored the flailing blows of her free hand. She whimpered, a helpless sound of futility that only made him laugh. There was the rending sound of tearing cloth, and night air chilled her breasts. Hoarsely, he made a wordless noise of admiration and lust, his fingers rasping over the tender skin of her breasts in a painful scour. He kneaded them in his rough hand, leaving marks that would bruise. He moved to lift her skirts, his hand snatching at the velvet to toss it up, and she clenched her legs together tightly.

"Aye, you will spread your thighs for a Scot, but not an honest Englishman. . . ."

His fierce mutter was heard as if from a distance as Catherine felt his hand pry her legs apart. She beat at him, but he shifted to wedge his body between her knees, and she managed a despairing cry like the wail of a tortured spirit. It only excited him.

"Aye, scream for me, my beauty. I like it best when they scream. . . ."

Gathering all her strength, Catherine gave voice to pain, terror, and sorrow as everything around her seemed to dissolve in a blur. She screamed again and again until her throat was raw, all the past days of fear and anguish injected into the lingering appeal for justice and deliverance.

And suddenly Percy was gone. The vise of his hand was snatched from her throat, and the crushing weight of his body atop hers rolled away. She lay still, with her skirts up to her waist and her bodice torn to expose her breasts, slow to comprehend that he had released her.

Then she heard a familiar voice, tender and angry and worried, urging her to get up as hands lowered her skirts over her legs and her bodice was straightened.

"Catkin . . . we have not much time. Rise, my love, for we must flee. You are safe . . . I have you. Catkin?"

Blinking tears from her eyes, she focused on the dark form leaning over her, then took his outstretched hands in hers and allowed him to lift her. She barely glanced at the lifeless body next to her, revulsion making her shudder as she saw the jeweled hilt of a dagger protruding from Percy's back.

"Alex. . . ."

"Shhh. I know, love. I know. I just wish I had taken more time to show him a bit of the pain he enjoys giving others, but we are in a hurry. Can you walk?"

She nodded, reeling a little as he took her by the arm and pulled her to him to fold her in a quick embrace. "Good. We have little time left to us before they figure out 'tis only a diversion . . . come, my sweet, for I think there are some friends waiting for us at the east gate."

"Yes." She laughed suddenly, a nervous bubble that sounded strange even to her own ears. "Robbie, I think. And John Elliot. And Tam . . . he wrote me a note in English, Alex, and it was very good."

He was taking her with him, bending to snatch up Percy's sword, then half walking, half carrying her across the bailey toward the east gate. "Then all your hard work was not in vain, catkin. Here . . . let me help you."

He boosted her up to a low wall, then leaped atop it more agilely than should be possible in light of his recent injuries, pulling her with him in a running walk along the narrow edge. She lapsed into silence, still shaken by her ordeal, but suddenly fiercely glad she was going with him, when she had never thought it possible.

And when he lowered her over the wall at the east gate and she saw Robbie MacLeod's bright hair shimmer in the black shadows, she felt oddly as if she were among friends again. Robbie caught her in his strong arms, grinning at her with a reckless light in his eyes, and said, " 'Tis good tae see ye ag'in, milady."

"Yea, Robbie, more than you know."

Alex set her pillion behind him on the horse, and she

wrapped her arms around his waist and clung to him as if she would never let go as they galloped swiftly over the rocky hills that fell away from Bothwell Castle. Exultation filled her. They were free.

The pounding of hooves on turf and the motion of the horse beneath her were safe and familiar, and she was reminded of once before when she had ridden almost this way with Alex Fraser. Then, she had been terrified of the savage Scot. Yet now she felt safe with him, even knowing that they would be fiercely pursued. She thought of Nicholas, and how angry and distressed he would be, but it could not be helped. He had chosen his life, and she must choose hers. God help her if she was wrong, but she knew that even if she died for it, this was where she wanted to be.

Nothing else mattered now, for she was with Alex.

26

Warily, Nicholas regarded the Welshman with frustration. "Curse you, man, let me pass!"

But terror appeared to have seized the man, and he swung at Nicholas again, the blade of his Welsh sword narrowly missing Nicholas's head. There was nothing for it but to fight back, and Nicholas turned in an agile pivot on the balls of his feet, bringing the blade of his sword back in a smooth swing that caught the Welshman across his ribs. The soldier grunted with pain and went to his knees, and Nicholas pushed past him, too impatient to reach Catherine to see to the man's welfare.

But when he reached the open door of the chamber, it was empty. Not even a serving maid occupied the room, and he swung about, storming back down the corridor to the wounded soldier. Grabbing him by the hair, he jerked the Welshman's head back and snarled, "Where is she? By all that is holy, if you have let something happen to her—"

"My lord." Beakin came toward him, striding down

the hallway with urgent steps. "The Scotsman has escaped."

Nicholas released the groaning Welshman and cursed long and hard, until Beakin's face went pale and he swallowed nervously.

"My lord . . . he must have had help, for his shackles were unlocked and the guard's throat was cut."

"Aye, he had help, of that much I am certain." Nicholas pushed grimly past Beakin. "If the assault on our west gate is a diversion, we needs check the east gate, for 'tis my guess that is where we will find Alex Fraser. God help the man who allows him through those gates. . . ."

Following behind him, Beakin offered, "Percy has gone to the east gate to ensure it is kept secure, my lord. He will not fail."

"No doubt. I have seen a sample of his work." Nicholas took the stairs two at a time, using his hands against the walls for balance as his feet skimmed the narrow, twisting stones designed to block easy access to the keep. A man descending could use his sword in defense, but a man trying to climb these steps would find his sword useless in the tight passage.

The bailey was a deafening clamor of chaotic action. Men shouted, and fires blazed as water was heated in hide tubs to pour onto the heads of the assailants. Light danced eerily over the ground and walls, fitful beneath torches, but beyond the wavering pools, there was only black shadow. He strode toward the east gate, sword in hand and murder in his heart, praying that he would find Alex Fraser.

And Catherine. . . .

"My lord!"

He paused impatiently, and swung around. "What delays you, Beakin?"

"Here . . . 'tis Percy, milord."

Another oath tripped from his tongue as he moved to where Beakin crouched beside a body. Beakin rolled Percy over to reveal his bloodied face, and the open staring eyes and slack jaw were evidence of his violent death. His breeches were unlaced and he was exposed as if he had been slain while relieving himself. When Beakin released him and Percy flopped back onto his belly, Nicholas saw the jeweled hilt of a dagger protruding from a reddish brown stain in the middle of his back. It had been plunged into him with such force that the dagger had snapped in twain. He touched the split hilt with a finger, frowning. Then his jaw tightened.

"By Christ, she killed him!"

"Grant pardon, my lord?"

He looked up into Beakin's face and muttered, "I have seem this dagger before."

Rising to his feet, he turned toward the east gate again. Even if it had not been Catherine's hand that plunged the dagger into Percy's back, she had killed him just as surely by giving it into the hand of the Scot. Ah, God, he would dearly love to see Alex Fraser pay for what he had done to his sweet, gentle sister. She was no longer the maid he had long known, but strange to him now, a woman who would betray her own brother and kill her own countryman to lend aid to the enemy.

And he knew, with sickening clarity, that his father had been right. It was oft better to lose the hand than the entire arm. He would have to cut Catherine from his life.

Torwood Forest was a vast wood with rocky outcrops that sprawled across the ancient Roman road from Edinburgh to Stirling, some five miles north of Falkirk. Since the end of April, Robert Bruce had been assembling an army there and training them for the coming battle.

Alex had made it safely to Bruce's camp, ensconcing Catherine in a small house in the nearby hamlet of Bannock that lay on the edge of the burn. There, with the growing Scots army surrounding her, she would be safe.

Yet it was now almost midsummer day, the time set for the battle near upon them, and the Scots army numbered between five and six thousand—scarcely more than a quarter of the English host that approached to engage them.

"Sir James, Sir Robert, and Sir Alex have just brought word to me that King Edward is now in Edinburgh," the Bruce informed his commanders in a meeting that included Alex. "The English are weary from their rush, with few halts for sleep and nearly none for food. A fool's reckless pace, for the horses, cavalry, and infantry will be worn out with exertion and hunger." He paused, then said with soft effect, "We are well rested and well fed, and wait for them with open arms."

A resounding cheer went up, and Bruce smiled. "By the time Edward's army replenished supplies from the ships at Leith and marched thirty-two miles to Falkirk, they were covered in dust and staggering from the heat. Yet we are here, shaded beneath the trees, with the burn to cool us when we grow heated."

Another cheer rose, and Bruce regarded them all with an assessing eye. "See that the men are made aware of our advantages, and of the English disorder, for 'twill be of great comfort. I will not have them discouraged by ill words." He paused before saying, "It is time for the camp followers, grooms, children, and those who are ill-armed to retreat with the wagon trains of food and equipment to the valley behind Gillies Hill. Those stragglers who are armed but arrived too late for training should accompany them, and wait until I summon them."

Again he paused, then said firmly, "We have neither the horses, the equipment, nor the men to attempt fighting the English cavalry with our own. We must fight on foot and depend upon the schiltron as our defense, as William Wallace did so effectively at Stirling Bridge. Yet, though that bristling wall of spears is superb defense, it can be used as an offense as well. It cannot remain stationary, but must be mobile. I intend for the Highlanders, with their expertise in ambush and assault, to wield their spears in this formation as offensive weapons."

"Grant pardon, sire," Sir Robert Keith spoke up with a grave frown, "but Highlanders are more used to independent fighting than as a group. Will they retain enough control to be effective in the tight formation of a shield-ring? Schiltrons require disciplined spearmen. . . . "

As one of the Highland chiefs present began to protest angrily, Bruce put up a hand and answered, "I understand your concern, Sir Robert, but I have personally supervised the training of the Highlanders who will be under my command, and vouch for their control and competence. Do you doubt me?"

Sir Robert, marischal and commander of five hundred light horse and a small company of archers from Ettrick Forest, shook his head and looked chagrined. "Nay, I would never doubt you, sire."

Bruce grinned. "Then I fear me you are unique in that sentiment, sir, for there are many English who yet do. But have we not come far? Have we not arrived at the moment when all of Scotland lies before us with hopeful hearts? Yea, and we will not betray that trust, none of us. Alone, I could not accomplish what these men with stout hearts and love for their country have done. Together, Scotland will once more belong to those who love the land and cherish its people."

Alex held to that hope, for only if Scotland was victorious would it survive. Edward I, the hammer of the Scots, had near destroyed it in trying to conquer it, and his son was little better.

Yet as Alex and Douglas surveyed the wood filled with men, he could not help a surge of pride in his countrymen. Through it all, they had persevered. Some out of loyalty to their country, some for their own gain, as with men of all nations. But there was a strongly connected sense of patriotism under the Bruce that had not existed with any other king. Perhaps it was because Robert Bruce took pains to speak to all his men, greeting them with good cheer and an encouraging word, learning their names to separate them one from another, and the men loved him for it. They would lay down their lives gladly for the man and the king.

"What think you," James Douglas said as they climbed a slope littered with campfires and men, "of the Bruce's choice of battlefield?"

Alex considered. " 'Tis a strategic site for a battle. The only means for the English army's approach is by way of the Roman road through the New Park, or perhaps to the east they can pass outside the New Park and under the lea of the escarpment at the Carse's edge."

"Yea, and since we have dug so many pits to trap unwary horses or men, and felled trees across any paths through the forest that can be used, they will be forced to advance along the route we want." Douglas paused, frowning, then added softly when they were past the camps and alone, "Sir Robert is greatly concerned about what we saw, Alex. He thinks the Bruce should inform at least the commanders of the truth of the situation."

Alex smiled wryly. "Yea, I can understand his concern. I have never seen so many English. The whole land is covered with mounted men, waving banners, columns of foot soldiers as long as the road to Berwick, and enough wagons to clog up the Firth of Forth."

Douglas fell silent, and Alex with him. It was June 22, and on the morrow, the battle would commence. So little time left, and he must see to Catherine.

He turned to Douglas. "I must ask a pledge of you."

Sir James looked at him in surprise. "A pledge of me, Alex? 'Twill be the first time you have ever done so. Ask it then, for I am curious what is so important that you would wait until now to broach it."

"My lady. Should I be killed, I would see her safely away."

"Ah. And you ask me to see to her safety."

Alex nodded grimly. "Yea, for I know of few other men who would be both capable and trustworthy to keep her from harm."

"Me? The Black Douglas whose very name frightens children into obedience and sends women running in terror? I vow, Alex Fraser, your wits must be addled, for I thought you wanted me far from your lady."

Behind the mockery lurked a trace of self-derision, and Alex heard it. He grinned. "Nay, for I think you put it out about yourself that you are so fierce just to enhance your reputation. Why, I have yet to see you be other than sweetly courteous and gallant."

Douglas laughed heartily, and clapped an arm about Alex's shoulders. "Aye, well that is just the face I show to you, Fraser, for I fear your wrath should I be other than courtly and kind." Then he sobered, and after a moment, said to him, "You know I will see Lady Catherine to whatever destination she desires, and will do so with utmost care and chivalry. As long as I yet live, she will be protected for you."

Alex nodded. "I did not doubt that you would, but

must ask for my lady's sake. She is wont to think herself able to manage on her own, and though I am constantly amazed by her success, I fear that should I fall and the Scottish army be demolished, she may meet with a dire fate at the hands of her own people." His mouth twisted in an ironic smile. "As she has championed me to her brother and over her own, she is reviled by them. Do not let harm come to her, but see her to the nunnery she has chosen should all fail."

Another silence fell between them, then Douglas said softly, "Take your leave of her, Alex, then meet us in our assigned positions before the midnight hour."

They parted, Douglas to join the division opposite the vanguard of Thomas Randolph, Earl of Moray, and Alex to the small hut on the edge of Bannock hamlet where Catherine waited. It was a long summer night, when the gloaming lingered without growing dark, and the sun rose again only a few hours after midnight. Purple shadows lay soft on the land, but it was yet light enough to ford the burn without a torch, for the moon cast silvery light over all.

Robbie prowled watchfully outside the hut, glancing up when he saw Alex. He waited until Alex dismounted before asking, "What news?"

"The English approach, and we go to join Douglas above the north slope of the Bannockburn. She must leave now to join the others at Gillies Hill. Is she awake?"

"Yea, she is awake and fretful."

Alex smiled at the sour tone of Robbie's words, and knew that Catherine must be waspish. Her moods were more frequent of late, a malady that was as mystifying as it was irritating.

Ducking to enter through the low door, he stood silent for a moment in the soft gloom that filled the one-room hut. A loft for sleeping was accessed by a small ladder on one wall, but Catherine complained that it was too hot and stuffy in the confines of the narrow space beneath the roof. Besides which, she added crossly, there were too many insects.

All of this, Alex knew, and knew that much of her mood stemmed from exhaustion and worry. How could it not? She had suffered much, and still awoke shaking from nightmares.

"Alex?" The voice drifted from the shadows, soft and weary. "Is it you?"

"Yea, catkin. 'Tis I who have finally come." He crossed the room as his eyes adjusted to the murky light. It smelled of candles and past meals, a not unpleasant scent that reminded him of his own hall. His throat tightened, for he thought of his mother and how she had wasted away, so that when she bore Jamie, her body was too weak to withstand the strain and yielded up what little strength she had.

"I am here," came the murmur, "by the window where I can see the fading light."

He went to her, and sat gingerly on the small cot where she lay beneath the window. Thin light illuminated her face, and there were circles under her eyes. She looked gaunt.

"Robbie tells me you will not eat," he lied, and she smiled.

"Poor Robbie. He is sorely tried by us both, I think. Do you stay the night?"

He shook his head. "I must join Douglas anon."

She reached for his hand and curled her fingers around it. Her grip was surprisingly strong, and he was encouraged by it. Bending, he kissed her, and she sighed softly.

"Alex . . . I must tell you something."

He tensed, for the tone of her voice foretold trouble.

He straightened and gazed down at her, still holding her hand as he waited. She looked away out the window as if searching for the words or the courage, then turned her head on the thin pillow to gaze into his eyes. His heart lurched. Ah, God, he could not bear it if she left him, whether of her own free will or fate.

He set his jaw and waited, and after a moment she said in a faltering voice, "Once, I told you I loved you. Do you recall?"

Silence fell. Yea, he could recall it well, for the words had shamed and alarmed him then. He lifted his gaze out the window, to where twilight shadows muted the summer night. A bird called, and the hum of insects was a steady drone. How could he say what was in his heart when he may well be killed on the morrow?

"Catkin . . . ah, God." Helplessly, he floundered, caught between his fierce desire to declare his love, and the fear that it would destroy her. He closed his eyes for a moment, and when he opened them he saw tears tracking her cheeks. It undid him. Touching the silvery paths with his finger, he said softly, "Yea, my love, I recall it well. 'Twas the night before we left to ride north, and when I asked you what was wrong, you said you feared to go with me. I knew then you lied. I knew you waited to hear me say it as well."

She drew in a deep, shuddering breath, and silence fell again. Lacing her fingers through his, she drew his arm upward to bring their joined hands between them.

"You clasp my hand, and you call me love. Yet you do not say the words. I languish without them, Alex. If you feel them, say them, and if you do not, I wouldst know that as well, for I cannot bear to think I may lose you on the morrow and never know for certain if you loved me."

"Have I not shown you how I cherish you?"

"Yea, you have. But I wouldst hear it."

There was no escape, and he did not know if he erred or did more harm than good, but he could no longer evade the truth. Pressing their joined hands to his mouth, he said against her soft skin, "I love you, catkin. God help us both, but I love you far more than I ever thought 'twas possible for a man to love a woman. You are my world, and I pray that I do not slay you by daring to love you."

A little sob caught in her throat, and she whispered, "How could you think your love wouldst kill me? 'Tis the lack of it that sorely wounded me, but now I will be whole. Oh, Alex, my love. . . ."

Bending, he kissed her, and tasted the salt of her tears on his tongue. Then he drew back, still holding her hand, and said, "All I have ever loved in this life has been taken from me, catkin. I did not want to risk you by loving you."

It sounded awkward and foolish even as he said it, but it was done. Her fingers tightened around his palm.

"Come back to me, Alex, and I will give you more love than you can hold." She brought his hand to her mouth, and holding his gaze as she pressed her lips against the back of his fingers, she said, "I am to bear your child. We need you."

Jolted, he sat staring at her for a long moment as the shadows lengthened and it began to grow dim. Her face was a pale oval shimmer in the fading light, and her eyes were like huge violet bruises as she waited for his response.

Then, gathering her into him, he crushed his face into the fragrant mass of her hair and said around the thickness in his throat, "I love you, Catherine, and if all goes well, I will make you my wife. Our child will grow up heir to the barony of Kinnison, and as Scotland grows and prospers, so will we."

He meant it. Despite the sudden surge of fear that she

would be taken from him as Catriona Fraser had been taken in childbirth, he knew that he would fight to his dying breath for the lands that would belong to the coming child. This would be his heir, and though none could ever replace the two beautiful children he had lost, it was as if all had been forgiven and he was being allowed a new beginning.

A beginning that included this fair English flower who meant the world to him.

27

It was the Sabbath, June 23. Just after sunrise, the Scottish army under Robert the Bruce heard mass, kneeling on the battlefield to pray for their cause. As it was the vigil of Saint John the Baptist, they observed it as a fast, and took only bread and water as sustenance.

Alex marshaled his men into formation with Douglas, their division numbering near a thousand. The marsh was at their back, and Edward Bruce and his thousand men on the left. Almost directly across the old Roman road, Bruce waited with his two thousand foot composed of the wild Highlanders, and to his right were the hidden pits and bogs. Randolph, Earl of Moray, was left of Bruce and up near Saint Ninian's Kirk with five hundred foot soldiers. Behind Bruce, Sir Robert Keith held his five hundred light horse in abeyance.

On the other side of the Bannockburn lay the English. The land sloped downward from their position, so that Alex saw Hereford's standard fluttering in the midday sun as the enemy milled about the edge of Torwood Forest.

"They do not hurry," he remarked, and Robbie laughed.

"Nay, why should they rush to defeat?"

Robbie's optimism was not isolated. After the divisions had been formed, Robert Bruce had it proclaimed to each that any man who may be faint of heart could depart at once. The answering shout arose from near six thousand throats as one: "We will conquer or die!"

The muted clank of sword and armor rustled around them, and the sun beat down with a vengeance from a cloudless sky. Alex removed his helmet and wiped sweat from his brow, then tugged it back down over his damp head and gazed across the valley that separated the armies.

As the English finally emerged from Torwood and onto the grassy meadow that sloped down to the Bannockburn, sunlight glittered on the brightly colored banners and from their polished metal armor. His throat tightened. The Earl of Hereford's pennant fluttered next to that of the Earl of Gloucester as they led the vanguard across the meadow and approached the ford over the burn. In the front, clad in full armor and mounted on a powerful horse, rode a well-armed knight bearing a spear and wearing Hereford's colors.

"Is that Devlin?" Robbie muttered, and Alex shook his head.

"Nay, he would be wearing his own colors. I would guess it to be Hereford or his nephew, Sir Henry de Bohun."

"Christ above, Alex—look!"

Blood ran cold as Alex saw the Bruce inspecting the tightly formed ranks of Scots who were partially hidden in the woodland near the burn. Alone, the king rode a small gray palfrey, and carried only an ax in his hand. The gold circlet around his helmet marked him as the Scottish king, and apparently, Hereford recognized it and saw his chance.

Spurring his huge destrier forward, he couched his lance as he rode straight at Robert Bruce. There was a stirring among the men as all waited anxiously to see the king's reaction to this bold challenge. Dare he answer it? Caution bid that he fall back within the safe ranks of his soldiers and let the armies decide the outcome of this battle, but that was not his nature.

"He must know 'tis his old enemy Hereford," Robbie muttered in a tight voice, "for de Bohun wears the crest on his surcoat. Christ have mercy, for the king is mounted on a pony and has no lance or spear, yet Hereford is well armed!"

But Robert Bruce turned his horse toward Hereford and waited for the charge; at the last moment, he swerved aside and stood up in his stirrups to bring down his great ax with such force that it split through de Bohun's helmet as he passed, so that skull and brains, along with his ax handle, snapped in twain.

For a stunned moment, there was silence on both sides as Bruce wheeled his small horse about, then the king's Highlanders broke with wild cries of exultation, swarming over the breastworks and onto the field. They charged the English cavalry as they attempted to line up in formation on the open ground below, hindered by the fact that many had fallen into the pits and were badly floundering. Swiftly, Bruce halted the pursuit of the English as they broke and ran, curbing the Highlanders from giving full chase.

Galloping back to the commanders who awaited him in consternation, he did not reply to their remonstrations for what might have happened had he fallen to de Bohun, but only lamented the broken ax handle. All eyes had been on the confrontation, and when Bruce looked up, he pointed to a body of English horse riding under cover of the bank along the Carse toward Saint Ninian's Kirk.

"Moray, a rose has fallen from your chaplet," Bruce called roughly, and Thomas Randolph, Earl of Moray, at once galloped to his men and deployed them in a schiltron to the open ground over which the English would have to pass.

From their position on the slope, Alex and the rest of the Douglas division watched as Randolph was assaulted by the English. The battle dragged on, and the Scots were hard-pressed to defend themselves as the dogged English cavalry tried to break their ranks with battle axes, swords, and maces. So great were their numbers that the tight-knit band of Scots was nearly hidden from sight by the mailed knights who assailed them.

Douglas asked the king if he could go to Randolph's aid, but Bruce sent him back to his post. As it grew more doubtful, Douglas fretted over Randolph's fate and was at last given permission to go to his aid. Yet as they drew close, Douglas halted his men and exclaimed, "The Earl of Moray has gained the day, and since we were not there to help him in the battle, let us leave to him the credit of the victory."

Alex watched as the English took flight, some north to Stirling Castle, and some south to rejoin their army. It was growing late in the day, and Randolph's men sagged to the ground to remove their helmets and wipe dust and sweat from their faces. When evening fell and the Scottish forces met with Bruce, the mood was jubilant as all crowded around to offer Moray's weary men praise.

Finally, Bruce spoke softly, and they grew quiet to hear him. "Tonight, there will be dismay in the camp of the English because of the double defeat of powerful knights by men on foot. Yet, if you feel you have shown mettle enough and wish to retire from the field, the decision is in your hands."

Their reply was unanimous. They would fight at first light. Bruce smiled slightly. "Sirs, since you will it so, make ready in the morning."

They dispersed, and Alex went first to Gillies Hill, so he could reassure Catherine that he yet lived. Supply wagons were scattered across the green slope and in the narrow belt of wood that edged it, and he found her sitting in the shade of a spreading oak where a cool breeze lifted her hair in gentle drifts.

Relief lit her eyes when she saw him, and she leaped to her feet with more vigor than she had displayed in some days. Flying to him, she was folded into his embrace as he caught her against his chest, and he held her that way for a long moment.

"Have you any wounds?" Her words were muffled against his surcoat, and he laughed.

"Nay, catkin. I did not even lift my sword, save to buckle it around me."

Her head tilted back. Late sunlight glinted in her eyes as she searched his face. "Is it over? Is the battle done?"

In answer, he squeezed her, and she buried her face against his chest again and shuddered. After a moment, she drew away and took him by the hand to lead him to the shade beneath the tree. It was cooler at the edge of the wood and with the approach of evening, and he sat quietly beside her as she laced her fingers through his and held him.

"Did you see my brother?"

Her quiet question was not unexpected, and he shook his head. "Nay, catkin. I did not. Though I did see Hereford's banner there. Most like, he fights under the earl's standard if his quarrel with your father still holds."

"Alex—"

"Do not say it. You know my answer."

She sagged against him, and he slid an arm around her. Nothing he said would help. He could not promise he would not kill Devlin if he had the chance. He still bore the red scars on his chest as a reminder of English mercy, and another reminder below his belt. It had been the last he had thought would kill him, but it may have saved his life. For when the hot iron had seared into his flesh with such excruciating agony he had lost his tenuous hold on consciousness. When he had roused, it was over. Devlin had arrived, and Catherine right after him, so that he was saved from being too brutally scarred. Oddly, it had been the first wound to heal.

It was John Elliot who had told him of her courage in demanding they cease the torment, for he had hidden nearby in the wood to watch. Brave little catkin . . . so tender and yet so strong. He wished he could tell her he would spare her brother, but Devlin would not make the same promise.

Sliding his hand over her arm down to her wrist, he felt the thin prominence of her bones beneath his fingers. "You are too thin, catkin. Have you eaten?"

She looked up at him with a smile. "Soon, you will be saying I am too fat, sir, so enjoy my lean frame while you still can."

Spreading his hand over her still flat belly, he thought of their coming child. What if he was killed in the battle on the morrow? What would happen to both of them? He had not wed her, and their child would have no name. There would be no generous stipend from his hand for the child or mother, nothing but scorn and shame. Perhaps it was not fair, but for a woman of Catherine's position to bear a child without benefit of priest was viewed more harshly than a village maid lying with a man of rank. And more than just ethics, there was the right to be suzerain that attended the birth of his child.

He leaned close and nuzzled her hair. "Catkin, wilt thou wed me?"

Drawing away, she turned to look up at him, her eyes serious. "Yea, I have said I would."

"Then we shall do so this eve, for I wouldst have it done before the morrow."

Her eyes widened, absorbing light from the setting sun. Reaching up, she traced her fingers over his mouth. "I fear me that you have a foreboding of the morrow that I dread to hear."

"Nay." He caught her hand. " 'Tis just that I have long delayed what should have been done."

"But what of your brother?"

He drew in a deep breath. "Jamie's fate is sealed on the morrow as well. It has nothing more to do with you, or even with me. He has become entangled with the fate of all Scotland, and if we win the battle, we win his life."

"Then yea, lord, I will wed you this eve should you find a priest willing to say the vows." She paused, and a smile curved her mouth. "My father should be pleased to learn that I am wed on Saint John's Eve, as he bade me do."

Alex laughed and pulled her to him with fierce emotion. "But I do not think he had me in mind, catkin."

"Nay, he did not. Nor did I at the time. Yet, I think I must have known that you would find me, though I did not know your name." She tucked her fingers into the edge of his dusty surcoat. "Shall we find the priest?"

Dawn broke on June 24, the feast of Saint John the Baptist, less than four hours after the sun had set. As the sun lifted over ragged crags and tree spires, rays of light glinted from the plumes and trappings of the English cavalry arrayed on the hard clay of the carse, and warmed the sodden English infantry scattered through the marshes beyond the Bannockburn.

To the west, the Scots stirred beneath the heavy leaves of the trees in New Park. After a light meal to break their fast, the men formed their divisions, their banners spiking the air like bristles. Scottish priests had conducted mass in each division, then retreated to the safety of Gillies Hill to await God's decision. After the customary knighting on the field of those chosen for that honor, the Scots were blessed by the Abbot of Inchaffray, who held a casket of the most sacred relics of the kingdom.

At the end of the solemn ceremonies, Bruce ordered the advance. Three divisions moved off in waves, while the fourth division and the cavalry stayed in reserve on the lower slope of the wooded park. Armed knights more used to doing battle from atop savage destriers arrayed themselves in the deadly line of the schiltron beside the foot soldiers, shoulder to shoulder, all with one aim in mind: unhorsing and destroying the English knights.

The battle began with an attack on Edward Bruce's schiltron—an attack quickly repulsed as the vanguard was beaten back by the hedgerow of bristling spears. When Randolph came to Bruce's aid, the English attack broke and turned back, setting off a stampede of wounded and riderless horses that clogged the field. Douglas entered the fray, barring the English from penetrating the tight circle in which they were held on three sides, and preventing their infantry from joining the battle.

Alex fought between Robbie and John Elliot, both good men, and thrust about him with sword and spear. In such close quarters, it became impossible for the English

archers to continue their deadly fire for fear of hitting
their own, and the rain of arrows slackened. The Scots
advanced slowly, pushing back the English with ferocity.
Horses screamed, and blood pooled on the hard clay of
the carse without soaking into the ground. Steel rang on
steel, and the brittle crack of breaking spear shafts and
the dying cries of men were deafening.

It was brutal. Alex moved forward with torturous
progress, using his sword to dispatch the fallen knights,
while Robbie wielded the spear with vicious efficiency.
Grimly, through the tumult of grunting men and slashing
weapons, the Scots beat back the English forces further
still. Knights tumbled from wounded destriers to the
blood-sodden ground, elegant garments trampled under-
foot and fouled. The Scots ranks were so tightly packed
that they pushed over the fallen in a wave, treading upon
men and beasts alike in their relentless advance.

The rallying cry of "Press on, press on! They fail!"
rang over the serried ranks as the Scots neared victory.
King Edward took flight, and the royal standard left the
field. With their king in retreat, the army began to falter.
Then Bruce gave the signal, and the Highland reserves
who had come too late to be trained and waited on Gillies Hill were called up. They streamed down the slope
with banners made of sheets fixed to poles and spears,
and at the sight of yet more Scottish soldiers, the might
of the English army turned and fled. It was a complete
rout. Every English knight who had not been unhorsed
spurred his mount in panicked flight.

Robbie gave chase and Alex found himself alone, his
bloodied sword in his hand as a path cleared before him
for the first time. He blinked sweat from his eyes and
looked up and across the field in time to see the Earl of
Hereford's banner quit the carnage. It fluttered, then
dipped and disappeared. A riderless horse careened

toward him, whites of the eyes showing, and Alex moved to one side to grab the dangling reins. Snorting, the beast reared and plunged, and he brought it down with a hard yank. It stood trembling, foam lathered on muzzle and chest, rich, ruined caparison hanging in tatters between its quivering legs.

Soothing the terrified destrier with calming hand and voice, Alex noted the red and white crest stitched onto the cloth that had once been white. His eyes narrowed. It was familiar, a red lion and black hawk—Devlin.

If Devlin had been unhorsed, no doubt he lay among the fallen, and he stepped over sprawled knights who lay dead on the field, searching for the lion and hawk shield among those slain. Around him men moaned, while in the distance came cries of battle as the enemy was yet pursued. The Scots would run them to the ground now, and take prisoner those of value to ransom or exchange. Alex wiped stinging sweat from his eyes with his sleeve, his sword in one hand and the leather reins in the other.

Christ Almighty, there had been work done this day that would not soon be forgot . . . so many English barons lay among the dead. But he did not see the man he sought. Slipping a little on gore, he progressed slowly over the littered field toward the burn. Then he stopped, watching in grim wonder as the routed English crossing the Bannockburn became bogged in its muddy depths and were crushed and rolled over by the panic of those who fled after them. Between its narrow banks, the burn became choked with struggling men and horses, many who drowned or were drowning as their comrades ran heedless over their bodies.

That was where he found Nicholas, Lord Devlin, on one knee with his sword still clutched in his hand and hot frustration in his eyes as he tried to turn his men back to fight. Bareheaded beneath the blazing sun, Devlin seemed not to notice or care that they were beaten, laying about him with the flat of his sword in an effort to create order out of chaos.

Despite the hatred he felt for him, Alex also felt a grudging admiration that Devlin showed courage where his comrades did not. With most of the English fleeing in panic, seasoned veterans among them, this young man preserved his courage and his calm, trying to marshal his men and get them to safety.

When Devlin saw him approach, he struggled to his feet and stood swaying, sword at the ready. Fierce hatred glittered in eyes as bright a blue as the cloudless sky over them. "Fraser . . . come and taste my steel, for I have long awaited this moment."

Alex halted and released the reins of Devlin's mount. The destrier seemed not to know what to do, and put down its great head to stand motionless. Moving in front of the beast, he caught and held Devlin's gaze.

"Your horse has already yielded the day, my lord Devlin. I claim him, your sword, and your person in the name of Robert Bruce, King of Scotland and my sovereign majesty."

"I do not yield."

Levering the bloodied tip of his sword toward Devlin, Alex said softly, "Then you will die."

"So be it." Devlin hefted his sword in both hands. His shield was gone, his helmet gone, and the once-white surcoat was ripped and bloodied. Dirt and blood streaked his face, as well. He was sorely wounded, yet held his weapon at the ready, and Alex understood. It was what he would do.

Blood surged through his veins as he parried Devlin's first thrust, catching it on the edge of his blade and forcing the swords upward. Twisting, he disengaged and swung back around, only to be met with an answering parry from Devlin's sword. The shock of the blow vibrated down his arm. They met, clashed, parted, and met again, each swinging impact a harsh buffet of muscle and stamina. Both were weary and drained from the fight, yet intent upon finishing the business between them.

They fought across the muddy banks of the burn, sliding in muck and blood, over fallen comrades and bushes. Sweat streamed, sunlight glittered along the blades and in their eyes. Then Devlin went down, his foot slipping on gore to send him crashing to the ground. Alex took immediate advantage of the opening and straddled him, his sword point aimed at Devlin's throat for the final thrust that would end it.

Devlin looked up, grim knowledge in his eyes now, along with the hatred. His lips were pressed tightly together, and he neither asked for mercy nor yielded.

Panting for breath, winded and filled with blood lust, Alex leaned on his sword so that the tip pushed harder into the mailed cowl protecting Devlin's throat. This one act would end it all, the months of simmering hatred and resentment, with a single hard shove of his sword. But it would end Jamie's life as well. Warfield, if he still lived, would not let this pass no matter what had happened on the battlefield this day. His daughter was gone to him, and if Alex took his heir as well, there would be nothing left for the earl to fear.

With the cries of the wounded and dying filling his ears and his enemy at his feet, Alex struggled between duty and vengeance, all that he had lost and all that would be his. Schooling his conflicting emotions into abeyance, he took a deep breath that smelled of death and blood.

It was over. . . .

28

———— ⚜ ————

Shivering despite the heat, Catherine waited. It was long after the victory, and yet he had not come. So many had died, the cries and moans of the wounded and dying pitiful and relentless. Twilight enveloped the land, and torches were lit as men wandered the battlefield in search of comrades or booty. They were like macabre fireflies bobbing over the darkened land, pinpricks of light among the lost souls.

Did he live? She hugged her knees to her chest and put her chin atop them, arms wrapped around her legs as she rocked back and forth in abject misery. A prayer rose to her lips, and she murmured it over and over, a litany of faith and despair, alternating between grief and fierce hope in an unending plea.

Around her were reunions, shrieks of joy as weary men climbed the slopes to kin, and she looked away. No one came for her, nor even glanced at her. Finally she rose from beneath the tree where she had promised Alex she would wait for him, and started down the hill. She could delay no longer. If he was dead, she must know it.

The waiting was intolerable, beset by fears that would not abate.

Before she reached the field, she smelled the blood and death that permeated the air. It rose in the soft currents that drifted over the torn earth, so thick and strong that not even the stench of burning pitch from the torches could obliterate it. She slipped, then gagged when she saw what made the ground slick beneath her feet, but pressed on. Eyes stared up sightlessly from unfamiliar faces. These men had families, loved ones who would wait vainly for their return. Scots or English, in death they were alike.

Someone was sobbing, and she realized the sound came from her own throat as she stumbled over the rutted tracks and dead horses and men, but she could not stop. Nowhere among the fallen did she see Alex, nor Robbie, nor any she recognized from Kinnison. Were they all dead? Gone from the field? Why had none come to tell her if Alex had died?

"Milady. . . ."

It was a faint whisper, but she heard it and stopped. Deep shadows drifted over bush and horse and man, so that in the gloom she could barely tell one still form from another.

"Milady. . . ."

Again it came, a whispered plea and a groan, and she turned toward the source. "Yea, I am here, but I do not see you."

"Here, milady. . . ." The feeble wave of a hand alerted her, and she moved over the lacerated earth to kneel beside a wounded man. At first she did not recognize him, but then she saw familiar bright eyes beneath the blood and dirt. "Oh, Holy Mary, Tam . . . you are wounded."

"Yea, milady. I die."

The words came out on a moan, and tears clogged her throat so that she could not answer for a moment. Then she managed to say, "You are sore hurt, but we will heal you, Tam. No, do not move . . . let me see. . . ."

She lifted the hand he had pressed to his chest, and knew with a sinking heart when she saw the raw, gaping wound that he would not live much longer. His breathing was shallow and swift, and his eyes were glazing. She took his bloodied hand in hers and held it, speaking to him softly. "Do not exert yourself. Here, let me wipe your forehead so the dirt will not sting your eyes."

His skin was cold and clammy beneath her palm, and she gently stroked her fingers over his brow and pushed back the damp, curling hair. Ah, God, he looked so young, with his pale freckled face and trembling mouth, and she wanted to weep but dared not distress him.

"My letters. . . ." His voice was a low, forced mutter as he strained to look up at her. "Di' ye read my message, milady?"

"Yea, Tam. You did very well. I am so proud of you."

He smiled, and took a shuddering breath. "Me mam . . . wilt be . . . proud o' me . . . too. . . ."

"Your mother will be most proud of you, as are we all, Tam. Rest now, so you can heal and tell her about it when we return."

He released his breath in a long sigh, and with the smile still curving his lips, died.

Catherine sat in stunned silence, holding his hand in hers, gazing down at him with aching grief. He was so young, with his life before him, as were so many of these men. Gone now. She bowed her head and gripped his lifeless hand, and murmured the prayer for the dead. "*Agnus Dei, qui tollis peccáta mundi: dona eis réquiem . . . Agnus Dei, qui tollis peccáta mundi: dona eis réquiem sempi térnam. . . .*"

As the words faded into the purple shadows, someone knelt beside her, and a hand moved to close Tam's eyes with the edge of his palm. She looked up, and saw Robbie MacLeod. Without thought, she leaned into him and sobbed, and he put his arm around her and murmured comfort in both Gaelic and English until she quieted.

Then he drew back and lifted her to her feet with him as he stood. "We maun go, milady. I hae brought men tae take Tam home wi' us."

"Yea . . . he needs . . . to be with his own." She drew in a shuddering breath, and asked the question that had haunted her for what seemed an eternity. "Robbie, does he live? Is Alex alive?"

"Yea, he wa' alive when last I saw him, milady."

She searched his face in the gloaming, and noted that he averted his eyes. Fear gripped her. "Is he wounded? Oh, God, tell me now, Robbie MacLeod, for I fear I will go mad unless I know!"

"He wa' whole and well, milady, wi' no' a mark on him tha' I couldst see." Yet still Robbie avoided her gaze, and she feared with sudden, heart-wrenching certainty that she would not want to hear the truth.

But she forced herself to ask: "Was he taken prisoner?"

Robbie laughed. "Nay, milady. 'Tis the Scots wha hae taken hostages this day, wi' the Sassenach fleeing for their lives like hares before the fox."

For some reason, James Douglas's story of the fisherman and the fox came to mind, and she stared up at him. "Is he with Sir James?"

Robbie looked surprised, then grinned. "Yea, milady, for they pursue King Edward and hope tae run him tae ground ere the night is o'er."

Relief mingled with anxiety, for if Alex was still involved in the fighting, he may yet lose his life. But at least he had survived the day, and she held hard to that knowledge as she went with Robbie to the camp.

It was in turmoil, with noble English hostages sitting in glum silence among the elated victors. Catherine scanned the faces, half-hoping, half-afraid to see her brother in the group. But Robbie steered her away from them to a small tent that had been erected, and bade her wait there while he found her decent food. She did so gladly, the tension of the day suddenly rendering her weak and weary. Ah, the coming child must be protected, though at moments she felt so worried and uncertain she could barely think. She perched atop a fallen log and rested her hands on her belly as she thought of the babe. A son, perhaps, with Alex's black hair and gray eyes. Or if a daughter—ah, if a girl, she would be granted more rights than her mother had been given, allowed to have choice instead of rigid stricture guiding her life.

A faint smile curved her mouth as she envisioned their child, for regardless of gender, it would be well loved. She would not be inaccessible as her mother was, nor would Alex be as cruel as her father was, for she had already seen how tender and gentle he had been with poor Christian and Sarah.

With the dreamy smile still on her lips, she looked up into blue, blazing eyes filled with hostility. *Nicholas.* . . .

Starting, she lurched up from the log and crossed the narrow space to where he was propped against a tree, his leg stretched before him and wrapped with filthy, bloodied strips of linen.

"Nicky . . . oh, God, you are hurt!" She knelt and put out a hand to examine him, but his leg jerked and he snarled an oath at her.

"Christ Almighty, do not touch me!"

Her hand stilled, and she looked up into his face to see simmering, fierce resentment. Her heart fell. "Let me help you—"

"Aye, if you want to help me, then give me a dagger as you did that bastard Scot. Ah, you do not speak. Is it that you will do for him what you will not do for your own blood?"

"Nicky . . . ah, God, Nicky, I cannot. You must know I cannot. Were your life in danger, I would do all in my power to free you, but you will be ransomed or exchanged." She drew in a deep breath at his short bark of laughter, and blurted, "Our father will do for you what he would not for me, and you know it."

He grew quiet, and his tone was bitter. " 'Tis the crux of it, I see. I never knew you hated me so. . . ."

"Nicky, you know that is not true. Please listen—"

"Nay, Lady Whore, you have naught I wish to hear said. Do you go back to your Scot and leave me be."

He turned his head and would not look at her, and yet she did not leave him. She knelt in the dirt beside him and waited for some sign that he did not hate her, that he would forgive her. His jaw was clenched so tightly a muscle leaped beneath the shadowed angle, and his mouth thinned into a taut, unforgiving slash.

Despair swept over her, rendering her powerless to offer any comfort that might matter. Ah, Nicky, Nicky . . . he looked so miserable, so angry and anguished, with blood and dirt streaking his face and matting his hair, and she wanted to find the right words that would erase all that and ease his pain, but knew she could not. It was up to him now to find his own redemption, and she prayed that he would.

Still, she could not leave him even though he did not

want her there and would not look at her, keeping his face averted. Robbie found her there, and gruffly told her she must return.

That earned Nicholas's attention, and his head turned at last to stare at the Scot with hard, narrowed eyes and an expression Catherine had never seen on his face before.

"Yea, take her with you now that she is ruined, and a traitor to her own people."

Robbie returned the hot stare coolly. "Aye, 'twill be my pleasure, for she hae a heart no' many do, man or woman. Wha' ere ye may think, ye maun know tha' she hae the same courage as do the men wha died here today. Men o' both sides."

Nicholas did not reply, but clenched his teeth and watched sullenly when Robbie urged Catherine to her feet, taking her back to the small tent only a short distance away. Then his head fell back against the tree and he closed his eyes, heartsick at the losses they had suffered this day.

Both his brothers had died on the field, Geoffrey cut down by the murderous advance of the schiltron, Robert slain after being unhorsed and thrown to the mercy of the Scots. He had seen it, but been unable to prevent it, another sorrow.

So much lost, and for a king who had not stayed to rally his men or marshal his earls. Disbelief had been evident in the faces around him, and the hearts had gone out of the men when their king fought through the disordered ranks to freedom, deserting them.

Until Alex Fraser found him, he had thought the worst was done. And now this. Now his own sister was decamped to the enemy, a part of them, a witness to the destruction of her own blood.

His leg throbbed, but 'twas small misery compared to

what he felt when he saw Catherine in the company of the Scots. Of all that had been lost to him, he mourned her defection most.

Ah, God, when he thought of how he had plotted and done all in his power to retrieve her safely, only for her to undo it all. If it did not pain him so greatly, he would laugh at the irony.

Worse, it had to be Fraser who captured him.

He would rather have been slain than suffer the humiliation of being taken prisoner by him. If he could get word to his father, he would demand that Fraser's brother and de Brus be slain rather than exchanged, but that was not possible. And it was another humiliation to see his father flee the field without honor, following Hereford and their craven king as if their tails were afire. Shame rose thick and hot in his throat at the memory of it.

Ah, God, he wanted to weep.

29

Flushed with triumph, the Scots rode back to Bannockburn at a swift pace to join their king. More weary than
he had ever been before, yet filled with hope for the first
time in years, Alex Fraser thought of Catherine. It had
been four days since the battle, but he knew Robbie
would heed his request to see her to safety. Now he
longed to see her, to put his arms around her and hold
her close.

But first, he had his duty. Though he had ridden with
Sir James to pursue the English king, Edward had some
five hundred men with him when they caught up to them
at Linlithgow, while they numbered only sixty. There
were too many to attack in a pitched battle, so they had
chosen to harry them relentlessly, killing any man who
fell behind or even stopped to relieve himself. The panic
in the English ranks was such that when King Edward
reached Dunbar, he and his followers flung themselves
from their horses to race through the castle gates, leaving
the expensive destriers milling outside the castle in con-

fusion. These, Douglas took back to the Bruce, with the information of the king's subsequent flight.

Alex would have gone to Catherine then, but the king sent him with his own brother Edward Bruce to pursue the nobles who had fled the field to Bothwell. If necessary, they would lay siege to the castle in order to take these nobles.

Yet upon their arrival at Bothwell, Edward Bruce was delighted to find the constable, Sir Walter FitzGilbert, with the Earls of Hereford and Angus, Sir Ingram de Umfraville, Lord of Berkeley, and Lord of Segrave already in his possession. The five men had taken refuge in Bothwell because FitzGilbert had kept one foot in the English camp, but when the constable heard of the outcome at Bannockburn, he had promptly switched allegiance to the Bruce and taken the nobles prisoner. Fortunately for a few, there had been no room at Bothwell for them, and they had been forced to continue on their way to Carlisle and northern England. The Earl of Warfield was among those, though two of his sons had fallen on the field at Bannockburn.

And I have his heir, Alex thought in grim satisfaction. If he does not exchange Jamie for Devlin, he loses all.

But what would he tell Catherine?

It was a question that weighed on him heavily, so that when finally he rode over the slopes that still bore scars of the recent battle to reach the tent where she slept, he was uneasy. That there was no love between Catherine and her father was a fact. But her brother was a different matter.

For good or ill, she loved him well, and if Alex harmed Devlin, he harmed her. Ah, God, what was he to do, for it was the way of things.

But how could he say the words that would hurt her? Of all men, he knew how it felt to lose those you loved, though there was scarce a man in all of Scotland who had not lost someone dear to him in this conflict.

Deep shadows shrouded tents and ground as his horse picked a way through the sleepy camp, until finally he saw his standard flutter from atop a tent pole. As he dismounted Robbie came to him and took the reins, then jerked his head toward the tent.

"She sleeps. Is all well?"

"Yea, Robbie, all is well."

"Is it true that Hereford and Angus have been taken prisoner?"

Grinning, he nodded. "Aye, they were guests of Sir Walter FitzGilbert, just as I was not so long ago. Bruce intends to hold Hereford in lieu of his queen, as Edward's wife is de Bohun's sister and will no doubt put pressure on the king to yield to any exchange demanded."

"What of Jamie?"

Alex's grin faded, and he shook his head. "No word. Warfield fled the field, but there was no room at Bothwell with the others, so he has not been taken. If he makes it to England, no doubt he will agree to exchange Jamie and de Brus for his heir, for his other two sons were slain on the field." He paused and glanced at the tent. "What news of here?"

"The lady had words with her brother."

Swearing softly, Alex could not help a glance toward the line of tents that held the noble hostages. Robbie intercepted his glance and grinned. "Devlin is under guard, for he would not give his word that he would not attempt escape. The lady has remained close to me, and other than their first meeting, has not tried to see him again."

Alex frowned. His weary destrier shook its great head

in a brittle jangle of metal bit and harness, and he put out a hand to stroke the damp muzzle and quiet the steed. It did not sound like Catherine to avoid her brother. Could it be that she felt a compunction to help him escape? He could not help a little nagging doubt that she might try from some misguided sense of loyalty that he could certainly understand, but would not tolerate for a moment.

He looked up, then slapped the destrier on the shoulder as he moved around it. "Take him, Robbie, and see that he has extra rations, for he has done well this day."

Ducking, he entered the tent, blinking at the absence of light save for a small lamp that dangled from the center pole. He stood still as the familiar fragrance of lavender wafted toward him. Closing his eyes, he breathed it in, and was startled by the sudden wave of comfort and love it brought with it. Perhaps he had wronged Douglas with his complaints, for the scented soap he had given Catherine had come to represent everything that was good in his life. And now it cleared away the residue of blood and death that lingered in his senses, to fill him with hope and tenderness.

"Alex?" The sleepy murmur penetrated the gloom, and was quickly followed by a glad cry. "Alex . . . oh, you are here at last!"

A shadow detached from the others and flew at him, and he caught her up and swung her into his arms. Pressing his face into her hair, he breathed deeply of soft scent and love. Suddenly, nothing else mattered now that he was here and holding her, nothing but the fact that they were together. He crushed her hair in his palm, letting the silky strands slide over his splayed fingers as he cradled her head, holding her to him as if he could not get close enough.

It was what he had been missing all these years, the

unfettered love that he had so long hungered for but not been able to put a name to. That it resided now in this one small woman who carried his child was a miracle.

"Catkin . . . are you well?"

"Yea, my love, I am now." She tilted back her head, and in the soft gloom he saw the misty joy in her eyes. He brushed a thumb over her cheek, and found it wet.

"Tears again? Poor catkin. Do you grieve?"

"Nay, my love. They are relief. Joy. You are here, and what I want most from this world is with me. I have you, and I have our child beneath my heart. It is enough for now."

He stroked her cheek. "And tomorrow, catkin? Will it be enough for you then?"

"Yea, my heart. And next year and the next."

Her swift response heartened him, and he could not speak so he pulled her to him again. For a time, he just held her. The beat of her heart was steady and sure, her fragrance sweet, and her skin soft and pliant beneath his hands. He did not deserve this. Not really. All his life he had fallen short when it came to doing the right thing. Everything he had touched, he destroyed.

Except this.

Ah, God, except this, and it frightened him that he may yet somehow manage to lose her despite all he could do to keep it from happening. It did not matter that a priest had said the vows, or that she said she loved him. There was yet the fear it would all be taken away, as so many had been.

What would he have left? His life would be empty without her. It had been empty before, but he had not known why. Now that he knew what it should be, the loss would be that much greater to bear.

She moved against him with a soft sigh of contentment, and he slid an arm down her back to lift her, then took her to the narrow cot against the limber wall of the tent. He lay her down gently, and knelt beside the cot on the dirt floor covered only by a few scattered rugs. For the first time, he noticed her garments, and smiled.

"I see you prefer the garb of a milk maid to the velvet gowns."

"It seemed more practical here, where it is so dusty and rough. Do you mind?"

"Nay, love. They are much easier to remove than all the trappings of a female in velvet."

Her laughter was soft, and as he reached for the laces of the leather girdle she wore, she whispered encouragement to him, French words that made him laugh, and the English vernacular that lifted his brow.

"I hope"—he kissed the bare skin of her shoulder— "that you do not"—another kiss on the cushioned slope of her breast as the linen gown was pulled away—"speak to our children"—this kiss made her gasp and arch upward as he found the nipple—"this way. Ah, yes, love . . . like that."

Conversation ceased, and in the close air of the tent, he made love to his wife for the first time. No other time they had lain together had been like this, for the vows that had been said created a bond between them that was stronger. It was sweeter, deeper, lasting.

It was forever.

A warm wind blew the unfurled banners with sharp, snapping sounds, and the red lion danced upon the field of white as the Earl of Warfield entered the bailey of Castle Rock. The contingent's arms had been taken from them at the gates, and the group of horsemen sat uneasily while the earl dismounted and climbed the stairs of the keep to greet the Scotsman.

Catherine watched without expression as her father

crossed the hall with a limping stride that bespoke the
wounds he had suffered at the battle on Bannockburn.
He looked aged now, with deep creases in his face that
revealed his years.

Warfield came to a stop before the dais and looked up
at Alex. "I brought the required hostages. Where is my
son?"

Alex remained silent as Robbie gave a signal and
Nicholas was brought into the hall. Catherine's throat
tightened when her brother still refused to look at her
and stood silently, flanked by armed guards. In the past
month, he had been a polite, distant stranger to her, held
hostage in a silken prison with all his needs met, but still
hostile.

Stiffly, the earl growled, "And my daughter?"

"She remains here." Alex lifted a brow at the chagrin
on Warfield's face, and Catherine almost smiled.

Then he blustered, "By Christ, Fraser, you have broken the terms of our agreement! Two for two, and now
you have reneged—"

"Nay," Catherine spoke up quickly, angrily, "it was
never that and you know it. I am worth not even one
hostage to you. Do not pretend otherwise."

" 'Twas understood that it would be a fair exchange of
hostages, by God!" Warfield's expression was dark, and
his gaze darted to Nicholas for a moment, then back to
Alex. "I will keep my bargain, but you must keep yours,
or I will not send the message that will bring in de Brus
and the young whelp."

Alex did not move, nor betray by gesture that he was
angry, but Catherine could hear it in the taut, clipped
tone of his voice.

"You cry foul, when 'twas you who played me false, my
lord. I negotiated for the return of your daughter, and

you came to my lands and slaughtered my people wantonly. That is not the act of a man with honor."

With an impatient gesture, the earl snapped, "They were only villagers. Do you regard them so highly?"

"Yea, my lord Warfield, so I do." Alex leaned forward, and the earl's eyes narrowed slightly at the ferocity now apparent in his face and words. "My children were in the village that day, and met their fates at your hands. 'Tis fortunate for you that I am bound by the rules of honor and chivalry not to play you as false as you did me, for by all that is holy, you should lose your life this day!"

For a moment there was only silence. Warfield stood as if carved from stone, staring up at Alex. Then, roughly, he said, "I still contend that the terms of the agreement will not be met lest there is an even exchange of hostages."

"Your king is not so discriminating as you, my lord Warfield." Alex sat back in his chair, but Catherine still felt his tension. "The Earl of Hereford brought the exchange of fifteen Scottish hostages, including Bruce's queen. If your son and heir is so valuable to you, perhaps I should ask for more."

Rage suffused his face as the earl glared at him. "Do you think yourself noble now that you have earned a barony?"

"Nay, my lord, I have always thought myself noble. My fathers were barons before me, and 'twas only your king who took away our title. It has been returned to me twofold, with all the trappings of my rank." He paused, and let his hand fall to caress Catherine's arm. "My lady is content to remain with me, and so she shall stay. You will exchange de Brus and my brother for Lord Devlin, or find yourself a guest at our table much longer than you anticipated."

"If I do not return or give the signal before the bell rings for vespers, my men will cut their throats." His eyes darted again to Nicholas, who remained strangely quiet, his gaze fixed upon the licking flames of the fire in the center of the hall.

"And you will have the pleasure of seeing your son's throat slashed before your eyes."

Catherine tried not to move, but could not help a sudden jerk of the hand Alex held beneath his palm. He exerted small pressure, and she remained silent, though her heart was thumping madly in her chest. Surely, he did not mean it! It had to be a bluff, to force her father to yield without strife.

But Robbie stood with a hand upon the hilt of his sword, and Nicholas was still flanked by two burly guards, and the earl was growing more furious by the moment. She could not bear it.

"Hold," she said into the tense silence. "I can hear no more of this. Do you wish for an even exchange by taking me as well? I vow, I am amazed to hear it, for you have never thought me worthy of aught but your anger. Yet now, I am to be a bone to be fought over. I will not have it. I do not choose to go with you. I choose to stay here with my husband, whom I love. Yea, you may well look at me with daggers in your eyes, but we were wed on Saint John's Eve by a priest at Bannockburn." She drew in a deep breath. "As for an even exchange, it would not be, for I am with child, and you would receive three hostages in place of two. Choose now whom you want, for if 'tis an even exchange you must have, then you will have to take me alone."

A long silence fell that was not broken until Nicholas began to laugh. Catherine flicked him a nervous glance, and even Alex stirred uneasily. Had the strain affected him? But no, for Nicholas began to shake his head, and looked at their father with amusement still marking his face.

"She has you, I fear, my lord. What say you, a Scots wife and her babe, or your heir? I can appreciate your dilemma, for none of it must appeal to you. But then, I have had much time to think in the past weeks of solitude, so perhaps I am unnerved."

"Yea, so you sound." Warfield looked irritated. "Curse it, I will accept your terms, Fraser, but I will not yield to you her dower lands."

" 'Tis done, for I want the lady more than I do her lands. In this, my lord, we are in accordance, for you want the lands more than you do the lady."

The earl did not look at her again and Catherine did not speak, even after Adam de Brus and Jamie Fraser were delivered into the hall, and Alex rose from his chair at last and left the dais to take his brother in his arms.

Then did she look at Nicholas, and with a heavy heart said softly, "I will miss you most sorely, Nicky."

To her surprise, he met her gaze, and a faint smile curved his mouth. "Yea, kitten, I think you will."

Then they were gone, Nicholas and her father—who had neither glanced at her nor spoken to her—departing the hall and Castle Rock.

As the tension drained from her body, she braced her hands on the table, and then Alex was there, his arms around her as he drew her to him. "I want you to meet Jamie, catkin."

A thin young man with a shock of black hair and a striking resemblance to his brother stepped forward and swept her a courtly bow. When he straightened, he said, "Your brother oft spoke of ye, m'lady."

"Did he?"

"Aye, most kindly." He smiled, and her heart clutched as she saw Alex in this young man, in the direct gaze and angular features that still bore traces of youth.

She thought then of Tam, who had been brought back to be laid to rest in the church yard with all honor as a fallen hero, and of the fees that his mother would receive in lieu of her son. These were people she liked, people she respected, and suddenly she knew that she would be content here. The animosity that had ignited after her father's assault had faded now that she was Alex's wife and bearing his child, and she thought she had Robbie to thank for diluting much of the village's resentment of her. While she did not know what he had said to the people, it seemed to have helped.

"Come with me, catkin." Alex pulled her with him, his arm around her shoulders, and walked her across the hall to the circular stairs that led up to their chamber.

When they were alone in the second-floor corridor, he took her in his arms, and his voice was rough with emotion. "I have never loved you so much as I do at this moment."

She toyed with the crest on his gilt-trimmed soutane, and looked up at him with a faint smile. "Have I told you how handsome you are dressed as a lord, my love? Though I think I much prefer the convenience of your tunic and plaid at times. . . ."

Soft laughter came from him, and he leaned against her to press her into the wall. "That can be easily remedied, catkin. Shall I show you?" His mouth found her throat, lips working against her skin.

"Alex . . . here?"

"Here. The hall. The kitchens. Wherever you like. Ah, wait. . . ." He kissed her mouth, and his hands slid down the velvet gown she wore to gather her skirts into his hands and lift them. She gasped, but it was swallowed by his mouth over hers. And then he was lifting her, his hands bracing her as he pulled her legs around his waist and entered her with slow, luxurious sensuality. She arched against him, and lost herself in the familiar, sweet sensations.

Never had she dreamed she would be so blessed, or that she would find the love she had once thought lay only in romantic tales. It was more than she had hoped for, more even than she imagined could exist. And it was not just a romantic poem or knightly tale of love, but real.

"I love you," she said in a husky whisper that brushed past his ear, and his arms tightened as he shuddered against her.

"Ah, catkin, I love you more than you will ever know."

She only smiled, for she knew well how much he loved her. And it was enough.

AUTHOR'S NOTE

I have tried to stay true to history, while incorporating my characters within the confines of the times and historical figures. Most of the incidents took place as described, or as legend dictates. A contemporary account, *The Lanercost Chronicle*, recorded many of the deeds, as well as the words attributed to the Bruce and James Douglas, as written in this story. Another contemporary source was John Barbour, who wrote the epic *The Brus*.

James Douglas was indeed the romantic, dashing figure he was portrayed as here, reckless and ruthless and boon companion to the Bruce. The incidents attributed to him in my story are recorded in history and legend. Alex, of course, is a fictional character, but could well have existed in very similar fashion. Men of that time were dangerous and intent upon victory, and hostages were frequently captured and exchanged.

For details of the Battle of Bannockburn I must thank an excellent source, a video by Castle productions, entitled *The Battle of Bannockburn*. It was informative and inspired. For the ballads, I used a book entitled *Scottish & Border Battles & Ballads*, which was very useful. As nearly as can be determined, these ballads were sung during the time of my story.

And finally, as always, I took liberty with the language of the times, incorporating it into a readable format for modern readers. For those purists who prefer the lyrical "thee" and "thou" or Scottish dialect, I apologize, and for those who cannot bear any kind of dialect, I apologize again. I can only say, you should have seen the first draft!

ABOUT THE AUTHOR

JULIANA GARNETT is a bestselling author writing under a new name to indulge her passion for medieval history. Always fascinated by the romance of *knights in shining armor,* this Southern writer is now at liberty to focus on the pageantry and allure of days when chivalry was expected and there were plenty of damsels in distress.

Ms. Garnett has won numerous awards for her previous works, and hopes to entertain new readers who share her passion for valorous heroes and strong, beautiful heroines.

**If you loved THE SCOTSMAN,
you won't want to miss the next
breathtaking epic of danger, temptation
and forbidden desire from one of
romance's brightest new talents.**

JULIANA GARNETT

**COMING IN AUGUST 1999
FROM BANTAM BOOKS.**

**Follow this award-winning author to
thirteenth-century England, where a
recent widow of a Norman knight, Lady
Jane de Winter, resolves to use her
position and her husband's wealth to
alleviate the suffering of the common
people. With the newfound freedom of
her social position, she is able to make
their cause her own—until one man steps
in her way. Not only is the new sheriff a
threat to her mission, but he endangers
the one thing she's sworn never to
surrender . . . her heart.**

**Furious to learn that the notorious outlaw
Robin Hood has renewed his nefarious**

activities in Nottingham and Lincolnshire, Sir Tré sets out to find and destroy the rebel and his loyal bandits. He must restore peace to the region or face the consequences from the king who appointed him . . . and the last thing he needs is the beautiful, intelligent—and willful—distraction of Lady Jane. Little does he know that he will soon be forced to choose between his life and saving the woman whose cause he set out to destroy—even as she's ignited the passion in his soul.